The SEMPER SONNET

SETH MARGOLIS

DIVERSIONBOOKS

Also by Seth Margolis

Closing Costs
False Faces
Losing Isaiah
Perfect Angel
Vanishing Act
Disillusions

Diversion Books
A Division of Diversion Publishing Corp.
443 Park Avenue South, Suite 1008
New York, New York 10016
www.DiversionBooks.com

For more information, email info@diversionbooks.com

First Diversion Books edition April 2016.
Print ISBN: 978-1-68230-056-5
eBook ISBN: 978-1-68230-055-8

For Jean Naggar

For Jean Naggar

A true knight is fuller of bravery in the midst,
than in the beginning of danger.

—Sir Philip Sidney

From the Diary of Rufus Hatton, Physician

20 March, 1555
Hatfield

I am driven to record the events of this evening, but I would rather it were not so. For these matters are not fit for the archive of memory—indeed, they should never have occurred. But occurred they did, and here I sit, quill in hand, a full pot of ink at the ready, as first light winks beyond my bedroom window; my diary, purchased many years ago but never used, now lies open to the first page, having waited all this time, it seems, for this moment to arrive. My hand, I think, longs to draw the pen across the page more than my heart or even my mind desires to write. These events will be recorded, it seems. But why? To what avail?

It has been the longest day of my life, but perhaps my lady will remember it as being even longer.

Impetuous whore.

There. I've written it. The day may come when these words deliver my head to the chopping block, a device much in use of late. Strange, that with my actions today I have dedicated my life to the coming of that day! But then these are strange times. Dangerous times. Few indeed know how dangerous.

I should blacken those words and save myself, but I cannot. Once again, my hand has its own will. For what purpose is a diary if not to hold communion with a lonesome soul? If I cannot and must not confide my thoughts to another soul, then I have no choice but to confide them to myself. I will hide this book, but even a fool knows there is no true hiding place when great men have great ambitions and think you an impediment to such. Yet I must write the truth, and the truth is this: She is impetuous, and a whore.

Oh, that my Jane were alive! I would whisper this thought to her, and take pleasure in her shocked expression, and comfort in her discretion. Then would I have no need of this diary. If our daughter Anne had lived beyond infancy, I might have recorded my treasonous thoughts and knowledge in her mind someday, and not upon this brittle parchment. But they were both stolen from me by plague, along with half the population of England, it seemed, and now my sole remaining confidant lies beneath my hand, awaiting news.

It began this morning. Or should I say, yesterday morning? My maid roused me with the news that I was wanted urgently at Hatfield. The night was yet dark, the windows shuttered. In the darkness I saw only her eyes and the occasional glint of her teeth. Lucy hails from the western coast of Africa. Since Jane's death, and then Anne's, I have had need of domestic help and companionship. Blackamoors are better workers than our native girls, and not as dear, and they have nowhere to run when they tire of servitude. Her knowledge of our tongue is imperfect, but she keeps my small house tidy and, I might as well confess, my body warm. Lucy (for that is what I have named her) has been the salvation of my body and my soul.

"A man here for you," she said, in a voice that sounds to my ears as if she sucks on a hard candy while speaking. "He wait you."

Nearly nine months ago, another man had sent for me. "Are you Rufus Hatton, the physician?" asked the servant sent to fetch me that time. He appeared nervous, as if he feared I was an imposter and that he would be blamed for involving the wrong person. "My lady is ill," he said, once I had reassured him that I was indeed the physician. "She is most violently ill." Her family worried for her health, he told me, and for their own futures (this last was unsaid). I don't flatter myself that my reputation caused them to summon me. In truth I am only recently returned from Cambridge. But I was then and am still the closest physician to the palace, residing below it in the village, a short walk from the back gate atop the gentle hill that begins almost at my doorstep. If I have a reputation at all, it is not for healing, I think, but for plain speaking, and for my loyalty to the new church, which I make no secret of, even now.

It was no secret about the village or even the countryside that my lady was at Hatfield, but her presence was rarely mentioned. I think it caused uneasiness in the village, as if she bore a plague. The plague of the new religion, perhaps, now out of official favor. No one ever saw her, of course, as few were allowed inside the gates, and she was never let out.

We mortals live below Hatfield Palace, in its shadow, only guessing what activities, grim and gay, take place above us.

It was her maid, Kat Ashley, who led me into her room that first time, after a short walk up the hill to the palace.

"We fear typhus." Kat's eyes brimmed with tears as she stepped closer to me. "Or poison."

I found my lady on her bed in a small room on the second floor, the curtains drawn against a bright morning sun. I confess I approached her with trepidation, for calamity attended her like a fatal odor, felling those who would get too close. When I was but steps from the bedside, the sprightly Kat circled in front of me and removed a chamber pot, but not before I had a chance to examine its contents.

The patient appeared to be sleeping. "Has my lady been able to hold down anything?" I whispered.

"Nothing," replied the servant, the word like a sigh or moan, heavy with despair. "You must help her."

I stood by the bed and observed her. I admit my examination was not, at first, entirely scientific. So this was the woman at the center of so much strife. She appeared smaller than I might have expected, though who would not have seemed so, given how large she loomed in the affairs of men. And she was, of course, not well, which did little to flatter her appearance. Her face was long, but with a rounded chin, and her mouth was small and likewise round. Her nose swelled in the middle, her only true deformity, and a minor one at that, though it must be said that overall she was not a great beauty. Her single claim to distinction appeared, during my cursory observation, to be her hands, which lay atop the bedding, unsullied by rings. Her fingers were slender and unusually long. One could imagine her an accomplished player at the lute or virginal. She had passed but twenty-two years on this earth, yet she appeared older to me. Or was it the heavy weight of expectations she bore on her slender frame that had aged her face beyond her years?

Perhaps sensing my presence, she opened her eyes. As she pushed herself into a sitting position, I watched fear give way to fierceness.

"Who are you?" Her voice was weak and hoarse from illness and sleep.

"A physician, my lady. Rufus Hatton. Your servant called for me."

"I want no physician," she said, her voice strengthening. "Leave me."

"But my lady has been ill. Mistress Ashley has—"

"Kat is a fool. Go!"

I had no choice but to heed her. As I was turning, I saw something on her bedside table: a small pile of garlic cloves on a plate. My heart felt suddenly heavy. While every instinct called to me to leave, I nevertheless found myself turning back to her.

"Was my lady able to smell the garlic?"

"I know not what you mean," she said quickly, glancing at the plate.

"Who brought you the garlic?"

"I know not why it is here. Or you, for that matter. Now, go!"

I obeyed this time, but I hadn't reached the door when I heard a softer, more plaintive voice.

"Is it always true?"

I turned. "My lady?"

"I could not smell it. For three days. Kat brings me fresh cloves from the garden every morning, and still I smell nothing. And the vomiting…."

I approached the bed and very carefully formed my next question, for much was at stake, not least my life, depending on how events transpired.

"Has my lady reason to fear that she may be with child?" I whispered.

Her eyes flashed with rage and then, after a long few moments in which I could not breathe, her expression softened. Slowly, almost imperceptibly, she nodded.

And so I became entangled in a most dangerous situation, one of a handful of men and women privy to a secret that could destroy any and all who held it. So many pregnancies never endure to term. It was my fondest hope, and that of others, that this one would so transpire. But God saw fit to dash our unholy aspirations, even after my lady availed herself of a purgative, devised by her loyal Kat, to bring down the term. Two months after that first visit the child quickened, and today, nearly seven months later, I was called to Hatfield once more.

As I walked the short distance to the palace, I said a prayer for which I am both ashamed and unapologetic. A stillbirth would solve many problems and ease many hearts, my lady's among them.

The gates of Hatfield were swung open for me, and I entered the park just as dawn's faintest light was casting a portentous glow over the palace. The red bricks of the facade appeared as smoldering embers, particularly on the center tower, which loomed over the two-story building with glowering disdain. It is not the prettiest palace in the land, and certainly not the largest, but all things considered, my lady is fortunate to be its tenant. There are worse places she could be, given the politics of the day, even were she not in her current condition.

A guard stepped aside to let me in through the main door. I made straight for the grand staircase, taking it two steps at a time. Outside my lady's room stood another guard, whose eyes, when they met mine, expressed what I could only interpret as deep shame. I had but a moment to contemplate this, for a series of sharp, high screams emanated from inside the room, indicating that the trials were well along. I opened the door with some trepidation. Men are not welcome in the birthing room, not even physicians, a situation I find unsatisfactory but am powerless to change. But this was no ordinary delivery room. I had been summoned not to attend to the child, if it survived, for precious few had an interest in that eventuality, but to see to my lady's well-being, should she need assistance.

I stepped inside. The wailing continued, but the source of it was obscured by a hovering circle of women. I recognized Kat and two other servants. Another face seemed to belong to Lady Longford, who lives close by and has been one of the few people allowed into Hatfield. Frances Sermon, the midwife, was in attendance, by long-standing arrangement. There were no kin in attendance, as there normally would be, for none of my lady's kin had been alerted to the situation, naturally. The curtains were drawn, as if to contain the noise. I think there were a hundred candles lit, most burned close to their nubs.

I knew better than to make my presence known, for I would be immediately ejected, but eventually Kat turned away from her mistress and spied me. She crossed the room and pushed me into the hallway. I knew her to be a pretty woman, with a lively disposition. But this night her eyes were shrouded in black circles. Unmarried, she had no need to wear a cap, and her hair looked ill-kept, even wild. I asked how long it had been since the labor had begun and was told that several hours had passed. "The child was breach, methinks. The midwife pressed on my lady's belly to right it. I know not if she was successful, but the howling…. I fear that my lady's insides are being ripped to tatters."

As if to lend credence to Kat's narrative, a new series of screams erupted from behind the door.

"We are losing her," she whispered through deep, heaving breaths. "Mother of God, we are losing her."

"The Lord will decide when to take his servant from us, not you, Mistress Kat." I heard little confidence in my voice, for it seemed to me that the Lord had scarce involvement with what was occurring at Hatfield this night. Perhaps the devil was more interested. "When the child is born, whether quick or still, I will attend to our lady and do what I can. Now back to her side, where you belong."

For the next several hours, I roamed the palace, trying in vain to escape the shrieking from that room and my own sense of dread. Both shadowed me wherever I went. In the great hall, with its arched timbered roof and walls lined with tapestries, I considered the sadness that suffused Hatfield, which had been the home of the bishops of Ely before it came into royal possession during the dissolution. Perhaps any house taken from its owners, no matter how justified the usurpation, would seem melancholy, but Hatfield felt… abandoned, like the lady lately imprisoned (for she had little opportunity to leave it) and now confined within its walls. I walked the length of the great hall, a considerable journey, and wondered when last it had held a grand banquet. Not in my lady's time, that much I knew. I had little need of the screams from the floor above to tell me that Hatfield had become a dark place.

"Sir, the child is born."

This announcement, from the lips of a male servant standing at the south entrance of the great hall, carried no intimation of joy but rather seemed to foretell a new tribulation, not merely in the life our lady but in the lives of all who attended her that day.

I returned to her room. Kat was at her mistress's bedside, but the focus of activity had shifted to the far corner of the room, where four women huddled about a small bundle of white swaddling. I confess my heart did not cheer when I heard the mewling of a healthy infant. Better for all in that room, myself among them, if the child had never taken a breath. I did not inquire after its sex. I wanted no further disappointment.

"Is my lady comfortable?" I asked Kat, who watched over the sleeping form of the new mother like a protective, adoring angel, which is perhaps indeed what she is.

"She sleeps, which is all the comfort she will have."

I took her arm and felt for a pulse.

"Was there much bleeding?" I asked, loudly enough for the midwife to hear.

"Too much," answered Mistress Sermon, crossing the room to join me at the bedside. "Now she must sleep. Your work is done, sir."

A midwife is always jealous of a physician's presence, so I took no offense at her impertinence.

"And the child?"

"A healthy boy. At least there is one in her family that can make such a thing."

"Dangerous words," I said quietly.

The midwife shrugged and rejoined the child, who was already suckling at the breast of a wet nurse. A moment later the boy was taken from the room, his retinue following.

My lady stirred and opened her eyes. Kat leaned over and whispered something.

"Bring him to me," I heard my lady ask in a weak voice. "Where is he?"

"It is better that you not see him," said Kat.

"Bring him to me." Now her voice was firmer, befitting her station.

"I'm sorry, my lady." Kat sounded close to tears. She retreated from the bed, leaving me alone with its occupant. My lady took my hand. Hers felt limp and cold.

"Will you watch him?" she inquired of me. "Take care of him?"

"Surely the family will have a—"

"Fie to my family. I am bidding you be his guardian, Doctor."

I could do nothing but agree, though the burden felt heavy already.

"I will call him Edward, after my late brother."

"A fine name, my lady. Now you must rest, to restore your strength."

"Yes, my strength," she said. "I will never endure that again. Such pain as I thought would tear me apart. I will never endure that again.... God be my witness, I will...."

With that, her eyes shut. I watched her for a while, wondering at her fate, which had never been secure but would now be even less so.

Princess Elizabeth, daughter of a King and an adulteress turned Queen, sister of two monarchs, including our reigning Queen, the Catholic Mary Tudor. Now she was the mother of a bastard. Stupid girl, I thought (yet another treasonous thought, if ever Elizabeth should be released from Hatfield, which seems more doubtful than ever). A bastard son would surely ruin whatever slim chance she had of succession. A healthy Tudor son, that rarest of commodities, but born a bastard.

I left her in Kat's hands. As I was leaving the house I nearly ran into a gentleman, also departing, and in much haste. Something about his manner told me he did not wish to be acknowledged, but my surprise at his presence loosened my lips before my mind had time to apply caution.

"Sir William, good day," I said.

Sir William Cecil, with his equine face and long beard of startling whiteness, could hardly expect to remain unrecognized. He appeared stunned nonetheless as he returned my greeting.

"Good day, Doctor," he said, barely moving his lips. His tone made my profession seem little more than that of fishmonger. "I trust your patient is well."

"Tired, but well."

He studied me a long while.

"You have a reputation for probity and discretion," he said at length. "We have need of such a person who lives close by Hatfield."

"I will of course attend to the Princess's health, and that of her child when—"

"You must not mention him again. He will be taken from this place and will not return. Even to talk of a child is treason." His eyes seemed to sweep the floor, as if the correct words lay there, waiting to be plucked up. He spoke the next line slowly. "There is no child." Then his eyes met mine, and I could only nod. "As for your part, stay close to the Princess. She will have ample cause to see you as she regains strength. Report to me what you know."

Again, I could but nod. Since the death of young Edward ten years earlier, Cecil has had no formal part to play on the political stage, and Queen Mary distrusts him, with good reason, it is said. Now he looks to be casting his lot with Elizabeth, a dangerous gamble even before the events of the past nine months.

Then again, there is no child.

Still, the Queen is healthy, and Catholic, and her sister a prisoner.

Outside, a retinue of men waited with swords and halberds. What were they about? As if to satisfy my puzzlement, one of the men turned to another and said, "We go now to Stafford."

The other, brandishing a mirthless smile, replied, "To offer felicitations on the birth of a son."

"Yes," said the first man. "But his joy will be short-lived."

I watched Cecil ride off with his men. The sun was already dying in the west. I hadn't realized how late the day had grown. I felt tired and burdened and yet restless with anxiety. Two people had charged me with responsibilities I had no wish to assume, first Elizabeth and now Cecil. Oh, how I longed for my Jane to share my burden. Lucy would slake my body's restlessness with her African magic, but could do little to assuage my mind's cares. As I left the palace through the village gate, the portal of servants, farmers, and physicians, my body felt twice as heavy as it had that morning. I sensed that my life, no less than that of Elizabeth or Miles Stafford or even their bastard son (Edward, who didn't exist), had changed that day, and not for the better.

The Sonnet

Poetry is nearer to vital truth than history.

—Plato

CHAPTER 1

Lee Nicholson walked carefully up the stairs to her third-floor apartment, balancing two cups of coffee and conflicting emotions. On the one hand, there was regret. How had she lost control of things last night and ended up with (she halted her climb briefly to recall his name) Alex? And how had he managed to remain there until the morning, resisting her efforts to rouse him until, craving caffeine, she left the apartment to fetch two large coffees from the Starbucks on the corner of Broadway and Eighty-First Street? She took hers black but didn't, of course, know how he took his, and spent several moments deciding what to do before splashing skim milk into his cup. How would she get him out of her bed and her apartment without having to make awkward small talk? She needed to get on with her day. What if he wouldn't leave?

On the other hand, there was pride. An appearance on the eleven o'clock news was hardly routine for a thirty-two-year-old English literature graduate student. She'd done well last night, smoothly describing how she'd come across the sonnet and built the case that it was by William Shakespeare, the first newly discovered work by the Bard in half a century. The Shakespeare establishment, a global industry of academics, writers, amateur historians, theater directors, actors, and critics, was still unconvinced of the sonnet's authenticity, and there were plenty of moments when Lee wondered if it was wise to risk her nascent academic career on a single piece of paper. But after last night, it was too late; appearing on the news program had been the point of no return. She'd staked her future on the sonnet.

The interviewer had seemed genuinely interested. Half her friends had been enlisted to record the show (Lee's non-cable reception was spotty, and she did not own a VCR, DVD player, or DVR). Her mentor at Columbia, David Eddings, had assured her that it was her looks and not her scholarship that had landed her a spot on the news. "Wear that cream blouse that falls open so becomingly, and make sure your hair's down, so it brushes your shoulders," he'd said. "When you pin it back you're a bit schoolmarmish, and that's precisely the image we'd prefer *not* to project to a mass audience. Anyway, you're hardly a schoolmarm, are you?"

He was always trying, in his smarmy way, to tease out details of what he probably liked to imagine was a libertine private life, and she'd been tempted, just to thwart him, to wear a turtleneck and bun. In the end vanity trumped revenge. He was, after all, the country's leading Elizabethan scholar and the man who would determine the fate of her dissertation. And she'd looked damn good, she thought, in the cream blouse that fell open perfectly to reveal just a shadow of cleavage. She'd availed herself of the network's hair and makeup people. Her eyes in the dressing room mirror had looked a deeper blue than usual, her cheekbones more pronounced. "Damn, I thought you were going to bring some *culture* to the show, but you look more like an actress than a grad student," the producer had told her as she was led onto the set.

Still high from comments like that, and from her mostly stammer-free recitation of how she'd found the sonnet and researched its provenance, she'd allowed herself to be seduced by the cameraman. Okay, they'd seduced each other. He was charming in a vaguely dopey way that was, thank god, nothing like the *can-you-top-this* wit she dealt with up at Columbia. He was a big guy, significantly taller than her five feet seven inches, in his thirties, she guessed, and the easy way he interacted with her, the confidence that came not from entitlement but from a profound lack of concern for where the encounter might lead, appealed to her. Everyone else in her life was so *invested* in the outcome of every interaction. And she hadn't wanted to be alone, not that night, when so much had gone right.

So she'd agreed to a drink at what turned out to be a dark, beery bar near the studio frequented by news folk, and after her second vodka tonic he'd escorted her home in a cab and then up to her apartment, and now she was carrying two large coffees upstairs and wondering how she'd allowed him into her bed in the first place and how she was going to get him out of it.

When she noticed her apartment door slightly ajar, her first thought was that he'd let himself out. Excellent. No forced chitchat, no awkward goodbyes between two people who had just shared life's most intimate and pleasurable experience and had zero interest in seeing the other ever again. *Love gave the wound, which, while I breathe, will bleed.* So wrote Philip Sidney, the subject of her doctoral thesis (a work in progress), more than 400 years earlier. Lee Nicholson would not be wounded.

She would not bleed.

She pushed the door open with her foot and went in.

Something seemed off—that was her first thought upon entering the living room. The drawers in the chest next to the sofa were slightly open. One of the cabinet doors under her bookshelves was also open. The stacks of books and magazines and papers that covered most horizontal surfaces were slightly askew, as if someone had gone through them and not straightened them afterward. The room would look perfectly fine to a stranger, but it looked all wrong to her. When you lived alone, you became hypersensitive to the presence of an outsider. Someone had gone through her things.

Had she slept with a freak? He'd seemed quite normal the night before. So why had he gone through her things and then left without even bothering to fully close the door behind him? Had he taken anything? He must have realized that she knew where he worked.

She put down the coffees and headed for the bedroom, directly off the living room. What she saw there threw her back against the doorframe as if blown by a sudden wind.

He was on the bed, face up, a small black hole through his forehead. Red-black blood covered his eyes and cheeks. The covers were bunched at his ankles, exposing his naked body. Legs slightly to the side, as if he'd been trying to get off the bed when the bullet—for it must have been a bullet—hit him.

She couldn't take her eyes off him, yet she was simultaneously aware that her bedroom, too, had been searched. Everything *looked* right but *felt* wrong. She also sensed—*knew*—that she was alone. Whoever had done this was gone, leaving the door slightly open in their haste to get away before she returned.

Her jewelry, which she kept on an antique ceramic tray that had been her mother's, was on top of the dresser. Nothing seemed missing.

She should get the hell out of there. Yet her mind kept processing the scene with unexpected detachment, as if taking in a movie. Clearly it wasn't a robbery. Had the intruder been after *him*? She forced herself to remember his name: Alex. Had someone followed them home last night and then waited outside until she'd left?

She reached for the phone and punched in 911, almost without thinking, as if she'd done it a hundred times before.

CHAPTER 2

The 20th Precinct on Eighty-Second Street near Columbus Avenue was a cheerless 1950s building that smelled of disinfectant. Lee had been taken there by the two policemen who'd arrived at her apartment within ten minutes of her 911 call. They'd called an ambulance moments after arriving, although they could see as easily as she that the man—Alex—was dead. They peppered her with questions about who he was. She told him what little she knew, vaguely embarrassed that a man found in her bed (found dead) was basically a stranger to her. They asked her to retrace every move she'd made since returning with Alex to her apartment the night before. When she reached the early morning walk to Starbucks, and then the return home to find the body, she became aware that their expressions had morphed from curiosity to skepticism.

"You left to get coffee, and came back to find a corpse in your bed?"

"That's what happened, yes."

"You could have made coffee at home, no?"

"I felt like getting some air." It sounded lame, even to her. "It's part of my weekend routine, going out for coffee."

And so it went, each answer she gave eliciting a new question, and greater skepticism. When a team from forensics arrived, the police told her to accompany them to the precinct.

She was led through the dimly lit lobby, the walls the same pale green ceramic tile used in her high school in western Pennsylvania, and into a battered elevator that lurched slowly to the second floor. She hadn't been handcuffed, thankfully. But the two cops gripped her elbows with such force she suspected she'd be bruised the next day. Their destination was a small room on the far side of an open office area containing several desks piled high with papers. No other officers were present. It was early, she reminded herself. Very early. The small room had a plastic sign on the door: Interrogation Room.

"That's reassuring," she said, nodding at the sign.

"Stay here, miss," one of the policemen responded. They left the room and closed the door behind them. She sat on one of two wooden chairs on either side of a small wooden table, deeply pitted and scarred, the finish peeling off in translucent flakes. On the wall to the right of the door, about two-thirds up from the floor, was a horizontal mirror—two-way, no doubt. She tried to ignore it but found herself glancing up every few seconds, intensely aware that she was probably being observed and convinced that she looked suspicious, perhaps even guilty. She glanced away, tried smiling, glanced back with a more somber expression. How was she supposed to look, under the circumstances? What did innocent look like?

When the door opened, after an endless wait that was probably no more than five minutes, she started so suddenly that her chair scraped the linoleum floor.

"I'm Detective Lowry." The woman was petite and attractive, with shoulder-length brown hair and a pale, smooth complexion that seemed at odds with the harsh, poorly maintained precinct building. Her eyes were light blue and seemed intently focused on Lee, even as the detective circled the small desk and sat down. She wore a tan wool sweater and gray slacks. A silver cross hung from a chain around her neck.

"May I call you Leslie?" The name on her driver's license.

"Most people call me Lee."

"Tell me what happened, Lee," she said as she opened a small notebook and clicked on a pen. It was stupid, really, but Lee had been expecting some words of consolation or empathy, given what she'd been through and the fact that the detective was a woman. The sudden launch of an interrogation—in an interrogation room!—was both disappointing and unsettling.

"I told the two officers who came to my apartment the entire story." Damn, why *story*? "The chain of events. They took detailed notes."

"I need for you to tell me what happened." She seemed disapproving. Had she never had a one-night-stand she later regretted?

"I think I should have a lawyer here with me," Lee said.

"You haven't been charged with anything, Miss Nicholson."

"But I can still call my lawyer." Not that she had a lawyer, or even knew one well enough to call so early in the morning, out of the blue. Was she even entitled to insist on one? "And I haven't been read my rights," she said, with a cringing sense that she was wading into the world of primetime cop shows without a sense of what really went on in these situations.

"You aren't Mirandized until you're charged. As for an attorney, if you want to call one, you may. How soon do you think he or she could be here?"

"I don't know, I—"

"Because if you answer my questions now we might be able to let you go sooner. But if you prefer to wait…."

Might be able to let her go?

"What was your question again?" she asked, her voice hoarse and faint.

She walked Detective Lowry through the past twelve hours, but this time she was stopped every few sentences with questions that sounded increasingly skeptical, at times borderline incredulous.

"Are you absolutely positive you never met Alex Folsom before?"

"Yes, positive." She couldn't help glancing up at the mirror. Who was behind it, and what were they thinking?

"Were you aware of anyone following you last night when you brought Mr. Folsom to your apartment?"

"I was not." She'd been aware of very little, in fact. "I suppose there might have been someone."

"You suppose?"

She bristled at the mocking tone. She'd already recited her academic credentials. They seemed to bore Detective Lowry, whose pencil, which scrawled frantically across the small notebook to record the events of the evening and morning, froze at any mention of Columbia or her dissertation. Was she coming off as a pedant? Well, you didn't go to jail for pedantry.

"I don't think I was followed."

"And you didn't invite anyone else into your apartment?"

She forced herself to avoid looking at the mirror, behind which she imagined a dozen or more salacious grins.

"It was just the two of us." She smiled primly.

And so it went, for two uncomfortable hours. Every statement, no matter how seemingly innocuous, was challenged.

"There was no sign of forced entry," Lowry said.

"I told the police who came to my apartment, and I told you, I never lock the door when I'm just running out for coffee. The door to the building is locked, and there was a man in there this morning, which is another reason I didn't lock up."

"Yes, there was a man in there." Lowry scribbled something on her pad.

Occasionally the detective would leave the room, no doubt to consult with the rubberneckers on the other side of the mirror, then return with a fresh line of questioning. The room was beginning to feel warm, and she had the strongest sense that it was shrinking, the walls closing in. She'd held off giving her theory of why Alex had been killed, a theory—more of a conviction, really—that had taken shape slowly over the course of the long morning. Once Detective Lowry heard it she'd understand, and Lee would be allowed to go home.

Home? Would she ever be able to sleep there again, even after the… crime scene had been cleaned up? Where would she go?

"Miss Nicholson?"

Detective Lowry was staring at her with something verging on concern. She was so pretty, Lee thought again, pretty in a delicate way that seemed at odds with her profession. But she sensed no empathy from her, a fellow single woman in New York (assuming the lack of a wedding ring could be trusted).

"Sorry, I was thinking…." Thinking about the rest of her life, which she suspected had just taken a gigantic detour. "You see, I think I know… well, in fact, I *do* know, what happened. Well, *why* it happened."

Detective Lowry's eyes widened ever so slightly, a very tepid invitation to continue.

"It's about the sonnet," Lee said.

In the long minutes before the police had arrived at her apartment, she'd had the strongest sense that everything was just slightly off. Even the hundreds of books on the shelves in the living room were askew, as if each one had been removed from the shelf and replaced, but without the admittedly obsessive care with which she habitually arranged her beloved collection. In fact, nothing was precisely as it had been. Her apartment had been carefully searched in the fifteen minutes or so she'd been gone, but it had not been ransacked. Everything had been scrupulously put back in place—*almost* in place.

She'd shared this observation with the police at her apartment, but they'd seemed less then convinced.

"Looks neat to me," one of them had said. "You're telling me someone searched this place?"

The sonnet. Whoever killed Alex had been looking for the sonnet. It was the only thing of value she owned, other than a diamond pendant, a gift from her father, which had been ignored (a fact the police on the scene had been very interested in). A newly discovered Shakespeare sonnet, written in faded black ink in the Bard's own hand on a brittle piece of paper six inches tall by three inches wide, might fetch fifty or even a hundred thousand dollars at auction, perhaps more if her authentication were endorsed by the global Shakespeare establishment, which she felt confident it would be.

And she'd had it in her purse all along, protected by a small wood-and-plastic frame she'd had specially made the day after she'd found it. Normally she kept it in a safety deposit box in Midtown (and she was already researching document preservation specialists), but she'd brought it with her to the taping last night, and the bank had been closed when she'd left the studio. At the bar the night before she'd kept the shoulder strap of her purse slung over her head, her left elbow pressing the zipped-tight bag against her side. Even after two vodka tonics, double her usual limit, she'd never lost awareness of the sonnet. In fact, she doubted she'd ever really lost awareness of it in the six weeks since its discovery.

Someone had been after the sonnet, had gone through every drawer and book in her apartment and killed Alex for it.

She put her purse on the table and removed the sonnet, which was swaddled in a small facecloth. When she placed it on the table, still in its frame, she sensed that it glowed, generating its own source of light.

"That's it?" Detective Lowry leaned over the sonnet, squinting.

"I'm convinced it's by Shakespeare. If it is...."

"It's worth a lot of money."

No, it was invaluable. Lee had the strongest desire to hide the sonnet back in her purse, away from the unappreciative eyes of the New York City police force.

"And this is why Alex was killed?" When Lee nodded Lowry asked, "Who would know about this kind of thing? How would they sell it?"

The questions had occurred to Lee. Any attempt to auction the document would call attention to the sellers and lead to the killers. Even a private sale of such a treasure would not go unnoticed, and the buyer would want to know its provenance. Before she could attempt to answer, there was a knock at the door. One of the officers who'd come to her apartment stepped in and motioned for Lowry to join him outside. Lee put the sonnet back in her purse.

"Okay," Lowry said when she returned a few minutes later. She didn't look pleased. "The server at Starbucks remembers you. You're there every weekend, but this morning you bought two coffees, not your usual one."

Despite everything, Lee couldn't suppress a smile.

"And the timing checks out, about ten minutes after they opened."

"Which is what I've been telling you all morning."

"Doesn't mean you didn't kill him and then go for coffee," Lowry said, but she sounded unconvinced herself.

"*Two* coffees?"

Lowry sighed impatiently. "Once we have the time of death nailed down, we'll know more."

"How about that test on my hands?" She was feeling more confident. A crime scene team of two men in white lab coats had arrived just before she'd been taken to the precinct and swabbed her hands for gunshot residue.

"The GSR was negative," Lowry said in a low voice, disappointment tinged with anger. "Doesn't mean you weren't wearing gloves." It occurred to Lee that Lowry *wanted* her to be guilty. It wasn't so much the desire to wrap up the case quickly. More like a sense of fairness: Lee had brought a stranger home to her apartment and slept with him. So she was guilty of something. Why not murder?

"Can I go now?"

It was close to noon before she was allowed to return to her apartment to collect her things. She was told she couldn't stay in what was considered a crime scene. Not that she had any intention of spending the night there after what had happened. She ran through the people she might stay with as she was escorted the short walk home by yet another cop. The list was depressingly short. She had few friends she felt comfortable enough with, or liked enough, to want to spend time on their sofa. And she had no family in New York. She'd lived alone since leaving home, and liked it that way.

Her apartment was more crowded than it had ever been since she'd moved in three years earlier. At least a dozen people were there, some of them busy dusting surfaces, presumably for prints, others who seemed to be standing around, observing. One man was taking photographs.

She was told she'd only be allowed back in with a police escort, so she packed a small bag with two nights' worth of clothes, and stuffed in toiletries from the bathroom. It took all her focus not to glance at the bed, though from the corner of her eye she could tell right away that

Alex's body had been taken away, leaving a lurid red stain that covered most of the surface.

"Leslie Nicholson?"

She turned from her dresser to face one of the plainclothes men sifting through every item in her bedroom.

"I'm known as Lee. Lee Nicholson."

"You know anybody by the name of Henford?"

"I don't—no. Why?"

"On this paper?" He pointed to a small, crumpled piece of paper next to her bed. It appeared to have been dropped. "You or someone wrote 'Henford' on it."

"I've never heard the word before. I didn't write it."

He considered her for a few moments, then returned to his work.

"I'm going," she told her escort when she was fully packed. A part of her felt uncomfortable leaving so many strangers in her place, picking through her things, her life. A larger part wanted—needed—to get out of there.

"We'll need an address. And you can't leave the country or even the city."

"So I've been told." Sensing that they wouldn't let her go without an address, she gave them David Eddings's address, along with her cell number.

CHAPTER 3

Lee flagged down a cab and gave the driver the address of the bank in Midtown where she'd rented the safety deposit box. As they headed down Broadway, slowed by the inevitable traffic, she opened her purse just to reassure herself that the sonnet was still there. She still couldn't believe that the police hadn't insisted she leave it with them. Then again, Detective Lowry hadn't really bought the sonnet angle. *Crazed sex addict shoots one-night-stand* was the story they seemed to be working on.

She paid the driver and went into the bank. The branches in her neighborhood didn't have safety deposit boxes. This one, much larger, catered to a business clientele. At the back, a staircase led to the basement, where a uniformed guard sat behind a metal desk. She showed him her driver's license, signed in, and, after the guard left for the back room, went to the small customer lounge, which contained a dozen or so privacy carrels. He returned a minute later carrying a steel box, which he placed in front of her. He inserted a key in one of two locks and turned it. After he left her, she put her key in the other lock, turned it, and opened the box. It was empty, of course. With a quick glance around to ascertain that she was alone, she took the framed sonnet from her purse and placed it in the box.

Even with all that was happening, she had to spend a few moments in awed contemplation of the slip of paper she'd discovered just weeks earlier. It seemed more mysterious than ever, an innocent trifle, a relic, but now also tinged with evil, the probable cause of a death. In the harsh, chemical fluorescence of the basement room, it also struck her as a bit pathetic. A rare manuscript written in Shakespeare's hand (or so she was convinced), relegated to a steel box in a soulless bank branch in a city that the Bard had never even heard of. History was one long irony, an unbroken chain of misspent energies and unintended consequences, equal parts tragedy and sick joke.

She shut the box, condemning the sonnet once more to obscurity, then called to the guard, who double-locked the box.

"Have a nice day," he said as he took it from her.

"Too late for that," she answered, and saw him check his watch as she headed back upstairs. On her way out, she stopped at a teller and emptied her checking account for cash: $1,830.

Philosophy Hall housed Columbia's English department. In front sat an original cast of Rodin's *The Thinker,* which she'd never particularly liked, suggesting as it did cloistered contemplation and self-absorption. She'd chosen Columbia because it sat squarely in the middle of New York, where it was almost impossible to disengage from the world.

David Eddings's office was on the second floor overlooking Amsterdam Avenue. He was at his big oak desk when she rapped on the partially opened door.

"Lee?" He looked a bit confused. "Did we have an appointment?"

David Eddings often appeared befuddled, as if his mind were stuck in Elizabethan England, leaving little brainpower for the mundane details of contemporary life. If anyone could disengage in the heart of Manhattan, it was David. The word "eminent" was usually inserted before his name in profiles in academic publications; no one had a better reputation in the tightly connected world of English Renaissance scholars. When he'd been assigned as her PhD adviser, Lee had been nearly overwhelmed and not a little bit intimidated. She'd become fascinated by Philip Sidney, who was not only a brilliant poet but also a soldier and statesman. She admired that combination—in fact, what drew her to the sixteenth century was the fact that poets weren't sequestered in quiet rooms but engaged in the rough-and-tumble world around them. Her thesis, years in the making and, she feared, years from completion, focused on how Sidney's political intriguing influenced his poetry, forging a sensibility that, though superficially romantic, was in fact more tragic and even cynical than starry-eyed. Her thesis would recast a great Romantic poet as a shrewd, if invariably disappointed, power player on the Elizabethan stage.

Eddings, always oblivious to the present day, was no Sidney. When his phone rang, he'd squint at it, not quite sure what to do next. Though he'd recently allowed a computer to be installed in his office, he still wrote his articles and books in longhand, turning over the manuscripts to a secretary for transcription. He was tall and perilously lean, giving the impression that even taking nourishment was an unwanted distraction from scholarship. In his mid-sixties, he had faded blue eyes and thick gray hair, with a deep, resonant voice that might have shaken the rafters in a sixteenth-century village church. Lee suspected he'd been quite handsome in his day, albeit in an ascetic way. He'd never married, and there was a lively debate among the masters and doctoral candidates as to whether he might be gay. Lee had always suspected that he was just oblivious to anyone not wearing a ruff collar, doublet, or velvet gown.

"I need your help," she said, entering his office, which was cluttered with books and manuscripts and smelled of damp paper. "It's about the sonnet."

"I saw you on that news program last night." His tone was condescending, but she knew he'd been excited by the reflected attention on the department. He'd even persuaded the Columbia public relations office to send out a press release on the discovery, though his quote in the release, expressing doubt about the sonnet's authenticity, had been infuriating. "Impressive."

"I was...." She decided not to tell him everything that had happened. He'd find out soon enough, but she needed information fast. "Someone tried to steal the sonnet. I need to know why."

"Steal it?" He swiveled in his chair to face her directly.

"I had it in my apartment last night. Someone broke in." Before he could respond she got to the point. "Didn't you tell me that it was worth at least forty or fifty thousand dollars?"

He smiled indulgently. "I told you that appraising manuscripts was not my forte. But I happen to know that if it were authenticated as being in Shakespeare's hand, it might go for at least that amount. In its current state, unauthenticated but almost certainly sixteenth century, it would probably fetch half the amount you mentioned."

Which hardly justified murder. She had another thought.

"I did authenticate the sonnet. You saw the draft of the paper I wrote, which has already been—"

"If I had a dime for every sonnet or play by Shakespeare that someone has quote-unquote authenticated, I'd be a wealthy man." He gave a tight smile.

Amazing, after what she'd been through over the past several hours, how angry and wounded she could be made to feel by his condescension. *Had* she become so invested in the sonnet's authenticity that she'd become blind to the possibility that it might be a forgery?

No, the sonnet was authentic. She'd sensed this the moment

she'd seen it in Grantham, Massachusetts. A handsome bond trader she'd recently met had invited her to an inn on the southern coast of Massachusetts for the weekend. She'd accepted in a weak moment. Matthew wasn't a bad guy. In fact, he'd seemed almost humble, which was refreshing in a financial titan-in-training. The inn was a surprisingly down-market choice for a Wall Streeter, and Saturday was overcast. After Matthew returned from a run (6.5 miles, he'd made a point of telling her), he suggested they visit a seventeenth-century house situated about ten miles from the inn. After the tour, she used the bathroom in an outbuilding and met Matthew in the small gift shop, which included a table of used books. One volume, sitting atop a pile of books, caught her eye. It was a compilation of Elizabethan love poems. The binding was plain red leather, worn to the texture of old skin. She wondered which of Sidney's poems it included—probably a sonnet or two from *Astrophel and Stella.* When she opened it, a small piece of paper fluttered to the wide-plank floor. She'd paid five dollars for the book, the piece of paper tucked inside.

The moment she touched the sonnet, she knew it was genuine. She felt it had been left there for her to find, that the entire weekend with Matthew had been cosmically arranged to bring her to the Taylor-Shipford house and guide her hand to the book with the plain red binding. True, as a scholar in the making, having a *sense* was hardly good enough. But she'd always let her instincts lead, then followed up with the facts.

"There hasn't been time for scientific tests, as you know," she said now, as evenly as she could. She hadn't gone to Eddings to debate authenticity. "But the contextual analysis is dead-on, as you—"

"The *contextual analysis,* as you call it, was dead-on in the 1790s, when Shakespeare's love letters to Anne Hathaway were discovered along with a completely new play, *Vortigern & Rowena.* There was a deed with his signature, and a lock of his hair. Imagine the excitement. Did you know that the play was performed by none other than Edmund Kean before it was exposed as a fake, along with the letters and the hair?"

Of course she knew. Next he'd mention the Second Folio.

"But that was nothing next to the discovery of the Second Folio, complete with manuscript annotations in the playwright's own hand. That piece of fraud was perpetrated by one of the most eminent scholars of his time. The truth is, there's not a single scrap of the Bard's own handwriting in existence, not one."

"But there are his signatures, six of them, and one of them matches the signature at the bottom of the sonnet."

"Even the signatures are suspect, as you know. They're nineteenth-century engraved copies."

"Copied from the original. Anyway, I told you I've been invited to present my paper at the World Shakespeare Conference next month in Melbourne."

"And you've appeared on the local news. But who has actually seen this thing, Lee? Other than the *legions* of viewers of last night's broadcast." That condescension again. Lee wondered if his skepticism about the sonnet, and disdain for the attention it was going to bring to her, were at least in part due to jealousy.

"I've been advised to keep it locked up. I've shown it to at least three scholars, one an expert in Renaissance manuscripts." She omitted the fact that Detective Lowry had seen it—and been less than impressed.

"But no one here at Columbia. Other than me, of course. Even if it's not genuine—even *though* it's not genuine—there are people out there who will believe that it is and try to take it from you. Where is it now? Have you brought it with you?"

"In a safety deposit box, where I should have put it last night."

"Running around on television vouching for its authenticity won't burnish our department's reputation in the event it's proven a fake. I have a responsibility."

Running around. One news program; a five-minute interview. And it had been his idea to issue a press release.

"You've worked with old manuscripts for years," she said. "You must have heard about thefts in the past. Who are these people?"

"There's an active black market in old manuscripts. *Authenticated* manuscripts. This is an entirely different situation. Why would anyone risk jail time to steal something that might be a fraud?"

"But on television last night I basically presented it as real."

"Still, anyone with knowledge of the field would want more proof before risking imprisonment."

She'd been standing during the entire conversation, but suddenly her legs felt heavy. She sat across from him in a visitor's chair, first removing a stack of student papers.

"I wish I had never found it." It was true. What had seemed a career-making gift only weeks ago now felt like a curse.

He reached out and took her hand. He'd never touched her before. She pulled back, then relaxed and placed her hand on his. Someday she'd find a way to get over the instinctive recoil from a man's uninvited touch.

"Lee, you have the potential to be a brilliant scholar. You know that. I've enjoyed our collaboration immensely. The undergraduates in your classes give you high marks. You're young, enthusiastic, and you see things that I don't, or don't anymore. Even Renaissance studies can benefit from youth. You must not let this derail your career." He gently squeezed her hand.

"I won't." Her words sounded unconvincing, even to her.

There was a long silence. He seemed to be working something out, his lips moving ever so slightly. When he finally spoke it was in a softer, deeper voice.

"There is something you should know, Lee. Something I found in the sonnet."

CHAPTER 4

She'd read only the first stanza on television, the first four lines of the sonnet's fourteen. The audience wouldn't sit still for more than four lines of poetry, the segment's producer had told her. Just show them the old parchment. "Not parchment," she'd said. "Paper. There were dozens of paper mills in sixteenth-century London, which is why—" He'd interrupted her mid-sentence to shout an order to a lighting technician.

David Eddings had written down the stanza she'd read. No one else had seen the entire sonnet, other than the document experts she'd consulted. The major "unveiling" of the poem would take place at the World Shakespeare Symposium in Melbourne next month. That was why she was going, to read the sonnet before the most eminent scholars in the world, and their acolytes.

Keeping the sonnet to herself had been Matthew the bond trader's idea. After she'd returned to the inn with the sonnet, he'd cautioned her not to show it to anybody. "As long as no one's seen it, it has value. Your only currency is the desire of people to know what it says. Tease the public with a few lines, if you want. But keep the rest to yourself."

Leave it to a bond trader to understand the power dynamics of academia. She'd followed his advice, letting it be known that she'd made a major Shakespeare discovery, but keeping the actual content of the sonnet to herself.

Except the four lines she'd read on the air, which Eddings had scrawled down. And in those four lines, he'd found something that she hadn't seen.

> Could I with love alone your safety grasp
> Then surely, love, my heart would lovely be.
> But lose a savior's lead and temper gains an asp
> As when for dying earth an apple quits the tree.

"You don't see it?" Eddings asked with impatience, pointing to the paper he'd written on, the stanza a mess of barely legible scribbling. "It's right there, in the fourth line."

She read it, to herself and aloud: "As when for dying earth an apple quits the tree."

"What does it mean to you?"

"It's a creation reference, obviously. The asp in the previous line, then the apple, a symbol of knowledge but also of destruction. It's about the relentless progress of time, the inevitability of death. The poet—Shakespeare—" she gave a tight smile— "is telling the object of the sonnet that he—"

"Nonsense. It's a clue. A buried word. The Elizabethans were addicted to wordplay, particularly puns, as you know. But now and then they would embed a word, or insert a palindrome."

"Henford," she whispered. The last three letters of "when," all of "for" and the first letter of "dying." In her mind she saw the key letters highlighted: "As w**hen for d**ying earth an apple quits the tree."

"But it could be a coincidence," she said. "The line makes perfect sense in the context of the first stanza. The poet wants to protect his love from the inevitability of death." Even as she spoke, she heard the crime scene officer describe the word imprinted on her notepad: Henford. She felt a shiver of panic.

"Nothing is a coincidence in the sonnets, which are rigidly constructed according to the fourteen-line, iambic pentameter rubric." He frowned. "Not that I am acknowledging the poem *is* Shakespeare's. Henford is a castle. I did some research last night. It's mentioned a few times in the literature, but there's nothing particularly noteworthy about it."

"But how did you see it?"

"Close examination of texts is my stock in trade." When he caught her skeptical frown he added: "When you showed me the original, before you locked it up, I noticed that the *h* in the word 'when' was darker than the rest of the letters in the line, almost as if it signified the start of a word rather than the second letter. And I also noticed that the spaces between the three words—'when' and 'for' and 'dying' were significantly shorter, as if the author *wanted* us to see them as connected, rather than apart. I've been puzzling over this for a while, and then when you read it last night it became clear, as if the word 'Henford' jumped out at me."

"May I use your computer?" she asked. The department had given every member a desktop. She'd never once seen Eddings use his.

He stood up and gestured toward his chair. She turned on the computer, opened a browser, navigated to Google, and typed in "Henford." A few names came up, several towns in the U.S. Nothing remotely connected to her or the sonnet, let alone to the murder the night before. Next she Googled "Henford Manor." Only a few links were returned, and none of them revealed much, other than that Henford Manor was about an hour north of London, had been privately owned since it was built in the thirteenth century, and was not open to the public.

"Not much to go on," he said, looking at the screen over her shoulder. "But if I were researching the authenticity of the poem, I'd begin at Henford."

"You're suggesting I travel to England?" Absurd. In fact, determining the authenticity of the sonnet hardly seemed important at the moment. On the contrary, proving the sonnet a worthless fake would probably be the best thing for her—presumably it would keep her safe from whoever murdered Alex. But whoever had killed Alex had written the word "Henford," and Henford was buried in the sonnet.

"The name is most certainly embedded in the poem," he said. "And consider the fact that you read four lines on a news program last night and that less than eight hours later there was an attempted robbery. Something about those four lines—something *in* those four lines—obviously attracted the thieves. The sonnet itself, until it's authenticated, just isn't worth a break-in, in my estimation."

Let alone a murder. Would the police follow a lead embedded in a bit of wordplay in a sonnet? Doubtful. They'd already dismissed the sonnet itself as more or less irrelevant. She thanked David and left, not quite able to ask if she could stay at his apartment that night. He'd probably agree, but it would be awkward, even without the explanation of why she couldn't go back to her apartment. They had almost nothing to do with each other outside of Philosophy Hall. She'd only been to his place once, to pick up some papers he'd asked her to grade. If she couldn't think of anywhere else to crash, she'd ask David. But there must be somewhere else she could stay.

Her phone buzzed as she walked across the campus. She fished through her purse to find it and saw "Unknown" on the screen. Warily, she answered.

"It's Detective Lowry. Where are you?" Her voice was tense.

Lee almost answered, but an instinct told her to extract some information first.

"What's going on?"

"Where are you?"

"At a friend's apartment," she lied. "And I won't tell you the address until you tell me what's happening."

A long pause, then: "Who is Josh Wilton?"

"I don't know."

"I repeat, who is Josh Wilton?"

"And I repeat, I don't know."

"Your boyfriend left a voicemail for Josh Wilton a few minutes before he died."

"My boyfriend? I told you, I only met Alex—"

"He sounded panicked on the message. Freaked out. Said you wouldn't let him go and that he was afraid you were going to turn violent."

"What?" She had left the campus and was on Broadway. Suddenly lightheaded, she leaned against a parked car.

"When Josh Wilton couldn't get in touch with his friend Alex this morning, he called the police. Why would Alex feel threatened by you? Did you show him your gun?"

"I don't have a gun."

"He was killed by a gunshot."

She had to squeeze her eyes shut to keep from shouting at the illogic of what she was hearing. She had no gun. She had no reason to want to harm Alex.

"We'd like to question you again," Lowry said. "Tell us where you are and we will come get you."

"What about Henford?" she said. "At my apartment one of the detectives told me he'd found the word on a piece of paper. I never heard the word."

"It was in the report. Where are you?"

"The word 'Henford' is in the sonnet I showed you. Well, not the word exactly, but it's buried in the second line."

"We've investigated the word. It doesn't appear relevant. And it has nothing to do with Alex and Josh Wilton."

"It's a manor house in England."

"As I said, it doesn't appear to be relevant. Perhaps you wrote the word yourself."

Clearly, *crazed sex addict kills one-night-stand* was still the operative theory.

"Shouldn't someone investigate it?"

"Only if it appears relevant. At the moment it does not. Now, tell me where you are."

She gave the address, on the East Side, of a friend who had long since moved out of the city.

"Do not leave the apartment, Miss Nicholson. Do you understand? We will be there within five minutes."

Why had Alex left that message? She had never threatened him. And she didn't own a gun. What was going on?

She flagged a cab and gave the driver the address she'd just given to Lowry. She would meet with Lowry, but not at the precinct. As the cab sped through Central Park across the Ninety-Sixth Street transverse, she saw that her legs were shaking. Literally shaking with fear. Great forces were acting upon her, mysterious plots that she couldn't begin to fathom. And yet she felt entirely alone, the center of something so big it left her feeling tiny and helpless.

She told the driver to stop at the corner of Eighty-Seventh and Third, a few blocks away from her friend's former building. Still carrying her tote bag, she walked slowly east, along Eighty-Seventh Street. When she got to Second Avenue she saw that Eighty-Seventh between Second and First had been sealed off by a patrol car parked across the street. Beyond it she saw that the street, where her friend had once lived, was choked with cars, some marked as NYPD vehicles, others not. Flashers blinked in syncopation.

This was all for her. No longer a victim whose apartment had been broken into, whose… friend had been murdered in her bed. No longer even a witness. They didn't send twenty cars for a witness. She was the suspect. The killer.

She stepped onto Second Avenue, heading toward the army of police cars and a future she felt certain she could predict: arrest, interrogation in another windowless room with a two-way mirror, questions about Alex, about his message. Maybe they'd demand to see the sonnet, and it would become a piece of evidence, dusted for fingerprints and then passed between unappreciative hands.

She stepped back onto the sidewalk. She would not go into custody, not without a better story to prove her innocence. She'd called the cops the moment she found Alex murdered in her bed. She'd let them interrogate her, answered everything honestly. And they hadn't believed a word. The voicemail was more than enough evidence to lock her up.

She would turn herself in eventually, but not without more information.

CHAPTER 5

Most flights to London departed early in the evening, which left a long afternoon to get through. Bone tired and needing a private place to think, Lee headed for the Broadway Hotel on West Seventy-Eighth Street. She'd stayed there when she'd come to New York for her Columbia interview and knew it was seedy but clean, and very cheap, the type of place that might not object to a guest who paid cash. She couldn't risk using her credit card.

She gave the hotel clerk a line about having her wallet stolen, a story he seemed neither to believe nor care much about. He did insist on two nights' payment upfront. The room was small, with a sagging double bed covered in an off-white chenille spread. Its one window looked out on a narrow, sunless courtyard. It smelled of furniture polish and mothballs.

She collapsed onto the bed but felt an immediate rush of anxious energy. How was she going to get through customs? Surely her name had been entered into some database of wanted fugitives. Even walking along Second Avenue to get a cab had made her feel exposed. Soon her face would be in newspapers and on the evening news.

A trip to the drug store and some quality time in the room's tiny bathroom would take care of changing how she looked, more or less. More problematically, she needed to change who she was. First things first. She put on fresh underwear and a new shirt from the duffle bag she'd packed back in her apartment and headed out. About three blocks south of the hotel, on Broadway, was a chain drug store, where she purchased scissors, hair coloring, and a tube of something called Tahiti Powder Bronzer.

Back in her room, she stripped off her clothes and positioned the scissors just below her left ear. Already, she didn't recognize herself in the mirror. It wasn't that she looked haggard or even frightened so much as *refocused.* The eyes gazing back at her saw beyond or perhaps through her; there was nothing familiar or friendly there. The image facing her was hard and wary, and alert, too, in a way she'd never been before. This was not a person who would sleep with a hunky cameraman after a few vodkas. This was not a person who would have intimate contact of any sort. This person was alone.

Snip. The first clump of hair fell into the sink. *Concentrate. Focus.* Another clump of hair, then another. Her beautiful chestnut hair, shoulder length or longer for most of her adult life, was now falling into a stained sink in a fleabag hotel. *Snip.* Expensive cuts at a posh salon on the East Side had been a regular splurge with her meager earnings from teaching Freshman Composition, and now she was massacring her hair with a two-dollar scissors. *Snip.*

Soon enough it was done. Not a terrible job. She had what would once have been called a bob, a short, bluntly cut hairstyle that angled up a bit in the back, exposing her neck. She shook her head to throw off any loose strands and was momentarily fazed when she didn't feel a thick mane of hair brush her neck and shoulders.

In the bathroom's stall shower she applied the hair coloring, "Champagne Blonde," carefully following the instructions on the box, for she'd never used hair coloring before. The process was longer than she'd expected and tedious, involving plastic gloves and the mixing of solutions and waiting times and a special conditioner. She paced the room between applications, half-sickened by the smell of the chemicals and still terrified at the course of events that had brought her to this room. When she was finally done, she dried her hair with a towel and smeared bronzer on her cheeks before facing the mirror.

Again, the sensation of confronting a stranger made her slightly dizzy. The coloring job wasn't awful. No one would take her for a natural blonde, but nothing about the color or the cut said "Look at me," either. With the blond hair and tan cheeks, she felt she could pass for a tourist from someplace cold and clean, Scandinavia, say, who'd just returned from a week of sunbathing in Jamaica. Or Tahiti. She smiled at the mirror and said "Hey," just to hear her own voice. After a long minute spent studying herself, she turned away and headed out with her laptop to take her new look for a test run and find a new identity.

She found a coffee shop on Amsterdam Avenue with free wireless access. After nearly an hour of searching, and a gallon of black coffee, she came across an organization called Eden Services, which was apparently a group of anti-government "bureaucrat" haters. Its physical location was not given, but she strongly suspected it was nowhere near New York. There was information about how to change your identity to avoid paying taxes (or, as the website put it, "acceding to government extortion"), how to acquire a new Social Security number, and how to live "off the grid." The site also listed multiple e-mail addresses for people with names like Troy Rebel, Nathan Hale, and Walt Waco. She opened a new Gmail account and sent the same message, from "Fed Up," to every address on the site:

Feds on my tail. Need new identity and credit card immediately. Can anyone help me in New York City? Will pay cash. Don't let them take me!

The message was suitably vague but with a paranoid edge that jived with the site's overall tone. She was counting on waiting a day or two for an answer, and was prepared to hole up in the hotel, perhaps even get some sleep, but a reply came through within minutes from someone identified only as Lucien. Perhaps these people did nothing else but monitor their e-mail for fellow anti-government travelers.

How much can you afford? was the terse reply.

She still had just over a thousand dollars in cash left. She typed, *Depends. How much for a credit card, social security number, and passport?*

The reply came a minute later. *$1,000.*

She'd gladly pay it to be able to rent a car, board an airplane, and check into a decent hotel, but felt she needed to conserve as much cash as possible. She typed *$500* and pressed send. Almost immediately the reply came: a telephone number with a local area code.

Worried that her cell phone was being monitored, she called the number from a payphone on Broadway—who even knew such things existed anymore? It smelled like cat litter. Perhaps, with a new identity, she'd be able to get a new cell.

"Is this Lucien? This is the person who e-mailed you just now."

"Fed Up?"

Fucked Up would be more like it. "I'm looking to establish a new identity. I'm… I refuse to support the system with my tax dollars, you see, and—"

"Yo, you can cut the bullshit with me. And it'll be seven-fifty. Got a pen? Write down this address."

144th Street just west of Broadway was a reassuringly ordinary block lined with mid-rise apartment buildings. A few had been renovated as Manhattan's relentless gentrification crept ever northward, and among the largely Dominican pedestrians Lee saw a few yuppie pioneers toting briefcases and bags from Crate & Barrel and Whole Foods. But most buildings retained an aura of benign shabbiness, including the address Lee had been given on the phone ten minutes earlier.

She pressed the button next to apartment 5A and was almost immediately buzzed in. The elevator had a handwritten "out of order" sign taped to it, so she trudged up four flights, feeling increasingly anxious with each one. What if she were stepping into a trap, a ruse to steal her money, or worse? No one knew she was there, and she was hardly in a position to call the cops.

But what choice did she have? She couldn't be Lee Nicholson any longer.

She knocked on 5A, one of three apartments on the top floor. The corridor was poorly lit and smelled of cigarettes and stale grease. After a moment the door was opened by a short, very thin white man with a thick, uneven beard, straggly moustache, and deep-set, rheumy eyes. He wore a white T-shirt—formerly white, actually, now a sickly yellow—and blue jeans that hung limply from his hips. At first she thought she might have woken him up, but once he'd gestured for her to enter she decided he must always look woozy and slightly dazed.

The apartment faced a narrow courtyard at the back of the building. Light from the single window in the living room cast a tired gray pall over the apartment. He switched on a table lamp, which only accentuated the gloom, and fell onto a sagging sofa of indeterminate color. She chose the only other option, a metal folding chair. Along one wall of the room was a long wooden board, supported by two filing cabinets, on which sat an impressive array of electronic equipment. She noted at least three different computers, two large flat screen monitors, several printers and assorted hard drives, all connected by a dense tangle of cords. Lucien struck her as the last person on earth who could master so much technology, but then he wasn't exactly building apps for Google.

She felt suddenly shy, like a patient on a first visit to a therapist. Where to begin? "I'm in some trouble with—"

"Who gives a fuck?" His first words, in a thin, scratchy voice that sounded like he could use something to drink. In fact, he projected an all-around lack of vital inputs: sunlight, food, water, companionship. "Just tell me what you need."

She took a deep breath. "For reasons that I really can't go into, I need a new identity. I've done nothing wrong, and I—"

"Okay, stop." He stood up so abruptly, for a moment she thought he was going to assault her after all. She rose almost immediately, hands clenched in fists.

"Relax, okay? Just relax."

She calculated that she could defend herself, if he tried anything, and assuming he wasn't armed. Without taking her eyes off him, she sat back down.

"Don't tell me nothing, okay? I don't need to hear shit about what you did." As he spoke his arms flailed arhythmically, adding to the sense of unfocused menace. "Just tell me what you need, right?"

"A credit card, Social Security number, passport, and driver's license."

"Okay, that's better. Just the facts, right?"

"You can provide these things?"

"S'what I do, okay?" Something approaching a smile appeared on his face. She'd expected an anti-government zealot, but he appeared to be an apolitical entrepreneur of sorts. He walked over to the electronics area and opened a small cardboard box that contained what appeared to be several dozen credit cards. He took one out and handed it to her.

"Sarah Cooper," he said. The name on the card. "There's like a few thousand bucks of credit on the card. I was you, I wouldn't charge nothing I didn't have to. Hotel rooms, car rentals, fine, but nothing else."

"Why hasn't Sarah Cooper reported this as stolen?"

"That wouldn't be easy, seeing as how she's dead." Another attempt at a smile. His inflamed gums were like grout around each tooth.

"Oh."

"Her family don't know she had this card, prob'ly. But when the statements start coming they'll figure things out, and then the card's no good. You got a few weeks, I'm guessing."

"Why don't you use it?"

"Me? Oh, no. You use stolen plastic enough, you get caught. Not right away, but 'ventually. What I do here, this is much cleaner." He gave the board that supported all the hardware an affectionate pat.

This didn't exactly inspire confidence.

"Will I get caught?"

"Most likely not right away. Depends when the family catches on. You don't want it?" He made a "give it to me" motion with his fingertips, like signaling a blackjack dealer for a card.

"No, no, I'll take it." Already, the credit card felt like a lifeline of sorts.

"So now we need a license for Sarah. New York State okay?"

She nodded.

"I'm assuming a U.S. passport? They're digital now, you know. Put me out of business. But I'll use an old date on this one. And what about the address? You cool with something upstate?"

"I guess it doesn't really matter."

"Cell phone?"

"You can get that, too?"

"Extra hundred bucks."

She nodded.

He employed an impressive array of materials and tools: computer, scanner, PhotoShop software, rubber stamps, sheets of Dura-Lar film, "Super Sculpey" sculpting putty (for the raised seal on the passport), X-Acto knife, and a tube of acrylic paint labeled "Interference Gold." He deployed these elements with silent, surgical precision. She watched, fascinated and horrified, as he created a license and passport for Sarah Cooper. His breathing was disturbingly aspirated as he worked, and slow, the sound of someone sleeping. At one point he stopped to take her picture with a digital camera, and when she saw her image on his computer screen—"champagne" blonde, spiky hair, bronzed skin, tense, unsmiling mouth and wary eyes—she wanted to tell him that she wasn't really that person, or she wouldn't be that person for very long. But she wasn't sure that was true, and he wouldn't care anyway. The image she saw wasn't Lee Nicholson, not anymore. It was Sarah Cooper.

An hour later, walking back toward the subway, she felt unexpectedly clearheaded and strong. She was a grad student, studying Renaissance literature. And she'd just acquired a new identity. What else was she capable of? Maybe turning herself in would have been more prudent, but she'd never been comfortable counting on anyone else. The person she'd trusted the most, her mother, had deserted her. And she'd been more of a parent to her hapless father than a daughter. She was used to going it alone, comfortable in that role. She had saved herself, and now she had the tools she needed to find the connection between Henford in England, the sonnet resting comfortably in a safe deposit box, and the murder in her apartment. When she had that information, she'd have the evidence needed to prove her innocence. She could be Lee Nicholson again.

CHAPTER 6

Lee tried without success to sleep on the overnight flight to London. After the nightmare of the day, and the anxiety of wondering if her new identity would work at customs, she'd anticipated a long, necessary slumber. But as soon as the plane took off she felt an almost irresistible restlessness that not only prevented sleep, but kept her walking the aisles of the 767, from one end to the other, as her fellow passengers dozed fitfully under dimmed cabin lights. She wished she'd packed a book, but in her rush to leave her apartment, swarming with police, she'd only managed to grab her laptop, clothes, and toiletries. Under normal circumstances, being bookless on a long fight would have been her worst nightmare. These were not normal circumstances.

What if she was wasting her time? Maybe she should not attempt to solve this herself. But what if the key to the invasion of her apartment was in fact at Henford? Would the New York police follow a lead to an old estate in England, when so much evidence—*all* the evidence—pointed directly at her? She'd sailed through check-in and U.S. Customs as Sarah Cooper, and boarded the flight unconvinced that she was doing the right thing but resolute in the importance of doing *something*, of taking action of some sort. She couldn't go back to her apartment. Her friends and probably David Eddings himself would soon be questioned about her, so she couldn't very well hole up with any of them. In fact, she didn't feel safe anywhere in New York. What if David was right, that the reason for the attempted robbery was not the value of the poem itself but the reference to Henford in the fourth line? What other clues might the poem contain?

She took the sonnet from her purse—not the original, which was still in the safety deposit box, but a copy she'd written out a few days earlier in preparation for the interview; reading fluidly from the original, with its elaborate script and idiosyncratic lettering and spelling, would have been difficult.

Could I with love alone your safety grasp
Then surely, love, my heart would lovely be.
But lose a savior's lead and temper gains an asp
As when for dying earth an apple quits the tree.

Heart, emeralds vainly exercise restraint
On those who for your station would aspire.
The peacock's astral plumage burns but faint,
Too dim to spare her brood from foul desire.

Must one deny my will? Pox will I bring,
A roiling storm will seem kind Pax's blow.
A plague when I uncap the bottled thing
From throne to grave no soul will comfort know.

When all the world in bootless ruin lies
I'll lie not more, but less my love belie.

"Henford" now jumped out at her, dominating the first stanza. Yet it still seemed like a slender thread connecting the sonnet to a murder and, now, a rash trip to England.

She rented a car at Heathrow—that is, Sarah Cooper rented it using her credit card and license—and drove to Henford. The pressure of navigating the one-hour journey, particularly the challenge of driving on the left side, took her mind off her predicament, offering a welcome respite from what had been a long and anxious twenty-four hours.

Henford was a village as well as a castle. Suddenly famished, she stopped at a tea shop in the village and ordered a black coffee and buttered scone. Henford contained a dozen or so shops lined up along a single narrow street. A few of the buildings appeared to have been built in the seventeenth century. At neighboring tables, women chatted over tea while outside, through the large plate glass window, people walked slowly by, carrying groceries and walking dogs. Compared to the city she'd left—had it really only been eight hours earlier?—Henford felt like another planet.

Fortified by the coffee, she made eye contact with an elderly woman sitting alone at an adjacent table.

"Excuse me, do you happen to know where Henford Manor is?"

The woman looked somewhat taken aback, as if Lee had asked the whereabouts of the Queen of England—or perhaps Sheba. She had a kind face ringed by buttery lemon hair teased into a diaphanous halo.

"I'd be an idiot if I didn't," she said. "Everyone knows the manor."

"Well, I'm not from around here…."

"Yes, I gathered that." The women peered at Lee over reading glasses. "American?"

"From New York."

"We don't get many tourists here. Not *quaint* enough, I suppose. Why Henford? It's not open to the public."

"Research," she said quickly.

"On Henford? I wasn't aware anything much had happened there."

"It is far from here?"

"Just up the road." She pointed out the window. "If you're hoping to get inside, you'll have a tough time getting past Lady Darman. She and Sir Benjamin bought the place a while back. He made a pile in investments, apparently. The knighthood's quite new. They spent a fortune restoring the place, which had been in ruins. I used to play hide and seek there as a child, much to my parents' disapproval. They were always afraid a piece of old masonry would fall on my head."

"You said I'd have a hard time with the owner."

"Lady Darman, yes. Her husband died not long after the place was finished. She doesn't come into the village much, and when I solicited her a few years ago for a house tour to benefit the parish church, she was quite rude. Wouldn't let me in the front door. That's the problem when city people buy up historic properties. They lack respect for local traditions. Still, perhaps your research will add value to the place, and that might encourage her to let you in."

Lee made a mental note to embellish her story for Lady Darman, and asked for detailed directions.

As promised, Henford Manor was a very short ride from the village. Lee found the entrance and drove between two stone columns and down a long drive that curved right and left for no apparent topographical reason, obscuring the house itself until she was almost at the front door. It wasn't enormous—nothing that a hedge fund manager might not commission for himself in Greenwich, Connecticut—and in fact it appeared in such excellent condition that it might have been a suburban "Tudor" built with a Wall Street bonus. After getting out of her car, she took a closer look. Three stories high, the building was made entirely of red bricks. Between the first and second floors, and over the windows and front door, the bricks were arranged in unusual patterns that added a touch of decorative whimsy. The house itself appeared pristine, but the landscaping was ragged; the lawn directly in front looked several weeks overdue for mowing, a number of dead, leafless trees swayed creakily in the breeze, and random tendrils from shrubs partly obscured ground-floor windows.

The front door was massive, made of wood, with a small, four-paned window just above eye level. She pressed the illuminated doorbell which, though tiny, looked ludicrously out of place. After what felt like a very long time, the door opened slowly to reveal a young girl dressed in a domestic's uniform: black dress, white collar, flat-soled shoes. She looked about eighteen, quite pale, her light brown hair pulled back into a short ponytail. She seemed more anxious than curious about Lee.

"Is Lady Darman at home?" Lee asked.

"Who should I say…." She shrugged, perhaps embarrassed by the formality of the question.

"It's urgent," Lee replied.

"But what exactly should I say?"

"Please, just get Lady Darman." Clearly the girl needed direction.

The girl frowned and pushed the door shut. Lee caught it before it closed completely and stepped into the front hall, a large, square space paneled in dark wood. A massive staircase led to the second floor, angling to the right halfway up. Suspended on a cord from the top of the stairwell was an enormous crystal chandelier; it struck her as embarrassingly out of place—more Miami, Florida, than Tudor England, and she noticed cobwebs between the crystals.

"I really must have that taken care of."

Lee turned to find a petite, elderly woman staring up at the chandelier. Like the doorbell and chandelier, she looked incongruously modern. She wore her lustrous silver-gray hair pulled tightly back, accentuating a classically handsome face with strong lines, preternaturally few wrinkles, and light blue eyes. She had on a pale lilac sweater set, probably cashmere, and black pants.

"Dust is like an invading army. The moment you turn your back it's upon you." She gazed up at the offending chandelier. From an interior doorway, the young girl who'd answered the door stood nervously observing.

"Lady Darman?"

The old woman turned to her guest, and nodded slowly as her eyes moved up and down Lee's frame. Suddenly Lee wished she'd changed out of the wrinkled blouse she'd worn on the overnight flight.

"I'm Sarah Cooper. From Columbia University."

"*Really*?" She sounded no less astonished than if Lee had announced her arrival from Tahiti. Or Mars.

Lee got right to it. "I've come across the name of your home in a newly discovered sonnet. I came here to investigate."

"Sonnet? What sonnet?" Her eyes narrowed with suspicion, as if Lee had mentioned not a poem but a newly discovered deed that might threaten her title to the manor.

Lee briefly summarized the finding of the poem and finished by reading the line that had brought her to England: "As when for dying earth the apple quits the tree."

"I don't understand."

Lee patiently explained about the buried reference to Henford.

"You came all the way here for that?"

Well, that and to escape a murder charge, she might have said. Not to mention the word "Henford" on a slip of paper by her bed.

"I need to learn as much as possible about this house."

"I'm afraid I'm quite busy." Even Lady Darman seemed unconvinced by the statement, uttering it in a faltering voice.

"I'm thinking that Henford may find its way into my book."

"Book?"

"On Elizabethan manor houses." Detecting a new sparkle in Lady Darman's eyes, she added, "A full chapter on Henford seems likely."

"Then I think you'd better follow me. Fiona, please bring us tea," she added, with an imperious nod to the young servant.

Lady Darman headed across the hall toward an open doorway on the left. As Lee followed, she noticed that the paneled walls were hung with portraits; all but one appeared to be of sixteenth- or seventeenth-century vintage. She was drawn to one picture by its jarring inappropriateness: a twentieth-century mogul posed stiffly in a Victorian wingchair before a giant open fireplace.

"My husband, Sir Benjamin. He died almost ten years ago, practically the day we completed renovations." She sounded less wistful than irritated by the irony. She led Lee into a vast room, also wood paneled. The tall windows were dressed in heavy, dark green velvet. On the floor were several large and apparently quite old oriental carpets. The furniture was classic rather than period—more Noel Coward than

Philip Sidney—comfortable sofas and chairs and tables arranged in four separate groupings. On the walls were more old portraits. The room felt impressive and tasteful and a bit unreal in its impeccable state of refurbishment. The only thing that was even remotely distinctive was the presence of two fireplaces on either side of the room.

"Two fireplaces?" Lee said.

"Yes, it's quite unusual," Lady Darman said. "Several of the bedrooms had two fireplaces when we moved in. We had most of the duplicates removed, but our decorator assured us that these two gave the room character. I assume this might find its way into your book."

She gestured toward a sofa, and Lee obediently took a seat. She immediately noticed a fine covering of dust on the table next to it. In fact, once she'd adjusted to the somewhat unreal opulence of the room, she began to realize that it was in fact quite filthy; to confirm this, she patted a throw pillow and saw a puff of thick dust emerge.

"It's just Fiona, you know," Lady Darman said, sounding a bit ashamed. Lee wished she'd been more discrete. "We used to have a full staff. But over the past few years the financial markets have taken away virtually everything I had. I've had to let everyone go except Fiona." Lady Darman leaned forward and added in a whisper, "She was the least expensive of the lot, though not especially talented in the domestic arts, I'm afraid."

As if to prove this point, Fiona appeared carrying a tray whose contents rattled precariously as she crossed the vast room.

"I'll pour," Lady Darman said. Fiona gave the tiniest of curtsies and hurried from the room.

"Frankly, a reference to Henford in a book would be welcome," she said as she poured tea into two porcelain cups. "It's a house without a provenance, unfortunately." She gave "provenance" a plummy French accent. "We were able to purchase it for far less than similar places, you know. Because of its history, or lack of one. But a reference in Shakespeare… perhaps I could charge admission. Sugar?"

Lee shook her head.

"Can you tell me anything about its history, Lady Darman?" Lee wondered if her ladyship had an actual first name. "I did a web search but there's nothing much to be found."

"Well, it's not exactly a distinguished house, though the renovation did merit eight pages in *Country Homes* magazine. Sixteen photos, three of this room alone." She slowly glanced around. "It's mostly fifteenth century. No one's sure of the exact date. There's a recorded deed from

1575 noting the sale of the house from a Robert Whittlesey to an Edward Filer. The Whittleseys are quite well known in this area; they're distantly related to the Howards, you know, and there are at least two other significant estates connected to the family, one of which is still owned by a family member. You see why my husband and I were never really accepted as locals. Perhaps if we'd had young children, and sent them to the local schools. But they were grown up when we moved here."

"What about Edward Filer?"

"It's unclear where he came from. His first appearance is on the recorded deed, which is odd. Even in the sixteenth century you'd have heard of someone who could afford to buy a place like this." She swept an arm from one end of the grand salon to the other. "But he appears out of the blue. My husband did some research on the Filers, you know. They spring up seemingly from thin air. An odd name, too, don't you think?"

Lee nodded. In all her readings of and about the sixteenth century, she'd never come across it.

"A lot of sixteenth-century names are of French origin, from the time of the conquest."

"You never said what exactly you specialize in, Miss Cooper."

"Renaissance literature. I'm writing my thesis on Philip Sidney, the poet and statesman."

"How interesting," she said, without a trace of enthusiasm. "Well, there's no record of him here, if that's what you're hoping for. We did have a royal progress, however."

"Elizabeth?"

Lady Darman couldn't suppress a stiff smile. "In 1576, a year after the house was deeded to Edward Filer. There's a rather lengthy description in William Cecil's diary from the time. Almost a full page."

Not quite as much space as had been allocated by *Country Homes*, but impressive nonetheless coming from the typically taciturn Cecil.

"We're not such a large house," Lady Darman said. "My sense is that Elizabeth usually stayed at grander places. I don't know where the entire court could have slept."

"She traveled so much, perhaps she had no choice. The progress was a way of defraying the costs of her household, which were expected to be picked up by her host. She'd go from house to house, with about fifty members of her court in attendance. To be selected as a host was a great honor, and a great expense. In addition to room and board, you were expected to provide entertainments and spectacles. Sometimes outbuildings were constructed specifically to house the court on a progress."

"Well, there are no outbuildings from that time here, other than the old stables. Cecil wrote that they stayed here a full two weeks. And you're correct about the entertainments. He lists actors and jugglers and musicians among those in attendance. I shudder at the extravagance."

"It was considered an investment," Lee said. "Royal favors usually followed—land grants, trade monopolies. Everything in Elizabethan England was a transaction."

"I don't know what Edward Filer got. His son, Charles, left for the New World eventually, a town in Massachusetts called Tunsbury. I only know that much because someone from the local historical society made a point of telling me. They have ships' manifests or some such thing from way back, the sixteen hundreds, I think. They tried to form some sort of 'sister city' arrangement with Tunsbury but were rebuffed. There just weren't any Filers left, apparently."

"So Edward's son, Charles, left for the New World—Tunsbury, Massachusetts—and that was the end of the family's presence in this area?"

"It was the end of them anywhere in England, as far as I can tell." Lady Darman shook her head, as if she personally were well rid of them. "There's no record of the house being sold. It appears to have been left in the name of Edward Filer to his descendants, but no descendants ever appear in any historical documents or records. The house became an orphanage in the eighteenth century, and then a school, though again, there's no record of a sale or even a donation. The school closed in the nineteenth century and the house was abandoned after that. I'm afraid that's the long and short of it. Are you very disappointed?"

She was, though she'd never been clear about what she'd expected.

"I would like to take a look at Cecil's diary for the reference to Henford. It can't be a coincidence that it's referred to in the sonnet."

"I've looked into offering tours of Henford, but there just doesn't seem to be much interest, certainly not of the fee-paying kind. Not authentic enough, apparently. The sonnet might help." She sipped her tea in happy contemplation for a few moments. "There is one thing I should show you. Something *authentic*. It's an old chest; we found it in the attic. The diary says it was presented by the queen herself during the progress. Would you like to see it? It's got a rather odd inscription."

• • •

Lady Darman led Lee back through the entrance area, up the grand staircase and down a long second-floor hallway. She narrated as they went, her tour more *Architectural Digest* (or *Country Homes*) than history lesson. "We had the drapes made from fabric we commissioned after seeing an identical pattern at Chatsworth," she'd said in the large library. "That rug was purchased at auction. Phillips du Pury. I was terrified we'd be outbid." There were some genuine antiques in the house, but they'd all, with one exception, been purchased recently to fill up the long-empty, cavernous space. And most looked like they had recently begun a slow decline into decrepitude.

The exception was the chest, relegated to one of many guest rooms, where it looked gloomily embarrassed amidst all the polished mahogany and riotous chintz. It was only about two feet high, but gave the impression of massiveness, with its heavy carving and dark, age-blackened finish.

"Imagine an entire house filled with the likes of this," Lady Darman said as Lee knelt before the chest. "I was tempted to sell it, but it belongs here, I suppose." She emitted a long sigh, perhaps troubled by the notion that the chest had more claim to Henford than she did.

"Are you sure it was presented by Elizabeth? Do you have a copy of Cecil's diary?"

"No, I don't. But one of the woodworkers who restored the moldings told me about it. The local people know these things, you see. Henford Manor is a point of pride to them."

Lee ran her hands along the deep carving, which depicted lush arrangements of apples, pears, and melons. When it came to furniture, the Elizabethans were not given to restraint, adapting Italian and Flemish designs with more gusto than taste. Only in the next century, under the Stuarts, would furniture-making achieve true distinction. But Lee loved the Elizabethans' enthusiasm and confidence, both of which were exuberantly reflected in the chest. Only the top had been left unadorned by carving, except for the inscription, which was included in an undulating ribbon running from one end to the other.

My heart no sympathy doth reject

She ran her fingertips over the inscription.

"Strange line, I've always thought," said Lady Darman. "Then again, I never could fathom half of Shakespeare."

Lee didn't bother telling her that Shakespeare, like Sidney, used "sympathy" to mean a deeper understanding of something, of a hidden truth, and not just a sense of pity or empathy. The words, though opaque in meaning, felt to her mind and fingertips like a pointed message from centuries ago. Why had the queen presented this chest with this odd inscription to this underwhelming household? Had it been created specifically for the progress of 1576? Or had it been given to the queen and then passed on to Henford as a last-minute house gift? Elizabethan regifting. The Elizabethans could seem so accessible through their words and at the same time so remote. It was part of what had drawn Lee to the period, this combination of the familiar and the unknowable. She imagined something similar drew people to science, in which new knowledge inevitably revealed new mysteries. When she was a girl her mother had read Shakespeare to her, scenes from the plays and the comedies as well as entire sonnets. Lee had been intrigued by Elizabeth I and her mother fed her fascination with books on the great queen, which Lee had devoured. Her mother had often quoted a line of the queen's, which seemed to define her own life in what must have been a loveless marriage, given that she'd ended it abruptly by running away: "If I were a milkmaid with a pail on my arm, whereby my private person might be little set by, I would not forsake that poor and single state to match with the greatest monarch." Lee sometimes worried that she was herself that milkmaid with a pail on her arm, well satisfied with the safety of the poor and single state.

When her mother moved out for good, Lee was just nine. But even at a young age she'd sensed her mother's unhappiness. When they were together, often in Lee's room, she got the feeling that her mother was seeking refuge, that she was there because there was no other place for her to be. Later she realized that her father wasn't cruel to her mother, and certainly not violent, just inadequate. He was clueless about what she wanted, let alone needed, and completely uninterested in anything that interested her. Lee always wondered why her mother had married him, given that they seemed to occupy separate planets. His motivation was easier to fathom; her mother was beautiful and intelligent and sophisticated. But what had drawn her to a small-town safety inspector at a local chemical plant? And when her mother finally did leave, she abandoned Lee to a father so devastated he almost couldn't bear to look at his daughter, who was so much like the woman who had broken his heart. Every time he looked at Lee, he must have seen a doppelgänger of the woman who had left him. So he rarely looked, seldom talked, and never touched. Lee escaped the emptiness the way her mother had, taking refuge in Elizabethan England, and the warmth of boldly expressed passions.

Running her fingers across the time-burnished surface of the oak chest, she felt at once close to the sixteenth century and hopelessly estranged from it. Who would ever know why the chest had been presented, or what its inscription really meant?

The inside of the chest offered no clues. It was filled with shoeboxes and contemporary linens. Lee stood up with some regret and cast one last look at the chest before heading for the door.

"I've been told that Edward Filer's son, Charles, took most of the good furniture with him when he left for the New World," Lady Darman said. Lee made a mental note to find out what happened to the Filers and their good furniture. "One can understand why he chose to leave this hulking thing behind. I imagine it would have sunk the ship. We had to hire two men from the village just to bring it down from the attic. It's a shame a Filer didn't end up a president or secretary of state. You'd be surprised by the increase in value when the Americans find a connection to Merrie Olde England. Speaking of which, that sonnet you found, is it considered first-rate?"

Lee was halfway down the long second-floor hallway when it hit her: a possible meaning of the inscription. She turned and ran back to the guestroom, Lady Darman hurrying to keep up.

"It's another embedded word clue, it has to be," Lee said. She knelt by the chest and read the inscription aloud.

"My heart no sympathy doth reject."

She studied it closely, running the words together to see if new ones appeared. Nothing. There appeared to be no hidden words, no embedded clue to anything.

"It's just an old chest," Lady Darman said, breathing hard.

"No doubt. But the word 'sympathy.' What deeper truth did the author of this line want us to see?"

"It's gibberish, I imagine, like a lot of old poetry."

"It would have taken weeks to carve this line. No cabinet maker would do that unless he was being paid by someone for whom the line was meaningful."

She stared at the words, ran her fingers across them. Nothing. The thought that the entire trip to England was a folly, worsening her position with the police when, inevitably, she returned to New York, fell upon her like a blow to the back of her head, causing her to lean on the old chest for support.

"Maybe you're right; it's just gibberish." She stood up, prepared to leave the room a second time, when she realized that the carved inscription included an instruction: *reject.* In Elizabethan poetry, the word meant to turn back, reverse. A mirror image.

She looked back at the chest. Now the line practically vibrated with potential meaning. She read it aloud—"My heart no sympathy doth reject"—and then ran her fingers from right to left, this time reading the line backward, letter by letter.

"T.C.E.J.E.R.H.T.O.D.Y.H.T.A.P.M.Y.S.O.N.T.R.A.E.H.Y.M."

If only she had a pencil and paper. She mentally ran the words together, trying to find links between them, still read reading from right to left—"rejecting" the letters.

And then she saw it.

"My son," she said.

"What?"

"Between 'sympathy' and 'no,' reading backward, the letters spell 'my son.' That's the hidden meaning in the line, the deeper meaning we were meant to find."

"I don't understand."

Lee felt the same nervous excitement she'd experienced when the sonnet had fallen out of the poetry book. The embedded words—"my son"—were significant, and she'd been sent to Henford to find them and determine what that significance was.

"More hidden words? Do you think this makes the chest more valuable? The sonnet, and now the chest—would people pay to visit Henford?" Lady Darman was breathless.

Lee needed to think, and while she hated to leave the chest she knew there was no way she could work things out with Lady Darman pressing her on the chest's value and the possibility of the sonnet attracting paying visitors to Henford. Reluctantly she stood up and left the room, Lady Darman just behind her.

"I may need to authenticate the chest with an expert at some point," she said at the front door. Night had fallen; she hadn't realized how long she'd been inside. "I'm convinced it's genuine, but—"

"Do you really think it's the genuine article?" Lady Darman's eyes glistened with hope as Lee said goodbye and left the house.

Henford looked gloomy but perhaps more authentic at night, the windows dark, as most would have been centuries ago. In fact the old place seemed forlorn in the near-darkness, as if all the money and effort and ambition applied to hoisting it into the modern age had somehow exhausted—or perhaps embarrassed—it.

With how sad steps, O moon, thou climbest the skies
How silently, and with how wan a face!

Sidney was superb at projecting onto objects, like the moon, the thwarted passions he felt in his heart and mind. Tonight the ghost of a moon, just visible on the horizon, did indeed cast a wan face over Henford. It shed a gray glow across the grounds, sending the landscape back to an earlier, black-and-white era. The night air smelled sharp and fresh, the slight chill bracing after the dusty stuffiness inside the house. Fishing her car keys from her purse, she still felt high from her discovery, though she was far from certain what "my son" could mean. She'd taken the first steps toward figuring out what had happened in her apartment, why Alex had been killed. It had to do with the sonnet, which had led her to Henford, and to the chest, whose hidden message would, she felt sure, lead her to the next step.

There was a slight rustling sound behind her, a few feet away. *Feet on the gravel*, she thought at first. Then: *No, just a small animal.* The crunching sound moved closer, got louder. *Bigger than a squirrel or even a dog,* she thought at the very moment her knees hit the gravel.

Only then, kneeling on the driveway, did she realize that she'd been struck on the back of the head. She started to turn and was struck again, this blow falling on the side of her arm and sending her sprawling onto the gravel. She pressed her purse into her face to protect it and squeezed the rental car key chain, all three tiny buttons, until she activated the alarm.

She heard a low grunt of surprise from her attacker at the sound of the alarm. She rolled over, twice, and was starting to stand up when she was pushed back down. As she fell she made out a large form, probably male, holding something in his hands, a club of some sort. The face, looking down at her, was silhouetted in shadow.

"No, stop!" she managed to say as he raised the club-like object above his head. She rolled to her right and attempted to scramble to her feet.

"What in God's name is going on?"

At the sound of Lady Darman's voice the attacker froze, then took off down the drive. Within moments, he'd vanished into the darkness.

"Who was that? What are you doing on the ground?" Lady Darman stood inside the doorway, one hand gripping the door itself, prepared to slam it shut.

Lee pulled herself up, dizzy. A dull ache radiated from the back of her head, her knees stung where the gravel had cut through her pants, and her right shoulder felt as if it had been injected inexpertly with a thick needle.

"Can't you turn that off?" Lady Darman aimed a finger at the wailing car.

Lee silenced the alarm, which had clearly drawn Lady Darman, as intended, and saved Lee's life.

"Who was *that*?"

"I don't know." Lee didn't want to alarm Lady Darman, who would call the police. Even as Sarah Cooper she didn't want attention from the police. What she did want was information, starting with what "my son" had to do with two attacks, first on Alex the cameraman, then just now, on her.

"A traveling companion," she managed to say.

"But where has he gone?"

"He wanted to walk back to the hotel."

"Walk? Whatever for?"

"I'm sorry if we disturbed you, Lady Darman," Lee managed to say as she got into her car, feeling unsteady and wondering if driving was really the smart thing to do. But what choice did she have? "It won't happen again," she added as she slammed the door. As she pulled away, driving very slowly, she saw Lady Darman in the rearview mirror, arms crossed, still standing in front of the door, a tiny, confused old woman dwarfed by the house and the history around her.

CHAPTER 7

She'd spent a restless night at the only lodging near Henford, an inn over a pub, the Coach and Horses. Her head throbbed where it had been struck, even after a fistful of aspirin, and she slept poorly. She woke early with a kind of hangover. Eggs and bacon in the pub downstairs, with copious amounts of coffee, helped a bit. As she ate breakfast, a plan took shape. She'd return to New York and place herself in the custody of the New York City police. Whatever happened, however guilty the circumstances of Alex's murder made her look, she'd be safe from whoever was trying to kill her. She'd survive. The attack last night had changed everything.

But she was in England, with several hours before her flight left for New York, which was ample time for research. Her immediate and strongest instinct was always to hit the books. She'd long believed that the answer to any dilemma could be found in writing. When she thought of being locked up in jail, even for a night, what terrified her most was not having access to books, to answers. It had always been that way. Growing up, after her mother left and her father abandoned her emotionally, she didn't take refuge in friends or sports or drugs. She read. English literature, mostly, and history. The books her mother had left her. After school she holed up in the town library until closing time. Fiction and history were alternative places to live. Even as an adult the smell of a library, the pungent mustiness of stacks of seldom opened books, could soothe her more reliably than friendly conversation or even the touch of a lover.

Cecil's papers were kept in several places, including the British Library in London, but most were housed at Hatfield, his ancestral home. A prolific writer, Cecil was an indispensable chronicler of Elizabethan England, having had a unique vantage point as the queen's chief minister. If, as Lady Darman claimed, there was a reference in his writings to the chest at Henford, with its mysterious inscription, it would be in his diaries, which were kept at Hatfield, the palace he'd built on the grounds of the estate in which Elizabeth herself had been kept a virtual prisoner during the reign of her older sister, Mary.

Lee drove to the village of Hatfield where, at eight o'clock, she found an open tea shop at the small train station. After several cups of coffee, she got back in the car, turned on her laptop, and drove through the still-sleeping little village until she detected a wireless signal on a street lined with densely packed homes of Tudor vintage, many of which looked recently renovated. She parked and navigated online to the *New York Times* site. There, on the homepage, was an article about the murder in her apartment. She clicked on the headline, and up came a photograph of the outside of her building, which evoked sudden and uncontrollable sobbing. It seemed so far away, that unassuming brownstone, so unattainable, now.

Alex Folsom was thirty-eight and had come to New York City a decade earlier to work in television after several years working construction. A pilgrim to the city, hoping like her to reinvent himself. She spent a few minutes trying to recall Alex—it seemed she owed him at least that—and tried without complete success to absolve herself of responsibility for his murder. If she hadn't brought him back to her apartment, if she hadn't let him stay the night—

Her name was identified in the first paragraph as the apartment's resident, "a graduate student in literature at Columbia University," and in the third, in which a police detective was quoted as saying that "Miss Nicholson is considered a person of interest at this time." He added that the police had not ruled out the notion that Miss Nicholson had herself been a victim of a violent crime. The existence of a phone message, identifying her as a threat to Alex Folsom, was not mentioned.

What must her friends, not to mention David Eddings and the others in the English department, be thinking?

The flight to London, the discovery of the inscription, even the attack at Henford, had somehow distracted her from her predicament. Now it came back to her, vividly. She clicked from the *Times* to the homepage for Hatfield House. Disappointingly, it didn't open until noon. The research library and archives, however, were surely staffed earlier than that. She read some more about Hatfield, which she'd visited several years earlier, touring the new palace and old house along with a dozen other paying guests. It was still owned by descendants of William Cecil, who'd been named Baron Burghley by Elizabeth in 1571. Cecil himself had never lived at Hatfield; his son exchanged the family's former home, Theobald's, for it in 1611, then tore down most of the old palace and built a newer, much grander one. But many of the first baron's papers were housed at Hatfield nonetheless.

Lee drove to the gate that was opposite the train station. She rapped on the window of the small guardhouse. The door was opened a few seconds later by a gruff-looking man wearing a corduroy jacket and khaki trousers. She flashed her Columbia University identification card and gave a story about an appointment with the chief librarian. Unfortunately, the guard insisted on calling the librarian, and informed her a few seconds later that she was most definitely not expected.

"Please, tell him I made the appointment weeks ago; I've come all the way from New York and my plane leaves this afternoon."

Perhaps it was the desperation in her voice, or the alarming gauntness of her face, despite the application of makeup and Tahiti Bronzer in the train station bathroom, but the guard handed her a pass and told her to walk up the long drive to the palace.

The Hatfield archives were housed in two large storerooms on the ground floor of the palace. Lee went to a side entrance, as instructed. The house appeared more massive than she recalled, perhaps because she now had the place to herself. It was built a few years after Elizabeth's death in 1603, making it Jacobean rather than Elizabethan—and therefore outside her area of academic focus. Its two red-brick wings splayed out from a central structure of white masonry, reminding her of a peacock displaying its plumage. Indeed, there was something preening about Hatfield, the way it sat brazenly at the center of acres and acres of grounds, unembarrassed by its immensity or ornament. In architecture the Elizabethans were more reserved than their descendants, and would have been appalled by the Victorian flourishes added to Hatfield by subsequent generations of owners (including the first desecration, the partial destruction of the old palace, many bricks of which had been incorporated into Burghley's monument to power and influence). But the estate, which included surviving portions of the old palace, was steeped in Elizabethan political history, and as she headed for the side door that led to the archives she felt a deep regret that she didn't have time to visit the old palace.

Inside a tall, thin man, about fifty, she guessed, greeted her with a skeptical half-smile.

"Miss Nicholson? I'm Jordan Collins. Apparently you believe we have an appointment." It felt good to hear her own name, after a day as Sarah Cooper. She doubted the news of Alex Folsom's murder had reached Hatfield.

She repeated the story that had worked with the guard, finishing with a plea. "If there has been a mix-up, I'm very sorry. But I have a flight back to New York this afternoon."

He frowned, accentuating the shadows along his craggy face, which was not unkind but struck her as professionally dubious.

"I only have a few minutes."

He led her back to his office, a small room in the basement that had probably been used as servants' quarters. She wondered what other pressing business he might have, as there was clearly no one else around and his office, with its neat stacks of papers and gleaming Macintosh desktop computer, hardly seemed a hub of activity. Nevertheless, she got right to the point.

"I'm researching a particular Elizabethan progress, from 1576. The royal party stopped at a place called Henford."

"Yes, a strange choice."

"Are you familiar with *all* the royal progresses?"

"Only the ones in which William Cecil participated. The 1576 progress was one of them. Why Henford?"

"I'm looking into the provenance of a large chest that was most likely presented to the household on the progress, by the queen, apparently. Perhaps it was mentioned in Cecil's diary?"

"I don't recall a chest." His eyes lost focus; he seemed intrigued.

"But you're not sure? Could we consult the diary?"

The Cecil diaries, along with other papers from his long tenure at Elizabeth's court, were housed in a vast, dimly lit room kept to a very cool temperature and accessed by entering a key code that opened a thick steel door. Her pulse quickened as he led her down the long central corridor, which was lined with leather-bound books and oversized folios of papers lying on their sides. The past felt tangibly present, and it took some effort not to wander down the various aisles labeled "Correspondence," "State Papers," "Legal Documents."

"We have about 30,000 documents," he said as they walked. "Most have been photocopied, and we are in the process of digitizing the collection. For the diary entry you're seeking, however, we must consult the original."

He seemed to relish the idea, and she shared his enthusiasm. Soon enough, documents like the ones in the Cecil Archives could be consulted online by anyone with a password—a great convenience for scholars. But a lot of the pleasure of historical research would be forfeited, and in her experience there was no substitute for consulting original documents. Simple variations in handwriting between manuscripts by the same author could indicate different moods or varying degrees of urgency. Such nuances were lost when a document was photocopied or digitized.

"Let's see, oh, right, here we are." He made a right turn and slowly walked down a short aisle lined with glass-enclosed shelves. Each shelf held a single book, lying on its side. "Fifteen seventy-six. Right here."

He put on a pair of thin cloth gloves, opened the glass, and removed the diary. Lee had been in several archives, and rarely did anyone use gloves any longer, except when handling photographs. But she appreciated the gesture, inspired more by reverence, she suspected, than necessity. Holding it in front of him like an icon at a religious rite, he retraced their steps to the entrance, walking more slowly on the return trip. Instead of leaving the archives the way they'd come in, he headed into a small, windowless room with a table and four chairs. Delicately, he placed the diary on the table and sat down. She took the chair next to him.

With one hand resting atop the volume, as if he were afraid it might fly off on its own, he looked toward the ceiling and began thinking out loud.

"Let's see, the progress was in the late spring, of course. There was quite a bit of international back and forth that year, the Peace of Monsieur in France, the death of the Holy Roman Emperor Maximilian. So I'm guessing we should start here." He gently opened the book about two-thirds of the way in. She leaned closer to him. "May 25," he said with a prim smile. "Not bad for a first shot."

Very slowly and carefully he began turning the pages, one by one. Cecil had written in a tight, vertical hand, using almost every available bit of the page. Lee had consulted hundreds of old manuscripts but she could see that Cecil's papers would be a challenge to decipher.

It took several long minutes of painfully slow page-turning to find the entry concerning the progress.

"Yes, here it is. June 23. They began at Greenwich." He moved his finger over the page, careful not to touch it. Then another slow-motion turn of the page and more finger-scanning. "Henford. June 30. Shall I read it?"

She nodded, and he cleared his throat, a self-consciously dramatic effect.

"'We stop at Henford. The house is small but well appointed. I have arranged for tents to be erected in the park, but even these fail to accommodate the full party, and there is grousing from a number of people. I share quarters with my Lords Rochford and Essex, which puts us all in an ill temper. Her Highness shows no such peevishness. In truth she is unaccountably happy, in spite of the hot weather that wilts her ladies, the youngest and oldest alike afflicted. Our host Edward Filer sets a fine table but does strike me as a performer thrust onto the stage without proper training. He is three and twenty but appears a callow youth, nervous and easily alarmed. Despite the heat he wears a heavy cloak, and I have seen his teeth chatter at divers times in the evening and early morning. He accepted a large chest from the Queen, which delighted him no small amount, as its carving is exceptional and required a wagon of its own to transport from London.'"

He looked up at Lee, who let out a long, slow breath.

"Is there more?" she said.

He carefully turned to the next page and continued.

"'June 25. I have tried to interest Her Highness with the news from France, where a treaty appears likely to end the religious fighting. This could bode ill for England, should that country finally right itself and gain strength through unity. She is unwilling to treat of such matters, preferring long walks with our young host, Filer, shooting parties, and the like. The evening entertainments are spectacular, perhaps too much so, for today Essex was ordered to solicit funds from the treasury for their support. Our host, it seems, is not bearing the cost. Most unusual.'"

Collins looked up. "That *is* most unusual. The host of the royal progress always bore the cost of the entertainment and everything else. It was part of the reason the queen liked the progress, the opportunity to freeload. Who is this Filer, anyway? I don't recall him." Collins sounded peeved, as if a dubious stranger had moved into his neighborhood.

"I haven't had time to look into him, but he appears to have come from nowhere. Henford struck me as kind of small to host a progress."

"Well, the Tudor houses weren't as grand as Hatfield. Just look at the Old Palace, or what remains of it."

"Is there anything else?"

He scanned the next few pages, running his finger just above the diary's surface.

"Ah, here we go. 'Her Majesty exhibits no intention of leaving Henford, which has made one and all peevish in the extreme, as the place is small and no breeze blows between its walls. I hinted to Her Majesty that it would be prudent to move the court as planned to Loughton Hall, but she was most aggrieved at the suggestion, and I have sent to London for still more funds. Affairs of state are of no interest. The boy Filer, for he is but a boy, I think, with his fair hair and pale complexion, always swaddled in heavy gowns despite the heat, like a young suckling, grows increasingly complacent in her presence, a cause of much disturbance in the court. I have sent to Brompton for news of this person.'"

Collins looked up from the diary. "Brompton," he said, "was Cecil's secretary. He would have stayed in London to carry on business while the entire court made merry on the road, as it were." He returned to the diary. "He writes, 'The Queen is fairly intoxicated by him, though I have seen no improprieties.'"

He scanned the diary in silence for a bit. "Ah, yes. 'July 9. We finally, after two weeks, depart Henford.' Two weeks!" Collins looked at her. "Unprecedented." He waited for her to acknowledge this, which she did with raised eyebrows, then resumed reading. "'I am sure no one save the Queen was sad to leave. She and young Filer spent the morning alone together walking the park, like two lovers, though theirs is by all accounts a chaste entanglement. Brompton sent word that Filer comes from an unknown family in the north of no distinction. Henford was a gift from the Howards, it seems, when he was but an infant and Mary still on the throne. We do not know the connection between Filer and the Howards. But enough of this frail boy who has captured the fancy of the Queen and near bankrupted the treasury. On to Loughton!'"

He read silently for a few pages.

"No more references to your Henford, I'm afraid. It does seem odd that the Howards gave him the house. They were early supporters of Elizabeth, during the Marian Restoration. I wouldn't have thought they'd part with even a smallish house while Bloody Mary was on the throne and their beloved Elizabeth was holed up here." He pointed behind him, presumably to the Old Palace. "Then again, it's all quite unusual. The progress remaining at such an undistinguished place for so long. Footing the bill from the royal treasury. The queen's obvious infatuation with this Edward Filer, who, by the way, never appears in a single court record that I know of. The man apparently never visited London."

"Her son," Lee whispered.

"What did you say?"

Of course, it could be nothing more than the infatuation of a forty-three-year-old woman with a man half her age. Elizabeth, God knows, wasn't immune to that sort of thing. But his ascendance to royal favor had clearly begun many years earlier, with the gift of Henford from the politically connected (and Elizabeth-aligned) Howards. If he'd been her favorite, then why hadn't he ever appeared at court? And there was the carving in the chest, which Cecil's diary confirmed was presented to Filer by the queen herself.

"My son," she said quietly, drawing a puzzled look from Collins. Born when Elizabeth was twenty, not yet queen, in fact a virtual prisoner at Hatfield, awaiting the fate determined for her by her older half sister, Queen Mary.

"Are there any records from 1543 of Hatfield Palace?"

"The Old Palace? We have household accounts, that sort of thing. We're digitized through 1560."

"Could I have a look?"

He frowned at her impertinence. "I still don't understand what it is you're seeking."

"Please, I won't disturb you."

They walked back to the office area, where he led her into a small room equipped with a desk and computer. He logged on and clicked and typed through a number of screens.

"Here you go," he said without much enthusiasm. "I've called up all records from 1543. There aren't many, as you can see. Household purchases...." He scrolled through old documents that had been scanned into the database, most of them lists written in impenetrable handwriting. "Quite a number of visits by a physician named Rufus Hatton."

"A physician?"

"From the letter sent by Sir Robert Welles to Queen Mary's Privy Council. Welles was the head of household at the time, Elizabeth's unofficial jailor, really. Hatton seems to have come quite frequently that year. Of course, we don't know if the doctor continued to make house calls, as Welles died that year, some sort of brawl or duel, the details of which are lost to time, I'm afraid."

Lee worked it out while driving back to Heathrow. An incredible story, but the deeper truth was detectable with *sympathy*, as the carved inscription had it. Elizabeth, then a princess and held captive at Hatfield, had delivered a child, a boy. A physician, Rufus Hatton, had been summoned to attend the delivery, which must have been a difficult one since births, even for the highborn, were handled by midwives, with physicians brought in only when there was a complication that threatened the mother's well-being. The father's identity was unknown, apparently. If the father had been named Filer, then the name would have appeared somewhere, since everyone who came into Elizabeth's orbit was observed and almost obsessively recorded. This Filer came from nowhere, it seemed, almost as if—

"Filer!" she shouted, then laughed out loud.

Elizabeth, like all royals at the time, was as fluent in French as English.

"Filer!" She had to concentrate to keep from veering off the road. *Fils* was French for son. But writers in the sixteenth century were reliably inconsistent in their spelling, dropping letters for no apparent reason. So, *fil* was *fils*. The *er*, of course, stood for Elizabeth Rex.

Edward Filer was Elizabeth's son.

CHAPTER 8

Hatfield
20 March, 1555

I know not how to record the events of this day, nor even if doing so is wise. Yet I must. For in what person can I confide that which has transpired at Hatfield today? What person would I burden with this news? Even if my beloved Jane were alive still, would I trouble her with this story? Would I put her so much at risk? Yes, I fear I would, for I am weak, and the events to which I bore witness cry out for description. Without Jane, I have only this diary.

I climbed Fore Street to Hatfield the day following the boy's birth. I had promised my lady that I would see to his well-being, though he appeared to be a robust child of sufficient weight and vigor. He has been removed from the palace, and the Princess's orbit, and placed in the care of a local family, a small landowner and his wife, who know nothing of the child's origins, only that its mother was high-born, and unable to keep it. The early morning shimmered with warm sunshine, and I was falsely comforted into believing that this story would unfold as comedy, not tragedy. A thundering storm would have better foretold what was to come, but I could not know that at the time.

The Hatfield gate was within view when I saw a woman's figure running toward me down the hill and away from the house. From afar I could see that she wore a white robe, perhaps a dressing gown, and her long hair was flying madly about her. As we neared one another I began to hear sounds, a low sobbing such as a person in great physical distress might make, and soon I was able to see her face and know her as Kat, the Princess Elizabeth's loyal lady-in-waiting.

I began to run toward her, impatient to learn the source of her distress, for it was clear she was greatly disturbed.

When we were but a short ways apart, I saw that her white dressing gown (for it was in fact such) was stained red round the middle. At once I knew it to be blood.

"My lady, what has happened?" I inquired.

She fell onto me, sobbing, almost pulling me to the ground. I feared perhaps she had died, so burdensome was her weight. I gently placed her upon the soft ground that bordered the drive and saw to my relief that she was indeed still breathing.

"You must hide me, sir," she said. "They will come for me."

"Who will come, Kat? Why must I hide you?"

"Please, put me away from the road. 'Twas only that the gate was opened that saved me. They will come and they will kill me as they have killed the others."

"What others, Kat?"

"And you, Doctor, they will kill you too."

"Why would they kill me?" I asked this in good faith, but quickly guessed what was occurring. I felt my heart begin to pound as blood rushed into my head. Cecil had lied to me when he asked me to keep watch over the Princess and report what I learned. Or perhaps he'd changed his mind. In either case, I was marked for death.

At that moment I heard men's voices from up the hill, near the gate. I picked up Kat and walked as quickly as I could into an alley a short distance away. From there I turned into a small yard, blessedly empty, and laid her upon the ground.

"Now, you must be still and allow me to examine you." I endeavored to maintain a steady voice, though I fear I was not successful.

I began to open the buttons along the front of her dress. She quickly grasped my hands and pulled them from her.

"Kat, I cannot help you if I am not permitted to see what has happened to you. Let go of my hands, Kat."

She turned her head to the side, her face stiff with distress, and released my hands.

I unbuttoned her gown and saw a gash the length of my thumb across her stomach. A sword wound, I thought. The opening did not appear to be bleeding profusely but I thought it best to stanch it nonetheless. I removed my jacket, then my shirt. I placed the shirt around her middle and across the wound, fastening a tight knot to hold it in place.

"You will be fine," I told Kat as I buttoned her gown. But would she? Would I? Just then I heard a contingent of horses clopping down Fore Street, and voices. Between us was the humble house whose yard was our temporary infirmary. Would they search the houses along Fore

Street? My prayers to the contrary were answered, for soon enough, though it felt an eternity, the party moved on.

"Who did this to you, Kat?"

"'Twas my lady's friend, sir, David Cecil, and his men. All who were there. The midwife, the servants, the guards—all of them who were there that day."

"The day of the birth."

"Yes, all who were there are now dead, save me and...."

They would be coming for me.

Elizabeth, if she could survive her sister's bloody reign, would be Queen, and Cecil would be the power behind the throne of a young woman unschooled in affairs of state. But a bastard son, a disgrace of a Prince, would destroy her chances, and theirs.

"The boy?"

"They wouldn't dare harm him, he has Tudor blood in him. But what of me? What am I to do? How will I save myself?" After a moment of sobbing she added, "And the boy. I promised my lady I would see after the boy."

My mind teemed with desperate thoughts. Look out for yourself! Ride to London and get word to Queen Mary that her half sister has foaled a bastard. That welcome news would earn me a great reward and royal protection. But I had no appetite for abetting the Catholic apostate. And had I not had a hand in birthing the son? Did that not in some way make me responsible for its safety, and that of its mother?

The only honorable way to save myself and Kat was to enlist the help of the Princess.

"Does your lady know of this?"

Kat shook her head. "She was yet abed when it began. All were taken by surprise. There were no shouts to rouse her."

"And the father?"

"I don't know who you—"

"'Tis no time for coyness, Kat."

"I fear he is dead, too. They went for him last night. To tell him the good news, they said."

"Miles Stafford?" I said, for I had heard his name uttered only the day before by Cecil himself.

"He is a nobody, young Stafford. He was sent to her last year by Queen Mary to guard her. A handsome lad, sweet of tongue. I believe the Queen sent him to Hatfield for that reason, to tempt my lady. She was so lonely here, never allowed to leave, treated like a common prisoner, and by her own sister. Oh, the poor lad."

Cecil's men had gone for Stafford the night of the birth. I fear he had scant time to enjoy fatherhood. The Tudors thought of little else but getting sons, yet the most recent generation had produced only one, Edward, who was never strong and had died, a virgin it was said, before begetting a son of his own. Now his sister Mary ruled the land, and had produced no heir of either sex. And here was a healthy Tudor son, but a bastard, never to be acknowledged. A King might sire a stable of bastards and create earldoms for them, though they could never rule. But a Princess or a Queen who foals a bastard is a whore.

"And the son, Doctor. What of him? I have placed him with a village family, but how long will he be safe so close to the palace?"

"He will be safe," I said, hoping my words would make it true. I knew not if any of us who attended her ladyship would ever be safe. "As you said, even Cecil would not shed Tudor blood and incur the wrath of a Princess who may be Queen one day. Now we must get to her ladyship. Only she can protect us."

"But the house is guarded by Cecil's men. No one can see her."

A plan took shape in my mind. I assured Kat that she was no longer bleeding, instructed her to stay where she was, put on my jacket, and left her. I assumed that the party of Cecil's men that passed us minutes earlier, in addition to searching for the wounded Kat, was on the way to my house to deal with me, leaving the road unguarded. If my assumption was incorrect, then all was lost. I had no choice.

As it happened, there were no men to stop me. I walked quickly down the hill on legs wobbly with fright and turned right at Park Street, which led out of the village. After a long while I came to the house of a farmer whose young son had broken a leg bone some weeks earlier. The leg had not been set properly, the farmer having not seen fit to call for a doctor, and it had become badly inflamed. I was summoned then and applied a poultice, and leeches, and the leg healed, though the boy would never walk properly again and was therefore of little use to his father. Nonetheless, the farmer was grateful to me, not least because I had not insisted on payment, and now I would test that gratitude. For the farmer, John Featherstone was his name, sold much of his produce, mostly barley and oats, to Hatfield.

I found him in his house, a tiny, ramshackle cottage at the edge of the village. He was seated at the table while his wife, a stout woman who had borne him many children, scurried about serving his midday meal. He looked alarmed to see me, perhaps thinking I was there to collect a debt or had perhaps been summoned to minister to a victim whose plight he had not yet been made aware of.

"Worry not, Featherstone, I come asking a favor."

His wife joined him at the table, placing a hand on his broad shoulders.

"You look as if you'd seen a ghost, Doctor," she said. "And I believe you are shaking."

"You said you want a favor," the farmer said. "What could I have what you might need?"

"First, you must swear to me that you will tell no one what I ask."

"You saved my boy's life, you did. 'Course I swear."

"Nor must you ask why. You must do as I say, and that is all."

He and his wife shared a nervous glance, and then he nodded.

The gates to Hatfield were closed, but they were opened soon enough as Featherstone's cart approached, for he was well known at the castle. Seated next to him, I wore a peasant's shirt and pants, my face smeared with earth, a hat pulled low over my face. Featherstone directed the cart to the far left of the palace, near the stables. He jumped down, signaled for me to follow, and knocked on the kitchen door. It was opened a moment later by a kitchen maid.

"Barley for the household," Featherstone told her.

"But you only just came with a bushel two days ago." The girl looked about fifteen or sixteen years, and her untroubled eyes told me that the horrible events that had consumed her superiors were unknown to her.

"I have brought my man to help. Step aside and let us do our work."

She shrugged and opened the door fully.

I helped Featherstone lower the burlap bag from the cart and together we brought it into the kitchen.

"Downstairs in the storage room as usual," the maid told us, pleased to have two men to order about.

"Might we trouble you for a cup of water when we return?" I asked the girl. I attempted to affect the coarse accent of the farmer, though the odd way she looked at me suggested that I had made poor job of it. Perhaps she heard the tremor of fear in my voice, for if I were discovered then all was lost, including my life.

I waited until she'd gone to the basin for the water, turning her back to us, to make my move. While Featherstone heaved the barley by himself and made for the basement stairs, I slipped through a doorway and found myself in a pantry lined with shelves holding pots and bowls and sundry other containers. I made quickly for a door at the far side and found myself in a long hallway. I followed it, pushed open a door at the end, and entered the house's great hall. To my right, at the far end of the vast room, was the great staircase that led up to the private quarters. Before it, ignorant of my presence, stood a guard.

I could ill afford to hesitate, for the maid would send an alarm when Featherstone returned unaccompanied from the cellar. Kat had told me that there was a guard posted outside the Princess's rooms, so my only hope was to lure him downstairs and then somehow evade two guards and make my way into her presence. I had no weapon, nor skill with arms in any case, while the guard possessed a longsword in a gleaming silver hilt at his side. I confess my heart pounded as if it would break through my chest, and I thought of turning back, accepting the cup of water from the maid, and leaving Hatfield, never to return. But I knew too that Cecil would never call off the search for me, and that I would be found and killed eventually. I reckoned I had nothing to lose by making my stand now.

I took a heavy pewter candlestick from a table and, standing in the doorway, threw it toward the center of the room. The racket drew his attention, as I had intended. I flattened myself against a wall, as he shouted something I could not interpret and ran into the great hall. Immediately a second guard came barreling down the stairs, his sword drawn. As soon as he joined his compatriot in the hall, both having run past me, I made my move, running toward the staircase. I had no illusions that my presence would go unnoticed. I only hoped to God I might outrun the guards to the Princess's door and, once inside, throw myself under her protection.

I had taken but one or two steps on the staircase when I heard a shout behind me. "Stop! Go no farther!"

I did not turn to look but instead took the stairs two at a time. I reached a landing where the stairs turned to the right for their final ascent to the upper floor. I could sense that the guards were coming closer and might overtake me before I reached the Princess. Without thinking, I lifted a heavy chair that sat on the landing, turned, and heaved it down at the guards. One of them fell backward, tumbling down the stairs, his fall as much due to the heavy weight of his sword and hilt and knee-high boots as to the chair itself. The other staggered against the wall but regained his balance even before I turned back. I picked up a second chair and hurled it at him. This time I did not wait to see what effect my action had. I flew up the stairs and then down the long hallway that I had last traversed the night before. Praying that the door to the Princess's apartments would be unlocked, I grabbed the handle just as the two guards reached the top of the stairs and shouted at me.

"Halt! You cannot go in there!"

Turning the handle, I pushed open the door, slipped inside, and slammed it shut behind me.

"Who are you? What are you doing here? Guard! Guard, come at once!"

My lady Elizabeth was standing in front of a window, hands at her neck, as if to protect it from the fate that had befallen her own mother. She wore a rich green gown with a pearl-studded stomacher across her middle. Her copper-colored hair was swept back, topped by a plain white cap. She looked surprisingly robust, given the ordeal of the previous day.

At first I could not speak. The pounding of my heart robbed the breath from my voice.

"It is I, your ladyship," I said at length. "Rufus Hatton, your physician."

I had hardly uttered these words when the door flew open. Within seconds, two swords were at my throat.

"Hatton?" After taking a cautious step toward me, she looked me up and down, eyes curious at my peasant's attire.

"Ignore my clothing, your ladyship. I had need of a ruse to enter this house."

"A ruse?"

"Leave us take this rascal away, your ladyship," said one of the guards. "He means you no good."

"A ruse, Doctor. Why?"

I began with the news that would have the greatest impact and thus the greatest chance of securing my safety.

"They have attacked Kat Ashley. I found her bleeding in the village."

"Kat? Attacked?"

One of the guards grabbed my arm and began to pull me toward the door.

"Stop!" she shouted. "Unhand him."

"Our orders are to—"

"I care not what your orders are. I command you, leave him be!"

I saw conflict play across the faces of both guards, the desire to heed the orders they had been given by Cecil, which undoubtedly were to keep everyone from Elizabeth.

"Leave us," she said, in a softer voice that nevertheless carried infinite authority. "Leave us at once or you will pay the consequence."

The guards glanced at each other. Finally one of them nodded and, with obvious reluctance, they left us.

"We will be outside the door, your ladyship," one of them said gruffly.

"Please explain yourself, sir," she said when we were alone.

Though it showed disrespect, I fell against the wall, my legs suddenly unable to support me.

"What has happened, sir?" she said with mounting irritation.

I felt I had no choice but to reply with a question of my own.

"Is your ladyship unaware of the course of events this day?"

She stepped forward, to within an arm's length of me.

"I have been told by my uncles to keep to my rooms. There is danger afoot, some sort of plot against me. What do you know?"

"The danger, my lady, is not to you but to anyone with knowledge of the events of the recent past."

"My son."

For a moment her regal facade appeared to crumble, changing her from arrogant young Princess to aggrieved mother.

"The midwife and her assistant. The guards who were standing watch that night."

"Dear God."

"My lady Kat, who is hiding nearby. I saw to her wound. She is no longer in danger from them."

"Her wound!" She covered her face with her hands.

"Stabbed, it appears, by a sword."

"Scoundrels!" she said, lowering her hands. "They dare not do this with my knowledge, so they keep me here, now twice a prisoner, first held captive by my enemies, now by my so-called supporters, while they ply their loathsome plot."

I felt it best to tell her all I knew, and in doing so establish my claim to her protection.

"They have already gone for Miles Stafford."

This news sent her staggering backward to a chair, into which she fell as if thrown by a sudden wind. I let her consider this last piece of news without comment. After a long silence, she spoke in a high, trembling voice.

"And my son?"

"They would not harm a child of yours, my lady. The boy is with a local family who know not his parentage."

"They will know soon enough. All the world will know."

I knew this to be false, for acknowledging the child would be fatal to her ambitions, and those of her supporters. She must have seen the doubt in my face.

"I will provide for him. He shall have a life fit for the grandson of a King, a Tudor King."

I forced myself to nod.

"Now, your ladyship, I have a request of my own. I have employed this ruse, this costume, to throw myself on your mercy. They will not stop until I too am silenced."

"You shall have my protection. They would not dare harm anyone if I forbid it." She stood and walked to a cupboard, on which sat a pitcher and pewter cups. She poured two draughts of ale, for all the world like a farmer's wife entertaining a neighboring peasant after Sunday services. The one lady-in-waiting allowed her, the ever true Kat, lay wounded in the village. "In return for my protection, I would ask something of you."

She handed me my ale, and I gave a shallow bow.

"Anything, my lady."

"You must help me look after Edward."

I needed a few moments to understand that she meant her bastard son, named for her late brother, Edward VI.

"His health will be my sacred responsibility," I said.

"More than that," she said a bit crossly, as if I'd missed an obvious point. "I mean for him to have a charmed life, the life of the son of a Princess, a future Queen." She waited for me to acknowledge her prognostication, which I did with a quick bow, though her sister was said to be in robust health. "I may not be able to achieve this without intercession. After today, I think you will understand my reluctance to enlist my so-called supporters." Here she gave a rueful laugh. "But I believe I can trust you."

"You may." I bowed again, as much from the sense, almost physical, that a great burden had been placed upon my shoulders as from obedience to a royal Princess. I wanted nothing to do with this royal bastard, and still want nothing, but I felt my life altering in a way that would make my comfortable life as a country physician a vanishing thing.

"You are a qualified physician, sir?"

"I studied at Oxford, ma'am, and later the College of Physicians."

"Created by my father by royal charter." She allowed herself a satisfied half smile.

"Yes, ma'am."

"Then why the life of obscurity in Hatfield, when greater distinction and more generous patrons surely lie in London?"

"I have little interest in advancement, and less in financial gain," I said truthfully. I could see this admission made her uneasy, for what sway could she have over me, who wanted nothing from her?

"Then you are unlike any man or woman I have ever known."

"I hardly think so, ma'am."

She frowned and sipped her ale, which reminded me that I had not touched mine. While she appeared to ponder matters, I drank some.

"Our first task is to get Kat," she said at length. "We will bring her back here and then decide on our course."

"Will the guards allow your ladyship to leave the house?"

"Allow?" she bellowed. As if to demonstrate the insolent folly of my question and the extent of her powers, she walked straight to the door and threw it open.

"I require a horse and cart, brought to the front of the house, at once," she said.

The two men hesitated. "By God, if you do not obey me I will have you both arrested for insubordination. Get me a horse and cart now!"

The two men hurried down the hall.

"I will find out if those two fools had any part in today's bloodshed, and if they did, they will pay dearly." She added, in a softer voice, "Come, good Doctor, let us go together and bring my Kat home."

Emeralds

"By November 1529, Anne was constantly at Henry's side, acting as if she were already Queen.... His Privy Purse accounts show that he spent the equivalent of £165,000 on gifts for Anne during a period of three years... necklaces, brooches, bracelets, gold trinkets to sew on her gowns, borders of jewels and pearls to edge those gowns, heart-shaped head ornaments, nineteen diamonds to wear in her hair, one ring set with emeralds and another with a table diamond, nineteen smaller diamonds forming lovers' knots, and twenty-one rubies set in gold roses, and even a crown of gold."

—Alison Weir
Henry VIII: The King and His Court

CHAPTER 9

Heathrow seemed unnervingly hectic after a morning spent in the cloistered archives of Hatfield. For Lee, even finding the gate for the flight back to New York was daunting, another challenge she might not be up to. At the same time, she felt safe amid the swarms of travelers, safely anonymous.

But for how long? Despite reassurances from Lucien that the Sarah Cooper identity wouldn't expire immediately, at least not until her surviving relatives got the first credit card bill for purchases made after her death, Lee feared the card and even passport would be confiscated at any moment and her true identity revealed. She figured that if she were caught, she'd hire a lawyer and hope to exonerate herself, as difficult as that would be while behind bars. And how would she pay the lawyer? Would a public defender take the time to investigate the tangled and still-unraveling story that led to Alex Folsom's murder? If she managed to slip back into the country without detection, she'd continue to follow the leads that had so far presented themselves, trying to answer the question that had led to the murder of an innocent cameraman in New York and an attack on her life in England: what was it about the sonnet—specifically, the single stanza she'd read on air—that was apparently so incendiary?

Was it the reference to Henford, which had led her to the discovery that Elizabeth I, the Virgin Queen, had been anything but, and had in fact given birth to a son? Fascinating, and a potential career-maker for a scholar, but worthy of murder? Who cared enough to kill?

She made it through security without triggering an alarm. Next she'd have to face customs at JFK. Waiting to board, she fired up her laptop and did a "people search" on Yahoo for the name Filer. Hundreds of people with that name lived in the U.S. There was no way to know if any of them were descendants of Edward Filer—"my son"—or descendants of *his* son, Charles, who'd left England for the New World.

After takeoff, she purchased a mini bottle of white wine from a flight attendant and drank it quickly. Within a half hour the wine had its intended effect, and she dozed off, sleeping for most of the trip despite considerable anxiety about what awaited her in New York.

As the 767 began its descent into JFK, she took the sonnet from her purse, the version she'd copied, and read it over. The name Henford jumped out at her, as it probably always would. But the rest felt so ordinary.

Could I with love alone your safety grasp
Then surely, love, my heart would lovely be.
But lose a savior's lead and temper gains an asp
As when for dying earth an apple quits the tree.

Heart, emeralds vainly exercise restraint
On those who for your station would aspire.
The peacock's astral plumage burns but faint,
Too dim to spare her brood from foul desire.

Must one deny my will? Pox will I bring,
A roiling storm will seem kind Pax's blow.
A plague when I uncap the bottled thing
From throne to grave no soul will comfort know.

When all the world in bootless ruin lies
I'll lie not more, but less my love belie.

She read it twice. *Was* it by Shakespeare? Fakes turned up all the time. Had she but world enough and time she could have the paper of the original analyzed, and consult more scholars to confirm whether the terminology and diction were "Shakespearean." In a way, the authenticity of the sonnet was irrelevant now; *what* it said, not who wrote it, was of greater significance to her fate.

What it said. She ran her fingers along each line, searching for words that had been buried, like Henford, between other words. Nothing. Then, just as she was folding it up to put back in her purse she saw it, hiding in plain sight.

Heart, emeralds vainly exercise restraint

It had been there all along, for half a millennium. Like Henford and "my son," a sly insistence from the past to be noticed, remembered. A clue.

At JFK, a customs clerk scanned the barcode on her passport and looked at her suspiciously from behind a Plexiglas screen. For a long moment, she felt a kind of peace wash over her; she'd be taken into custody, questioned, incarcerated—she'd be safe, and unburdened of the need to take action.

"Just one night in England, Miss Cooper?" he asked.

She nodded.

"Business or pleasure?"

She almost laughed. "Business."

Finally, he stamped her passport with a loud thwack and slid it through the opening.

"Welcome home," he said.

There was no question of visiting David Eddings at his office on the Columbia campus. Her failure to turn herself in might well have made the local news. Even if the police weren't specifically monitoring the campus, someone was sure to recognize her. Eddings himself might call the cops. By now he knew what she had been accused of. So she stood across from his apartment on West End Avenue at six o'clock, after a taxi ride into Manhattan from JFK, waiting for him to return from his office uptown. Eddings was a man of regular habits, leaving his office at precisely six every evening and taking the 104 bus down Broadway to Eighty-Sixth Street.

He appeared at 6:25, walking toward West End from Broadway. Wearing a dark, well-tailored suit, white shirt, and unassertive tie, and carrying a thick briefcase, he could have been a banker or corporate lawyer returning from an office tower in Midtown. She intercepted him on the corner, before he could cross to his building. It took him a moment to recognize her.

"My God, Lee, what are you doing here? And what happened to your hair?"

"I need to talk."

"Yes, well, the police feel they need to talk to *you*."

"Just a few minutes. I found something, in the sonnet. I need to know what it means."

He looked like he thought she might be armed or at the very least dangerously unhinged.

"It's me, David, it's Lee. I didn't kill that man, I haven't done anything wrong. I just need to prove that I'm innocent, and I need your help."

He studied her for several long moments before emitting a long sigh.

"Why don't we walk in Riverside Park?"

• • •

It was a beautiful New York evening. The sun was setting over the New Jersey side of the Hudson River, casting a mellow, forgiving glow on the joggers and dog walkers and nannies with babies taking advantage of a warm evening. She might have been among the joggers, panting out four miles after a sedentary day of teaching and research. Instead she walked slowly, Eddings beside her, along the esplanade that paralleled the river up to Ninety-Sixth Street.

"You didn't tell me, that day in my office, that there had been a murder," he said. "I would never have advised you to leave the country if I'd known about that. The police questioned me quite extensively."

"Did you tell them about England?"

A long pause. "Actually, I didn't mention that you'd come to see me."

"David, you didn't have to—"

"No, please, don't make this worse by thinking I fell on my sword for you. When the police came and told me what had happened, I simply omitted your visit. I don't know why exactly. I'm unused to this sort of scrutiny, and I suppose I was afraid they'd see me as an accomplice. About five minutes into the interview I had second thoughts, but by then it seemed too late. The lie had taken root. And now you're back."

She summarized what she'd learned at Henford.

"This would be huge, if you could prove that Elizabeth had a child. It might explain so much about her subsequent life." For a moment he seemed lost in scholarly contemplation, anxiety momentarily banished by the prospect of being associated with a major historical breakthrough.

"But why would someone break into my apartment, kill that man, frame me for the murder, and attack me at Henford just because of a reference to something that happened five hundred years ago? I kept thinking there's something more to this, and then I discovered a new clue in the sonnet." She recited the line from memory: "Heart, emeralds vainly exercise restraint."

"I don't understand…."

Despite everything, she felt a twinge of pleasure at being able to explain something to the great David Eddings.

"The first letters in each word spell Hever."

"The Boleyn family's ancestral home. It's where Elizabeth's mother, Anne Boleyn, was raised."

"It solidifies the connection between the sonnet and Elizabeth, if nothing else. But I keep thinking there must be something more."

"Read the line again."

"'Heart, emeralds vainly exercise restraint.' H.E.V.E.R."

He stopped walking, slowly shaking his head. "I don't believe it."

"What?"

"Too extraordinary."

"David, what is it?"

He took her elbow and practically dragged her up a short, steep hill to the nearest park exit.

"There is something you need to see, in my apartment."

CHAPTER 10

David Eddings lived in a sprawling top-floor apartment in a grand prewar building on West End Avenue. The foyer was the size of Lee's entire apartment—she felt a momentary pang, thinking of that place, small as it was, which she hadn't been back to in three days and feared she might never see again. David's apartment was as densely crowded with *stuff* as a consignment shop. Against the walls were mismatched chairs and oil paintings stacked one in front of another. Overlapping oriental rugs made the floor an uneven hazard for visitors. He led her into the vast living room, which was similarly crammed with what appeared to be three times the appropriate amount of furniture. She made her way to one of several sofas and sat down. Eddings walked to the far side of the room, which was lined with floor-to-ceiling bookshelves, and began searching the shelves.

"Forgive the clutter," he said with his back to her.

Clutter seemed a ludicrous understatement, but she assured him there was nothing to forgive.

"This was my parents' apartment. They had two other homes, one in Florida, the other in Maine. When they died, I had to sell both houses. But I couldn't bear to sell their things. So I had a lot of it sent here."

The contrast between the riotous chaos of the apartment and David's rigidly controlled demeanor was unsettling. He seemed curiously smaller in his own home, dwarfed by the claims of his own past.

"Ah, here it is." He pulled a large volume from a low shelf, blew a covering of dust from the top of the pages, and sat on the sofa next to her. "Now, let's see." He began flipping through what looked to be an art book, lavishly illustrated with color plates. "Eureka!"

He moved the book onto her lap. It was open to a portrait of a woman.

"It's Elizabeth, but I'm not sure I recognize this particular portrait," Lee said.

The portrait was the typical Elizabethan extravaganza, the queen herself almost lost amid a mass of embroidered cloth, puffy sleeves, chin-high ruff, and masses of jewels around her neck, her wrists, and along her tiara. In most portraits Elizabeth looked confident and authoritative, but in this one she looked almost sheepish, self-conscious of her finery.

"I'm not surprised you don't recognize it. It's probably by Nicholas Hilliard, who did several portraits of her, but its whereabouts are unknown. Thankfully, the queen had it reproduced during her own lifetime as a gift to Burghley, and what you're looking at now is a reproduction of that copy."

"What does this have to do with Hever Castle?"

"Nothing whatsoever to do with Hever Castle. Look closely, Lee. You're a scholar of the English Renaissance. Tell me what's unusual about this picture."

"She's in typical Elizabethan dress. The three-quarters pose is standard for the period. The Tudor roses and the fleur-de-lys embroidery symbolize her claim to both crowns, English and French."

He sighed his displeasure. "The jewels, Lee, the jewels!"

She studied the necklace, a double strand of emeralds, each the size of a shooting marble and separated from one another by significant diamonds. On the middle finger of Elizabeth's right hand was a ring with an emerald of equally impressive size.

"The Hever Emeralds," David said. "Given by a smitten Henry VIII to a young, allegedly virginal Anne Boleyn. She had left the court for her family's home at Hever, furious that the king hadn't made sufficient progress in divorcing his first wife, Catherine of Aragon. He followed her there and gave her these." He tapped the portrait. "At the time, the necklace and ring were considered the most impressive jewelry ever created."

"Not a bad consolation prize."

"But the emeralds were more than a sop," Eddings said. "For Henry and his court, the emeralds had a specific subtext, a second layer of meaning. Since ancient times, emeralds have been a symbol of fertility. Henry would have known that, and so would Anne, and so would the entire court for that matter. Presenting her with emeralds was a sign that Anne's fertility was important to him—that she would bear him a son. A legitimate son."

"Well, the emeralds didn't lie," Lee said. "She *was* fertile. Only she bore him a daughter."

"She might as well have been infertile." He frowned and shook his head, as if still disappointed by the thought. "Emeralds were also thought to reveal a lover's true intentions, which make them an interesting gift for a married king to give his wounded mistress."

"So much in Elizabethan England had a double meaning, particularly in literature," Lee said. "Little could be taken at face value."

"That's why the period still attracts people who enjoy wordplay and puzzles. I think that for Henry, giving his mistress these emeralds had yet another meaning. Emeralds were looted by Spanish Conquistadors from the Incan royal treasury and mined by natives forced into slavery. The violence didn't end there. English pirate ships, given free rein by Henry, attacked the Spanish galleons and plundered their cargo. Many, many people died horrible deaths to bring these jewels to the English court and, ultimately, to the delicate neck of Anne Boleyn. They died in the mines of South America and in the middle of the cold Atlantic. For a man like Henry, I think that was part of their allure, the cost in human terms."

Lee nodded her agreement. "After Anne was executed, the Hever Emeralds must have gone to her daughter, Elizabeth."

"They might have gone to one of the subsequent wives and then, once she became queen, to Elizabeth. I don't know. By wearing them in a formal portrait she communicated yet another subtext: 'I am Anne Boleyn's daughter as well Henry's. These emeralds, the finest jewels in the land, were a symbol of his love for her, and they live on beyond the chopping block.'"

"Are the jewels still in the royal collection?"

"That's the great mystery. They disappeared." David emitted a shallow, almost wistful sigh. "There is no record of them after Elizabeth's reign. In fact, before this portrait the Hever Emeralds were noted in several diary entries—you simply can't ignore gems of this size and quantity. But after the portrait was painted, nothing."

"They were lost?"

"Well, I don't think they fell behind a bureau at Hampton Court. I believe, and most historians agree, that they were hidden. You just don't lose two hundred carats of flawless emeralds."

"So the mention of Hever in the sonnet—"

"Is a clue," David said. "What is the line again?"

"'Heart, emeralds vainly exercise restraint.'"

"You see, the word 'emeralds' is associated in the same line with 'Hever.' The sonnet could be a clue to the location of the Hever Emeralds."

Which might explain the attack in her apartment and at Henford.

An old and as yet unauthenticated manuscript was valuable but hardly worth homicide. Two hundred carats of emeralds, on the other hand…

"May I see the rest of the sonnet, Lee?"

She retrieved the copy from her purse and handed it to him. He read it silently.

"Nothing strikes me as an overt clue. There is, of course, a subtle reference to Elizabeth in that same stanza. Did you catch it? She was often compared to a peacock, which was itself a symbol for the Greek goddess Hera. I like the pun in the last line on the word 'foul,' which when read sounds exactly like a synonym for a bird, the peacock's brood." He handed back the paper just as a buzzer rang out.

"The doorman is calling. I'll just be a moment."

He walked swiftly to the front hallway and lifted the house phone. A moment later he returned.

"The police are downstairs, Lee. They're coming up."

CHAPTER 11

"The doorman must have recognized you from the papers," Eddings said. "My name was in the *Post*, apparently, refusing to comment." For once, he looked at a loss, glancing around the cluttered living room like he was seeing it for the first time. "Even with your new look, he must have guessed it was you. I have so few visitors."

She got up and grabbed her purse and duffel bag.

"I can't let them take me. I have no money for bail, and someone framed me to make it look like I killed that cameraman."

"I'm afraid you have no—"

"Is there another way out of here?"

"The service stairs to the basement."

"A back exit?"

"The service exit, yes."

"Show me." She started to leave the room, but Eddings seemed unable to move, less panicked than confused, trying to work something out. She grabbed his arm and shook it.

"David, *show me the service stairs.*"

She pulled him from the room.

"Through the kitchen," he said in a stronger voice, a sense of urgency now apparent.

They went through a pantry and into a vast kitchen, which looked like it hadn't been updated since the building was built.

"That door," he said, pointing to the far end of the kitchen.

"Unlock it for me."

"Lee, I—"

"*Unlock it!*"

He complied, and she stepped out onto a back hallway. There was a service elevator and a staircase leading down.

"Thank you, David." She touched him briefly on the shoulder.

"I shouldn't be doing this," he said as she began running downstairs.

"*You* shouldn't be doing this. I'm going to have to tell the police that you insisted on leaving." His voice grew fainter as she went down, taking the steps two at a time, practically in freefall. "In fact, I hear the passenger elevator now. They'll be at my door any second. I'll have to tell them how you left, and then they'll…."

His voice faded. All she heard now were her own steps, though her feet hardly touched the stairs as she flew down. When she reached the fifth floor, she heard voices above, and then footsteps. The police were coming after her. It was unlikely that they'd catch her on the stairs, but what would happen out on the street? What if they'd already radioed to put someone at the service entrance? She placed one hand on the railing and basically levered herself forward, skipping over four steps. She repeated this for five flights, accelerating her descent by precious seconds.

In the basement, she followed the lit exit signs and found the service door. She threw herself against the panic bar to open it and stumbled out onto an alleyway. An alarm immediately wailed. A ramp led up from the basement level to the street. Thankfully, there didn't appear to be anyone watching the service door. She raced up the ramp, pushed open a metal door, and plunged onto the sidewalk. Again, no sign of the police. Desperately panting and unsure what to do next, she headed toward Riverside Drive, away from West End Avenue and the front of David's building. She forced herself to walk slowly so as not to attract attention from pedestrians. Once she reached Riverside, she turned the corner and headed downtown. After a few blocks she managed to flag a cab.

"The Broadway Hotel," she told the driver. The fleabag she'd briefly stayed in before flying to England.

CHAPTER 12

The four-hour drive to Tunsbury, Massachusetts, was unexpectedly relaxing. Lee had rented a car as Sarah Cooper and also bought some new clothes using her alter ego's credit card. Just being out of New York was a relief, and the car itself felt comforting, a cocoon in which the outside world flew by in harmless abstraction. Her main purpose was to find out what had happened to Edward Filer's son, Charles, once he left England. Lady Darman had said that Charles emigrated to Tunsbury, though she'd added that there didn't appear to be any Filers left, or none that wanted a sister city in Henford.

On the way, she called David Eddings's home phone from Sarah Cooper's cell phone. She knew he wouldn't be there, but wanted to leave a message.

"Thank you for yesterday," she said. "Here's my cell number if you think of anything else about the emeralds. I really need to figure this out." She slowly recited her number.

She pulled into Tunsbury at about noon. Its location on Buzzard's Bay had led her to expect a resort town: clapboard houses and a charming harbor. But Tunsbury was an old industrial town dominated by empty factory buildings that had processed the tuna once abundant in the waters off the shore. Today an air of neglect permeated the town, including the harbor, where even the small fishing boats looked ill-maintained and infrequently used.

It didn't take her long to find the town hall, a one-story brick building from the fifties, a block in from the marina. The receptionist sat behind a cloudy slab of thick Plexiglas perforated with holes for speaking. Handwritten signs provided instructions for paying various fines and license fees, most having to do with litter disposal and fishing permits. Lee explained to the young woman behind the Plexiglas that she wanted to look at real estate records dating back to the seventeenth century. The woman seemed entirely uninterested, as if such requests were routine.

"Through that door, then the second door on the right."

A harsh buzzing sound unlocked the door that led into the back office.

The heavy-set, gray-haired woman in charge of recorded deeds was not much more encouraging. She seemed utterly incurious about why Lee was interested in old real estate transactions. She led her to a locked closet, which she opened with some difficulty.

"Don't get much call to open this," she said as she struggled with the key. "Sales from the last ten years are computerized."

The door finally opened to reveal a walk-in closet lined with shelves.

"The oldest are these ones," the woman said, pointing to a stack of ledger books.

"Is there some place I can take the books?"

The woman sighed. "You can use the desk next to mine, I suppose. Noreen's on vacation this week. Lucky her."

Lee took the oldest ledger books and followed the woman to a large room that contained eight metal desks. When she walked in, everyone looked up briefly and then returned to what they were doing.

She opened what appeared to be the oldest book. The pages smelled musty and felt brittle. The historian in her hoped that the town was planning to digitize these old records so that the originals could be left alone. At the top of the page, in a very thin, faded hand, were the words "Recorded Deeds." There were several columns below. In the left-most column was the property name. To the right were dates and amounts, in pounds. The dense and faint handwriting was hard to read.

She began at the top of the page. The earliest recorded deeds were for families named Sherwood and Allen. She ran her finger down the date column until she found the first reference to a Filer. It was in 1634, and in fact there were two transactions that year. The first recorded the sale of 200 acres to "C. Filer." The second recorded the sale of 85 acres to the same person. The next mention of a Filer came forty years later, in 1674, when "Edward Filer" purchased 40 acres from "Job Haddam." This transaction was recorded on the second page of the ledger. Edward was probably the son of Charles, named for the latter's father. A third reference, on the ledger's third page, noted the purchase of an additional 50 acres by Charles Filer, no doubt named for *his* grandfather, in 1732. Apparently the Filers were prospering, or had been, until the mid eighteenth century, after which there were no further Filer references.

Unfortunately, none of the purchases recorded an address or location, merely the name of the buyer and seller, the size of the property and the money exchanged. Several, though not all of the other purchases included some reference to location—"adjacent to Parsonage Creek" or "between Stony Hill and the bay." Still, it seemed unlikely that a property of 200 acres, even in colonial times, when land was abundant, would go unnoted in local histories. Perhaps the town library had a book on Tunsbury's history.

Lee was about to close the ledger when something caught her eye. In the third Filer reference there was a very faint smudge in the "description" column. It had almost escaped her notice because the paper itself was faded in parts, giving it a blotchy appearance. But the smudge under the "50 acres" reference was different. There were faint but definite horizontal bands within it, almost as if there had been an erasure. She flipped to the previous page and found a similar smudge in the same column next to the reference to the 85-acre purchase. The smudge was also on the first page, adjacent to the original purchase of 200 acres by C. Filer.

She scanned the first three pages and found no smudges other than the three next to the Filer purchases. It seemed that someone had deliberately erased a notation in each transaction, and it became quickly apparent what that notation had been: the location of the Filer purchases.

The whereabouts of the properties they bought had been rubbed out. She lifted the ledger book so that it rested vertically on the table. Carefully, she adjusted the pages so that the first page was isolated, then angled the book until the overhead fluorescent light shone through the first page. The erasure next to the first land purchase, in 1634, revealed nothing, although after a few moments of close study she thought she could discern a single letter: a florid capital C, on the left side of the smudge.

"Rip those pages and there'll be hell to pay." The woman who'd taken her to the deed closet stood over Lee, frowning.

"I'll keep that in mind," Lee said. She turned to the second page and tried to make out what the erasure might have said. Again, nothing was immediately evident, although after a few seconds she thought she could detect another faint "C," again to the left of the smudge. On the right side of the erasure she just barely made out the word "river." The property was near a river that began with a C.

"You can't replace these old books," the clerk told her. "Don't know what we'd charge you if you damaged one."

Lee ignored her and turned to the third page. This time the erasure revealed nothing. She placed the book on the desk and closed it.

"Do you know the Filers in this area?" she asked the clerk.

"No I don't. I'm from a different county. Ask Grace; she's lived here since the flood." She pointed to a young woman at a desk across the room. Despite the warmth of the day, the young woman wore a thick wool cardigan sweater buttoned to the neck. Lee walked over to her.

"May I ask you a quick question?"

The young woman, who'd been typing on a keyboard, stopped abruptly, looking startled. Her face and hands had a mottled quality, like rose-tinged marble. Lee noticed a small space heater glowing red under the desk. The woman nodded tentatively.

"Do you know anything about the Filer family? I believe there are several Filers in this area."

"Filer?" She rubbed her hands together, as if against the cold. "I don't know that name." Lee guessed she was about twenty, perhaps as old as twenty-five. Her ring finger was bare.

"Grace Belleview, how can you be so thick?" The speaker was a much older woman who sat at a nearby desk. She was heavyset, gray-haired, and dressed much more appropriately for the late-spring weather in a white cotton blouse and khaki slacks. "Everyone knows about the Filer property."

Lee turned to her. "Filer property?"

"It's the oldest historical site in town. The house isn't much, just a few rooms with sagging floors, but it's worth saving, I guess, since they're moving it somewhere."

"Why are they moving it?

"Some developer is building a new subdivision and the Filer place was in his way, I guess. So they're putting it up on a truck and moving it. Any day now. Me, I'd tear it down. Not much to it, as I said. The contents were all sold a long time ago. Half the furniture went to the Taylor-Shipford house, about a half hour east of here. They needed to fill it with stuff from the same period."

Taylor-Shipford—where she'd discovered the sonnet.

"Were the books from the Filer House sold to the Taylor-Shipford house as well?"

"That would be a safe bet, seeing as how everything else went there. We got too much to worry about in the present to spend much time or money on the past. But we're not tearing down the Filer place. Although moving it is wrong, you ask me. Houses should stay put."

During this discourse, Grace Belleview continued rubbing her hands together, glancing nervously between Lee and the speaker.

"I live in the country," Grace said in a tremulous voice. "I don't come into town except to work here."

"Still, it's hard to believe you never heard of the Filer House. Everybody knows about it." The gray-haired woman sounded dismissive.

Grace started to defend herself.

"Is there a river in town that begins with the letter *c*?" Lee interrupted.

When both women shrugged, Lee asked for directions to the Filer House, then thanked them and left.

CHAPTER 13

The Filer residence was on the outskirts of Tunsbury, where the houses began to spread out a bit, though the level of maintenance didn't improve much. Zoning seemed nonexistent; gas stations and small convenience stores interrupted most residential blocks. It seemed an unlikely area for a seventeenth-century survivor; most of the homes in the neighborhood looked early twentieth century, and had been left alone to slowly deteriorate. But there it was, on an undistinguished street of small, single-family homes, a two-story shingled colonial with black shutters. Lee pulled up in front and considered the distance between Henford, where the first recorded Filer had lived, and the Tunsbury house. The distance seemed vast, in miles as well as years, from the stately Tudor home surrounded by acres of parkland to this small, dilapidated farmhouse set in a depressing working-class neighborhood. Was this where the grandson of a queen had ended up? Could there be a connection between this place and a trove of emeralds of incalculable value?

Lee walked up to the front door of the house along an overgrown brick path. In preparation for its move, the house had already been stripped of landscaping, exposing two vertical feet of foundation. This lent it a vaguely embarrassed appearance, like an old woman whose skirt had inadvertently hiked up. The front stairs had been replaced by a plywood ramp.

She knocked on the front door and got no response. After a second knock she tried the doorknob, which turned easily, and stepped inside. On either side of the small foyer, the rooms were empty of furnishings. Even empty, however, the house felt more impressive from inside. The rooms were unexpectedly large, and though disfigured by peeling paint and scratched floors they seemed nicely proportioned, with generous eight-over-eight windows that let in a great deal of sunlight. She stepped into what was probably the main parlor and right away noticed something odd—and familiar. Like several of the rooms at Henford, this one had two fireplaces, about eight or ten feet from each other along the same wall.

She crossed the foyer to what had most likely been the dining room, a handsome square room with two corner fireplaces across the room from each other. At the back of the house was a large kitchen without a fireplace, which had no doubt been removed once central heating and modern appliances had come into use. Upstairs there were three bedrooms and a single bathroom, which had probably been converted from a fourth bedroom. The two smallest bedrooms did not have a fireplace, though they would have in colonial times. But the largest bedroom, which was over the living room, had two fireplaces along the same wall. Its walls were covered in floral wallpaper that, although faded, provided the only hint of recent habitation. Otherwise, everything in the house had been stripped away—not just the contents, which had been consigned to the Taylor-Shipford House, but the light fixtures, carpeting, doors, and window hardware, even. Lee imagined the room furnished; the bed would have sat between the two fireplaces, warmed from both sides.

She walked to a rear-facing window and looked out onto another world entirely. Whereas inside the house all was still and abandoned, the scene behind the house was bustling. New houses were in various stages of completion, at least fifteen or twenty of them. They appeared to be quite large, with ample space between them. She felt like she'd stepped through the looking glass. On one side of the Filer House, everything was working class and ramshackle; on the other, a subdivision of double-height foyers, spacious decks, and three-car garages.

One man stood out. He wore a business suit and held what looked like rolled-up architectural plans as he talked to another man wearing overalls and a hard-hat. At one point he glanced at the Filer House, and Lee knew instantly that he'd seen her in the large, bare window. She saw him point her out to the construction worker, and then both of them walked quickly toward the house.

Something in the two men's expressions, and the speed with which they approached the house, made Lee very uncomfortable. She was, after all, trespassing. She hurried downstairs and was in the front foyer when the two men entered the house from the back.

"Who the hell are you?"

The man wearing a suit was tall and thin, with pale skin and hair that, while thin with middle age, had a slight reddish tinge. The other man, in overalls and hardhat, was equally tall but much heavier, with the ruddy complexion of a man who spent much of his life outdoors. Despite his size, he seemed less menacing than the suit, who glared at Lee through faint blue eyes beneath very thin, almost invisible brows.

"The door was unlocked," Lee said. The foyer felt suddenly quite small.

"What do you want?" The suit's right hand slid up and down the rolled architectural plans.

"I'm researching the Filer family," Lee said. Which was the truth, though hardly a complete explanation. As the man's eyes continued to bore into her, she worried that he'd see beyond the cropped, dyed hair and recognize her from newspaper photos.

"What about them?"

"Everything. I'm particularly interested in what happened to them. As far as I can tell, there are no Filers left in Tunsbury."

"Damn straight. The title was free and clear. I'm moving this heap at my own expense."

So that's what the grim expression and threatening mien were all about: concern about title to the property.

"Why this house?" she asked. "You're not moving any of the others on the street, and they seem to be equally in the way."

"Because of the back acre. It jutted right into the center of the subdivision. With the Filer property I got three more lots. Without it, the entire project wouldn't have made economic sense."

"One acre? I thought the Filer's owned hundreds of acres."

"You thought wrong."

"But at the town office the deed archives had three—"

"What were you doing at the town office?" He stepped closer to her. His lashes were reddish-blond, like his hair, and the whites of his eyes had a milky quality that suggested a recent illness.

"Researching the Filers."

"There are no Filers here. Period. They died out long ago. This land is mine. Is that clear?"

"I'm not interested in who owns the land. I'm just interested in finding—"

"Next time I catch you on my property, I won't be so hospitable." He placed a hand on her shoulder. "Got it?"

She jerked his hand off her with enough force to send him staggering back a few steps.

"What the hell's the matter with you?" he said.

"Just don't touch me, okay?"

His small, round eyes fixed on her for a few moments before he turned to the construction worker.

"Get her out of here, Pete." The suit turned and left the house by the back door. Pete seemed about to take her elbow.

"I said, no touching. "

He held up his hands. "Look, I don't want trouble. I just need to get you off the premises."

Together they left through the front door.

"Is there some dispute over title to this place?" she asked when they were outside.

"Dispute? I don't know about that. I just know that Mr. Aspinall has put every cent he has into property and he don't want trouble with it."

"Do you know any Filers?"

"Me? No. And I've lived here all my life. Like my parents."

"Anyone related to a Filer?"

"Well, there's some here who are related to the Filers, I've heard that. None of them called Filer any more. A bunch of them live on the outskirts, is what I hear. But they keep to themselves." He shrugged.

The outskirts. The Filers had owned hundreds of acres in Tunsbury, and there was no record of a property sale, only purchases, so perhaps there was Filer property somewhere nearby.

As with so many of the things she'd done since the attack in her apartment, the visit to the Filer House had at first appeared crucially relevant to her predicament and now seemed futile, for what had she learned that might explain anything? If Henford felt light-years away, then the Hever Emeralds, given by a besotted king to his wife's reluctant lady-in-waiting, and then handed down to a young princess, were in another galaxy altogether.

"Look, you don't want to come back here. Aspinall's a tough customer when it comes to his projects."

"But how am I a threat?"

"Just stay away."

She watched him climb the ramp back into the house. It bowed under his weight, and she was waiting for it to snap completely when something caught her eye. To the left of the ramp, in the brick foundation. She walked over to the house.

"Now, what did I just tell you about staying away?" Pete looked down at her from the doorway.

She squatted in front of the foundation, which consisted of about ten rows of reddish-brown bricks neatly separated by dark gray mortar.

What had caught her eye was an irregularity in the brick pattern. About three feet to the left of what had once been the front stairs, the regular pattern of bricks was interrupted by a pattern that appeared decorative: bricks were placed vertically, or cut in half, or angled, like giant mosaic tiles. From close up the arrangement revealed nothing, but when she took a few steps back the design coalesced into two clear letters: an *s* and an *e*.

"You need to get out of here. If he comes back and finds you…." His cell phone chimed, and he answered it. "She's still here; I'm waiting for her to leave." He hung up and lumbered halfway down the ramp. "Don't be stupid, miss. Get the hell away from this place."

She was peering under the ramp, trying to see if the letters continued along the foundation, but the brickwork was obscured by a vertical support that held up the front of the ramp. Ignoring Pete, she circled the ramp and almost shouted when she saw two additional letters patterned into the brick: E and R.

"Elizabeth Rex," she said aloud. Perhaps Henford—and even the Hever Emeralds—weren't so far away after all.

"I don't care who you are," Pete was saying as he lumbered down the ramp. "Ed Aspinall's on his way back here and you don't want to see him mad."

As the big construction worker approached her, she backed away toward the sidewalk, unable to take her eyes off those two letters. Half a world away, a grandson had embedded the name of his royal antecedent in the very foundation of his new home, homage to a relationship, a heritage, he could never acknowledge.

"I hear him in the house," Pete was saying. "Get out of here before he makes me do something."

Reluctantly, she turned away from the Filer House—the House of the Descendants of Elizabeth Rex—and got into her car. Her mind was consumed by more mysteries than ever, beginning with the significance of the other two letters in the foundation, *s* and *e*. But her trip to Tunsbury had revealed one thing at least: the sonnet led from England back to the New World, back to this house.

Just before driving away, she glanced at the house. Aspinall stood at the top of the ramp, before four centuries of history, glaring at her, hands fisted at his side, shouting something unintelligible.

CHAPTER 14

Lee headed for the Tunsbury Public Library, where she intended to research the Filer family, convinced that there had to be some record of what had happened to them. Once they had owned the largest tract of land in the area, the specific location of which had been deliberately erased from town records. They'd owned a significant house right in town as well, probably unconnected to the land, but how that property had passed out of family hands was a mystery. And now a developer seemed unusually anxious about her inquiries into the history of the house. Why?

She didn't see the stop sign until she was almost past it. She was tempted to continue straight across the intersection without stopping but saw a car starting to head through it. Rather than broadside it, she hit the brakes. Almost immediately, another vehicle slammed into her from the rear, pushing her car into the center of the intersection. When it finally stopped, she found herself panting, as if she'd just sprinted. Turning around to see what had hit her, she felt a stinging pain run down the back of her neck into her shoulders. She was reaching cautiously for the door handle when a rapping noise at her window caused her to start.

Crouching next to the car, peering through the closed window, was a man. He moved his hand in a signal for her to roll down the window, which she did.

"Are you okay?"

"I don't know. My neck…."

"Do you need an ambulance?"

"No, no ambulance."

"Can you move the car out of the intersection, or do you need help? I could call a tow service."

"No, I can do it."

She drove slowly across the intersection and parked the car on the shoulder. After a moment's thought she drove a bit farther and turned into a driveway. She didn't want to attract any more attention than necessary. A few seconds later the other car pulled up behind her.

She got out of the car, careful not to engage her neck in any sudden movement. The man approached her. He looked about forty, tall and lean, with a face that was appealing in a pensive, almost distracted way, like he was processing an alternative reality as opposed to what was directly in front of him. He wore a faded blue polo shirt and loose-fitting khaki pants that needed ironing. A small part of her mind, some vestigial instinct from her life prior to the sonnet's appearance, registered the fact that he was attractive. The rest of her calculated how best to deal with the situation and move on without drawing attention to herself.

"Look, I'm sorry about what happened, but you stopped short back there." He examined her rear bumper. "A few dings, not much more."

"How about your car?"

"No damage."

She nodded, and winced.

"I think you need a doctor. Are you from around here?"

She almost nodded but thought better of it.

"No, but I'm fine. If there's no damage to your car then I'll just get going."

"I didn't think you were from here. Tunsbury people have a certain grayness about them."

Faint praise, to say the least, and she could easily have returned it. Although his hair was flecked with gray, he was far from dull-looking.

"I'll see a doctor when I get home."

"Where's home?"

"New York," she said, and immediately regretted it. The less anyone knew about her, the better.

"You heading there now?"

"Actually, I'm going to the library. Can you point me there?"

"About a mile that way." He pointed to his left. "But it closes at five. You came all the way from New York to visit our library?"

She'd forgotten about the time.

"I guess I'll have to stay over. Is there a motel near here?"

"Nothing I'd recommend. I have a spare room." He smiled in a way that suggested that, while the offer wasn't totally serious, he wouldn't be totally surprised if she agreed to stay with him. She liked that.

"How about directions to a motel?"

He shrugged and told her how to get there. As she was getting into her car, he called back to her.

"You haven't asked me about restaurants."

"I'll find something near the motel."

"Uh-uh, not here."

"Then where?" Restaurant chitchat, a staple of her pre-sonnet life, felt almost surreal to her now. People really cared about that stuff?

"I'll pick you up at seven." He got into his car before she could respond.

He knocked on her motel room door precisely at seven. She'd showered and changed and put on some makeup (but not bronzer) for the first time in days, doing her best to overlook the room's stale odor and overall dinginess. Three aspirin erased the ache in her neck. She was still not used to the blond hair, and the weight she'd lost since the attack in her apartment made her look a bit gaunt, she thought, though a touch of neurasthenia probably went with the bottle-blonde look.

"How did you find me?" she asked in the car. "I never gave you my name."

"There are exactly six people checked in. I asked the manager for the blonde."

"Good thinking."

"Actually, I asked for the attractive blonde."

Given what she'd been through, it would take a lot more than a line like that to soften her up.

"I don't know your name."

"Mark Warren."

"Sarah Cooper." She'd come close to giving her real name.

A few minutes later he stopped the car in front of a small, fake-shingled house with a large front porch.

"What kind of restaurant is this?"

"Best place in town. Mine."

"Uh uh, you told me—"

He held up both hands. "Nothing tricky, I promise. Just a home-cooked meal, which you look like you could use."

He was a terrific cook. She watched him prepare dinner in the small kitchen of the house, drinking red wine and feeling, with each sip, that a normal life might somehow be within her grasp. The house was compact—just a living room, dining room, and kitchen on the ground floor—and casually furnished. She sensed a woman's touch in the decorating, which was heavy on floral fabrics and botanical prints. While he seared tuna steaks crusted with peppercorns, she steered the conversation to the subject of relationships. He'd been living with his wife until a few months ago, when she had left him for a lawyer at the firm that employed her as a legal secretary.

"She got a big step up from marriage to a fisherman," he said. "I think that's what she really wanted: a better life. She should have known what she was getting into when she married me. I'm third generation. Maybe because I got a scholarship to college, Tufts, she thought I'd make a different life for myself, for us. But I always figured I'd be back on the boats."

The ex couldn't possibly have upgraded her cuisine with the lawyer, Lee thought after tasting the tuna, the Brussels sprouts sautéed with garlic and bacon, and the rice pilaf.

"This is amazing," she said.

"I haven't been out on a boat in a few years. You ever hear of the National Oceanic and Atmospheric Administration? Neither had I, until they started telling local fishermen how much cod they could catch. It hasn't been worth going out in a decade. I finally quit three years ago."

"What are you going to do?'

"Make coffee." His grin, equal parts self-effacing and cocky, set off alarms that should have been triggered when the cameraman asked her out for a drink a few days earlier. *Ask him to drive you home. Now.*

"How about more wine instead?"

He opened a second bottle of red, and they drank it in the living room, she on the sofa, he on a chair.

"You haven't told me why you're here."

"For the waters," she said.

"What waters?"

"I was misinformed." He smiled faintly to show he got the *Casablanca* reference, and also to register that her diversionary tactic hadn't worked. "Actually I'm researching the Filer family. I'm getting a PhD from Columbia." She didn't mention that it was in English literature, not U.S. history.

"Why the Filers?"

She told him that the name had come up in her research and asked him if he'd known any family members growing up.

"Not a one. There's the Filer House, over on Mason Street. You been there yet?"

She told him what had happened that afternoon. They talked for a while. When she felt the wine softening her mind, she did the sensible thing and asked him to drive her back to the motel. First she went to his bathroom, which was on the second floor, and when she came back down he was standing in the front hallway, holding her purse.

"I thought you said your name was Sarah Cooper."

She lurched at him and grabbed her purse from his left hand, but his right hand held onto her wallet, which contained her real driver's license and credit cards, and the white envelope in which she kept her *new* identification.

"Give that to me."

"You lied to me."

"And you searched my purse."

"Correction. I was moving it from the kitchen counter and dropped it. A driver's license fell out. And a wallet. I noticed another driver's license sticking up out of it."

"You *noticed*?" She made another grab at her wallet, but his free hand caught her arm just before contact.

"I said give them to me." She struggled to free her arm.

"I heard you, relax."

"Don't tell me what to do, just give them to me." She managed to free her arm.

"Okay, okay, here." He started to hand her the wallet and envelope but pulled them back just before she could take them. Then his eyes widened.

"I know who you are."

CHAPTER 15

She told Mark everything, from the discovery of the sonnet to finding the royal initials on the foundations of the Filer House. She even let him read her handwritten copy of the sonnet. She had no choice. Once he figured out who she was, her only hope was enlisting his support—or at least, convincing him not to turn her in. He listened intently, asking few questions, sitting on a chair across from her on the sofa. As she spoke, she felt a heavy burden fall away, and for the first time in days the crushing sense of isolation began to lessen. When she finished, there was a long silence followed by a question.

"What are you going to do?"

She felt so relieved she almost sobbed; he believed her, and he wasn't going to call the cops.

"Someone heard something in the sonnet, the part of it I read on the air, and what they heard was enough to make them come after me. Twice. Because of the reference to Henford, in England. I know it has something to do with the Filer family. And because of the coded reference to Hever, I know it has something to do with emeralds. That's why I was heading to the library, to see if there's anything there about the Filers, who seem to have disappeared after buying up half the town. Then I'll head back to New York and see what I can learn about the emeralds. I don't know what else I can do."

"Should I call you Leslie?" From her driver's license.

"Call me Lee." He nodded, and she asked quietly: "You're not going to turn me in?"

He waited for a few moments before speaking.

"You should turn yourself in. You've attracted some dangerous people. At least in custody you'd be safe."

"In custody I'd wither and die trying to prove beyond a reasonable doubt that I didn't murder Alex Folsom. They'd play his voicemail for the jury, the one where he claimed I was threatening him. And what would I offer in my defense? A four-hundred-year-old sonnet?"

"This must have been horrible for you, finding the body," he said quietly.

"I haven't had much time to wallow in it."

"It's not wallowing. You're allowed to feel things."

She shrugged and took a swig of wine.

"For someone writing her dissertation on a writer of love sonnets, you're—"

"Surprisingly unromantic." She got that a lot.

"It's almost like you—"

"Compartmentalize?" She raised her wine glass, but it was empty.

"Don't you ever feel like, I don't know, just letting it go? After what you've been through, most people would want someone to trust."

This was a conversation she most definitely did not what to have. Philip Sidney was a man of action. *A hard man.* He'd fought a duel *and* created *Astrophel and Stella*, to her mind the most glorious love poem ever written. He was her beaux ideal, the quintessential Elizabethan—body and soul, equally accomplished. She'd taken the required courses on the Romantic poets—Byron and Keats and Shelley, contemplating love and nature and the human spirit in safe tranquility. But the Elizabethans had captured her soul.

She stood up and felt dizzy. He must have sensed her unsteadiness because he came right over to her and placed a hand on her arm. She shook it off. There was something about his expression then, a look of revelation, but not a pleasant one, that had the effect of holding up a mirror to her. She didn't like what she saw. *A hard woman.* She hadn't been born that way, and she didn't feel tough. Quite the opposite, in fact. Why couldn't anyone see that? She stepped toward him and lightly kissed his lips. After what felt like an eternity, he pulled her closer and returned the kiss.

Something dissolved inside, that part of her that balanced risk and reward, action and reaction. She was going to sleep with Mark Warren. She'd learned nothing, apparently. All her life she kept busy, kept moving, convinced that activity would forestall connection. Elizabeth, as always, was her muse on this: "Love is usually the offspring of leisure, and as I am so beset by duties, I have not been able to think of love." But even now, beset by urgent troubles, she found herself thinking, if not of love, then of loving. She was, after everything that had happened, despite the new hair color and the tan and the new name, still Lee Nicholson.

• • •

The next morning, he drove her back to the motel to check out and collect her things. From the moment she'd woken up in his bed Lee had felt the onset of remorse, the deflating and familiar conviction that she'd broken a promise to herself. She tried to make the case that, since Mark had figured out who she was, she couldn't risk leaving him. But there was no denying, in the sharp morning light, that self-defense in the legal sense was only part of her motivation for spending the night.

Outside the motel room, she prepared for the familiar awkward goodbye of two strangers in daylight who'd just shared dimly lit intimacy. He seemed uncomfortable and finessed the situation by offering to show her the way to the library. She followed him in her rental car to a one-story brick structure not far from the municipal building downtown. They pulled up in front. Before he had time to get out of his car, she left hers and walked quickly to the library, waving with her back turned. Bye-bye, Mark Warren.

The young woman behind the front counter greeted her with a cautious smile, perhaps surprised by the appearance of a stranger at nine in the morning.

"I was hoping you could help me," Lee began. "I'm researching a family that settled here in the early seventeenth century, the Filers."

The librarian gave her a history of the town, a volume published in the early twentieth century that, because of its age, was kept in a back room. Disappointingly, the book dispatched with the colonial years of Tunsbury in a single chapter. Charles Filer was mentioned as one of the town's earliest settlers. His entire life was covered in a single paragraph.

> Charles Filer purchased several acres of land on what is today the edge of the town's commercial district. He established a small farm, producing primarily vegetable crops. It appears that he brought a wife with him from England, whose name was Katherine, and that they had at least two children, a boy and a girl. Nothing remarkable seems to have occurred, until 1632, when most of the family disappeared. Due to the frequency of raids by the Narraganset Indians at that time, it was assumed that the Filers had been abducted and perhaps murdered. Other such abductions were not uncommon during the period, although it was rare for an entire family to be carried away; typically, only the female members were taken, the men left

behind dead following a violent struggle. The house was sold to the younger son of the Winford family, though, perhaps as a result of the family's strange disappearance, it was always known as the Filer House.

That was it. A single paragraph. There was no mention of the land purchases, which had occurred *after* the family's alleged disappearance in 1632. Had the book's author known the identity of Charles Filer's paternal grandmother, he would no doubt have spent a bit more time investigating the disappearance.

She returned the book to the librarian.

"Did you find what you wanted?" she asked.

"Not exactly. This is really the only reference you have about the town?"

"We don't attract a lot of researchers, I'm afraid. We never produced a president or even a senator. That might have put us on the map. You might try Derek Martinson. He knows everything there is to know about Tunsbury history. If anyone can help you, it's Derek."

Lee got directions to his house, which wasn't far, as well as a warning.

"He's kind of peculiar, if you ask me. Take him with a grain of salt and you'll be okay."

Outside the library, she saw Mark leaning on his car.

"You're still here," she said.

"You never said goodbye."

Just then, a man left the library. She hadn't noticed anyone else inside—he must have been in the stacks while she consulted the town history. He looked directly at her, then immediately turned away. For a moment he seemed about to turn around and head back inside, but he walked quickly—very quickly—down the front path, not looking at her.

Something about him, some aura of menace in the hunch of his shoulders, the swiftness of his gait, the way he'd started when he saw her, then studiously avoided looking at her, caused her to grab onto Mark's arm.

"What is it?" he asked.

The man had to walk within a few feet of them in order to reach the sidewalk. As he passed he glanced at her for a moment, like he couldn't resist, then quickly walked toward the center of town. Watching him hurry off, Lee found herself shivering.

"What's the matter? You're trembling."

She just shook her head, because she wasn't exactly sure why she was suddenly cold. She wasn't frightened by the man in any way she could verbalize, but when he'd passed close by her she'd felt an unmistakable chill. The day was sunny and warm, and yet the man seemed to move in a wintry aura that she'd felt quite strongly.

"That man," she said, "did you notice? He had on a wool coat and gloves."

Mark peered down the street toward the stranger, who was already a full block away.

"He's overdressed, so what?"

She let go of his arm. "Nothing, I guess." She fished from her purse the scrap of paper on which she'd written Derek Martinson's address. "Do you know where this is?"

"You seem nervous. I'll take you there."

They got into their respective cars, and she followed him, quickly overtaking the stranger, who'd slowed his pace some. As she drove by, he glanced up. She couldn't, of course, feel a chill from within the moving car. But she felt the unmistakable coldness in his eyes, something bordering on a threat.

To calm herself, Lee recited the sonnet in her head. She knew every word by heart. She focused on the first stanza, and then on a line that had puzzled her from the beginning, "But lose a savior's lead and temper gains an asp." It had never made much sense to her, and during the drive to Derek Martinson's house she recited it out loud over and over again until, suddenly, it was less a line of poetry and more a string of random words. That was when she figured it out.

She pulled over behind Mark in front of an imposing old house. Mark started to head up the slate walk, but she stopped him.

"Wait, listen to this." She read him the line she'd been reciting.

"What about it?

"For the Elizabethans, temper didn't mean anger per se; it referred to personality or mood. The asp of course is a symbol of temptation and ruination, from the Garden of Eden. This is confirmed by the next line, with its reference to the apple of knowledge. The asp is also a phallic symbol. I think the line means that without faith, the writer is subject to ruination. But look at it another way, in a literal way. What is the most common symbol of Christ?"

"The cross."

"And the cross is essentially the lowercase version of the letter *t*, correct? So what happens if the word 'temper' loses the cross?"

"You mean, loses the letter *t*?" She nodded. "You get 'emper.'

Which isn't a word."

"But what happens if 'emper' gains an asp?"

"You lost me."

"What letter is most like a snake? The letter *s*. In medieval iconography, the snake was usually depicted in a wavy 'S' shape, not coiled as if it were about to strike. It wasn't always used as a symbol of temptation alone. It also symbolized eternity. Eternal temptation, perhaps. The snake's shedding of its skin was thought to represent man's shedding old sins and moving forward untainted. Shakespeare's Cleopatra applies two asps to her body and asks her maids, 'Dost thou not see my baby at my breast, that sucks the nurse asleep?' It's an image of immortality, of life-giving, even as she's ostensibly committing suicide." God, it felt good to be back in the world of symbols and metaphors, if only for a few moments. Reality, in contrast, truly sucked.

"Not sure I'm following you," he said.

"Put it all together. Start with 'temper.' Take away the cross, the *t*, and replace it with an asp—the letter *s*."

"Semper. Latin for 'always.'"

"Eternity. The line, 'But lose a savior's lead and temper gains an asp,' is a hidden reference to semper."

"The line is a riddle," he said.

"It could be the…." After all that had happened, attributing the sonnet to Shakespeare felt like an unnecessary—and unimportant—complication. "…The poet showing off his talent at wordplay. The Elizabethans adored wordplay."

"As do you, apparently."

"So the reference to semper is about the poet's eternal love for the object of the sonnet."

"But if Hever refers to emeralds, and Henford to a specific place, why should semper have no meaning outside the sonnet itself?"

He had a point. In all likelihood, 'semper' wasn't just a Latin word. It was an embedded clue.

CHAPTER 16

3 November 1572
Hampton Court

I was summoned this day to appear before Her Majesty. I feared for her health and made haste. My rooms are in a dark corner of the palace, not nearly so comfortable as those at Greenwich or even Whitehall, yet as the Queen's physician I have no influence on where I lay my head at night. She desires me near, but summons me infrequently, as she is in robust health. She moves often from palace to palace, for when the court has occupied a place for but a handful of weeks the stench becomes intolerable. It is said that Her Majesty has a sensitive nose, which I do not doubt.

Still, I would prefer to remain longer in a place, no matter how rude the accommodations. The upheaval, even for a gentleman without a wife, is wearing. But I must be near at hand, for I am ordered to be so. I have husbanded a secret for eighteen years, and therefore I keep her trust.

I made my way to her side, through the great hall and the guard chamber. Gold and silver glinted from the tapestries lining the walls like a thousand eyes blinking at me. In the presence chamber I occasioned to meet William Cecil, engaged in hushed conversation with other members of the Privy Council. He has a lush white beard and calculating eyes, and it is said that the Queen dares not spend a shilling without consulting him. He was at Hatfield that night eighteen years ago and therefore he alone understands the nature of my relationship with the Queen. He would prefer me dead, I know this, but he is wise enough to know that the Queen and I share an unusual bond. I am protected by her.

"Good Doctor, is the Queen ill?" he asked me, breaking away from his whispering cabal. The concern for her health is genuine, though it springs from his mind, not his heart. Her Majesty is not married, and has no heir. No legitimate heir, I might add, were I not concerned with my well-being. Marriage negotiations with the Duke of Anjou, brother to Charles IX, have not as yet been successful. The Queen is suspicious of the French nobleman's reputation for promiscuity and perhaps his young age, for he is but nineteen and she two decades his senior. The uncertainty of succession makes our time a perilous one. Passions trump reason. Only recently Her Majesty had to intercede to prevent a duel between the poet Sidney, who opposed the French match, and Edward DeVere, who championed it. Then Thomas Howard, Duke of Norfolk and the Queen's own cousin, was executed for his role in the plot to assassinate Her Majesty and place Mary of Scotland on the throne. It matters not where the court resides, as these are uneasy times for all. The stench of intrigue, no less than that of bodily origin, follows the court from palace to palace.

"I have not yet seen her," I told Cecil.

"There is talk of a progress to Henford this spring."

The mention of Henford caused a shiver in me, for this is where the Queen has installed her son, Edward, known as Filer. She has not seen him since his birth, but she has sent me there often to monitor his well-being. He is but eighteen years of age.

"I am not privy to the Queen's plans."

"Henford is a small house, unfit for the court. Don't you agree?"

"It is indeed a modest house," I replied.

"The negotiations with Anjou are in progress. Nothing must interfere with them. Any hint of scandal…."

I looked closely at those small, knowing eyes. Since the Queen granted Henford to the obscure Filer boy, the court has thrummed with gossip about his influence, or rather that of the people surrounding him.

"I am but a humble physician," I said, with a shallow bow in deference to Cecil's lofty station.

"A humble physician with great influence in certain matters. I would be grateful, quite grateful, if you could persuade the Queen that a visit to Henford would be ill advised."

"If she is well enough then I—"

"Do not trifle with me." He stepped so close that I could feel his mead-scented breath upon my face. "Your life hangs by a slender thread, Doctor. The Queen wishes you near, but even the royal physician is subject to misfortune. You recall the fate of the others at Hatfield?"

I did indeed. I could only bow once more and make my way across the room to the door to the privy chamber. The usher, recognizing me, pulled open the great doors, and I passed through.

• • •

She was alone at the far end of the long table around which sat her Privy Council, though they were absent now. I was struck by how small she appeared, for she loomed larger than life in my memory, even after a short absence, sometimes occupying my mind to such an extent that she crowded out all other thoughts and desires. Perhaps it was the portrait of her father, dominating the room as he had in life, that diminished her. In Holbein's picture, Henry glared at the visitor, lips pursed disapprovingly, his beard as luxuriant as the ermine that lined his waistcoat. What would he think of his second daughter, his unlikely heir, his only equal among the ill-fated Tudors? What trouble he had brewed to marry the Queen's mother, Anne, only to send her to the block three years later. Perhaps we would be better off if he had kept Katherine and the old religion. Had things improved since shaking off the Catholic yoke?

Heretical thoughts, these, which could cost me my head. Standing before her, I shook that same head to banish these ideas and cleared my throat softly to signal my presence.

"Doctor, come here!" She patted the table.

I bowed and crossed the great room. She remained seated.

"I trust Your Majesty is well?" I said.

"Perfectly so. I did not summon you about my own health."

"Praise be to God."

She waved her hand at this. "There is someone else I wish to discuss."

I could easily imagine who this was. "Your Majesty?"

"I wish to discuss Edward Filer."

"He is ill?"

"Must you dwell on disease like a poet on love?" Before I could reply to her outburst she added, in a softer tone, "He is perfectly fit. But I am uneasy all the same. You have heard of Norfolk's treason?"

"I have, Your Grace."

"I am surrounded by enemies, Doctor. Each day could be my last, and no medicine in your repertoire can save me."

"Surely you are beloved of your subjects and protected by the grace of God."

Another wave of the long and pale royal hand. "I have not seen him for eighteen years." I have never seen him, she might have said. "But I plan to stop at Henford during the progress this spring. I will make myself known to him then."

"Is that wise, Your Grace?" I was stepping over the line that separated my duties as physician with those of counselor, but I felt she wanted advice. "What can be gained from this?"

"He must be prepared for what may happen. There are fewer than five souls in England who know who he is. You, Cecil, Kat, and perhaps two or three more. I know not who they are, but they exist. They will use this information if it benefits them. He will never be allowed to take the throne. I am well aware of this." She frowned and glanced away for a moment. "But if the succession is in doubt, he could still be reckoned a threat, and that could imperil his life. I must secure his future. That is the only thing I can do for him, Doctor. He must understand who he is and what the dangers may be. He must stand on equal footing with his enemies."

"You make an excellent argument, Your Grace."

"But knowledge is not enough. I want to give him power. If it cannot be the throne, then it must be something else."

"Power, Your Grace?"

"The power to survive. It begins with knowledge, knowledge of who he is. But it must not end there."

"You cannot be thinking of elevating him to an earldom, Your Grace. That would surely bring attention, which would contradict your intentions."

"Damn!" She pounded the great table with her fist. Her pale face reddened, nearly matching the color of her hair, which today fell to her shoulders in soft undulations. When she turned from me to gaze out the window, I was reminded of the faint crook in her nose and saw her lips, already thin, all but disappear into a frown. A plain collar, rather than the usual ruff, revealed a long, pale neck. Even sitting, she impressed by her stature. I thought her more handsome than beautiful, yet the cares of her position were evident in small lines about her eyes and atop her brow.

"My father's bastard with Bessie Blount was made Duke of Richmond when he was six! But were I to acknowledge my son I would endanger the realm itself." She stood up, and I bowed, taking a step back. She was nearly as tall as me, and I am not short. "You were there, Doctor," she whispered, close to my face. "You saw how I suffered, how I was torn in two and almost died. I will not endure such torture again. I will not throw England into chaos by dying in childbirth. Let the negotiations with Anjou continue. They occupy my ministers and cause my enemies to fight amongst themselves, which is all to the good. But I will not marry."

I wondered, at that moment, how much her declaration owed to loyalty to the realm and how much to fear, understandable fear, of enduring once more the pain of childbirth. Nigh half the noblewoman at court have died while giving birth since the Queen took the throne.

"Your Grace's concern for the security of the realm is admirable."

She shot me a skeptical look, and I feared I may have betrayed myself.

"Wait here."

I bowed again, and she hurried to her private rooms. In the empty chamber, I felt for the first time the weight of her office, the great solitude that a monarch bears. 'Tis a shame, I thought, that she will not marry, for though negotiations with this monarch or that lord never cease, the Queen herself sending ambassadors and ministers to do her bidding across Europe, I knew now she would never take a husband. She had known childbirth, marriage's inevitable and violent consequence, and did not care to repeat it.

She returned shortly and dropped something on the table.

"There, what think you?"

I could only gasp at what she had tossed onto the table so thoughtlessly she might have been depositing a stack of dull papers. A necklace of emeralds, each stone the size of a large playing marble, shimmered with life. Diamonds, only slightly smaller, sparkled between the green stones, as if in conversation with them. Though I have been at court for many years, I have never seen anything so magnificent.

"My father gave these to my mother at Hever," she said. "In 1553, the year they married."

When the future Queen, still simply Anne Boleyn, was already pregnant with Elizabeth, I thought, but of course did not say.

"They came into the possession of my mother's family, the Howards."

Delicately put, I thought, for no doubt much was plundered from the royal apartments once it became clear that Anne Boleyn's tenure as Queen was coming to an end.

"My great uncle Howard told me they were captured from the Inca savages in Peru, where emeralds grow in the ground as common as mushrooms. One of my father's ships intercepted a Spanish galleon returning from the New World and brought these back as tribute."

"Most worthy tribute indeed," was all I could think to say, the jewels distracting me.

"I plan to give these to my…."

She turned away, and I leapt into the void.

"To Edward Filer?"

"Yes," she said, the word almost a sigh, for it must be a relief to

Her Majesty to share her great secret with a sympathetic and discrete subject. "I won't always be alive to protect him and his heirs. I cannot give him new estate and titles without arousing suspicion. Henford gave me trouble enough. The Howards were not pleased to part with it, and the progress I am planning will set tongues wagging. But these are worth two estates, and they shall be his and his sons and their sons, to do with as they please. I shall present them, in private, during the spring progress."

"Your Majesty is truly generous, and I believe your plan to endow Master Filer with wealth in this form is a clever one."

"You cannot expect me to ask the Privy Council for funds to give to a mere Hertfordshire squire. But these...." She gently ran her fingers over the jewels. "These belonged to his grandmother, a great Queen."

Some would cavil at the notion of Boleyn as a great Queen, but not I, or at least not aloud. I ventured a bit of flattery instead.

"And to his mother, a great ruler."

She could not suppress a satisfied smile, which quickly faded.

"Jewels are not enough, Doctor. They will purchase some security, but Edward will never be truly safe with money alone. Do you know what makes a man truly secure, Doctor?"

"The protection of an interested monarch?" was all I could venture.

"Power! To possess power is to possess security. I must find a way to endow him with power."

"An appointment to court would be—"

"Out of the question. We must be ingenious, you and I. We must find another way, as yet unthought of, to furnish Edward with power."

I cannot say I felt flattered at being included in her conspiracy, for the stakes seemed perilously high, and the dangers incalculable.

"I will do my very best, of course, Your Grace."

"Some potion, perhaps. Some elixir."

Her eyes were gleaming like the emeralds, almost too brilliant to be trusted. Such passion can enfeeble reason.

"Surely Your Majesty does not believe that a potion can bring power. There has never been such a thing."

"You must find one, then. Consult with the eminent doctors at Cambridge. You yourself were there as a student. There must be something." Her voice had begun to tremble. "I know no one else to consult. There is no one I can trust."

Then power does not bring security, I might have said, had I not feared for my life. For the Queen might rule a people with serene confidence, but safeguarding a person was perhaps a more vexing challenge. She was deeply distraught at the thought of her son, who was almost certain to be her only child, powerless to defend himself in a world in which she no longer held sway. Given the conspiracies swirling around her, that world might be closer at hand than I liked to think.

"I shall make it my cause to find something," I said.

She turned to me, her eyes now glistening with tears.

"I nearly died that morning at Hatfield. Do you remember? He was ripped from my loins. I vowed, afterwards, that I would never risk my life that way again. I owe it to England to survive."

Some would say she owed the country an heir, but this was yet another thought I husbanded.

"So I will not marry, not Anjou nor any other. I will keep them interested, these men who think they can claim me. It is good for a woman to be desired. Good for a Queen, as well. But I will not marry. I cannot risk it."

Many a woman dreads the pain and peril of childbirth, but husbands demand heirs, and their wives have no choice but to provide them. The Queen was fortunate in this respect, for she had no one to answer to but herself.

"Edward will never be King," she said. "But he will be safe, as will his heirs." Her eyes were dry now, her voice steady. "You will assist me in this, Doctor. I command it."

I bowed. "Of course, Your Grace."

"Now leave me."

I backed away from her, turning only when I had reached the door, on which I rapped my fist. Immediately it was opened, and when I had passed through I let out a long breath which felt like the first one I'd taken since entering the chamber.

CHAPTER 17

Derek Martinson lived on the outskirts of town, where Tunsbury began to turn rural, in a large house with a steeply pitched roof, pointed-arch windows, and high dormers. The wood siding was painted a pale yellow, with elaborate trim along the roof edges in a contrasting white. It appeared to be in very good repair, and was set amid a carefully tended lawn and manicured shrubs.

"Gothic Revival," Lee said as they walked up the flagstone path to the front door. "Probably 1840s. Not my period, or my taste."

Mark gave her a look that showed he was impressed with her knowledge and at the same time suspicious of it—and her. She sensed that he wasn't entirely convinced of her innocence, so that anything new she revealed—such as a knowledge of Victorian architecture—was evaluated in the context of a woman wanted for homicide.

She rang the doorbell. After a short while, the door was opened by a very small and quiet old man who peered at them with hostile curiosity.

"Derek Martinson?" Lee said. When he nodded, she introduced herself as Sarah Cooper and explained that the librarian had suggested she stop by for information about the town's history.

"Must be my age," he said without a trace of humor.

Like the house, Martinson was fussily well-tended. He had a full head of white hair, combed in a part that revealed a perfectly straight line of pink flesh. His features were small and delicate, with lips that seemed pursed in a permanent expression of judicious disapproval. No more than five four, he had on an expensive-looking white dress shirt and light gray slacks made of carefully pressed linen. Dressed for visitors, Lee thought.

Martinson led them into a large parlor furnished with low-slung, richly upholstered sofas and chairs and tables polished to a luminous gleam. The walls were covered with moss green paper flecked with gold fleur-de-lys. Paintings of fruit and flowers hung by wires from picture molding.

"What a beautiful room," Lee said. She despised Victorian froufrou, but she did appreciate authenticity, and the room was nothing if not true to its period.

"I cannot take credit, I'm afraid. My great-grandfather built this house in 1856, and I have done little other than maintain it. I see it as my birthright, and therefore my obligation. I became the unofficial town historian largely so that I could maintain this house appropriately, and encourage other owners to do the same. I'm afraid I haven't been successful in the latter pursuit. Would you like some refreshments?"

Even his slightly mannered speech sounded Victorian.

They both declined, but he called out for someone named Hugh anyway, and a moment later they were joined by a much younger man of about fifty, tall and thin, wearing a heavy cardigan sweater.

"Iced tea, please, Hugh. Nothing for my guests."

Hugh gave them a vaguely resentful look and left the room.

"I notice that he's wearing a heavy sweater," Lee said. "I've seen other people in Tunsbury wearing heavy clothing despite the season. Why is that?"

Martinson looked at her disapprovingly.

"I thought you were a historian."

"That doesn't mean I'm oblivious to what goes on around me."

"You'd be well advised to stick to history, Miss Cooper. Much less trouble. As to why people dress the way they do, I haven't a clue."

Hugh returned with a tall glass of iced tea, which he placed on a coaster on a marble-topped coffee table. His hands were chapped and red, as if he'd been exposed to extremely cold weather and only just come inside. His pants were gray flannel.

"I'm interested in the descendants of Charles Filer, who arrived here in 1639. His father was Edward Filer, of Henford in Hertfordshire."

"Have you been to the Filer House?"

Lee nodded.

"Then you know what there is to know about the Filers. They all but vanished after the seventeenth century, like so many families in that perilous time." He glanced suspiciously from one end of the room to another. "Indians," he whispered.

"But recorded deeds indicate large land purchases by Charles."

"He couldn't have known his line would die out."

"But there were purchases after Charles, well into the eighteenth century. So there must have been descendants."

"None that I'm aware of."

He said this with a smug certainty that immediately raised Lee's hackles, and her suspicions.

"And the land?" Mark asked. "What happened to all that land?"

"When taxes went unpaid, the land was usually sold at auction by the town. These transactions may not have been recorded, as they were often less than transparent, shall we say? Foreclosed land went to those with connections, often quite cheaply."

"Someone mentioned a group of descendants living on the outskirts of Tunsbury," Lee said.

"Really? I'm sure I would have heard of such a group."

"The original purchases must have been expensive," Lee said. "Where did Charles Filer and his descendants get the funds for that?"

"He was the only child of a landowner in England."

"And yet he apparently abandoned his home to come to New England and purchase land, only to disappear a few years later."

"What does the term 'semper' mean to you?" Mark asked.

"It's Latin for 'always.'"

"It has no special connection to the town?" Lee asked.

"None that I know of."

"Are you sure about that?" Mark's tone had turned a bit aggressive.

"If there were a connection, I would know about it. Sadly, we are a town that does not value the past. Houses are torn down here every day, or left to rot. 'Semper' would be an ironic word for us, under the circumstances."

Mark stood up and crossed the room, where he closely examined one of the several ornately framed paintings.

"This looks like a portrait of a map maker."

"A cartographer, yes."

"An ancestor of yours?"

"Not at all. My great-grandfather purchased it. It's English, early eighteenth century."

"I don't see a signature."

"Alas, there isn't one, which makes its value quite low. Still, I think it's well done."

Mark gestured for her to join him at the painting. She complied, unsure why Mark was suddenly fascinated by this one painting, the only one in the room that wasn't a still life.

"What does the inscription mean?" Mark asked.

"Inscription?" Suddenly Martinson was at their side, squinting at the painting as if seeing it for the first time.

"On the map. 'I divine the future holding an empty map.' What does it mean?"

"I haven't a clue." Martinson said this lightly, but his voice had developed a tense edge.

"The map *is* empty, in a way," Lee said. "You can see the outline of some sort of land, but there's nothing delineated inside the outline." In the painting, a prosperous-looking man in a dark robe, depicted in classic three-quarter view, held a parchment map on which a large tract of land appeared to be uninhabited.

"An empty tract of land," Mark said. "It might be a reference to the disappearance of the Filer property."

"Nonsense, this wasn't even painted in this country. In any case, the painting wasn't intended to be a literal depiction of a map, but rather an allegory. Geography is destiny, it tells us. One's future, our collective future, is determined by the contours of maps. There was a great fascination with the New World in the eighteenth century, a sense that this vast tract of open land did indeed foretell the future."

Mark looked skeptical. "Kind of a roundabout way of putting that—'I divine the future holding an empty map.'"

"Yes, well, everything isn't always as *literal* as we might like."

His tone oozed condescension. While the two men continued to discuss the painting, Lee took out her phone and snapped a few photographs of the inscription. When she was done, she interrupted what had evolved into a tense conversation about Tunsbury, Martinson arguing that the town had shown a negligent disregard for its past, Mark pointing out that the slow evaporation of the fishing industry required hard choices, including selling off old houses to build new developments for people lucky enough to still have jobs.

"It's a tragedy, what's happened to this town."

"What's tragic is the disappearance of the fishing industry. I've lived here my entire life and never once run into you in town or even at zoning meetings. Where do you come off wishing things stayed quaint and cozy?"

"I never said quaint and—"

"We need to go," Lee said, practically pulling Mark away from Martinson. In the front hallway they were joined by Hugh, still swaddled in wool despite the warmth of the day. He said nothing, but stared intently at her, perhaps fearful that she was going to pocket a precious artifact. She thanked Martinson, who merely nodded in response, and left. Just before getting into her rental car, which was parked behind Mark's, she turned and saw that both men, Martinson and the overdressed servant, were standing inside the house, the door still open, watching them.

CHAPTER 18

In darkness, the Filer House seemed larger than Lee remembered, a looming and not altogether benign presence. The half-moon and swaying branches of the two ancient oak trees on the front lawn conspired to cast jagged, moving shadows across its blank facade.

All day she'd wanted to return to the place to confirm a hunch, but she'd decided to wait until night, when the construction crew would be gone and darkness would obscure their presence from neighbors. She would have gone alone, but Mark had insisted on accompanying her.

They had spent the afternoon at his house, some of it in his bed. His idea, not hers. Mostly his. Afterward she fell into the deepest sleep since the night she'd read the sonnet on the evening news. "The certain knot of peace," Sidney called it. "The poor man's wealth, the prisoner's release." When she woke up, it was dark outside and Mark was downstairs, preparing dinner. While he cooked she used her laptop to google "semper," which turned up in dozens of seemingly irrelevant links. She refined the search to "semper + filer" and got nothing of interest, then "semper + Elizabeth I." Again, nothing relevant. She combined semper with Tunsbury, Hever, and emeralds. Still nothing.

"I'm heading home after the Filer House," she said after turning off the computer.

"What home? Riker's Island?"

"Cute. No, New York. I need to learn more about the Hever Emeralds. They don't seem connected to this place, but there must be experts in the jewelry district who know something about what happened to them."

"You can drive down tomorrow morning. Tonight, you're staying here."

She hated being told what to do and almost said so. But under the circumstances, it felt okay to go along. And he was right. What "home" did she have, in any case? Her instincts told her to keep moving. They also told her to stay put. When he offered a glass of red wine, she took it, and then watched him whip up a marinade for the swordfish he'd gone out to buy while she slept.

"Why are you doing this?" she asked at one point.

"Because I like to cook, and you need to eat."

"No, I mean, why are you helping me? You could get in serious trouble."

"I don't have a whole lot to lose, I guess. No job. No wife. No kids. Soon, no house unless I scratch together six months of back payments."

"Still…."

"And I like you."

She ignored this. "Do you believe I'm innocent?" He squeezed lemon juice into the marinade. "You're not answering."

He turned to her. "I guess I don't really know, and I don't really care. You seem like a good person, so whatever you did you did because you had to. And you've got a great ass."

"So you're not sure."

"About your ass?"

"About my innocence."

"Not interested. But when my car slammed into yours yesterday, I felt this conviction that my shit-show of a life was about to change course. And I promised myself I would go along with it. I just want to see what happens."

She was disappointed, though not entirely surprised, that he harbored some doubt about her innocence. And there was nothing she could say to defend herself beyond what he already knew. So she shut up and watched him cook. Later, she focused on the meal, which was delicious.

Mark had brought a flashlight to the Filer House, which he trained on the white clapboards. The house seemed to absorb the light and swallow it, almost reluctant to be seen.

"I don't like this place. Even as a kid it gave me the creeps. I don't think anyone ever stayed here more than a year or two. What was it you wanted to see?"

"We need to move the temporary ramp," she said. "It doesn't look heavy."

She was right about ramp, which was made of unpainted plywood. Working together, they were able to lift the structure an inch or two off the ground and pull it away from the house. After they set it down, Lee took the flashlight and shone it at the brick foundation, starting on the left side.

"See the pattern in the brick?"

"The letter *s*," Mark said.

She moved the light to the right.

"An *e*," he said. "Someone went to a lot of trouble to create this fancy brickwork, only to bury it underground."

She moved the beam to the right, where the temporary steps had been.

"I was right."

The light fell on a third letter, an *m*, that had been obscured by the steps. She moved the beam farther to the right and revealed a *p*. Slowly she directed the light onto the remaining two letters, the two that she had originally assumed denoted a queen: *er*.

"Semper," Mark said. "Amazing."

"The word has some meaning beyond 'always,'" she said. "Some meaning special to the Filers, otherwise why go to the trouble of embedding it into the very foundation of their home? It's hidden in the sonnet, and it's hidden here."

They stood silently, contemplating the significance of the word, Lee moving the light back and forth across the foundation. The letters seemed to come alive as the beam crossed over them, a signal from the past, at once clear and unintelligible.

"We should get out of here before someone calls the police," Mark said.

They dragged the steps back into place and headed for the car. In the street, Lee turned once more, feeling a strange reluctance to leave the house where Charles Filer, son of Edward, grandson of England's greatest monarch, had put down roots in the New World. She shone the light on the foundation one last time, moving it from side to side, illuminating only the four visible letters. What were they trying to say? After a few seconds she flicked off the light.

"Wait a minute, turn it back on," Mark said. "What do you see?"

She read the four visible letters one by one: "'*s, e, e, r*.'"

"Exactly."

"The middle letters are blocked by the steps. We knew that."

"Yes, but what do they spell, these four letters?"

"Seer."

"*One who can divine the future.*"

"From the inscription on Martinson's painting," she whispered. "I can divine the future holding an empty map."

"The inscription must refer to a seer, a diviner of the future. But what's an empty map?"

It came to her instantly.

"If you *empty* the word itself, 'map'—take out its middle letter—you get the two outside letters, *m* and *p*."

"And if the seer is *holding* the empty map, you put the *m* and *p* inside it...."

"*Semper.*" The word hung in the air around them. "Derek Martinson lied to us. That connects him to this place, to the Filer family. He must have known what that inscription meant."

She became aware of a crackling sound, faint but distinct, and looked around. The overhanging branches of one of the old oaks obscured the moonlight, cloaking them in near total darkness.

"Do you think Martinson—"

The crackling grew louder. Closer. Tires moving slowly on asphalt. But there was no car, just the darkness.

Suddenly, the roar of an engine, accelerating. Then a blinding light. Headlights flicked on. She and Mark turned to look. A car, speeding toward them. In a second it would pin them against the back of Mark's car.

She could dive to the side, but the car could swerve that way too.

"Jump!" she screamed and simultaneously leapt onto the trunk of the car. Mark did the same, just a split second before the car plowed into it. The impact threw them both onto the street, on either side of Mark's car. The oncoming car, lights still blinding them, backed up with a screech of tires, then jumped forward, this time aiming for the driver's side of the car, where Lee was sprawled on the asphalt.

No time to stand and run. Instead, she rolled toward Mark's car and squeezed herself under it. The attacking vehicle sped by, so close she detected the sour smell of heated tire rubber. The car stopped abruptly about ten yards ahead. Lee stood, opened the driver's door of Mark's car and dove in. Before she could shut the door the other car backed into it, slamming it shut. Mark got in a second later.

"Drive!" he shouted, handing her the keys.

She fumbled the ignition key into the slot, started the engine, and yanked the shift into drive. She floored the accelerator, and the car lurched forward.

"Drive to the end of the street!"

The attacker was behind them, perhaps two feet from their rear fender. Halfway to the corner it pulled parallel and jerked into them, forcing them onto the curb. Lee tried to get a look at the driver but couldn't. She swerved to avoid a tree, then swerved back onto the street. The attacker jerked the car into them again, and once again she was forced onto the curb. This time she slowed almost to a halt before steering the car back onto the street, so that the attacker was a good twenty yards ahead of them. She turned the steering wheel all the way to the left, floored the accelerator, turned the car around, and took off in the opposite direction.

"Turn right at the corner!"

She glanced in the rearview mirror.

"He's not following." She was gasping for breath. "I think we're safe."

CHAPTER 19

They drove through the night toward New York, Mark behind the wheel. Lee only stopped shaking an hour into the drive. Back in Tunsbury, her rental car sat in front of Mark's house, racking up charges on the late Sarah Cooper's credit card. Mark seemed equally freaked out, staring intently at the road without speaking. He broke the silence shortly after they crossed the border into Connecticut.

"At least we learned one thing from the attack. Someone really is after you. You're innocent."

"It took another attack to convince you?" She turned away from him.

"If I thought you were a killer, I'd have called the police the moment I realized who you were. But I couldn't help thinking that maybe you were involved in something that brought on that first attack in your apartment."

"In my mind I run through everyone I know, wondering what they're thinking about me. They must assume I killed that guy, all of them." The New York papers were still featuring stories about the case. Descriptions of her ranged from "person of interest" to "prime suspect" to "fugitive."

Her father had no doubt been contacted, and had no doubt told the cops—and perhaps reporters—that his daughter was innocent. Had Tom Nicholson also told them that his daughter's most reliable communication with him was an annual Christmas card? And her mother. Assuming she was even alive, had she seen the story? Would she care? She'd left her young daughter in the hands of a kind but remote father; after that bit of betrayal, would Lee's current predicament cause any anguish? At every milestone in her life, graduating second in her high school class, summa cum laude from Penn State, even completing the New York Marathon, Lee inevitably wondered what her mother would think and hoped, irrationally, that she knew. She used to read Lee stories about Elizabeth and Mary, Queen of Scots and Lady Jane Grey. What would she make of her current predicament, triggered by a Shakespeare sonnet?

Lee and Mark checked into a 1950s-era tourist hotel on the far west side of Midtown, near the Hudson. Mark used his credit card to pay for the room. They slept for several hours on separate beds. Lee awoke first, at about ten, and called David Eddings.

"Lee, where are you?" He sounded more peeved than truly concerned, as if she were merely late for an appointment. She got right to the point of the call.

"I need information about the Hever Emeralds. Is there a book, a manuscript somewhere I could consult?"

"I've done some research since you were last here," he said. "Nothing turned up. The emeralds were passed from Anne Boleyn to her Howard relatives and then to her daughter, Elizabeth, who wore them as a young queen. There's no mention of the necklace after 1575."

"Except in the sonnet. Someone must think that the sonnet holds the key to finding the emeralds."

"I did turn up one thing. There's a chap on Forty-Seventh Street, the world's foremost expert on emeralds, apparently. If even a single stone from the Hever necklace turned up, he'd know about it."

"Who is he?

"Lee, I really think you need to turn yourself in. The police already suspect me of helping you." He lowered his voice to a whisper. "I think they're watching my office."

"What's his name, David?"

The office of Maurits Immersheim was on the second floor of a small, unremarkable office building on West Forty-Seventh Street, which was lined with similarly undistinguished buildings, each of which housed a jewelry store or an arcade of jewelers' stands on the ground floor. His office was behind a sturdy metal door, with three locks, on which had been stenciled nothing more than his name in large block letters.

"Not exactly classy digs for the world's foremost authority on emeralds," Mark said as Lee rapped on the door. A few moments later they heard a faint man's voice from the other side of the door.

"Who is it?"

"Sarah Cooper," Lee said. "I called earlier." She'd phoned with a made-up story about inherited jewels.

There was a faint scraping noise as he slid the keyhole cover to the side.

"Yes, I remember, just one moment, please."

One by one he opened the locks and then the door.

Maurits Immersheim was a small, very thin man, dressed formally in a dark suit, white shirt, and striped tie. He looked at least eighty, with a deeply lined face. A black yarmulke was bobby-pinned to his wispy white hair. He seemed very light on his feet as he returned to his desk across the large, sparsely furnished room. There was a sense of compact efficiency about him, a reluctance to take up more than a minimal allotment of time and space.

They sat across from him in two wooden armchairs. The room was dominated by an old, very large steel safe whose combination dial was at least three inches in diameter. The room's single window looked out over Forty-Seventh Street.

"I would offer you refreshments, but as you see I am alone here, and generally take my meals in a restaurant," he said. He spoke with an accent, northern European, Lee guessed. "You had a question about emeralds?"

"The Hever Emeralds," Lee said.

Immersheim frowned and slowly shook his head.

"If I had known it was the Hever you wanted to know about I would not have encouraged you to stop by. Unless, of course, you have brought them with you?" He chuckled quietly.

"We may have some information about where they are," Lee said.

"If I had a dime for every lead to the Hever Emeralds I'd be a rich man. In Antwerp, where I began in this business before the war, I would hear a new story every week. But I quickly learned to ignore them." Though he spoke in a fluid, calm voice, Immersheim's hands roved nervously across his desktop, occasionally moving to his lap or scratching a leg.

"How can something so valuable disappear? Mark asked.

"A great mystery. We know they were given by Henry VIII to his then mistress, Anne Boleyn, and that they eventually passed to her daughter, who became Elizabeth I. Elizabeth wore them several times, as remarked upon by several diarists of the period, who were understandably dazzled by them. Even for Elizabeth, a woman obsessed with jewels, the Hever Emeralds were considered unusually opulent. She sat for a portrait wearing them, which is the last time they were seen as far as we know. There is no further record of them."

"What would they be worth today?" Mark asked.

"If the portrait is accurate in its depiction, the stones alone would be worth between forty and fifty million dollars, depending on their quality. But there's also the provenance to consider. How much more would someone pay to own a necklace worn by the greatest monarch in British history? A necklace bequeathed to her by her mother, one of history's great tragic figures? That we do not know, and never will."

"Someone must know where they are," Lee said.

"Perhaps. Over the years there have been intriguing hints that the Hever Emeralds might not be lost altogether. In 1824, a large stone was sold on the Antwerp market whose shape matched that of the Hever pendant stones. Then, twenty years ago, another such stone appeared, this time in my office. It went for $1.3 million dollars, a record for a single stone without a setting."

"You think it was from the necklace?" Lee asked.

"The cutting was the same. And the quality was flawless. But the seller was adamant that it was not part of an ensemble. I probed him about its provenance. I handle perhaps one-third of the world's trade in raw emeralds, and much of the secondary market in cut stones. It is highly unlikely that the existence of a stone of that size and quality could have escaped my attention. The seller claimed he had inherited it from his parents, who had purchased it in Hong Kong some years earlier. It sounded dubious to me, but what was I to do? We are fortunate in the gem business. Unlike art dealers, we do not need to document the provenance of our goods. Otherwise we would all be out of business."

"Do you have the stone?" Lee asked.

Immersheim smiled indulgently. "Another reason I'd be out of business. To keep something so valuable in inventory would be ruinous. I reset it into a pendant and sold it within a week. At a substantial mark-up, I might add."

"Do you recall the seller's name?"

"In my files, of course I have his name."

"Could you look it up for us?"

"Absolutely not. That would be a breach of trust."

"We're talking jewelry, not doctor-patient confidentiality," Mark said.

"If word got out on the street that I had disclosed the name of a seller, I'd be ruined." He shook his head slowly, lips pursed, contemplating such a fate. "He was an odd duck, I will give you that. It was summertime, August, I think, and I had the air-conditioning turned on, naturally. He asked me to turn it off the moment he arrived, even though he was wearing a heavy sweater and a jacket. He seemed to be shivering, too, which I initially took to be a sign of nervousness at the size of the proposed transaction, but which I eventually came to realize was a sign of being cold. The poor man just couldn't get warm."

Lee had to shiver herself, recalling the clerk in Tunsbury and Derek Martinson's servant, both dressed for winter on a warm late-spring day.

"Now tell me something," Immersheim said. "What is this lead you talk about? What have you discovered?"

She wasn't about to tell him about the sonnet, which would only alert him to her real identity.

"Nothing specific," she said. "A passing reference in an old manuscript."

He considered her for a few moments, clearly skeptical.

"A word of advice, then," he said at length. "Leave the Hever Emeralds, wherever they are, at rest. They never did anyone any good, I think. Emeralds were meant to symbolize fertility, but look what good it did Anne Boleyn."

"She produced the greatest ruler in the history of—"

"She was executed. And they hardly boosted her daughter's fertility, did they?"

Lee smiled, thinking of Edward Filer.

"It isn't just these stones," Immersheim continued. "Emeralds have a long association with violence and treachery. There were dealers in Antwerp who wouldn't touch them, back when I was just getting started. The whole sordid history of the conquest of South America by conquistadors began with emeralds, which were looted by the Spanish from mines and plucked out of native headdresses. Once European royalty had a look at the green gems they sent more and more ships across the Atlantic with instructions to do whatever it took to bring back stones. Untold people were ultimately slaughtered."

"And yet you specialize in them."

"I had no choice. My family was in the gemstone business in Antwerp. I wanted nothing to do with it. I went to university to study philosophy. But after the war. . . ." A long pause. "I was the only one left. I came here, to New York, to start fresh. I only knew the gem business."

Mark stood up and crossed the room to the window. Lee immediately knew what had drawn his attention: a flashing of red light from the street below.

"In medieval times," Immersheim continued, "scholars wore emeralds to strengthen their memory and improve their eloquence."

"Three police cars out front!" Mark swerved around to face Immersheim. "Did you call them?"

"Why would I call the police? *How* would I call them?"

Mark walked to the desk and yanked Immersheim's chair, with him in it, away from the desk.

"What in god's name are you doing?" the old man shouted.

"This button, what is it for?"

Lee, already standing, peered over the desk, where a small doorbell-like button was screwed into the leg well of the desk.

"I don't know, it's just something that was there when I—"

"It's a panic button, for the police, in case of robbery. We need to get out of here." He grabbed Immersheim by the shoulders. "Is there a back exit?"

"Please, I am sure they are here for something else."

Mark shook him violently. "*Is there a back exit?*"

Immersheim looked suddenly small and terrified.

"Down the hall and to the right."

"*Take us there*!" Mark pulled him up from the chair and shoved him toward the door. "*Now*!"

Immersheim led them down a short corridor that angled to the right. At the end of the hallway was a door with an illuminated exit sign over it.

"This door. It leads to a service exit, also on Forty-Seventh Street." He was panting, his voice faint.

Mark waved her into the stairwell and immediately followed. They raced downstairs, taking the steps two at a time.

"I know who you are, from the news!" Immersheim shouted after them. "The blond hair didn't fool me. I know who you are!"

Lee pulled open the service door, triggering a loud alarm, and they stepped into the street.

CHAPTER 20

The service door opened directly onto the Forty-Seventh Street sidewalk, about fifteen yards west of the building's main entrance.

"This way," Lee told Mark, turning toward Sixth Avenue. "Don't run. Try to fit in."

The sidewalk teemed with pedestrians, many black-suited Orthodox Jews who worked in the street's countless jewelry stores. Mark took her hand as they walked. It wasn't easy maintaining a slow pace when every instinct said *run*. Only once did she look back, catching a brief glimpse of several patrol cars, lights flashing, in front of Immersheim's building.

Pedestrian traffic slowed as they approached Sixth Avenue. She quickly saw why: the intersection had been blocked off by patrol cars parked in the middle of the street. Uniformed officers stood at the corner, screening everyone coming from Forty-Seventh Street. She pulled Mark into the nearest store.

"Immersheim may already have given them a description."

The store was a collection of small stalls. Down the middle, a narrow corridor was lined on both sides with low, glass-topped display cases of jewelry. Behind the counters stood women dressed conservatively in long-sleeved blouses and skirts.

"May I show you something?" a woman behind the nearest counter asked.

Ignoring her, Mark said, "We'll separate. They'll be looking for a man and a woman together."

Lee nodded. "There's a coffee shop on Broadway and Seventy-Fifth Street. Meet me there."

"I'll head that way," Mark said, pointing to the east. "You go the other way."

They separated on the sidewalk. He crossed the street mid-block to avoid having to walk in front of Immersheim's building. She headed west, toward Sixth Avenue. As she approached the corner, pedestrian traffic slowed considerably. Ahead, she saw three cops standing across the sidewalk. The one in the middle stood with his arms extended, effectively halting everyone who tried to walk past him. The other two examined each pedestrian before the center man lowered his arms. The same scenario was taking place on the sidewalk across the street.

She had no choice but to proceed. All around her, people speculated on what was happening. There was talk of a robbery, a jewel heist. As she shuffled with the crowd toward the corner, her heart began to pound so insistently she feared the cops would notice. When it was her turn to step up, she stopped about a foot in front of the cop with his arms up, willing herself to make eye contact.

"Okay," the cop to her right said, and the arm in front of her went down. With a rush of relief, she stepped forward.

"Wait!"

She forced herself to continue walking, turning right onto Sixth Avenue. Perhaps the call hadn't been meant for her.

A hand gripped her right arm. Turning, she found herself face-to-face with a policeman staring intently into her eyes.

"Your name?" he said in a flat voice, his grip tight on her arm, his gaze never losing focus on her eyes.

Name? Even her pseudonym was no good, since she'd used it with Immersheim. She said the first name that came to mind.

"Hever, Anne Hever." When he didn't respond, she added, "Is there something wrong?"

The cop called to a colleague over his shoulder. "Get that jeweler over here for an ID. This one looks like a match."

CHAPTER 21

13 June 1572
Whitehall

I am still much troubled by the Queen's discomfort, but today I received information of a most startling nature, information which, if it proves true, will have momentous, perhaps I should write monstrous, implications not only for Her Majesty but for God's entire world. I must add that it is not the Queen's health which troubles me, for Her Majesty is robust in body. It is her spirit which unsettles me, for how shall a monarch rule if her mind afflicts her spirit? Her counselors whisper that she is distracted, prone to outbursts of temper with no seeming cause. They talk of loneliness, of the need for a husband to fortify her resolve against Spain and her enemies at home. Earlier this week, at Hampton Court, I chanced to see her pacing in the great court, eyes fixed on the clock above the gate, willing the passage of time. It is ever a mistake to will time away.

Her counselors may whisper of her distress, but I alone know it is her son and not the threat from foreign powers which gnaws at her. Even to write these words, "*her son*," sets my hand to trembling. She fears for his safety above all else, for if his identity were to be known he would become a target of envy and intrigue. Marriage negotiations, though I know them to be bootless, would cease, for what Prince will want to marry a whore, as she would be called? She desires to provide for his future comfort, and that of his heirs, who are her heirs, too, but any show of favoritism will only draw attention to what is already so obvious to me, the uncanny resemblance he shares with his natural mother; the russet hair, small green eyes, and slender fingers.

During the last progress, the court spent an uncommonly long time at Henford, causing whispers as well as griping among the court, for the house is not great nor the grounds especially generous. Master Filer himself was hardly gracious, keeping to his rooms for most of our stay. He is a frail young man, prone to chills and ague, ever swaddled in robes and scarves more suited to winter than glorious June. I do not know how he liked the Hever Emeralds, for no one at court was privy to the Queen's gift, although I can easily enough imagine what he thought. He will take a wife soon, but she must not wear them, I think, for jewels so rare and precious are like signposts to a deeper story, in this instance a story that must not be revealed. Someday, when the Queen is no longer on earth to protect and support Filer and his heirs, then he may find it expedient to sell the jewels, all at once or, more likely than not, one by one. Each pendant emerald could support a generation of Filers, I think.

But I digress, having so little time to record my thoughts here and no one with which to share them. Even my devoted Lucy, who shares my bed wherever the court takes me, must never know of these events, though I trust her wholeheartedly. It is a burden I will not place upon the shoulders of a servant who has already forfeited her home and family for a new land and an old master.

Last night, just after dusk, there was a knock at my door. I was reading Thomas Linacre's translation from Greek into Latin of Galen's *Methodus Medendi.* His mastery of human anatomy is second to none, and I will be ever grateful to Linacre for making Galen's medical writings accessible to a country-raised wretch such as me with no training in ancient Greek.

"There is a man to see you; he won't give his name," Lucy said from the door to my private apartment, where I have been given new lodgings fit for a foreign ambassador, which causes no end of chatter among the court. The walls of my bedroom are lined with tapestries that show a great feast, tables laden with fruit, and other delicacies. The room is ablaze with candles, for I am allotted as many as Cecil, I think. Such is my rising stature with the Queen.

"Tell him my surgery is closed for the day."

"I did so, my lord, but he tells me it is not your healing he wants."

"Send him away. I have appetite for supper, nothing more."

She curtsied, as always with a sly smile to remind me that there are times when she is not quite so obedient, and left me. I miss Jane with a husband's true soul, but Lucy brings the savage alchemy of Africa to my bed, and I confess that when she administers the dark arts upon my body my soul takes leave, carrying reason with it, and I am the slave, she the master. I shall be damned for eternity, it is true, but when Lucy lies in my bed I cannot help but think that if she shall join with me in Hell, then I shall resign myself happily to eternal damnation.

A minute later my room was invaded by a most peculiar figure.

He was tall and alarmingly thin, about thirty years of age, I guessed. His clothing was that of a poor man, and his hair, which fell to his shoulders in greasy clumps, that of a person of little pride. His face was the color of old rhubarb, suggesting a man who had spent a great deal of time out of doors, perhaps at sea. But it was his eyes that were the unavoidable focus of my attention. They appeared to be unblinking, and they seemed to look beyond me and my room to some place else, a place of untold horrors. The man looked terrified of something that only he could see.

"Physician, I must have a word with you," he said. His voice was as thin as his physique, and equally unsteady.

"My servant told you my hours are—"

"I am not ill!" he shouted. "Not in any way you can cure." With this strange outburst he threw himself into a chair across from me, next to the fire. "I have come because it is said you are close to the Queen." His unblinking eyes never left mine.

"I am Her Majesty's physician, it is true."

"Then you must tell her at once. A most terrible thing. More awful than all her armies and ships. It has come from the New World. It is here, in London, as we speak. It can destroy us, all of us. Please, tell the Queen."

His eyes lost focus, or rather they focused more intently on that thing or place I could not see. I saw that his hands were shaking, and he appeared to be nodding constantly, as if agreeing to some unspoken assertion.

"What in God's name are you talking about, sir?" I asked. "What is this 'thing' you mention?" I had already dismissed him as a lunatic, yet I confess I was intrigued by his tale, for haven't our best storytellers often been men of unbalanced temperament?

"The savages call it Amdilia, because it lives forever, or so they think. But my captain has given it another name." He let his head flop back on the chair and gazed upward, mouth slack, as if on the ceiling there was a sign from God that perhaps all was not lost. "My captain, he calls it Semper."

CHAPTER 22

Maurits Immersheim was being escorted toward Lee by a uniformed policeman. She had seconds to act—he'd recognize her even before he reached the corner.

What if she just let it happen? Identification. Arrest. Jail. Trial. Could she prove her innocence, in the face of all the evidence, beginning with the bogus voicemail on her answering machine?

No. She had to get out of there.

The jeweler was now ten yards away. Only the throng of pedestrians in front of him prevented a clear view of her.

"How about letting go of my arm?" she said to the officer holding her. "Any tighter and you'll cause gangrene."

"Nice try. "

"You're hurting me!" She squirmed her right arm and shoulder, but his grip never relaxed.

"That's her!" The jeweler was just a few feet away. His finger pointed right at her.

She jerked to her left, but the cop holding her never lost his balance, and pulled her right back.

"Time for the cuffs," he said. "Harry, you wanna cuff her?" he shouted to the policeman escorting Immersheim.

Then, from nowhere, came a man's voice from behind the officer who was holding her.

"Excuse me, officer?"

He turned and immediately staggered back, releasing his grip on her. Only when he'd fallen away did she see Mark and realize, in an instant, that he had slugged the cop in the face.

Having succeeded in freeing her, he seemed momentarily unclear about what to do next.

"This way!" she shouted, grabbing his hand. They ran up Sixth Avenue, the two of them forming a kind of battering ram through the midday crowd of pedestrians. Behind them she heard the jumbled shouts of the police ordering chase.

At the corner of Forty-Eigth Street she made a quick decision, plunging down into the Rockefeller Center subway station, Mark now right behind her. It was significantly less crowded down there, though she knew that would only make it easier for the cops to catch up to them. She threw herself at the emergency exit next to the turnstiles. It flew open, triggering a shrieking alarm. They ran straight ahead and then down another flight of stairs to the subway platform. From behind them, she heard shouts and footsteps getting closer.

There were no trains in the station. They kept running along the platform, pushing away anyone who got in their way. At the far end, they raced up another set of stairs and continued running. Rockefeller Center sat atop a network of tunnels connecting the various buildings in the complex as well as the subway. Stores and cafes lined the tunnels. They ran through them, dodging and occasionally colliding with oncoming pedestrians, turning right or left as the tunnel snaked east toward Fifth Avenue.

As exhaustion began to slow their pace, Lee sensed the cops were catching up. From the corner of her eye she saw a staircase heading up, and grabbed Mark's arm. They took the stairs two at a time and found themselves inside the lobby of one of Rockefeller Center's original Art Deco office buildings. The elevators were protected by turnstiles and a security guard, so she headed for the nearest door, plunging through it onto the sidewalk.

They were on Forty-Ninth Street, just south and west of the sunken plaza that, in wintertime, contained the famous ice skating rink. Lee saw two uniformed cops standing under the row of flags on the southern edge of the plaza and signaled for Mark to follow her in the opposite direction, to the west. Midway down the block, halfway to Sixth Avenue, a long line had formed outside of 30 Rockefeller Plaza. Tourists waiting for the NBC tour, or for the elevator to the observation deck. She assumed the cops were still close behind them. They were forced to slow to a walk as they went by the line, which took up most of the sidewalk, weaving through oncoming pedestrians who had to move in single file. Fearing that they were about to be overtaken, Lee made a sudden decision.

She yanked Mark's arm and pulled him into the back of the line. Almost immediately a young family—parents and three children—joined the line behind them.

"May I borrow that?" Without waiting for an answer, Lee grabbed a tourist map from the father's hands and held it in front of her and Mark, shielding them from the sidewalk. A few moments later she heard the police.

"Police! Clear the sidewalk!"

It was all she could do to keep her hands steady; even so, the map fluttered like one of the flags over the sunken plaza nearby.

"Come on, people, let us through!"

The voices were now behind them, heading rapidly toward Sixth Avenue.

"I think we lost them," Mark said quietly, still panting.

She nodded and peered over the top of the map.

An unoccupied cab came into view. She shoved the map into the tourist's hands and strode out on the street, hailing the cab. Inside, she gave the address of their hotel uptown. They both slouched as the cab crossed Sixth Avenue, heading west.

CHAPTER 23

Lee and Mark sat on the side of the king-size bed in their hotel room and caught their breath—literally and figuratively. Not until the cop's hand was clenched around Lee's arm had the full implication of getting caught sunk in. She'd felt doomed, condemned. She had always insisted on being the sole architect of her life, and she'd felt helpless.

"I still can't believe Immersheim recognized me," she said after a long silence. "I look in the mirror and don't recognize myself."

"Don't forget, I figured out who you were, too," Mark said. "I think Immersheim is always on the lookout for frauds and con artists. Goes with the business."

"Is all this really about the emeralds? Did someone hear the sonnet, figure out that it referred to the Hever Emeralds, and then kill Alex Folsom to get them?"

"And then attack you in England, and then again in Massachusetts."

"But I don't know where the emeralds are. I don't even care. And what about Semper? The attack in Massachusetts may have had nothing to do with emeralds; it may have had to do with my getting closer to something called Semper, whatever it means or stands for." *And it's all about the sonnet*, she thought. Discovering a sonnet by Shakespeare had seemed, in itself, momentous. It *was* momentous. But Shakespeare was communicating something more than an homage to eternal love.

They sat silently for a few minutes.

"Maybe you should go," she said at length. When he looked at her with surprise, and perhaps hurt, she tried to explain. "You're getting too involved. I think it's called aiding and abetting. You could also get hurt, or killed. This isn't about you; it's about me."

When he didn't respond, she stood up abruptly and crossed to the window, which overlooked the tops of a row of four-story brownstones on the far west side of Midtown. Despite the cloudless blue sky, New York looked drab and deserted.

"You can't help me," she said.

"What do you call what I just did on Sixth Avenue?"

The room was chilly, in the artificial, refrigerated way of hotel rooms. She touched the window to feel the reassuring warmth from outside.

"You don't understand," she said, "I have to—"

When his arms touched her shoulders, she pulled away.

"I'm going to call you Domino if you keep this up."

"Okay. Why?"

"My old cat. Even after ten years, she'd swat at me when I first touched her. Each time I'd have to prove to her that I wasn't her enemy. I did it with soft, very gentle strokes." His hand moved up and down her arm, just barely touching her. "After a while she'd climb onto my lap, and I'd think maybe we had something going. But the next time I went near her, she'd arch her back and attack me like a stranger."

Lee said nothing, her back still to him, though he seemed to want a response.

"You want me to call you Domino?"

"No."

"The specialist in romantic poetry who avoids romance."

"Renaissance poetry. Philip Sidney was a Renaissance poet."

"Who wrote about love."

"Oh, *love*. People toss that word around like some sort of mantra or cure-all. Yes, Sidney wrote about love, but he had no illusions about it. *Astrophel and Stella* is a sonnet sequence with 108 individual sonnets and 11 songs. They're about the love of Astrophel for Stella, but it's thwarted love, frustrated love. Omnia vincit amor—love conquers all. People think Virgil meant that love can surmount all difficulties. But he meant that love conquers *us*, destroys us. 'Love gave the wound,' Sidney wrote."

"Is that your mantra?" he asked. "You will not be wounded, or conquered?" When she turned away he asked, quietly, "Do you want me to leave? Say 'yes' and I'm gone."

After a few moments, she shook her head.

"Okay, then no more talk about me leaving."

His hands continued to stroke her arms and shoulders. She wanted to stand there forever, feeling close to him. But she forced herself to get back to business. When she turned, abruptly, to face him, his arms went to his side.

"It goes back to Shakespeare," she said, something she still had trouble wrapping her mind around. "We know that something in the sonnet, in the part I read on the air, triggered the attack in my apartment.

We know that the sonnet alludes to Henford Manor in England, where I was also attacked, and indirectly to the Filer family, which is descended from the illegitimate son of Elizabeth I." She took a deep breath. Under other circumstances, what she had discovered was a career-maker; now the best she could hope for was that the information would exonerate her and save her life. "David cued me to the fact that the sonnet also references the Hever Emeralds, which Immersheim told us have not been seen in four centuries."

"Except for one or two stones that are thought to have come from the set."

"Which have come to market periodically, maybe because some group is raising money by selling individual stones piecemeal."

"There's also Semper," Mark said.

"Which we don't understand at all. It's in the sonnet, so it connects the Filers to everything that's happened. It could be nothing more than some sort of motto for the family. It means 'always,' which isn't bad for a family motto."

"I think it's more than that. Why would you go to the trouble of creating that elaborate brickwork on the house, and then bury it in the foundation where no one can see it?"

"Good point. Mottoes are supposed to represent a family or organization to the outside world. You don't hide them." She sat on the bed, feeling hopeless. "So now what?"

"Here's what I'm thinking. You read the sonnet on TV, and that triggered a reaction. But once you read the poem, whatever information it contained was out there, so why were you attacked? You knew nothing more than anyone with access to a replay on YouTube would know."

"Except I didn't read the entire poem."

"Exactly. So whoever is after you wants to know what's in the rest of the poem, or wants to prevent you from figuring out what's hidden in it."

She fished out the copy of the sonnet from her purse and read it aloud.

"Could I with love alone your safety grasp
Then surely, love, my heart would lovely be.
But lose a savior's lead and temper gains an asp
As when for dying earth an apple quits the tree.

Heart, emeralds vainly exercise restraint
On those who for your station would aspire.

The peacock's astral plumage burns but faint,
Too dim to spare her brood from foul desire.

Must one deny my will? Pox will I bring,
A roiling storm will seem kind Pax's blow.
A plague when I uncap the bottled thing
From throne to grave no soul will comfort know.

When all the world in bootless ruin lies
I'll lie not more, but less my love belie."

She finished reading and looked at Mark.

"The sonnet gave us Henford, then Hever, then Semper. Is there anything else in it?"

Mark took the paper and studied it for a bit, then shrugged.

"There has to be something more to it, otherwise you wouldn't have been attacked. I just can't see it."

"So far, the Hever Emeralds seem to be our best line of investigation. Immersheim said that someone sold a stone that was most likely from the necklace. He has the name, but he wouldn't give it to us. We need that name."

"Somehow I don't think calling him and asking would do us much good."

"It's probably in his files."

"You saw the locks on his door. We'd never get in there unless we were let in."

The apparent dead end stifled further conversation. She lay back on the bed, eyes closed, trying to clear her mind so she could rest but struggling to figure out what to do next. Mark used the remote to turn on the TV. He surfed through several channels until he came to a local news broadcast.

"Shit," he said.

She sat up. On the screen, a cop was being interviewed on the corner of Forty-Seventh Street and Fifth Avenue. Behind him, crowds of onlookers strained to be seen by the camera.

"No, we don't know if either of them was armed. They did not pull a weapon at any point, that's correct. But we have to assume she is dangerous, seeing as how she's wanted for murder. Mr. Immersheim did provide details about their conversation with him. No, we are not releasing details of that conversation at this time."

"Turn it off," Lee said. She fell back onto the bed. "Now they know what I look like with short blond hair and this fucking tan. What should I do, get a wig or shave it off? I'm running out of options."

He joined her on the bed, pulling her toward him. She tried to focus on the feel of him, the warmth and strength, but all she could think about was their next move. After a minute or two, she sat up abruptly and turned to him.

"I know how to get into Immersheim's office."

CHAPTER 24

19 June 1572
Whitehall

I confess I know not why I followed the man down to the Thames to investigate this "semper" of which he spoke with such undisguised torment. Perhaps it was his invocation of the Queen's name. "Please, tell the Queen," he'd said.

"Tell me your name, sir," I demanded as we made our way along Southwark, which thronged with humanity, many of them foreigners speaking in exotic tongues. On either side, shops did a brisk business in all manner of commerce. Furniture makers were particularly in evidence—joiners, carvers, and upholsterers. Praise God we live in prosperous times when so many can afford the fruits of their labors. Oftimes we were made to swerve to one side or another to avoid farmers in from the country with their flocks of sheep and carts laden with fruit and vegetables.

"Mulcaster, my lord," he shouted above the din. I did not point out that I was hardly worthy of such a title, for to this lowly sailor I was as good as an earl. "Thomas Mulcaster."

"Tell me more about this 'semper,' Thomas," I said. The bridge came into view, and with it the reek of the Thames at low tide.

"That I cannot do, my lord. I will show you to my captain, and he will tell you everything. But I must warn you, he wants a dear price for it."

"For 'semper' or for information?" I asked.

"'Tis one and the same, my lord. For once you have the information, you will need to have the thing itself."

The masts of the great ships in harbour now loomed over the building tops, and the crush of human traffic coming from the quays slowed our progress to a crawl.

We finally reached the quays. There must have been 100 ships in port, stretching the entire length of the city from the tower to the bridge. Spanish galleons. Portuguese caravels. Flyboats from Holland. And of course our own English ships, traders and warships alike. A man could be forgiven for thinking London the center of the world, for here were boats that had returned from all known places, many of which had been discovered only lately. Giant cranes of ingenious design removed cargo from the decks, while carts trundled up and down the wharves, laden with goods coming and going.

Thomas knew precisely where his ship lay at anchor, and in a short while we were climbing the plank onto a large English galleon. Like most of the great ships in port, it was fitted for trade, not combat. I have been told that it requires a few hundred carpenters, pitch-melters, blacksmiths, coopers, and shipwrights to make seaworthy a single galleon. To pay for all this labor and material she must ply the seas in search of gold and spices and rum, not battles, though many a good England merchantman had been refitted for warfare after capture by the Spanish or Portuguese.

The Lansdale, for that was her name, had a long beak, four masts, and a square gallery at the stern off of the captain's cabin. Atop each mast flew the red St. George's Cross. A sharp breeze from upriver set the flags aflutter, joining the general cacophony of clanking chains, lapping waves, and a veritable Babel of voices in unrecognizable languages.

She appeared deserted, her cargo having presumably been taken off some time earlier, its men enjoying the fleshly consolations of our city after months at sea. As I followed Thomas across the main deck I observed that she was truly a fine vessel, in good repair, a credit to our country's industry.

He led me to the ship's stern, where an elevated, open-air gallery extended around the entire stern of the ship. We climbed a short staircase to this gallery and stood before a closed door, upon which Thomas, after coughing to clear his throat, rapped his fist.

The voice that answered was gruff and none too coherent. Nevertheless, Thomas opened the door and showed me in. The chamber into which we stepped was quite large by ship standards but cloaked in darkness. I noticed two small windows on the port side and wondered why curtains had been drawn across them, the day being pleasantly bright. To the right was a comfortable-looking bed, built into a nook in the wall, piled with blankets and clothes. In the center of the room was a table, covered with plates of food, some of which appeared to have gone rancid, and empty pewter tankards. Across from the bed was a chest whose drawers hung half open. The dishevelment of the room was in stark contrast to the rest of the ship but not, I noted at once, to the condition of the man who occupied one of the three chairs around the table.

"Cap'n, this is the doctor I was telling you about, what knows Her Majesty the Queen." Thomas squared his bony shoulders, proud to have brought on board such illustrious cargo.

"Knows the Queen, does he?" The captain squinted as he looked me up and down. He appeared to be a man of considerable though indeterminate age, perhaps fifty or even sixty. His skin was the texture of old strawberries, and quite nearly the same color, having spent too many days exposed to the elements. His beard was a sickly gray with patches of darker brown. But he was nearly bald on top, his gleaming pate sprouting unruly strands of greasy gray hair that extended nearly to his shoulders. His narrow eyes, seemingly locked in a squint, as if against bright daylight, were rheumy, the whites having dulled to ivory tinged with watery pink. I wondered if the Lansdale's owners had seen him of late, and whether they felt sanguine about the safekeeping of their investment if they had.

"Sit," he said, indicating a chair across from him. "You, go," he barked at Thomas, who hesitated. "Go!"

When we were alone, the captain filled two tankards with ale from a pitcher. He pushed one toward me, spilling some of its contents.

"So, you know the Queen," he said, his eyes narrowing to watery slits.

"It is my honor to serve as Her Majesty's personal physician." I allowed the ale to sit untouched before me, for I feared it had absorbed the unsavory atmosphere of the fetid-smelling cabin.

"The old sow must be in a state, what with the Spanish attacking her ships and threatening to invade."

"You will not talk so of the Queen in my presence." I stood up, prepared to leave.

"Come off it," he said with a smirk. "I was only saying that she has a weight on her shoulders, quite a burden she bears. And I may have something to lighten that burden."

Intrigued despite my better judgment, I sat.

"Semper," I said.

"Aye, for that is what I have called it. The savages have their own word. It is said to last forever."

"What is it? Why would Her Majesty be interested in acquiring this Semper?"

"For a good price." He drained his ale. "For a royal price, you might say."

"Yes, for a price. But what is it?" I looked around the gloomy cabin. "Where is it?"

"Now, I would be a fool if I told you where it was, would I not?" His grin revealed an uneven row of yellowed teeth anchored in black gums.

I must have cast a superior glance just then, for he pounded a fist on the table and began to shout.

"Don't imagine I was always like this, you with your superior airs and your royal appointment. What kind of fool would give a ship to a man who looked like this?" He stroked his greasy beard and raised his chin, challenging me to answer. I did not answer. He stood and walked to one of the port-side windows. He parted the curtains and glanced out, then turned back to me.

"'Twas Semper what made me the man I am. In the Amazon, two months past. A place called Ateeka. Fifteen men set out to see for ourselves what this… what this power was. One of us returned. He stands before you now, but not the man he was."

I could hardly contain my curiosity.

"Why did you change? What happened?"

He sat down and poured a full tankard of ale.

"I saw the devil is what happened."

CHAPTER 25

For Lee, it felt unsettling—make that terrifying—to walk down Forty-Seventh Street so soon after she'd nearly been arrested there. At least the street looked different after dark. Metal gates had been lowered over display windows now emptied of jewelry. The sidewalk was nearly deserted.

"It's the next building," Lee told Lucian, who nodded. He seemed more comfortable with gestures than actual speech, which was unnerving. When she'd called him earlier and introduced herself as the woman who'd changed her identity, with his help, to Sarah Cooper, he'd merely grunted. "Do you remember me?"

"I might," he'd replied.

She hesitated. "Is it safe to talk on the phone?" When he answered with a dull "Uh huh," she took a deep breath. "I need help breaking into an office. I know that this isn't necessarily what you do, but I don't have many contacts in your world. I mean, with people who might be able to help with this sort of thing."

"Government office?" he said, and she recalled that she'd made contact with him through a website for anti-government extremists.

"A jeweler." She gave him a few details about the type of building and office and assured him, not that he'd asked, that she was not interested in stealing jewels.

"Okay."

"You can do this?"

"I said okay."

They met on the corner of Forty-Seventh and Sixth. Lucien looked even shorter and thinner than she recalled, his body supple and sinuous, ferret-like. His thick black beard overwhelmed his narrow face so that his eyes and mouth appeared to fade into the background. He wore a black T-shirt, black jeans, and black running shoes, a messenger bag slung over one shoulder.

"Who's this?" he said, nodding at Mark.

"A friend," Mark said quickly, perhaps fearful that she was going to formally introduce him.

"You didn't mention a friend."

"He's fine. Look, I don't feel comfortable standing here, so let's go," Lee said.

She had bought a Yankees cap earlier and now pulled it down over her forehead.

The front door to Immersheim's small office building was made of gray-painted metal. Lucien examined it closely, running his fingertips over the two key locks.

"You two watch the sidewalk. If this is alarmed we walk away, okay? You head east, I head west. But I don't see an alarm, so I think we're okay."

He removed a small case from his bag. Inside were several long strips of metal—they looked like very narrow nail files. He selected one and gently eased it into the top lock. Then he took a second, smaller file and fiddled it into the same lock. Handing the case to Lee, he used both hands to manipulate the two picks. After a few moments she heard a faint click. Lucien removed the two picks and used a similar procedure to open the bottom lock. He replaced the picks and put the case into his bag.

"Pray for no alarm," he said, as he slowly pushed the door. Lee held her breath and waited for the sirens, prepared to run.

The door slowly swung inward.

Silence. The door was not alarmed. Lucien stepped inside. She and Mark followed.

"Second floor," she said in the small, dark entranceway, whispering, though there was clearly no one there. They used the service stairs.

She directed him to Immershiem's door, also made of metal, this one with three locks and "Maurits Immersheim" and a room number stenciled on it.

"Three fucking locks," Lucien said, casting an accusatory glance at Lee. "And this one's an Abloy." He ran an index finger around the top lock.

"Is that a problem?" Mark asked.

"Gonna take a while."

Lucien crouched before the door and laid his pick set on the floor.

"I may have to drill this one, if the picks don't work." He chose a pick and began with the top lock. Looking almost reverential before the dreaded Abloy, he slowly inserted the pick into the chamber.

"What the…."

With his free hand he pressed the door.

It swung slowly open.

They stood in the hallway, stunned silent, staring at the half-opened door. Was Immersheim in the office? Someone else? Should they go in? Leave?

"I don't like this," Lucien said, gathering his tools and shoving them into his bag.

Lee whispered to Mark, "If someone's in there they would have heard us already. We might as well go in."

"I don't like this." Lucien was slowly shaking his head.

Mark pushed open the door and stepped into Immersheim's one-room office, Lee right behind him. The room was quite dark, with only faint illumination from the streetlights on Forty-Seventh Street.

"Hello?" he said softly. There was no answer.

Once their eyes adjusted to the darkness, Lee pointed to the large desk in the center of the office. There was someone sitting behind it.

"Mr. Immersheim?"

Whoever it was didn't respond. Fighting an urgent desire to run, Lee felt along the wall to the right of the door and found a light switch. She flicked it on, blinked at the sudden blast of fluorescence, and gasped as she fell back against the wall.

"Holy god!" Mark covered his mouth and staggered back.

A man sat behind the desk, leaning back in the tilting chair, his pose strangely normal, as if he were conducting negotiations of no great urgency. His hands were folded on his lap. But there was nothing remotely normal about the condition of his face. Blood covered it, from the eyes down, leaving only his forehead clear. And his eyes: they seemed to have sunk back into his skull in retreat from what they had witnessed. Circling his skull, at eye level, was a deep impression, about an inch wide, a bloodied trench that seemed to cut right through to his skull.

Lee felt herself retching. She took deep breaths to avoid throwing up.

"It's Immersheim," Mark said. "At least, I think it is."

Cautiously, as if the killer might be crouching next to the victim, he walked around the desk, Lee close behind him. The cord leading to the panic button that had summoned the police during their visit had been severed. From the back, they saw a raw bruise encircling the victim's neck.

"Strangled," Mark whispered.

"And something else," she said, pointing to the indentations in his skull. "What happened to him?"

"He was tortured."

"Why?" But she knew the answer, or some part of it. Someone had come there because of Immersheim's connection to her. He had asked the gem trader for information, information that he was probably unable to provide because he didn't have it. So he'd tortured him and then finished him off by strangulation.

A second murder, following two attacks on her. Was it really all about emeralds?

"Let's get the fuck out of here." Lucien hadn't moved any closer to the body, standing just inside the doorway.

"He's right," Mark said.

"We came for the files." Lee turned to the row of tall, three-door file cabinets. All the drawers were opened, and folders were sticking out, as if they'd been pulled up for inspection and then not replaced.

"Someone had the same idea," Mark said. "We should leave."

She started rifling through the top drawer of one filing cabinet. Each hanging file contained copies of invoices and bills of sale, all handwritten in precise lettering. The tabs appeared to indicate last names and sometimes just dates. There was no discernable order to the files; it would take hours to work through them to find a reference to an emerald with a sixteenth-century provenance.

"Whoever did this probably got the file he was looking for," Mark said. "How long was Immersheim going to hold out? It looks like his head was crushed somehow. We need to get out of here. It's almost midnight. What if someone misses him and calls the police?"

He was right, but she felt a sense of hopelessness return as she headed for the door. Another murder she'd be blamed for. "Two hundred dollars," Lucien said as they hurried down the service stairs. "Don't matter if the door was open, I still collect."

Lee took the money from her jeans pocket and handed it to him. As they parted in front of the building, heading in opposite directions, Lucien had one last request.

"Don't call me no more, okay? I don't need this shit."

With that, he headed west toward Sixth Avenue. As they walked the other way, Lee felt her phone vibrate. The caller ID showed the name David Eddings.

"David?"

"Lee, you must… you must come here… right away." His voice sounded wheezy.

"David, what's—"

"Just come, *now*." He made an ugly, gargling noise, almost like static on the line. "And come alone. I… I won't let you in if… if you're with someone. Do you understand?" Another deep, gargling sound. "Just you."

The line went dead.

CHAPTER 26

The service entrance to Eddings's building was held ajar by a small piece of cardboard inserted between the door and the jamb. He had told her to use the service door, rather than risk being identified by his doorman. His voice had sounded pinched and panting, but his instructions had been clear: come alone, and quickly.

It had taken some work to convince Mark to wait for her at the hotel. "I can trust David," she'd insisted, "without him I'd be in jail now."

She took the service stairs up to Eddings's apartment. By the time she reached the twelfth floor she was quite winded. She entered the elevator landing and rang his doorbell. After a few seconds the door opened.

Blackness.

And pain, stinging pain, in her eyes.

Someone grabbing her and pulling her into the apartment.

Still unable to open her eyes.

"David?" Her voice was faint, even to her own ears. "David, what happened?"

Her hands were yanked behind her back. Something else… string? No, rope. Rope being wrapped around her wrists.

"What the *hell* are you doing?"

She jerked her arms to the side with as much force as she could muster and heard a low groan. Forcing open her eyes, David's apartment came into watery focus. She was in the foyer, facing the living room.

"Christ, what—"

Her arms again, being pulled behind her.

She spun around, or tried to. But her arms were immobilized by a powerful grip.

What the hell? Was that David on the floor? What had happened to his head? Blood from his mouth, his ears—holy god, from his eyes. And above his ears, and on top of his head, it looked as if his skull had been crushed. Next to him, a wooden stand pierced by wooden rods and a kind of oversized screw, and a bowl. A cruel, medieval thing.

First Immersheim, with similar wounds on his head. Now David.

Sickened and terrified, she whipped around, trying to free herself from whatever was holding her hands together behind her back. She caught a quick look—a man, tall, expressionless, *normal.* But just before she tumbled to the floor, having lost her balance because her hands were now tightly bound behind her back, she saw something else.

On one side of his face. Something wrong. A scar so deep and wide it was almost a trench, running from the top of his ear down to a corner of his mouth.

"Don't fight me." The voice, like one side of the face—bland, expressionless. But with an angry edge, like the other side.

She looked up and saw a hand thrust toward her face, holding something. A small atomizer.

A faint hiss.

Then that excruciating stinging in her eyes, forcing them shut.

She felt herself being lifted from the floor. He was strong, preternaturally strong, hoisting her like a bag of groceries.

"Tell me about Semper."

Not even winded, his voice betraying no strain as he carried her, from behind, hands under her armpits.

Semper. Had he said "Semper?" To the extent that she could think, she had expected to hear "Hever." Immersheim had endured what David had. Wasn't this about emeralds? But he'd said "Semper." She thought of the line in the sonnet, of the painting in Derek Martinson's house, of the letters embedded in the foundation of the Filer home in Tunsbury.

"Let me go," she said. "Whatever you want…"

"Tell me what you know about Semper."

"It has something to do with Elizabeth. She had a son."

The chair stopped moving. She continued.

"While a princess. At Hatfield. Called Edward Filer. I found the word 'semper' in a picture in an old man's house in Massachusetts, and in the foundation of a different house." She was talking quickly, unsure whether she was making sense.

"Filer," said the monster. "The name on the receipt Immersheim gave me."

"*Gave* you?" The thought of Maurits Immersheim, his head like a pulped orange, turned her stomach.

"Where is Semper *now*?" The voice was flat, robotic.

"I don't know what you're talking about. It's just a word."

That apparatus next to Eddings. Suddenly she knew what it was. A head crusher, invented during the Inquisition but used in the Tower of London during the Tudor dynasty. David had been tortured and killed like one of Elizabeth's prisoners.

"You recognize it. I can see that," he said. "Your professor did, too. The Elizabethans liked to use it on pretty people because of the special way it disfigured them. Adulterers, court favorites fallen out of favor—the prettier the face the more likely this would be the torture device of choice. I think I've chosen well."

He placed a hand behind her head and started to tilt her backward. One hand on her neck, the other on her left arm. Rage shot through her.

"Get off me!" She shimmied from side to side, rocking the chair, her hands tied behind it.

"Where is Semper?"

She raised her feet and pressed them against the front of the cabinet and pushed off with everything she had. The chair shoved into him, the force sufficient to elicit a groan. Perhaps she'd forced the back of the chair into his groin. She sensed that he'd backed away, if only a few inches. She repeated the move. This time the chair tipped back and fell to the floor.

She caught a glimpse of him, standing over her as she lay on her back, still bound to the chair. From below he looked huge, his shoulders impossibly wide.

He left her momentarily.

Still on the floor, she quickly shifted position so that the chair's back pressed against the chest of drawers. Then she jammed the chair into the chest and pressed as hard as she could. This had the intended effect of pushing her bound hands up the back of the chair.

She heard his footsteps returning to the room.

Her bound hands were almost at the top of the chair. She gave her arms a hard yank, twisting from side to side. The chair jerked back and inch or two, enough to free her hands from it.

He was a few feet away, carrying a kitchen knife.

She sprang to her feet in time to see him raise the atomizer. She closed her eyes and turned away until the hissing had stopped. Then she spun around and threw herself at him. With her arms tied behind her, she would have tumbled onto the floor if she hadn't hit him dead on.

A wall. Like running into a wall. If he reacted in any physical way to the impact, she didn't detect it. He stood before her, immobile, unblinking. Except for a pulsing on either side of his jaw. And that fissure on one side, it seemed to glow as if molten. Then his right hand moved. The knife.

"You *fuck*!" she screamed as she leaned into him and rammed her right knee into his groin. "You sick fucking bastard!"

This time he reacted, lurching back with a low, feral grunt. The knife fell to the floor.

She charged at him, landing a second knee to his groin.

His moaning escalated into a high-pitched keening. She'd bought herself some time. Five, maybe ten seconds.

She ran to the front door and turned her back to it. Her bound hands scrambled for the knob, turned it, pulled.

Locked. And the deadbolt was at least a foot above where her hands were tied.

Shit.

She sprinted into the kitchen. On the counter was a wooden knife stand. Leaning over the counter, she grabbed the largest knife with her teeth. When it was securely clamped in her jaws, she raced from the kitchen into the guest bathroom, which was off the hallway that connected the living room with the bedrooms. Inside, she rammed her shoulder into the door, flinging it shut, and turned around. On her toes, she fumbled until she found the small knob above the door handle. Turned it.

The door was locked.

He would have little trouble breaking down the door. She'd bought herself another few seconds, perhaps a minute.

Bending over the sink, she opened her mouth and the knife dropped into it. She turned around, back to the sink, and managed to grab the knife with her right fingertips. Slowly, she wriggled her hand until she had a firm grip on it.

Footsteps, running down the hallway to the bedroom area. Looking for her.

Carefully, she angled the knife so that it pointed toward her back, then down. She levered her wrist, wedging the knife between her back and the rope.

The knob on the bathroom door turned. Then it shook, rattling the entire door.

She began sawing, up and down, painfully slow, trying to put pressure on the rope. Her right wrist felt close to snapping.

An explosion of sound as the door shuddered. He was hurling himself at it. Fortunately the hallway was narrow—he couldn't get a running start.

But he was strong. She'd seen that. Felt it.

The knife cut through one coil of the rope. How many more times had he wrapped it around her wrists?

Another crash. This time it seemed as if the door itself bowed in from the impact. But the lock had held.

A second coil of rope gave way.

The next impact splintered the door just above the lock and sent flakes of white paint to the floor. The lock held—but the next blow would be decisive.

The knife cut through a third coil. There wouldn't be time to continue. She let the knife fall back to the sink and wriggled her hands and wrists. The three cuts had loosened the rope. She crouched and pressed the rope under a corner of the porcelain sink, forcing the rope down.

A low, guttural cry from the hallway. He was girding for a final assault on the door.

The rope slid off and fell to the floor.

Grabbing the knife, she jumped into the stall shower, which was next to the door, pushing aside the fabric curtain.

The door exploded open, sending shards of wood into the bathroom. He stumbled in as the door gave way. She thrust the knife at him.

"You *sick fuck*!" she screamed, the words meant to give her strength as she plunged the knife into his side. She pulled back, prepared to stab him a second time, but he crumpled to his knees, his right hand reaching around to his left side to stanch the flow of blood from the wound.

Despite the blood, she guessed he was more shocked than gravely wounded. A part of her wanted to carve him with the knife for what he'd done to David. She suppressed that part in favor of a saner voice that told her to get the hell out of there.

As she angled around him she kicked him hard with her left foot. The monster's head jerked to the side, but his eyes didn't appear to register the impact. Eyes glassy and still, like those of a dead fish, but he was alive.

She ran across the foyer, where she couldn't help glancing into the living room. The wreckage of David Eddings lay sprawled on the carpet. She squeezed the knife until her arm shook and fought hard to keep from turning around.

Moments later, she was racing down the service stairs to the ground floor, where she threw open the door leading to the sidewalk. Only when she was nearly to the corner of West End Avenue did she realize she was still carrying the bloody knife. She dropped it into a garbage can and hailed a cab.

CHAPTER 27

Lee took a cab from David's building to the hotel in Midtown. She shoved a twenty-dollar bill at the driver and jumped out, sprinted across the small, fluorescent-lit lobby and, eschewing the elevator, climbed the emergency stairs to the fourth floor. She fumbled in her purse for the room key but was too flustered to locate it. Instead she pounded on the door. When Mark didn't open it immediately, she began to shout.

"Open the door!" More pounding.

When it finally opened, she rushed in.

"What happened?" Mark asked, as she raced by him and into the bathroom. She slammed the door, locked it, leaned over the toilet and began to vomit. She thought she might suffocate as she fought for breath between heaves. When she had nothing left to throw up, she flushed the toilet, stripped out of her clothes, and got in the shower. Standing under the shower head, she gradually turned the dial all the way to "hot." The water scalded her shoulders and back. When it ceased to sting, she slowly turned around and let it wash over her face, parting her lips to let it cleanse her mouth. After she turned off the water, her skin throbbed. Wrapped in a towel, she returned to the room.

"Do you want to talk about it?" Mark sounded wary.

She sat on the far side of the bed and tried to tell him what had happened. But she found she couldn't. Images of David and that person, that monster, flashed in and out of her mind, and when she tried to describe them she sounded incoherent even to her own ears. He crossed the room to her, but she shrugged off his attempt at an embrace.

"No, no. Not now. I need to think. Think. Who is he? *What* is he? What is Semper? Why did he do that to David and to Maurits Immersheim?" Her voice was flat and a bit slurred, words running into each other.

"Who are you talking about, Lee? What happened at David's apartment?

"His face was crushed."

"Lee! Try to be calm. We need you to be calm. Tell me what happened."

"I am calm; I am calm. He had this device from that time. I know it; I recognized it. He used it, he—"

"Lee!"

Abruptly, she stopped talking, but her mind continued to race ahead, or rather back, back to David's living room. Mark was heading for the door.

"I'll be right back."

She was too dazed to question where he was going, or why. Alone was good. No talking. No explaining.

When he returned some time later—a minute? An hour?—he carried with him a plastic shopping bag and a plastic ice bucket. Without saying anything he got a glass from the bathroom, filled it with ice, then removed a fifth of scotch from the bag and poured it until the glass was full.

"Drink," he said, handing it to her.

"No, I need to think, I need to understand, I have to figure this out."

"*Drink*."

He held the glass to her lips, and she took a tentative sip. The scotch burned on her tongue and cut a warm trail down her throat. Another sip, then she took the glass from him and had a few gulps.

"Thank you," she said when the glass was half empty. Scotch never failed her.

He waited her out, sitting across from her, saying nothing. After a few minutes she placed a hand on his leg, as if to reassure herself he was actually there, and told him what had happened.

She felt marginally better. Now someone else knew.

"I don't know what to say." Mark looked shaken. "I wish I had—"

"No sympathy. I want a way out of this."

He nodded. "Did this creature say anything specific about Semper? Something that might lead us to it?"

"Lead us to *what*? What is Semper?"

"Tell me what he said about Semper."

"Nothing. He just wanted to know what I knew, where it is. I kept thinking, why isn't he asking me about the emeralds? Isn't this about the emeralds?"

"The emeralds were a distraction. This is all about Semper."

"But Hever was in the sonnet."

"And so was Semper: 'But lose a savior's lead and temper gains an asp.'"

"It keeps coming back to the damn poem." She grabbed her purse and found the handwritten copy she'd made. They read it silently.

"It took me to Henford," Lee said. "It mentions the emeralds and Semper. Could there be something else that we've missed?"

"What about the stanza after the Semper clue."

She read it out loud.

"Must one deny my will? Pox will I bring,
A roiling storm will seem kind Pax's blow.
A plague when I uncap the bottled thing
And, then, at last, a lasting love you'll know.

"It feels out of place," she said after reading the passage. "It's about violence and vengeance, which are not exactly the typical subject of a Shakespeare sonnet, assuming he even wrote this."

Despite everything, she found herself smiling.

"What?" he asked.

"A few days ago the fate of the universe, or at least my universe, depended on whether Shakespeare actually wrote these lines. Now it seems like the least important thing in the world."

"It'll be important again, soon," he said.

"You think?"

"Start with the first line: 'Must one deny my will? Pox will I bring.' Is there a double meaning we're not seeing?"

She started at the line and then had an idea.

"Not a double meaning, an instruction," she said. "What if the poet is telling us what to do? In the sixteenth century, 'deny' didn't have exactly the same meaning as today. It meant to turn away from, to ignore."

"So the writer wants us to ignore—"

"The words that come after 'deny.'"

Mark repeated the words. "'My will? Pox will I bring.' But those words don't appear anywhere else in the sonnet."

"Maybe he wants us to ignore the *letters* in those words."

She got a pen and paper from the desk and wrote out the line that followed the one Mark had just read:

A roiling storm will seem kind Pax's blow.

"Read the letters from the previous line, the letters in the words that follow 'deny.'"

Mark read them one by one, beginning with *m*, then *y*, and so on. As he read each letter, she crossed it out in the line that followed.

A ~~ROILING STORM WILL~~
~~SEEM KIND PAX'S BLOW~~

When he was done, she was left with six letters:

ATEEKA

Their shared disappointment at the meaningless word was almost palpable.

"Well," he said, "it was a good theory."

The word meant nothing, and yet she felt sure that the line contained instructions. Sometimes, when doing research with original documents, she felt a sudden connection to the author that shot through the centuries separating them and pierced the haze of academic objectivity. At such times she felt the author's breath on her neck, asserting his presence, and she understood in a way that she could never describe in an academic paper why he had written what he'd written, what he'd really meant to say.

She felt the breath now, though the document was a copy written in her own hand. The poet, whoever he was, was speaking to her.

ATEEKA

She jumped from the bed and got her laptop. Her legs felt a bit unsteady from all the scotch, but her head was clear. She powered on the computer and googled "Ateeka."

In seconds, the search returned a page of matches. She clicked on the first, from Wikipedia, and read it out loud.

> "A tiny, indigenous tribe in South America, on the border between Brazil and Peru, sometimes referred to as the 'Lost Tribe of the Andes.' The Ateeka were first contacted by Europeans in 1582, on an expedition led by Spanish explorer Francisco Pisarro. In 1598, a second Spanish expedition, headed by Alfonso Somero, made contact with the Ateeka. When this expedition was not heard from, a search party was sent under the command of Diego Rodriguez. Rodriguez discovered that Somero's entire force of approximately ninety-five men as well as every member of the Ateeka tribe had been wiped out by some sort of virulent infection or disease.

> The nature of this disease has never been discovered. In the 1970s, archaeologists discovered a number of tribal objects from the Ateeka settlement which are today owned by the National Museum of the American Indian, which is part of the Smithsonian. No other remnants of the Ateeka survive."

When she finished reading, they both stared at the screen for a few moments. Lee broke the silence. "Is it possible that Shakespeare—" despite everything, she *knew* he was the author— "was pointing us to a lost tribe in South America? It seems incredible."

"We can't ignore the fact that the word 'Ateeka' appears in the poem. If we've learned one thing, it's that virtually every line in the sonnet was intended to signal something. This maniac who tortured and killed Immersheim and David Eddings clearly believes that you know where Semper is, and the only thing that you possess that no one else has is the sonnet."

"So if we learn more about the Ateeka we may find out what Semper is, and why someone is willing to kill for it?"

"I don't see any other way to move forward," Mark said.

The Internet contained little additional information on the Ateeka: they had existed; they had vanished. Perhaps someone at the Smithsonian knew more. According to its website, the main, public facility of the National Museum of the American Indian was on the Mall in DC, but virtually all of the artifacts in the museum's collection were housed in Suitland, Maryland, which was just outside of Washington, in Prince George's County.

"To Washington, then," she said with forced jollity. "To find the lost tribe."

Ateeka

We Spaniards know a sickness of the heart
that only gold can cure.

—Hernando Cortez

CHAPTER 28

19 June 1572
Whitehall

The captain—for I never knew him by any other name—told me a story so fantastical that my mind had to work with great diligence to credit it. Yet I did believe him, for he appeared to take no pleasure in the telling. Rather, he seemed in need of release, as if his health, his very sanity depended on sharing the burden of knowledge with another.

"'Twas a few months back," he began after a long drink of ale. "Off the island of Trinidad. My quartermaster, a fine man by the name of Robert Hobbes, now deceased…." Here the captain went quiet for a good while. "Hobbes alerted me that a Spanish galleon lay off our port side. She appeared to be heading east, away from Trinidad and perhaps back to Spain. She was low in the water, which I took to mean her hull was likely full of treasure bound for the King of Spain. As she was alone, I gave the order to prepare for battle. Such were my instructions, you understand. It weren't my idea, though I confess I lusted for a fight after months in port."

I nodded, full aware that Her Majesty turns a blind eye to piracy, so long as it is committed by our own ships against those of our enemies. Soon enough our looting of Spanish galleons will lead to retaliation and perhaps war. But for now the Queen's coffers are overflowing with jewels from the New World, her kitchens turning out strange but delicious dishes laced with spices once unknown to English tongues. These are good times to be at court.

"I am sure Her Majesty is grateful for your service," I told the Captain. "Particularly as you no doubt render the required one-third of your haul to the Crown."

The captain studied me. We both knew that captains were notorious for cheating the Crown of its just share of the spoils of piracy.

"I am a loyal subject, there's all ye need know," he said, and I nodded my agreement, eager to hear more. "This Spanish ship, La Vela she was called, was an easy mark. She was gravely undermanned, having lost half her crew already in a manner that I will shortly describe. We boarded her with little resistance and took a dozen men prisoner. The Spanish captain, name of Diego Rodriquez, was lying on the foredeck with a deep wound in his chest. I was headed with my men down to the hull to appraise our spoils when the captain made a groaning noise and banged his fist on the boards. Even a Spaniard deserves some respect on his deathbed, I say, so I knelt beside him. He started to speak but as I cannot understand Spanish I called over my boatswain, who apprenticed in Cadiz back when our popish Queen was married to the Spanish devil."

"Queen Mary and Philip of Spain," I said, feeling it necessary to defend our late monarch and her husband. She was, after all, Her Majesty's sister, though a Catholic and unwise about marriage and religion in equal measure.

The captain shrugged and continued. "'You will find a vessel,' Rodriguez told my boatswain, who translated for me. 'Made of gold, with jewels of all colors set in the side.' Now I was particularly eager to get down to the hull, but the Spanish captain had more to say. 'There is a cap, a stopper, of solid gold with a single ruby on its crown.' Here he made a circle of his thumb and forefinger to indicate the size of this ruby. He took hold of my jacket and pulled me closer. 'Do not open this vessel,' he said. 'I would not wish the evil within even upon my enemies.'"

The captain seemed to lose focus, as if his mind were not in that small, dark cabin on the Lansdale but across the great ocean on the Spanish galleon La Vela.

"Did Rodriguez describe what this 'evil' was?" I asked, in an attempt to bring him back.

"He did indeed. He told me it came from a tribe called Ateeka, where the Amazon branches from a mighty river to a mere stream, that was how he described it. He told me he and his men went to the Ateeka in search of an earlier party, another group of Spanish who went to the Ateeka and were never heard from again. There was meant to be gold and jewels hidden somewhere, was what he told me. So this earlier party, about seventy men in all and heavily armed they were, traveled by boat up the Amazon to find the treasure and bring it back."

The captain refilled his cup. I placed a hand over mine.

"But this first party never came back, like I said. So a year later, maybe longer, Rodriguez and his men set out to find them. He told me it took more than a month to reach the Ateeka, or what was left of them, for when he got there he found nothing but rotted corpses. The tribe and the Spanish, all dead. He told me it looked as if they had been in the midst of some kind of ceremony when they all died. The savages were gathered on one side of the city, the Spanish on the other. But there were no signs of injury or fighting. Just hundreds, maybe thousands of people lying on the ground, mostly skeletons, their flesh eaten away. And he told me one other thing I won't soon forget. All along the ground, where the people were lying dead and farther out into the jungle, were animals stopped dead in their tracks, now just bones, and birds that looked like they had dropped from the sky. He told me he thought he had wandered into hell. There wasn't a sound to be heard, not a single bird or animal or insect moved. All dead."

"What did he do?"

"He ordered his men to search the area for treasure, same as any man would. Most of what they found wasn't worth much. Jars and such, painted with scenes of primitive life. Some of the men took a few of these things just to have something to show for their trouble. But there was this one object."

"The vessel."

"As magnificent a thing as you'll ever set eyes on. Mind you, there are drawings on it as would turn your stomach, scenes of agony and death. But the jewels!" Here the captain paused, eyes lit by the reflected memory of rubies, emeralds, and diamonds. "Rodriguez told me he thought this must be just the beginning, that there must be other treasure somewhere in the village. But he found nothing more, just this one object. He and his men left the day they arrived, glad enough to be out of that hellish place. On their way back up the Amazon they stopped to rest, and a native from another tribe, not the Ateeka, caught sight of the vessel. He became excited, said Rodriguez, pointing to it and calling to his fellow savages to come have a look. But they wouldn't dare get close to the thing, almost as if they feared it. They had a name for it, and kept shouting it over and over while pointing. It sounded to the Spanish like 'Semper,' and that's how this object got its name. The Latin word for eternal, is what I'm told, though I never had much education in that or any language other than what you hear now. The natives treated Semper like it was a god, a fearsome god. Many of them, upon seeing it, fled into the bush. But one of them, a very old man, tried to communicate something to Rodriguez and his men. A warning, you could say. He made as if to remove the top of the vessel, only of course he didn't actually remove it. Then he fell over, dead, or pretended to be, and them near him, the few who hadn't run off, they fell over likewise. Rodriguez understood this to mean that inside the vessel was some sort of powerful spirit that inflicted death on all who came near it. The drawings on the vessels itself told a similar story. He told me he knew right away that it was this Semper that had annihilated the Ateeka and the Spanish. The vessel had been opened. And he resolved to keep the stopper in the vessel as long as it was in his possession."

"But then you became its owner," I said.

"Rodriguez died right there on deck. I believe he had a fearsome need to tell the story of Semper, and this kept him alive until he had done so. I went to his cabin where I found the vessel, which was every bit as magnificent as he described. You shall see for yourself, if you are interested." Avarice gleamed in his eyes. "I took it back to the Lansdale myself while the men went below to find what they could. There wasn't much of value, though true to the captain's word there were a goodly number of Ateeka pots and such covered with crude designs."

I was anxious to see this vessel, this Semper, but I did not want to appear so eager that the captain would drive up the price.

"Legend and superstition," I said. "That's all I've heard. Third-hand accounts of massacres and the hallucinations of a dying man."

"I wish it were so, though it would lose me a fortune. But it is all true, and I know it for a fact."

"How can you know it?" I inquired.

He studied me for a short while. I supposed he was considering whether or not I was worthy of his confidence, or would be sufficiently credulous.

"They say you have the Queen's ear. Do you apply leeches to the royal arse, then?"

I stood up, prepared to leave. I have indeed employed leeches on occasion, usually on Her Majesty's forehead when she is wracked by fevers and sharp pains in her head brought on by the exertion of statecraft. And I have bled her on many occasions to keep her in robust health, for the good of all England. But I will not tolerate insolence from a drunken sailor.

"Only a joke, Doctor. Rest easy."

"A poor joke, and treasonous to boot."

"Come!" he said suddenly, shoving back his chair and standing. "I will show you."

He led me up onto the deck, then crossed it to the hatch that opened onto a ladder. Despite his age and apparent lack of fitness he easily managed the descent into the hull. I had considerably more difficulty, though I refused his offer of a hand.

We plunged from bright daylight into murky darkness. Shafts of dim light shot through the ship's windows, but they did little to allay the overall feeling of gloom. I wondered that anyone could stand to live in such a place for the weeks required of a crossing to the New World. For a moment I thought of my Lucy, transported from Africa in such a place. I hope I have been able to make her forget that passage. It was no surprise that not a soul was down there now, not when London beckoned, with all her carnal temptations.

The captain led me to the bow end of the hull, which was largely empty, its cargo already sold to an eager public, save that which was given in tribute to the Crown. He stopped before a large wooden chest, which was girded by two thick chains, each secured by a padlock. With two keys he removed from his pocket, the captain opened each of the locks and flung aside the heavy chains. After a glance at me which I can only describe as contemptuous, for I had doubted his story, he pried open the chest, reached in, and removed the vessel.

I had intended to present a stoical disposition so as to maintain a position of advantage should I decide to purchase the vessel on the Queen's behalf, but no such equanimity was possible once I beheld the thing.

It was as the captain had described it, yet no words could capture its magnificence. It seemed almost alive, so radiantly did it shimmer in the gloom, as if creating its own light. The vessel came up to the top of my boots. It took the form of a naked male figure, thick-set, seated on a small platform, legs slightly apart to reveal an erect phallus thrust forward like a weapon. The figure's hands and feet were crudely sculpted, suggesting the paws of a great beast. The eyes were widely set, the nose as prominent as a hawk's beak, and the lips as thick as bread dough. Its ears jutted like twin sails.

Jewels covered much of the surface, emeralds and rubies and diamonds and other stones I did not recognize, their colors of a palette I have never before encountered. Atop the effigy's head, like a crown, was a stopper formed by a single ruby set into an orb of gold that seemed to burn with an inner flame of incalculable heat. I would not have been surprised to find it hot to the touch, so passionately did it gleam from atop the vessel.

But even a description of the gold and jewels does not convey the true power of this thing called Semper. It had a power beyond mineral and stone, something awesome and sinister. As my eyes adjusted to the dim light, and to the brilliance of the vessel, I saw that it was covered with crude drawings that were almost invisible next to the magnificent stones. Drawings of pain and suffering, quite hideous. They covered the figure's body, its bald head, the simple platform on which it sat.

And yet even these drawings did not explain the power of the thing. Semper was alive, I felt certain, as if I could feel its warm breath on my face.

"You are made mute," the Captain said, glancing at his possession as if at a favorite child.

I composed a thought and managed to express it in a voice that sounded faint and hoarse even to my own ears.

"A magnificent object, true. But the stories you have told me, of death and destruction, these I still cannot credit. Why should I believe what you have told me, of what you yourself were told by this Rodriguez?"

"Why?" He stepped closer. Faint light from a nearby porthole glanced off the vessel and illuminated the Captain's ruddy face. In fact, the light appeared to gain strength from the jewels. "Why? Because I saw its power. I bore witness." He thrust the vessel toward me, until it almost touched my chest. "I hold the most powerful weapon the world will ever know."

"But proof," I whispered. "What proof have you?"

"My crew is the proof."

I looked round, at the patently deserted hull.

"I see no one present who can substantiate your fantastical story."

"Oh, my crew is here, Doctor. Although they have not made themselves known to you."

With that he walked to the very bow of the ship, where a large white sail covered an uneven mound. As the rest of the hull was empty, I wondered what cargo might have been left behind. Still cradling the vessel, the Captain bent over and took one corner of the cloth.

"My crew," he said, as he pulled sharply on the cloth.

"Mother of God," I cried, for I could not censor my tongue in the face of what I saw. A pile of bones and skulls, perhaps twenty or thirty skeletons in all, one draped over the next, tossed there like harvested vegetables.

"What is this?" I asked when I regained my voice.

"The finest crew in Her Majesty's service," replied the captain. Then he held aloft the vessel. "Behold the work of Semper."

CHAPTER 29

As with the drive from Tunsbury to New York, the four-hour trip from Manhattan to Maryland was unexpectedly relaxing. Lee felt cocooned in Mark's Toyota, which he drove at a deliberately cautious speed of precisely 55 miles an hour. Inside the car she was impervious to Semper, whatever it was, and to whatever evil forces the sonnet had unleashed. But at the first sign for Suitland she felt herself begin to tense up, and by the time they pulled up to the security gate in front of the National Museum of the American Indian Cultural Resources Center, she felt a powerful reluctance even to lower her window.

"No one knows we're here," Mark reassured her. "We're safe."

"It feels like every move I've made since reading the sonnet on TV has been monitored. It's like someone's been watching me."

"We're getting closer to an answer," he said quietly. "Once we know what we're facing, you'll be safe."

Information is power—she'd always believed that. It was what kept her in the library late into the night, poring over manuscripts for that one bit of information that no one else had come across before, one corroborating piece of evidence for a case she was building. Information was power over the past, power over *her* future. But now she wasn't sure. Information had almost gotten her killed, and more than once.

"Who is your appointment with?" The guard was an imposing man. His demeanor suggested that he controlled access to Fort Knox rather than a storehouse of artifacts.

Lee had prepared a lie. She reached across Mark and handed her Columbia ID to the guard, hoping he wouldn't recognize her name or notice the stark difference between the photo and the bleached-blonde in the car.

"We're here to see Amy Meyers." On the NMAI website, Meyers was listed as a specialist in South American Indians. They did not have an appointment; she figured it would be easier to talk their way in once they were there than over the phone.

After a cursory glance, he handed back her card and directed them to the visitors parking lot. As they drove off she saw him lift the phone in the small booth.

The Resources Center was surprisingly large, given that it was intended not for the general public but for scholars. She'd expected a warehouse but found instead an unusual piece of architecture. Set on a large tract of land, it was a vast nautilus-shaped structure that seemed to open up to the heavens, probably reflecting some aspect of Native American culture or design. Her confidence in her ability to talk herself into the archives diminished as they approached the imposing main entrance.

Inside, they were met by an attractive young woman wearing a pale blue sweater set and black trousers. She had dark hair and eyes and rather pronounced cheekbones; Lee wondered if the woman was perhaps part Indian herself. She looked to be in her mid-thirties. She introduced herself as Amy Meyers but did not extend a hand.

"I'm sorry, but I have no record of an appointment."

"I sent an e-mail last week." Lee put as much conviction behind the lie as she could, adding, rather lamely, "From Columbia University."

"Columbia. Then you must know Ike Mazulla," Meyers said.

Lee had never heard of him and sensed she would not be able to pull off the lie much longer and switched to a new tact: honesty, up to a point.

"I am from Columbia, but not the history department. We're here for a personal reason. We're looking for information on the Ateeka tribe."

"You have a *personal* reason for wanting to know about the Ateeka?"

"It's urgent," Mark said. "We may have come across an Ateeka artifact, and it appears that someone is threatening to take it from us."

Lee turned to him, impressed by the lie, considering they hadn't rehearsed their cover story. She continued:

"We need to know as much as possible about the tribe so that we can evaluate what we have. We think we might be in some danger."

"Then you really should talk to the police."

"Yes, that's our plan," Lee said. "But first we need information."

Meyers studied them for a few tense moments.

"Ateeka artifacts are quite rare," she said at length. "In fact, I don't believe there's been a new one discovered since I've been in this field. Virtually all of them are in museum collections, most of them here at the NMAI. What type of object is it?"

"A pot of some sort," Mark said quickly.

"Decorated?"

"Yes, with scenes from daily life," Lee said, recalling a few of the items she'd seen on the museum's website.

"Do you have it with you?" Meyers's skepticism had begun to dissolve into something approaching curiosity.

"That didn't seem prudent," she said. "But of course we'd be happy to show it to you once we know what we're dealing with."

Meyers looked from Lee to Mark and back, then shrugged.

"Okay, I'll take you to the archives. But you'll have to let the security folks check your purse for cameras or cell phones."

As the guard inspected her purse, Meyers grew more enthusiastic about the story they'd told.

"If what you have is in fact Ateeka, it would be remarkable. We know so little about the tribe, and what we do know comes primarily from artifacts."

"There isn't much on the Internet, other than that the tribe vanished in the sixteenth century."

"That's because we don't know much. The Ateeka were quite isolated. To the west, the Andes formed a natural border that kept the Inca from invading or even having much influence. To the east was thick jungle. They appear to have developed independently. We estimate that at their peak, in the sixteenth century, there were perhaps two or three thousand members. A small tribe, miniscule in comparison to their neighbors. The Inca had no written language, but there are pictorial references to a tribe living across the Andes. For reasons that have never been clear, the Inca feared this tribe, though they far outnumbered them—there were perhaps ten or twelve million Inca at their peak. The Inca expanded aggressively across the western edge of the continent, using intermarriage as a way of consolidating their power. But they never bothered with the Ateeka. Excavations at the Ateeka site show that they were primarily hunter-gatherers, though they practiced limited agriculture, root crops, mostly. There was no mineral wealth to speak of—no major source of gems—which might explain why they were ignored by the Inca, though it doesn't explain why they were feared, of course."

"They vanished suddenly," Lee said. "Why?"

The guard had removed her phone, placed it in a clear plastic bag, and now handed her a receipt. Mark surrendered his phone as well, which the guard placed in the same bag.

"No one really knows why they disappeared, though we suspect it had something to do with the arrival of the *Europeans*." Her lips curled around the word with mild distaste. "They brought a variety of diseases with them against which the indigenous populations had no defense. Many native populations were wiped out entirely. Still, it was typically a slow-motion holocaust, lasting several decades. What happened to the Ateeka was quite sudden. Anthropologists have found an enormous number of bones at the Ateeka site, randomly scattered, as if there were no time for proper burial. As if they all died at once. And there were a great number of animal and bird skeletons mixed in with the human remains, as if some sort of ritual slaughter had taken place."

"Were they annihilated by the Spanish?" Mark asked.

She shook her head as the three of them walked through a metal detector. Lee had the sense that they were entering a military facility and not an archive.

"We would see signs of bullet or stab wounds. There are none. The only clue we have comes from a single mention of the Ateeka in a letter from a Spanish explorer, Diego Rodriquez. In 1582, he wrote to his patron in Seville that he had *acquired*—I use the word loosely, for it was obviously plundered—a jewel-encrusted effigy of a seated male figure, worth a fortune, apparently, from a tribe called the Ateeka. He added that he and his men had gone in search of an earlier party who had disappeared in the jungle. He wrote that when he found that party they were all dead, along with every member of the tribe itself. He implied that the annihilation had something to do with the effigy, basically a small clay statue, though he wasn't specific. It's the only clue we have to the disappearance of the Ateeka. Rodriguez himself vanished shortly after sending the letter from Trinidad. It is thought that his ship, La Vela, was attacked by English pirates, who were encouraged by Queen Elizabeth to plunder Spanish galleons."

"And the effigy?" Mark asked.

"Never found. There are some intriguing clues, however."

Meyers waved a card in front of an infrared scanner to open a steel door. She led them into a vast and unexpectedly cool room lined with white metal cabinets.

"If it *is* Ateeka, I hope you'll offer us right of first refusal. There hasn't been an Ateeka discovery in decades."

Meyers navigated aisle after aisle of storage cabinets, some with doors, others with rows of wide drawers. They were quite tall, at least nine feet high; occasionally they came across fork-lift-like carts that allowed access to the higher-placed objects. Meyers walked swiftly, obviously well acquainted with the space and the whereabouts of the Ateeka artifacts.

"We have over 800,000 items here from more than a thousand indigenous cultures throughout the Americas. But only about ten percent of our collection is from South America."

There was something inescapably sad about the area, full of ancient relics wrenched from their natural habitats and relegated to a fluorescent-lit storeroom. As if reading her mind, Meyers said, "Many of these objects are still considered sacred by the tribes who created them. They want us to be very careful about how they are handled, and who gets access to them."

Meyers stopped in front of a large metal case identified by a number. She opened both of the two tall doors to reveal a series of deep shelves. There were about ten objects in the case; in front of each was a small barcoded label.

"Our entire Ateeka collection, I'm afraid. The label corresponds to our database, which has information about each piece. This is the one I wanted to show you. It tells us more about the Ateeka culture than anything else we have."

She pointed to a large clay urn at shoulder level, on the right. It looked to be about two feet high and almost as wide. It was covered with very detailed designs. She carefully turned the urn 180 degrees, revealing that what had appeared from the front to be an intact pot was in fact only half a pot: the entire back was missing. A jagged edge revealed where the pot had been broken. A triangular metal stand held it up.

"It's badly damaged, obviously. It's the story told by the pictures that I wanted you to see." She turned it back to its original position. "Here, on the left, we see some sort of statue, a male effigy." The effigy was mounted on a sort of platform, perhaps an altar. In front of the altar, a small crowd of people were crouched on the ground, heads facing downward, hands stretched in front of them, as if in supplication before the vessel. "The brushwork is crude, but it's still among the best pre-Columbian pictographs we've seen."

"The colors are amazing," Lee said. It looked as if it had been painted only recently.

"No question. The reds and blues and greens on the vessel probably represent jewels, including the large red orb on the head, which appears to be a kind of stopper, which indicates that the effigy may be a vessel of some sort. It's unclear where these jewels might have come from, as the Ateeka had no mining of their own and did little if any trading with their neighbors. We never found anything remotely similar to the vessel depicted here. If we had...." She smiled wistfully.

"If you had?" Mark asked.

"Well, it would be of incalculable value, not only for the jewels but for what it might tell us about this obscure tribe. Perhaps someday," she said with a shrug, then pointed to the picture to the right of the first one. "This is where things get strange. The red stopper has been removed from the effigy—see it lying here?"

The second decoration, to the right of the first, was a close-up of the jeweled statue.

"There's no indication of who removed the top, or why. It's almost like we're watching a movie, and the cameraman has moved in for a close-up of the statue. Notice that there appears to be a vapor emanating from the statue, a cloud."

"A genie escaping from the bottle," Lee said, though the "cloud" was little more than an ill-defined smudge on the pale orange background.

"Now look at the third picture. The artist has pulled back to the perspective of the first illustration. The effigy is still uncorked, but the supplicants appear to be running away from it. Look at their faces."

Their mouths and eyes were distended in terror, transforming them into horrific masks. Arms seemed to be flailing, as if they were fighting each other in their desperate need to flee. The scene had a powerful simplicity that magnified its impact.

"What was in that statue?" Lee asked, her voice lowered to a whisper.

"Probably nothing, but the Ateeka believed the vessel held vast powers, apparently. It's a shame we don't have the other half of the urn; we might have learned more about what the vessel meant."

"Is it definitely lost?" Mark asked.

"The Ateeka site has been exhaustively excavated. I doubt there's anything there. And Ateeka artifacts are so rare, it's really unlikely anything as important as this would escape attention. Well...."

She appeared to stop herself.

"You were about to add something," Lee said.

"Only that I always had the sense that the archaeologist who excavated the Ateeka site knew something more about this piece. He was sent by the Smithsonian to South America, and everything he found belonged to the museum. *Legally* belonged."

"Are you saying he may have kept something, including the back of this urn?" Mark asked.

"No, no. Miles was scrupulously honest and really dedicated to this institution. Miles Truman, the archaeologist who headed up the Ateeka dig. He would never withhold anything from the collection. I just always sensed he knew something about this vessel. He sent a letter from Lima to our director, following his second major excavation of the site, saying he'd found the missing link to the Ateeka story—those were his exact words, 'missing link.' This was before my time here, you understand. When Miles returned to Washington, he had quite a number of pre-Columbian tools and potsherds—nothing of great importance—but nothing that explained the tribe's disappearance. No 'missing link.' And when he was asked about the back of this urn, he became evasive, or so the director told me."

"Is he still alive?" Lee asked.

"Miles? He lives in Washington. But I don't think you'll learn anything more from him, and I strongly doubt you'll find the back of the urn." Nevertheless she smiled, perhaps imagining the breakthrough.

"We'd like to speak to him," Mark said firmly.

"Why? If you have a genuine Ateeka artifact, bring it here for evaluation. And safekeeping. You don't need Miles."

"We do need information," Lee said. "The more we know, the—"

"In fact, you seem a lot more interested in how the Ateeka vanished than in determining the authenticity of your pot."

"If this archaeologist can provide details about the tribe, then maybe we'll be able to—"

"Fine. I'm still unclear about exactly what you're after, but you could probably find Miles's contact information on the Internet anyway. Come back to my office, and I'll give you his address." She closed the glass doors and locked them. "I must warn you, however, that Miles Truman is a difficult man."

CHAPTER 30

Lee called Miles Truman several times from the museum, but each time an answering machine picked up. "I'm not home, leave a message if you want," said a man's voice, flat and annoyed. She left a message the first time, indicating that they wanted information on the Ateeka, nothing more specific. She didn't hear back. Amy Meyers had told them that Truman was quite old and rarely left the house. They decided to visit him.

Truman lived in an attractive brick colonial in the northwest section of Washington. A slate path led up a slight incline from the street to the front door. The small yard was neatly tended, and the house seemed well maintained, with its crisply white shutters and aura of prim self-satisfaction. An upscale enclave of large but close-set homes located just a few miles from the Capitol as well as the seedier areas of the district, the neighborhood felt like an oasis, *in* the city but not really *of* it.

Lee rang the doorbell, and they waited. She rang it again. Nothing. After a third try, they headed back toward their car.

"Damn it, I thought we were getting close to an answer," she said.

"To what question?" Mark asked.

"Why did the sonnet point us to the Ateeka? What is Semper? They have to be connected."

She circled the car to the passenger side and took one last glimpse at the house before getting in.

"There's someone inside," she said, pointing to the second floor. A shadow of a figure behind white curtains, looking down at them. "The last window on the right, I saw someone."

Lee retrieved her phone from the car and pressed redial. After the gruff, impersonal "greeting" and beep, she spoke slowly and forcefully.

"Look, Mr. Truman, we know you're in there. This is very important, it's about life and death, not archaeology. We're not leaving until you talk to us." She clicked off and turned to Mark. "Come on." She headed back up the slate path to the front door, where she rang the doorbell several times. A few minutes later she pounded on the door. Then, after a short wait, she rang the doorbell again. When this failed to draw a response, she redialed Truman's number and left a new message. "How long can you stand this, Mr. Truman? Because we have all night."

"He'll call the cops," Mark said.

"I don't think so." Lee tried the doorbell again. "Amy Meyers said he hates attention of any kind."

From inside the house they heard faint footsteps, moving slowly. A few moments later the front door opened.

"What the hell do you want?" said the man in the doorway. He was tall and thin, his body angled forward from the waist, as if frozen mid-bow. His thinning hair, white tinged with yellow, badly needed combing. His skin was nearly as colorless as his hair; even his eyes seemed bleached, though there were traces of faint blue in the corneas. His pale lips were so thin and bloodless as to be nearly invisible, giving him a suspicious, disapproving expression. He wore a white dress shirt that was frayed around the collar and missing a button halfway down the front, and pants that must have been purchased when he weighed significantly more; they were cinched by a black belt that acted like a drawstring, pleating the waistline.

"Amy Meyers suggested we visit you," Lee said, reverting to politeness after essentially besieging the man's home. "About the Ateeka, specifically a large urn that's missing half its surface."

"Get away from here," he said, and began to close the door. Mark grabbed the door to keep it from closing, which wasn't difficult, given Truman's frailty.

"Just a few questions," Lee said.

"I have nothing to say about that." His voice faltered and his head-shaking turned almost violent.

"Someone is trying to kill me," Lee said. "And I think it's because of that urn. Please, just tell us what you know and we'll leave."

"Kill you?" He peered out the door, looked both ways, eyes wide and darting, lizard-like, from side to side. "My god, what have you done?" He stepped aside to let them in. "What in god's name have you done?"

CHAPTER 31

The interior of Miles Truman's house was much like the exterior: prosperous, well-tended, and conventional. It was the sort of house that always made Lee uneasy, since it offered no clues to its occupant's personality. A book without a jacket, she thought as he led them to the living room, which was directly off a narrow center hall that connected the front door to a back door, through which Lee spotted a patch of green lawn in the dim evening light. He limped as he walked, lurching dramatically to the right with each step. Surprising that he didn't use a cane, since he appeared to be in quite a bit of pain, his eyes squinting with each step, almost a spasm.

In the living room, she and Mark sat on a traditional sofa covered in beige fabric; Truman sat across from them in one of two matching club chairs covered in a floral pattern. The room was handsome but lacked personality. She searched in vain for any indication that Miles Truman was a world-renowned expert on pre-Columbian civilization. There were no family photos.

"I'm sorry we had to force our way in," Lee began, but Truman waved his hands, cutting her off.

"Get to the point."

"Amy Meyers showed us an Ateeka urn in the archives of the National Museum of the American Indian. Or more accurately, the front of an urn. She said that the back half is missing and presumed lost, but that if anyone knew where it might be, assuming it exists, it would be you."

If she'd thought this would flatter his professional pride, she was wrong. He scowled and shook his head.

"It's gone. End of story."

"You discovered the urn, correct?" Mark asked.

"On my second dig, correct."

"Was the urn broken when you found it?"

A hesitation, just a moment, then: "Yes."

He was lying. His skin was pale to the point of transparency; Lee saw a faint reddening of his face, and the left side of his jaw began to pulse.

"Are you sure?" she asked.

"Of course I'm sure." No hesitation this time. He leaned forward and adjusted a small pile of magazines on the coffee table that separated them, squaring their edges. *Time*, the *Washingtonian*, the *New Yorker*. Lee looked around—the entire room was like that pile of magazines: rigidly well-kept, almost military in its precise orderliness.

"Did you find the back of the urn?" Mark asked.

"I told you, no."

"Actually, what you said was that it was broken when you found it," Mark said. "You didn't say that you'd never seen the back half."

Now his face turned crimson as he sucked in his pale, narrow lips so that they disappeared entirely. He must have been a fearsome man back when he had meat on his bones; now, he appeared harmless, and frustrated by it.

"Why the hell are you so interested? I know everyone in the field, read every journal that's published. You're no one."

"I've been attacked. Twice. I'm not sure why, but the motive of whoever is after me is linked to the Ateeka."

"Then why the urn?"

"There's very little left of the Ateeka." Mark leaned toward Truman. "Apparently their disappearance is one of great mysteries in your field. Most of the artifacts we saw earlier today deal with daily life. But the urn is different. It tells a story, and that story seems to pertain to some sort of great fear. There's a male figure, an effigy, of great reverence. It's at the center of why the tribe vanished."

"Primitive superstition."

"And yet the tribe vanished. When the Spanish arrived there, they found a scene of annihilation, not only Ateeka but the Spanish explorers who had preceded them months earlier. Everyone dead. Animals, birds. That's not superstition, that's history, and the urn may hold a clue to how it happened."

"But the urn in the archives tells only half the story," Lee said. "We were hoping you had at least seen the other half and could tell us what happened once the male figure was opened."

"I can't."

Again a slight hesitation, and his eyes, which had bored into them since sitting down, shifted momentarily to the side. He *had* seen the urn intact.

"Please, tell us what you know," she said.

"Get out of here," he said. His tone was arrogant and defensive at the same time.

"Just tell us—"

"No! I have been out of the field for almost twenty years. I know nothing that you don't already know. Now, go."

"Why did you leave the field?" she asked.

"I retired."

Lee looked around the room, then back at him.

"There's nothing here, not a picture, a photo, *anything*, having to do with pre-Columbian civilization. Why did you turn your back on it? You were practically a celebrity in that world."

Truman shifted in his seat, hands running back and forth along the armrests.

"There was nothing else to learn. I discovered the Ateeka, I dug up everything there was in that Peruvian hellhole, I published books, articles. My work was done two decades ago."

"Then why is there nothing here from that period, no indication at all that you had this life, this amazing life?"

"I gave everything to the Smithsonian." He hesitated a moment. "Everything."

"As you were required to, since they sponsored your expeditions to Peru," Mark said. Lee turned to him, surprised by a new, more aggressive tone in his voice.

"Yes, as I was required to." Truman sucked in his lips as he glared at Mark.

"What do you think the urn means?" she asked. "You must have a theory."

He considered the question for a few moments without taking his eyes off her. Finally he placed both hands on the armrests and pressed himself up to a standing position.

"I've told you everything I know. Now leave."

"A theory, that's all. Just tell us what you think those pictures mean."

He headed toward the front hallway, lurching with each step, and picked up a phone on a table near the door.

"I'm calling the police."

He punched in three numbers. Lee jumped up, and so did Mark.

"Okay, we'll go," she said.

Slowly he replaced the receiver and then watched intently as they headed for the front door.

Just before leaving Lee turned back, prepared to plead for information. He knew more than he was saying, and he was the only apparent link between the sonnet and the maniac who had attacked her in David Eddings's apartment. But his face dissuaded her. He looked depleted. He was hardly a sympathetic character, but he was frail and empty, somehow. Hounding him further would be cruel.

Even saying goodbye would be an intrusion, she felt. So she left the house silently, Mark behind her. She'd taken just one or two steps along the slate path when Mark grabbed her arm.

"I'm not leaving here," he said quietly but with an unfamiliar edge to his voice. "Not yet."

He had stopped just outside the front door, which Truman was in the process of closing behind them. Suddenly he whirled around and charged back in, flinging the door open and sending Truman staggering back. He might have fallen, but Mark grabbed him under the arms and, practically lifting him off the ground, threw him against the wall. Truman let out a low, guttural gasp on impact.

"Tell us what the fuck you know! *Now*!"

"Mark, don't do this." Lee ran back into the house. "Let go of him."

Her words had no impact on Mark, and Truman merely stared blankly at his assailant through hollow, eerily indifferent eyes.

"I'll kill you before I leave here without information." Rage deepened his voice, adding a hoarseness she'd never heard before.

"Mark, stop. Let him go."

He jerked Truman away from the wall, then slammed him into it. Truman's head left a jagged dent in the plaster.

"You're lying to us." When Truman didn't respond, Mark shoved one hand against his throat. Truman let out a gurgling sound.

Lee began pounding Mark's back, shouting at him to stop.

"I'll *kill* you," he said, placing his mouth right up against Truman's left ear. "Is that what you want? Because I'll do it."

Truman's eyes lost focus, as if contemplating, not unhappily, his imminent death. Lee continued to pound Mark's back. Then, suddenly, Truman's eyes, which had rolled up into his lids, returned to focus, and he began to nod, if only slightly, given the pressure on his neck.

"Ready to talk?" Mark said without releasing him.

"Mark, let him go, he can't say anything with your hand—"

"Are you ready to talk?" Mark tightened his grip, lifting Truman so that he was forced onto his toes.

Truman managed to gasp a weak, "Yes." Mark let go and stepped back. The old man slunk to the floor, panting audibly.

"Talk!"

Truman continued to struggle for breath, not looking up at them. Lee squatted next to him.

"Are you okay, do you want some water or—"

"Get away from him!" Mark pushed her right shoulder, sending her into the wall. He was panting as hard as Truman, his face an angry red. "*Talk*!" His voice, almost a roar, filled the narrow hallway.

Truman began to say something, but his voice was too weak to make out, even to Lee, who was still on the floor next to him.

"*Louder*!" Mark kicked him on the leg, not especially hard but enough to cause him to groan.

"Stop. Please. I'll tell you what you want to know."

CHAPTER 32

"The Ateeka were my family. They vanished more than 400 years ago, but I felt closer to them than anyone alive."

They were seated around the small table in Miles Truman's kitchen, which looked unchanged from the 1950s: knotty-pine cabinets, speckled Formica countertops, ancient appliances, and vinyl flooring made to resemble ceramic tile. Lee had helped Truman get to his feet, and he leaned heavily on her as she led him back to the kitchen, where she got him a glass of water. She couldn't bring herself to look at Mark.

Truman began to speak the moment he was seated, even before Lee and Mark joined him at the table. And once he started to talk, he seemed unable to stop. Words tumbled from his mouth like one long, faint sigh that had been stifled for too long.

"Every archaeologist dreams of the big discovery, and if you're lucky you find a grain storehouse or a cluster of houses adjacent to a site that's already been picked clean by your predecessors. But I found an entirely new tribe, and one that was quite isolated, so that its culture was not polluted by any other, including the Incas. There were very few records from other sites that pointed to the Ateeka. We'd found Incan drawings that suggested a tribe to the east with some sort of fearsome power, but nothing more. The Ateeka seemed to have existed in a kind of ethnic bubble."

"How did you come across the tribe?" Lee asked.

"Blind luck. I was interested in Incan trade patterns, particularly along the Amazon. The Inca stayed mostly to the west of the Andes, but there was evidence that they crossed the mountains to the east and used the Amazon to trade with other indigenous tribes. I followed one suspected trade route, across a mountain pass heading northeast to the Amazon. This was 1962. I was with a group from the Smithsonian. We came across a large area, perhaps fifteen square miles, that had been mostly covered by volcanic ash from an eruption in the late sixteenth century. The volcano, which still exists, though long dormant, is called Cerro Auquihauato. We decided to make camp there, and while preparing our site, one of our crew members, who was digging a pit for a fire, dug up a potsherd. I thought at first that it was Incan, evidence that they had crossed this route on their way to the Amazon. But on close inspection it was like nothing else I'd ever seen. The style of drawing, even on this small fragment, was not as refined as that of the Inca, and the content of the pictures was unique. The faces were rounder than those you find on Incan objects, with jutting ears, long, narrow noses and unusually large lips. I knew this didn't necessarily reflect reality. Depictions of humans reflect a culture's perceptions and values, not what people actually look like. Of course, an isolated tribe will tend to present distinct physical features, even deformities, due to inevitable interbreeding. This may have added to the strangeness of the drawing. In any case, this illustration clearly was not drawn by an Inca. I ended up staying at that site for the better part of five years, with occasional breaks to return to Washington for progress reports to the Smithsonian. Eventually I concluded that I had discovered the site of the Ateeka, the so-called Lost Tribe of the Andes."

Lee gently interrupted him. "Amy Meyers said that there were very few Ateeka artifacts discovered."

"Very few worthy of museum collections. We excavated thousands of tools and everyday implements that were of immeasurable help in piecing together the contours of the Ateeka culture. Most were quite crude, without any sort of decoration. The Smithsonian wasn't interested in these items, nor was any other institution."

"Right, so what happened to the Ateeka?" Mark sounded impatient.

"It's possible to piece together a credible story, though of course we'll never know for sure. Pizarro came across them in 1582 but left them alone, which wasn't typical of him. No doubt the lack of significant gemstones or gold made them unworthy of his murderous attentions. A few years later, another expedition traveled down the Amazon and made contact with the Ateeka—we know this because they sent a party back to their base camp at the mouth of the river. But this expedition, headed by Alfonso Somero, was never heard from again. A search party was sent out, this one headed up by Diego Rodriguez. They found Somero and his men, all of them dead. Also wiped out was the entire Ateeka tribe—every man, woman, and child. Our excavations confirmed this, a mass extinction."

"Could it have been the volcano?" Lee asked.

"No. Think of Pompeii, bodies found in the streets, life suddenly interrupted by a cataclysmic rain of ash, evidence of panic, and attempts to flee. But most Ateeka were found in their homes—huts, really—huddled together. Parents and their children, tightly connected, as if they'd been comforting each other."

"And the Spaniards?"

"Their bones were all found in the same place, near the edge of the settlement, as if they were at some sort of gathering. There were a number of Ateeka skeletons with them. And here's something really odd. There were hundreds of animal and bird remains, littered all over the site, like some sort of mass slaughter, perhaps a ritual of some kind, had taken place. We found very little in the way of weapons or armor, by the way. Our supposition is that Rodriguez's men stripped their bodies of anything of value. Likewise the Ateeka themselves. Whatever they might have had of value was apparently looted by the search party. And then, approximately three decades later, the Cerro Auquihauato erupted and buried the entire scene in five feet of ash. The Lost Tribe of the Andes was buried for half a millennium."

"You still haven't told us what happened." Mark's voice had lost none of its aggressiveness.

"I've told you what I know." Truman's voice quavered as he looked across the table as his assailant.

"Not everything."

"Mark, come on, try to—"

"*No*! We need to understand what happened, and he knows!"

"But you don't have to—"

"It's okay," Truman said quietly. "He's right. I do know."

The room felt suddenly still, preternaturally so, as if the wind outside the windows had stopped blowing, the refrigerator shut down, and their own breathing ceased. Neither she nor Mark moved, waiting for Truman to collect his thoughts.

"I discovered the truth of the Ateeka, why they had been left alone for so many years, and why they vanished. It was recorded on the urn."

At the mention of the urn Truman dropped his head and went silent.

"Have you seen the entire urn?" Mark asked. When Truman didn't respond, he banged a fist on the table. "Have you *seen it*?"

Truman looked up slowly, then began to nod. Without a word, he stood up, took a key from a drawer, and slowly left the kitchen.

In the long hallway, he unlocked a door that led to the basement staircase. Gripping the banister, he descended very slowly, using the strength of his left arm to support his bad leg. Lee and Mark followed close behind in the darkness. At the bottom of the stairs, Truman found a wall switch and flicked it on.

The basement appeared in a flash of fluorescence, one large room running the width of the house, its walls lined with metal shelves. The shelves were empty.

"Behold the world's finest private collection of Ateeka artifacts," Truman said, waving a jittery arm at the empty displays.

"What happened?" Lee asked. The room, though clinically lit by long fluorescent bulbs, felt spooky, as if inhabited by watchful spirits. The absence of whatever had originally been in there was strongly present.

"I gave the good stuff to the Smithsonian, as I was required to do," Truman said, slowly turning to take in the empty shelves. "As I said, I only kept the things no one was interested in displaying—crude tools, unpainted household objects, and small fragments. I had this room built for the collection. Nothing here was what you'd call beautiful, but taken together there was something magnificent about the collection. A civilization. *My* civilization."

"The urn, Truman," Mark said. "Tell us about the urn."

Truman looked at him a long while before saying anything. When he began to speak, he turned away and faced the floor.

"That was the one important thing I kept. The urn, or part of it."

"You stole it, you mean," Mark said.

"I had planned to give it to them, that was always my intention. But I knew it held the key to understanding the Ateeka, why they'd remained untouched for centuries and why they'd vanished. I didn't want to relinquish it right away. Every year I promised myself I would give it to them, to the Smithsonian. But I never could."

His voice was so tender, almost wistful, he might have been talking of a lost child.

"Where is it, Mr. Truman?" Lee asked gently.

"You've seen one half of it."

"In the museum, yes," Mark said quickly. "But the other half, where is it?"

"Gone," Truman said. "Stolen."

"Someone broke in here and… and took everything?" Lee found it difficult to believe that thieves would have looted the entire collection, most of which, according to Truman himself, was of little value.

"Not took, destroyed. Every single piece, smashed to bits. Except the urn. That was left in two pieces. I gave the half I had to the museum."

"And the other half?" Mark asked.

"He has it."

"Who, Truman? Who has it!"

He said the next two words as if uttering a curse, whispering them so as not to summon ancient demons.

"My son."

CHAPTER 33

"My son." The words hidden in the inscription on the chest at Henford.

"Daniel was a golden child in every way. Extraordinarily beautiful, he had a glow about him, an aura. And his brain was every bit as beautiful. Truly magnificent. He was our only child; we couldn't have any others, and it seemed at first that we'd been compensated for this with perfection."

Truman had led them back upstairs and, after locking the basement door, out of old habit, Lee guessed, since there was nothing of value left down there, he took them back to the living room. His limp seemed even more pronounced, his pace even slower. They retook their seats, and he began talking about his son, Daniel.

"Sometime around his fifth birthday it became evident that he was far from perfect. He was reading adult texts, solving complex equations. We were in awe, really. I had finished my on-site work in South America and was working full-time at the Smithsonian. My wife, Ann, taught history at George Washington University. Since he was an infant we'd employed a sitter for Daniel, but once he turned five they never lasted very long. He was uncontrollable, they told us. Impossible. Undisciplined."

"Had you noticed this behavior yourselves?"

"Of course. And perhaps we indulged him a bit, given that he was our only child, and we'd had him late in life. And of course there was his obvious brilliance. In school they had him skip two grades—he went directly from kindergarten to third grade. It was thought that if he were challenged academically it would help calm him down, and that being with older kids would also have this effect. It didn't work."

Lee was aware of Mark shifting on the sofa next to her, impatient to get to what had happened to the back of the urn, and what it revealed about the meaning of the word "semper."

"He became increasingly unruly as he grew older, almost unmanageable. We tried everything: private school, psychiatry, behavior modification therapy, group therapy. He continued to achieve outstanding academic results, but at home he was disruptive to the point of violence. Sometimes, when my wife would discipline him for something he'd…." His voice fell off, and his head dropped. "He would strike her. I became worried for her physical safety. He was a strong boy, and although he didn't play any sports for more than one season he was very focused on fitness. Every morning he performed a regimen of exercises in his room. We'd hear him panting and straining. Frankly, it was disturbing in a teenager, that level of… I suppose I'd have to call it obsession. My wife was a small woman. Petite, I'd say."

He took a long, slow breath.

"What happened to your wife, Mr. Truman?" Lee asked.

"She died when Daniel was fourteen. She was crossing Virginia Avenue on her way home from her office at GW when a van hit her. I thought at the time and I still think that she must have been distracted by worries about Daniel. He was at his most violent then, and she had determined to take a tougher stance against his outbursts."

"Tougher stance?" There was something oddly vague about Truman's recollections, something almost generic, Lee thought.

"We would often insist that he stay in his room as punishment. He would go to his room and then, after five minutes at most, he'd come downstairs and watch television, brazenly ignoring us. So Ann had a lock installed on his bedroom, on the outside. Our plan was to lock him in there for the specified period. But the first time she tried this, he broke through the door, smashed it to pieces. This was the day before she was killed. It must have been on her mind when she stepped into the street."

"Fascinating," Mark said with undisguised sarcasm. "But what does this all have to do with the urn?" Lee shot Mark a look, but Truman seemed oblivious to his impatience. He was telling his story on his own terms.

"So Daniel and I were on our own. He never showed the slightest interest in my work. I tried to get him to help me with my exhibit in the basement, but he wouldn't cooperate. With his intellectual gifts, he might have been a great scholar. He seemed to have no interests at all. He was teased at school and had no friends."

"Why was he teased?" Lee asked.

"I don't know," he said quickly, perhaps defensively. "He had no real connection to me, not in any emotional sense. He would look at me…." Truman closed his eyes for a few moments. "He would look at me as if he'd never seen me before, not with contempt so much as complete indifference."

It occurred to Lee that Truman had never really described what it was that his son had done wrong, other than fail to connect emotionally. He was just a bad kid. End of story. But kids were bad in specific ways, weren't they? They did drugs. They stole. They got into fights at school. Truman seemed unwilling to specify what his good-looking, brilliant son had done wrong, other than resist being locked in his room, which was hardly unusual behavior for a headstrong teenager.

"And when he left for Yale, it was as if a great tension went out of my life. He rarely came home after that, not even for major holidays. I don't know what he did or where he went. I paid the tuition for four years and after that I heard nothing more from him until ten years ago. He simply showed up at the front door. 'Hello, Father,' he said. He was not a welcome sight, I have to be honest. He looked well, and prosperous, even, but I hadn't given him much thought in the six or so years since he left for college, or I tried not to. And when thoughts of him did creep in, I forced them back out as soon as possible. I have no fond memories of Daniel, nothing I would want to relive."

"What did he want?" Mark asked.

"He said he was applying for a job in the government. He wouldn't tell me what kind of job, or even what part of the government. He needed his birth certificate as part of the overall background check. Well, I had no idea where it could be. My wife handled that sort of thing, and she was long gone. I checked the most likely places and couldn't find it. I could see this disturbed him. He became more and more agitated as I continued to search the house. I was afraid he'd turn violent, that's how enraged he was. Finally we ended up in the basement. There is a walk-in storage closet off the gallery. I went in there to look through the various boxes and cabinets and when I couldn't find the birth certificate I came out and told him the bad news. At that point, he lost control."

Truman's voice had grown fainter and he'd begun to talk slower as he replayed this episode, as if he were fighting a great, almost physical reluctance to continue.

"I'll never forget what he said," Truman continued. "He said, 'You managed to keep all of this crap. You catalog it, dust it, salivate over it, show it off. But you can't bother to keep one small document about your own son?' He grabbed the nearest object, I think it was a small incense burner, and smashed it on the floor. He was about to demolish a second piece when I ran at him to try to stop him. He threw me to the floor, just as he'd thrown the object, and began destroying my collection.

Everything. Piece by piece. And every time I tried to stand up he'd strike me, on my face, in my gut, anywhere he could hurt me, and throw me back down. I told you he was very strong. His rage was the most terrifying thing I'd ever seen, far worse than the specter of my life's work being obliterated. He was out of control, but at the same time quite methodical. That was the most terrifying thing, the combination of blind rage and cold-blooded determination. And when he'd smashed everything in the room, he let out a great roar and pulled down the cabinets themselves. One by one. They're made of steel, the sturdiest available. The last one landed on my right leg, nearly cut it in half. When he saw that there was nothing left to destroy, he abandoned me. Not a word, not a glance, as if I were just another ancient artifact he'd thrown to the floor. It took almost an hour to get out from under the cabinet. I was in excruciating pain. I may have passed out once or twice. I dragged myself upstairs, half surprised that he hadn't burned down the house, and dialed 911. I told the EMTs nothing about Daniel's visit; I only said I'd fallen from a ladder while cleaning the gutters. That kept them from going down into the basement. I didn't want to implicate Daniel. Not out of any sort of pity or paternal feelings, but because I never wanted to see him again, even in court. As you've no doubt noticed, I never fully regained the use of my right leg."

Telling the story seemed to have diminished Truman even more than age. He looked shrunken, hollow, the words having emptied him out.

"What does this have to do with the urn?" Mark asked.

"Yes, the urn. I told you that I kept the urn for myself."

"Why?" Lee asked. "Half of a piece of pottery can't be worth much."

"It wasn't a question of value. When I dug up that urn, it was intact. A magnificent find, potentially the centerpiece of the collection. The drawings told an intriguing story that seemed to point to some sort of mysterious power the tribe had, which might explain their rather remarkable independence from the Inca. Priceless from an artistic and historical perspective. As with most of the artifacts I discovered, I kept the Ateeka urn here, at my home, where I could clean it properly. I planned to keep it a few weeks, a month perhaps. In those days, I'm talking decades ago, we didn't have sufficient staff at the museum to handle all of the incoming finds from pre-Columbian excavations. And, frankly, the Ateeka weren't exactly a top priority. Everyone was focused on North American indigenous peoples; that's where the funding was. If it was South American it had to be Aztec or Inca, something with a *name* that would attract benefactors and swell the ranks of our members. The

Ateeka were something of a stepchild, and so I did much of the cleaning and cataloging work on my own, some of it right here. I lavished particular attention on that urn, for obvious reasons. I suppose it was something of an obsession. I thought it would make my reputation, you see, this intact, unusually large piece with an intriguing story to tell. Then, one evening I came home from the museum, went downstairs right away, as I always did, to gaze upon my masterpiece, and found it on the floor, shattered."

"What happened?" Mark asked.

"Large pieces of pottery don't fall to the floor on their own."

"Daniel?" Lee said.

"He was an intuitive child, and though he was only ten at the time he knew how important that urn was to me. There were dozens of other Ateeka artifacts in the basement at the time. Why did this one alone end up in pieces?"

"Was he jealous of the attention you paid to it?"

"I don't think Daniel cared enough about me to be jealous of anything or anybody. Destroying the urn was an act of pure evil. It was beautiful, it was valuable, and it was important to me—hence, it had to be destroyed."

"This is your son you're talking about," Mark said, slowly shaking his head. "A ten-year-old. You make him sound like a freak."

"Hardly a freak. He looked like an angel, a golden boy. He was freakishly perfect, if anything."

It occurred to Lee that Truman was describing his son as some sort of priceless artifact, a mint-condition offspring who, like the Ateeka urn, had in the end disappointed. No doubt Daniel would have a very different perspective on life in the Truman household.

"Of course he denied having anything to do with what happened. And I had no proof. It had broken into nine pieces. One large segment, which represented half of the original urn, and eight smaller ones. I couldn't turn the entire thing over to the museum, that was out of the question."

"Why?" Mark asked.

"The conservators who would have been charged with putting it back together would have seen right away that it had been recently broken. Questions would have been asked. That would have been very embarrassing for me professionally. As with medical doctors, 'First do no harm' could be our motto. We use tiny brushes to excavate through layer after layer of soil and ash, all to avoid the possibility of damaging even a fragment of something that might turn out to be valuable. And here I'd destroyed a priceless urn in my very own home? Donating all nine pieces was out of the question. One large piece would attract less scrutiny. Besides, the intact portion that I did turn over was in itself quite remarkable. That's the portion you saw today."

"What happened to the other eight pieces?" Lee asked. Finally, they were getting to the point of the visit.

"He has them."

"Daniel?" Mark asked.

Truman nodded.

"I had reassembled them as best I could into one fragment, not unlike the one you saw displayed in the archives, but of course with disfiguring scars running up and down the surface. I didn't keep it downstairs, because I didn't want it to be seen by visitors. I often had experts over to view my collection. I kept it upstairs, in a closet. I didn't want to be reminded of it, you see. It is still my greatest shame. When Daniel came that day for his birth certificate and destroyed everything in the basement, he took the fragment."

"Why would he take that one thing, rather than destroy it?" Lee asked.

"Perhaps to add to my punishment?" Truman sighed. "I never really understood Daniel's motivations, other than to torture his parents."

"And you haven't seen him since that day?" Mark asked.

"Not for ten years."

"What was on the back of the urn?"

"At last we come to the reason for your visit. You saw the paintings on the front, earlier today, correct?"

"They depicted a male figure of some sort, a ritual object, being opened, and a sort of gas being released that caused great terror," Lee said.

"Precisely. But what you saw wasn't really the 'front' of the urn. For one thing, an urn doesn't really have a front and back. But in this case, what you saw in the museum was, if anything, the middle."

"How do you know this?" Mark asked.

"Because the story told by the pictures begins *before* the portion you saw and continues after. There's no numbering, of course; I can only go by the narrative flow. There's a scene of a kind of lake, really more of a swamp. Three Ateeka men, in ceremonial garb, are gathered by the water's edge. One of them is kneeling and seems to be dipping the vial into the water, as if to fill it up. I believe this is the beginning of the story."

Mark sat forward. "Was there anything unusual about the swamp?"

"It seemed to give off the same kind of gas that the male effigy did when it was opened. If we didn't have the other illustrations, we might assume that this gas was just morning mist, or fog."

"But you don't believe this?"

"I'm an archaeologist, not a scientist."

"What happens next?" Lee asked.

"We see the vial in a sort of temporary platform in a small clearing, nothing nearly so grand as the platform depicted on the portion of the urn you saw today. Lying next to the vial are the three men, including the one who presumably filled the vial. All three appear to be dead. In fact, judging by the way their corpses have been depicted, they appear to have died a painful death. Their mouths are distended, their limbs in almost impossible positions, as if they were in unspeakable, wrenching pain at the moment of death."

"Similar to what we saw on the front of the urn, only there were dozens of people who had died," Lee said.

"Yes, the three Ateeka who filled the vial died from the effort. Later, when the bottle is uncorked, hundreds of people die—or so the illustration suggests."

Lee thought of the sonnet: *A plague when I uncap the bottled thing.*

"The next drawing is something of a departure. We see the swamp again, but this time it appears to be raining, only it isn't raindrops falling but large rocks. The back of the swamp is filled with the rocks, and the foreground seems to be filling up."

"A volcano?"

"Undoubtedly. There were a number of smaller eruptions before the big one that covered the Ateeka village decades later. The next illustration is the one you saw, of the effigy on a pedestal, apparently worshiped as some sort of ritual object."

"An object with the power to kill," Mark said.

"Yes, well that would seem to be the point of the narrative. We're dealing with tribal superstition here, of course."

"And yet the Spanish explorers reported finding an entire expedition wiped out, along with every member of the Ateeka tribe," Mark said. "Mass death not unlike what was painted on the urn."

"Europeans brought any number of diseases to the New World to which the indigenous peoples had no biological defenses, and vice versa."

"And they all died at once? Come on."

"Well, you can believe what you want. I choose not to believe that an ancient vial contained some sort of powerful vapor that decimated an entire tribe. The Ateeka may have believed in such a power. They also believed that the volcano was a god, as were the sun and the moon. I find these beliefs fascinating, but I don't share them."

"We mentioned the word 'Semper' earlier and you didn't respond," Lee said. "Does it mean anything to you?"

"Again, I don't like to speculate. Archaeology is based on the accumulation of fact, one by one, to build a case."

"*But?*" Mark's impatience bordered on aggression.

"The Inca, as I noted, made reference to a tribe over the mountains with mysterious powers. Perhaps the mysterious vial in the illustrations—who knows? The Inca had a fascinating system of written language that used knotted cords, called khipus, to create words. Only about 700 khipus have been discovered, mostly in tombs. The rest were destroyed by the Conquistadors, who thought they were decorations. But archaeologists, with the help of computer scientists, have been able to decode many of the khipus. Most of them had to do with trade, accounting for shipments of grain and tribute given to tribal leaders. But some were of a ritual nature, and some, as I mentioned, referred to a tribe across the Andes. There is a word used to describe the sun and the mountains. It suggests something permanent, eternal, unchanging. This same word appears in the context of the Ateeka references, if these were indeed references to the Ateeka. Something eternal."

"Semper, meaning always," Lee said.

"Yes, historians have used that term to translate the khipu, and in the very small world of Ateeka scholars, Semper has become shorthand for whatever mysterious power the tribe had, perhaps embodied in the vial. There is also reference to 'semper' in a letter written by a Spanish explorer to his patron in Cadiz. He refers to a mysterious power described by tribes located near the Ateeka—not the Incas but smaller tribes along the Amazon. They used a similar locution for this power, a reference to eternity."

"Why didn't you tell us this when we first brought it up?" Lee asked.

"As you might guess, I have little interest in excavating my own past. The destruction of that urn represents my greatest professional failure as well as my greatest personal failure."

"Do you have any idea where your son is now?" Mark asked.

Truman looked almost alarmed by the notion. "None whatsoever. And I hope never to see him again. Why?"

"Because he has the missing half of the urn."

"But I've told you what's on it. Seeing it for yourself would add nothing to your understanding." Truman placed his hands on both armrests and lifted himself to his feet. The effort was evident in his face. Lee already had her phone out, searching for a nearby hotel. "I've told you what I know. Everything. Now I hope you'll leave me alone."

He left the room, heading toward the front door.

"We should go," Lee said to Mark. When he started to argue for staying longer, she changed the subject. "I found us a hotel, the Georgetown Suites. We can talk there."

"Thank you," Lee told Truman by the front door. "And I'm sorry if we frightened you." He said nothing, offering no absolution. But she sensed a kind of relief, an unburdening. He didn't look at them as they walked out, but started to speak when they were a few feet along the slate path.

"I've come to believe that the Ateeka are a cursed tribe, and not just because of their sudden disappearance. I wish I had never heard of them, much less devoted my career to them. Not a happy way to look back on one's life work, but there you have it. My advice to you is to forget all about Semper. It's brought me nothing but heartache and disappointment, and I don't doubt it will bring the same to you."

With that, he closed the door.

CHAPTER 34

Mark spoke as soon as they pulled away from Truman's house, pausing only to listen to the nasally insistent female voice of the GPS unit direct them to the Georgetown Suites.

"I think we're getting closer to figuring out what this Semper is."

"What happened back there?"

Mark shot her a puzzled look.

"What were you doing? You assaulted an old man. I thought he might die, literally. It took him fifteen minutes to breathe normally."

"What was I doing? Trying to save your ass, that's what."

"I didn't recognize you. You scared me as much as anything that's happened."

"Would you have preferred we left without the information we got? I knew he was holding back. So did you."

She didn't answer, couldn't. She was driving through a strange city next to a stranger. She'd spent far too much time with strange men. It had always gotten her in trouble, most recently deadly trouble. For someone who studied history, she was pathetically unable to learn the lessons of her own past.

The Georgetown Suites was a seven-story modern hotel in the heart of the city's historic neighborhood. Mark parked the car across the street, and they walked silently into the lobby.

"Two rooms," she told the desk clerk once he'd confirmed that they had a vacancy. She heard Mark let out a long, exasperated sigh.

The tense silence continued in the elevator. She was about to get off on the third floor—his room was on the fourth—when he pushed the button to hold the door open.

"I'm starving. How about meeting in fifteen minutes in lobby and we'll find a place to eat?"

"I think I'll just find something on my own," she said and headed down the hall for her room.

Her suite was two rooms decorated in a tasteful, modern style. There was a view from the living room over the rooftops of Georgetown, brick chimneys atop dignified old houses, the occasional church steeple. She closed the blinds. She would have preferred a single room, something smaller. The expanse of useless space made her feel more vulnerable and lonely than she already was. The lack of a free wireless connection was also disappointing.

After a quick shower, she headed back down to the lobby, relieved not to find Mark there. In the hotel's business center, she logged onto the Internet and started googling. Her goal was to locate an expert on whatever it was that had been or still was inside the Ateeka effigy. She first searched for "viruses," which seemed a logical place to start. More digging led to the conclusion that virologists were a subset of microbiologists, who worked mostly in industry, including the food business, where they studied food-borne illnesses and spoilage. Not really what she was after. It seemed likely that the best source of information would come from a university-affiliated microbiologist. She googled "microbiology + Georgetown" and was pleased to find that the university, located just a few blocks away, had a microbiology department. An agenda for the next day was taking shape. She closed the browser and left the hotel.

She wasn't really hungry but thought she'd buy some fresh clothes with whatever credit remained on Sarah Cooper's Visa card. The warm evening filled the sidewalks of M Street and Wisconsin Avenue with pedestrians. She stopped into a Gap store on K Street and bought a pair of black pants and a white knit top. The card went through. Not yet ready to face her hotel room, she walked down to the Potomac waterfront. It felt less crowded and therefore less safe than the commercial center of Georgetown up the hill, so she turned around and headed back.

The grade was steep, slowing her pace a bit, and about halfway up, midway between the river and Wisconsin Avenue, she realized she was completely alone. She'd stumbled onto one of the least active streets in the area, Thirty-First Street, lined with storefront businesses that were closed for the evening.

A moment later, she sensed that she wasn't alone after all. She turned, still walking.

Nothing. The sidewalk behind her was empty. Turning back, she walked a bit faster.

But there was someone there. She heard something, not footsteps but a rustling, of clothing perhaps, or maybe just breathing.

Without breaking stride, she turned again.

Nothing.

No, not nothing. A flash of movement. An arm, a shoulder, covered in a black shirt, ducking into a recess—perhaps an alley, or just a doorway. She began to run.

CHAPTER 35

Lee fell into a deep, dreamless sleep within minutes of returning to her hotel room. She was awakened the next morning by a pounding on the door. Panic quickly gave way to anger when she heard Mark's voice.

"Lee, open up. We need to talk."

She put a pillow over her head, muffling his voice, and waited. Eventually he left.

She showered, dressed in her new Gap clothes, and called the number she'd written down the night before.

"Microbiology department, Janice speaking."

"Good morning. I was hoping to make an appointment to speak to Stephen Minton," Lee said. "Can you tell me if he has office hours today?"

"I'll connect you," she said before Lee could explain that she wanted an in-person interview. "Please hold."

"Minton," came a male voice a second later.

"Professor Stephen Minton?" she said, buying time while she collected her thoughts. She had hoped to have the morning to figure out exactly what she wanted to know.

"Yes."

"This is Sarah Cooper. I'm with the history department at Columbia. I was hoping to arrange an appointment to speak to you about a book I'm writing."

"History department?"

She'd been tempted to say biology but had worried that she wouldn't be able to carry out the ruse. The truth, Columbia's English department, seemed too far-fetched. History felt like a reasonable compromise.

"It sounds strange, I know. I'm working on a history of virology, and I've been referred to you as someone who knows more about viruses than anyone else." Flattery never hurt in academic circles, as she well knew.

"Who referred you to me?"

"Edward Filer, at Columbia." The first name in her head.

"Never heard of him."

"Do you have some time today?"

"Did you say *today*?"

His tone suggested that she'd just proposed a weeklong cruise together. The academic world moved at a snail's pace: introductions were made, bona fides checked, e-mails exchanged, and finally a meeting was arranged, perhaps at a long-scheduled conference in a far-off city. Months could elapse between introduction and the first face-to-face.

"Last-minute, I know, but I'm here in Georgetown and I—"

"I'm not your man. I'm a virologist, but my research focus is phages—bacteriophages."

"I thought—"

"I don't know who told you I'd be a source for a history of the field. If you were interested in the impact of viruses on bacteria, I'm your man, though I have no free time today, or this week, for that matter."

She didn't tell him that a website had mentioned him as a prominent virologist, and that she'd called him only because she was staying in a hotel within walking distance. Instead, she plunged right into her story, improbable as it sounded even to her own ears as she unraveled it.

"What I need to know is whether a virus, or perhaps a bacteria, can live indefinitely in an enclosed space, say a kind of bottle, for many years—centuries, actually. How would it survive without outside resources? I mean, a virus has a short lifespan, correct?" She didn't wait for him to respond, keenly aware that she sounded at best ignorant, at worst insane. "So how could it last for years in a closed environment? Wouldn't they—the viruses—just die out from lack of, I don't know, food or oxygen?"

"Don't you mean without a host?" He sounded utterly condescending.

"Yes, exactly."

"There is a hypothesis, which has quite a few adherents, that viruses once had the ability to survive outside a host cell, but that over time, their parasitic... call it lifestyle, caused them to lose the genes that enabled independent life. This is called the streamlining hypothesis. I suppose if you accept this hypothesis then you could also posit that there once lived microorganisms capable of living independently, outside a host. They would have to possess some form of self-replicating DNA."

"Yes, that's exactly what I'm thinking of," she said, bewildered but sensing that his mini-lecture supported in some vague way the notion that whatever the Ateeka had locked up in that vial might still be alive and lethal.

"I'm not suggesting that such organisms still exist. All the viruses that I know of, that anyone knows of, live within a host. It's just that they may have evolved from microorganisms that could self-replicate and live independently. What period is your book focused on?"

"The sixteenth century," she said, sensing that she was about to be ridiculed.

"Impossible. We're talking about an evolutionary process that occurred over millennia, if it occurred at all."

"But isn't it at least possible that—"

She heard a loud sigh, as if he was blowing cigarette smoke directly at the mouthpiece.

"Talk to Reginald Phelps," he said. "Up at Columbia, your home turf. Do you know him?"

"I don't have much contact with the science departments."

"Well, if there's anyone who believes in the possibility of self-replicating viruses, anyone with any standing in the field, it's Reg. I believe he wrote a paper on the subject some years ago. Widely ridiculed, as I recall, but the man is highly respected nonetheless."

"Reginald Phelps." She was scribbling down the name.

"A word of advice, and then I really must go. I would take a softer tack with Reg if I were you. I'm not sure what you're after, frankly, but you don't sound particularly knowledgeable about the subject of microbiology, even for a historian. Imagine if someone contacted you as a source for information on the sixteenth century and had never heard of the Spanish Armada. You wouldn't be eager to spend precious time with such a person."

"Point taken," she said.

"But Reg is an interesting fellow. A bit quixotic, actually. He truly believes, against all evidence, in the possibility of self-replication among microorganisms. A frightening thought—perhaps that's why he's something of an outsider, even for a man with eminent credentials. Is there anything else?"

She was still thanking him for his time when he clicked off.

What she would have asked him, if he'd given her the time, was why self-replication among viruses was such a frightening thought. She'd have to learn the answer on her own.

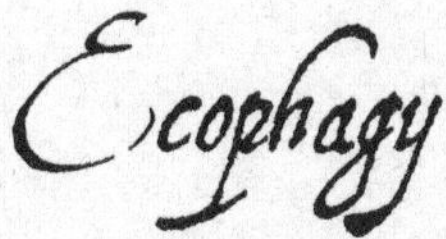

"Scientists found the microbes living in a remarkably inhospitable environment, drainage water as caustic as battery acid from a mine in Northern California.... Scientists say the discovery could bear on estimates of the pervasiveness of exotic microbial life, which some experts suspect forms a hidden biosphere extending down miles whose total mass may exceed that of all surface life."

—*New York Times*, January 18, 2000

"The Mayo [Clinic] study found that nanobacteria do indeed self-replicate, as [Finnish biochemist Olavi] Kajander had noticed, and endorsed the idea that the particles are life forms."

—Pasquale Urbano, University of Florence, and
Francesco Urbano, Italian Army Medical Corps
"Nanobacteria: Fact or Fancies."
Public Library of Science (May 25, 2007)

CHAPTER 36

The Acela raced through New Jersey on its way from Washington to New York City. Lee gazed out the window. Town, factory, river, town, highway, city—landscapes flickering in and out of view too quickly to be fully absorbed. The train did not achieve its maximum speed of 150 miles per hour on the DC to New York leg, but it moved quickly enough to give the impression of watching a travelogue in fast-forward.

She'd checked out of the hotel less than half an hour after hanging up with Professor Minton at Georgetown. During that time, she'd returned to the hotel's business center, which had a free printer for guests, and googled Reginald Phelps. His official bio on the Columbia website included an impressive array of degrees and published books and papers with titles like "Force Transduction by Triton Cytoskeletons" and "Phosphatidylinositol 4,5-bisphosphate Functions as a Second Messenger that Regulates Cytoskeleton-plasma Membrane Adhesion." How or whether any of this related to a five-hundred-year-old sculpted clay effigy dipped into a South American swamp was beyond her. His photo revealed a white-haired man of sixty-something with a cropped white beard and trimmed moustache and bright blue eyes. A friendly face, she decided.

Still, there was no way she was going to walk onto the Columbia campus, where the chances of being recognized, even with her new look, would be too great. So she typed his name into Yahoo's "people search" window and found his home address in Mount Kisco, New York, about an hour north of New York City. She printed directions to his house along with the Acela schedule and the commuter schedule from Grand Central to Mount Kisco.

Mark was not in the lobby when she left, which was a relief. The outburst at Truman's house had unnerved her, and reinforced her instinct for going it alone. She glanced around the car. It was only a third full. There was little conversation, a few irritating cell phone calls, mostly just the whoosh and shudder of the train hurtling through the flickering landscape. She took her notes and the maps she'd printed from her purse and studied them for a while to distract herself from a sense of encroaching loneliness.

Somehow, in that moment of isolation, it wasn't old boyfriends she recalled, or close friends now reading about her, she guessed, in lurid newspaper articles, but her mother, whose face she could barely recall. It was the nights she returned to in her mind, the two of them in Lee's bed, taking turns reading to each other. Novels, mostly, and occasionally a Shakespeare sonnet, which her mother would explicate for her, line by line, unlocking the secrets of a puzzle.

After the train left Newark she made her way to the bathroom at the back of the car. In less than ten minutes they'd pull into Manhattan. When she came out the train was in the Hudson River tunnel, and she had the disorienting sense that in the minute she'd been gone day had turned into night. Back in her seat, she gathered her papers to put them back in her purse.

Odd. She was certain she'd left them more or less scattered on the empty seat next to hers, but when she got back from the bathroom they were gathered in a single messy pile. She glanced around the car. Had someone gone through them? Looking forward, there were only the backs of heads. She turned around and quickly studied the dozen or so faces behind her. No one familiar or even suspicious. As the train pulled into Penn Station she got up, grabbed her purse and overnight bag, and walked quickly toward the front of the car. When she got to the end, she turned around and scanned the people who'd been sitting in front of her. Again, no one familiar. No one suspicious in any way.

But then, who might she have been expecting? The monster who'd murdered David had no idea where she was. Neither did the police.

She shook her head to clear it of paranoid thoughts and stepped off the train, joining a tightly packed stream of exiting passengers inching toward the stairs and up into the station. Threading her way through afternoon rush-hour pandemonium, she was distracted as she passed a newsstand by the headlines of both New York tabloids. "Grisly Death in Georgetown," screamed the New York Daily News. On the Post's front page: "Museum of Death." Under both headlines was a photo of Miles Truman.

She bought both papers, managed to find a quiet corner amid the chaos, and scanned the articles, which were short on details but told her what she needed to know. The murder had occurred about an hour after she and Mark had left Truman. And he had been tortured, his head crushed in a way that seemed identical to what had been done to David Eddings and Maurits Immersheim.

She threw the papers into a nearby garbage can and found the entrance to the subway, where she bought a one-trip pass and swiped her way in. She couldn't help looking over her shoulder every few seconds. First Immersheim, then David, now Truman. Everyone she visited in connection to the sonnet ended up brutally murdered. Tortured in the style of the sixteenth century, then murdered. She turned sharply around. Where *was* he?

The uptown Number One train took her to Times Square, where she transferred to the Queens-bound Number Seven, getting off at Grand Central. After purchasing a Metro-North ticket to Mount Kisco (round trip, though she wasn't sure at all what she'd do when she got back to New York, or where she'd stay) she waited in the very center of the vast station, feeling protected by the fast-moving currents of commuters streaming around her. At least she'd learned one thing: Truman must have heard her tell Mark where they were staying, and told whoever had killed him, and the monster had followed her there last night. Had he been on the train, too? Was he in Grand Central?

The fifty-minute ride to Mount Kisco took her underground to northern Manhattan, then through the Bronx and Westchester County, the landscape growing steadily leafier and less populated. She knew she should have contacted Professor Phelps in advance, but after her phone call with Steven Minton she was afraid that her ignorance of microbiology, coupled with the implausibility of her quest, would put him off. By the time she arrived it would be late evening, and he would, she hoped, be home. If he wasn't home, she'd wait for him. If he was out of town, she'd try to find out where he was and meet him there. There was just no way she was going to set foot on the Columbia campus.

She got into a waiting taxi at the Mount Kisco station and gave the driver Phelps's address. He drove her through an upscale village, a mix of local stores and the usual national chains, and then into a very affluent neighborhood of large homes on expansive plots of land. The feel was more country than suburban, and many of the houses appeared to be genuinely old, clapboard colonials meticulously maintained amidst carefully tended lawns and manicured shrubs.

"Do you know this address?" she asked as they drove deeper into the countryside.

"I take many people here, many people. People from all over. And I bring them back to the train."

The taxi turned into a long gravel driveway with no home in sight for a good two hundred yards. A ghostly white full moon was just barely visible in the early evening sky. There was a stillness about the landscape, the earth itself holding its breath in anticipation of nightfall.

Finally, a house appeared. Or loomed. It looked immense, forbidding, inviolate. Unlike its clapboarded, symmetrical neighbors, Phelps's house was made of stone and appeared to be a jumble of jutting wings and dormers. Two stories high with a steeply pitched slate roof, it was dominated by a three-story tower to the left of a massive stone porte cochere. Most of the windows were tall and narrow, bisected into two panels, with peaked tops. Over the porte cochere and on the tower were more elaborate windows, great arches with inset panes of rectangles and domes. On either side of the porte cochere were verandas covered with stone arches. It was all quite impressive and gloomy.

The driver stopped under the portico. She paid the fare and considered asking him to wait for her. But she didn't know how long she'd be, and despite the gothic gloom of the house she was, after all, visiting an eminent scientist, though clearly one who lived well beyond the means of a college professor. She asked the driver for a card so that she could call him to take her back to the station.

The cab sped off even before she pressed the small doorbell button. She heard nothing from inside the house, but within seconds the large wooden door was opened by the white-haired man whose picture she'd seen on the Columbia website. He had on a dark suit, white shirt and solid blue tie.

"Professor Phelps?" she said with as much confidence as she could summon, as if showing up at a house in the late evening without calling ahead was the most natural thing in the world.

"And you are?"

"Sarah Cooper," she said. The false name came easily to her lips.

"And what is it you want?"

"I was told by professor Minton at Georgetown that you are an authority on self-replicating viruses. I'm doing research in this area."

"And so you just show up here, unannounced, to ask questions?"

"I know this is unusual. But it's a matter of urgency." He looked at her with a combination of incredulity and scorn. He appeared to be at least seventy, older than his official Columbia photo. His thin white hair was combed back from his forehead, and his white beard and mustache were neatly trimmed. His eyes were a very pale blue and his voice matched his appearance, crisp and formal but not unkind. "I may be in danger, you see. I need your help. Please, just let me in."

He continued to study her, his gaze more analytical than judgmental, and completely without fear, which was perhaps odd, given the circumstances. Finally, he stepped aside to let her in.

CHAPTER 37

As Professor Phelps led her across a vast entrance hall, she tried to take in as much as possible: the double staircase twisting up to the second floor; the walls paneled in polished wood with oversized portraits dimly illuminated by overhanging lamps; the oriental carpets on the floor, muffling their footsteps. In fact the entire place felt hushed, deserted.

"Have you lived here long?" was her not-very-brilliant opening gambit. Her voice sounded small and flat, not quite up to the challenge of filling the space.

"For quite some time," he replied without turning around.

His tone discouraged further inquiries of a personal nature. She would like to have asked, for example, who else lived in the house. A wife, children, servants?

"When was this built? It appears to be gothic revival."

"Yes, gothic revival. Are you an amateur historian as well?"

As well as an amateur biologist, he seemed to imply.

"Professional historian," she replied.

He opened a door between the two curving staircases and led her into a library. It was magnificent, two stories high with bookcases rising from floor to ceiling on four walls. On either side of the room, beautifully carved ladders on brass tracks provided access to the higher shelves. The books appeared to be leather-bound, gold-embossed, and quite old.

The moment they entered the library, two large dogs jumped to their feet. With long, glossy hair the color of mother-of-pearl, fluffed out as if recently blow-dried, they seemed as sumptuous and unreal as the house itself. Neither animal made a noise, but they glared at her through narrow, unblinking eyes.

"Sit," Phelps said quietly, and the dogs instantly obeyed, eyes still focused on the stranger. He pointed to a burgundy-leather sofa, one of a matched set that faced each other in front of an enormous stone fireplace. She sat down as directed.

Perhaps it was Phelps's apparent frankness, or the imposing grandeur of the library, or the embarrassment of her conversation with Minton earlier that day, when she'd revealed her ignorance of all things scientific, but she found she had no enthusiasm for inventing a story. So she told the truth, or something approaching it.

"I believe I've discovered a deadly virus, an ancient virus with the power to kill vast numbers of people. I came across it by accident. I have no scientific background. I stumbled across a reference to it in a poem. Now someone is trying to kill me, and he's already killed at least three people, and I believe it's because of this virus."

She took a deep breath. There was so much more to tell: the connection to Elizabeth I and her bastard son. The Hever Emeralds. The Filer family in Massachusetts. But she wanted to stay focused on Semper, which seemed to be the motivation for whoever was trying to kill her. Phelps said nothing, staring at her with the mild curiosity one might show someone describing a recent vacation to a well-known destination. The dogs seemed more intent than their master on following her story, their gaze never leaving her.

"Have you heard of the Ateeka?" she asked. He shook his head. "Not surprising. They're a tribe in South America who vanished in the late sixteenth century. They discovered this virus in a swamp, apparently, and preserved it in a clay object, an elaborately decorated male effigy. The neighboring tribes, including the Inca, seemed to know about the power of this virus, because they left the Ateeka alone for centuries. There's an urn in the Smithsonian that shows the virus being taken from the swamp, then placed in the effigy and then worshipped on an altar. Well, there's half an urn. It shows the virus being released from the effigy, and masses of people dead from it."

"You've seen the complete urn?" Phelps spoke quickly, running his fingers through the silky hair on the head of one of his dogs.

"No, it's missing. But I spoke to someone who has seen it, the archaeologist who dug it up. Are you familiar with the urn, Professor Phelps?"

"Archaeology is hardly my bailiwick," he said.

Something about his attitude, the forced serenity, his willingness to let her in… was it possible that he'd been expecting her? Perhaps he was just oblivious to danger. She'd spent enough time in academia to recognize two types of inhabitants: those terrified or at least befuddled by the world beyond the academy, and those blissfully unaware of it. Perhaps Phelps belonged to the latter category. "I know it sounds bizarre, but I believe this virus is real, and that someone wants it badly."

"And what do you want from me?"

"I want to know if this is possible, if a virus, or whatever it is, could have lived inside a bottle for five hundred years and remained potent."

"Have you…." His fingers froze on top of the dog's head; it jerked its head toward its master for a split second before returning its gaze to Lee. "Have you seen this effigy?"

"No."

"Do you know where it is?"

For reasons not clear to her, she decided to lie, and nodded with some vigor. Perhaps she wanted to elevate her standing with Phelps, impress him with her investigative prowess and tempt him with the prospect of studying the virus first-hand.

"Where do you think it is?" His voice had thinned nearly to a whisper.

"I can't say," she answered, then turned the conversation in a new direction. "Is this feasible, Professor Phelps? Could there really be a deadly virus inside the effigy? And could it have survived all these years?"

"That depends who you ask," he said with a touch of irony.

"I'm asking you."

"Then the answer is yes. But there is much debate about this point. Actually, not much debate at all, as I am one of the very few scientists who believe that viruses can self-replicate. Viruses seem to cause a lot of arguments, in fact. There's the age-old debate over whether or not a virus is a living organism. Most virologists consider them non-living, since they don't meet the criteria of the generally accepted definition of life. They don't respond to changes in the environment, for example, and they aren't composed of cells, which are viewed as the fundamental unit of life."

"Which side of the issue are you on?"

"Neither. The debate is purely academic to me. As long as we understand the organism, what does it matter how we label it? The origin of viruses *does* interest me, however, and is relevant to your inquiry. Here, again, there's considerable debate. Viruses don't fossilize well, unfortunately, which has impeded our ability to study their history. The most commonly held belief is called the 'streamlining hypothesis,' which holds that viruses were once independent organisms that developed parasitic relationships with a host organism. Over time, the viruses lost the genes that were not required by their parasitic existence. They became incapable of living independently outside a host cell."

"Then a virus kept inside a clay vessel must have some sort of host to live on," she said. This would disprove the notion that the virus had endured inside a sealed effigy for five centuries.

"Not necessarily. I believe that viruses were originally stand-alone organisms with the ability to replicate themselves, much as humans and other living creatures perpetuate their species. While it is unarguable that the viruses we know of today have lost the ability to survive independently, without the sustenance of a host, there is an argument to be made that a virus may exist that never lost its self-replicating DNA."

"So, the virus could exist within the vessel."

"I believe so. Of course, every independent organism needs nourishment of some sort. It must feed on something."

"So the Ateeka must have put something in the vessel to feed the virus."

"For five hundred years? That seems unlikely."

She frowned. Every time she thought the Semper story was becoming scientifically plausible, another objection appeared.

"However, it *is* feasible that the organisms could feed on themselves. This would make them the ultimate self-replicating creatures. The vessel itself becomes an ecosystem, a completely independent world unto itself. The swamp you mentioned might have been one such ecosystem in which the virus continually fed on itself. Inside the vessel, it would have been no different, with a bit of water in which the virus could live and reproduce without fresh input from the outside world."

"And if this virus were released?"

"Anything would be possible. This swamp you described was clearly isolated and so the impact of the virus was contained."

"And at some point it was covered with volcanic ash."

"Which not only hid it but more than likely neutralized the virus, which, by interacting with its surroundings in a controlled environment, would have been able to adapt over time and lose whatever unique qualities it once had." He stopped talking and seemed temporarily lost in thought. "However, if the virus were not allowed to adapt, as would be the case in this vessel you describe, and if it were released into the general population…." Phelps's tone had grown more somber as he talked, losing the air of casual disinterest he'd given off when she'd first arrived.

"What could happen?"

"Have you ever heard the term ecophagy?" Before she could answer he waved a hand at her. "No, of course you haven't. It was coined by Robert A. Freitas of the Institute for Molecular Manufacturing in Palo Alto. Its literal definition is the consuming of an ecosystem. As

I mentioned, I believe that inside the vessel there might be a complete ecosystem, with all that is needed to sustain life. The earth contains many ecosystems: coral reefs, rain forests, deserts. Cities are ecosystems as well. But if you were to look at the earth from another planet, you might consider the earth itself an ecosystem, a single, natural, self-contained unit in which all components work together to sustain life. What Freitas meant by ecophagy was a scenario in which out-of-control, self-replicating organisms consume an entire ecosystem. Taken to the extreme, this could mean the extinction of all life, human and non-human alike."

"This could happen? From a single vial of water and microorganisms?"

"Freitas was talking about molecular nanotechnology, in which humans engineer mechanical systems at the molecular level. This has led to the hypothetical existence of self-replicating nanorobots capable of functioning autonomously in the natural environment. The nanorobots could quickly convert that natural environment, or biomass, into replicas of themselves. On a global level, this scenario could lead to ecophagy, global ecophagy."

"But we're not talking about engineered robots."

"No, but the impact would be the same. Extinction. Of course, we're assuming that these viruses inside this vessel of yours are potentially harmful."

"The images on the urn show mass death."

"Yes, the urn." He appeared to ponder this for a few moments. "It is unlikely that the virus would be benign, I'm afraid. You see, a virus may feed off itself, so to speak, when no other external sources of nourishment are available. But this is hardly an ideal situation. Every species is hardwired to proliferate. We have no reason to believe this virus is any different. In the swamp it had what it needed and so remained contained. In the vessel it has no choice but to feed off itself. Once it is freed from the vessel, we have to assume that it would seek alternative sources of sustenance."

"How would it do this? I mean, how would it travel?"

"Worst case scenario? It could be transmitted through the air. The scenario depicted on your urn suggests an airborne virus. But it could also be placed into the water supply of a major city. Remember, it once lived in water. Either way, the potential for ecophagy is very real."

"Do you believe the virus is real?"

He didn't answer right away. Nor did he move or change his

expression in any way. Yet Lee detected a profound shift in his demeanor, the way she could sometimes sense that someone was about to cry, even without physical confirmation. It was an atmospheric change, as real as the metallic scent of oncoming rain.

"Do I believe?" he said finally. "Do I believe that my home will burn to the ground? Of course not. Do I have fire insurance? Of course I do. Some eventualities are so devastating we prepare for them even if we don't really believe they will occur."

"So you believe there's a small chance that the Semper virus is real."

"I believe that it is theoretically possible that such a microorganism could exist. Only a few years ago scientists discovered a new form of life, entirely new. It's called nanobacteria. These organisms are far smaller than what had been, until their discovery, the smallest accepted limit for life. It could be nanobacteria inside your effigy, not a virus. Already, these creatures are being blamed for a whole host of diseases, and we didn't even know they existed until quite recently. So you see, it is important to keep an open mind as a scientist. Unfortunately, the minds of many of my colleagues are shut firmly against new ideas."

"Then what sort of insurance have you taken out?"

Another long silence, then, in a very soft voice: "What kind of insurance could there be?"

She couldn't begin to imagine, so she shifted gears. There didn't seem any reason to disguise who she was any longer. At least not with this very old academic.

"This all began with a sonnet I discovered. I believed it was by Shakespeare and read a portion of it on television. Within hours, my apartment was broken into and my companion killed. Since then I've been stalked, and there have been other murders. I believe that the Semper virus is the cause of all this."

She expected him to indicate that he'd heard this story—the murders had been in the headlines, after all, as was mention of her television appearance. Instead he asked: "What does the sonnet have to do with the virus?"

"There's a coded reference to it in the poem, in the portion I read on the air. Someone must have heard it, spotted the reference, and come after me."

Phelps sat forward, causing his dogs to spring to their feet, anticipating that he was about to stand up. But their long, disdainful snouts never pointed away from Lee.

"Do you have the sonnet with you?"

"No." The word rolled off her lips before she'd even had time to consider why she'd lied. The original was still in the safety deposit box in Manhattan, but her handwritten copy was with her, as it had been from the beginning. Phelps's sudden interest in the sonnet felt intense verging on inappropriate. He was a scientist, after all, a dealer in facts. If she'd learned one thing over the past days, it was that withholding at least some information was almost always smarter than sharing it.

"Have you memorized it?"

"No."

He inched forward on the sofa until he was almost off it.

"You mentioned that you knew where this vessel is."

"I lied," she said. "I really don't know where it is, but someone thinks I do, obviously, because they're trying to stop me from finding it. Someone else believes that this virus is real, and that it has great power."

"Destructive power. Whoever controls the virus could control the fate of mankind."

He'd gone from skeptic to true believer in minutes. She wished she had time to decode what he was all about, but he was sitting inches from her now, staring at her like his dogs, hanging on her words.

"Should I contact the government? The FBI?"

He shook his head, almost sadly, and sat back. The dogs, too, relaxed slightly. "You should probably do just that, in the interest of self-protection. But I must warn you: no one will believe a word you say. I assure you, I almost ruined my career over the existence of a self-replicating virus with ecophagic capabilities. I don't know who you'd get to even listen to you."

Particularly once they realized she was really Lee Nicholson, wanted for murder. At least Phelps hadn't made the connection.

Or had he? She still had the sense that she'd been expected.

"What will you do now?" he asked.

Again, she decided not to share her plans with him, vague as they were.

"I don't know. Stay alive, I guess." She stood, and the dogs instantly followed suit, snouts in the air like rifles trained on her face. She thanked him for his time as he led her from the room into the front hallway. Once again she was struck by the vast emptiness of the house. The silence was a presence, a crowd of ghosts all around her. It seemed improbable that Phelps lived alone in such a massive house, and wasn't the place a bit grand even for a physician—an academic physician, no less? The portraits lining the entrance hallway were half-length, all of men, and appeared to span several centuries. One in particular caught her eye, and she walked over to it. The subject was a man of about forty, with cropped hair and a neatly trimmed moustache and beard. He wore a snug-fitting, cream-colored doublet, buttoned down the front, with narrow white ruffs around the collar and wrists. In his right hand he grasped the Rod of Asclepius, a serpent-entwined staff associated with medicine, often confused with the caduceus—a symbol of commerce, not health. A small plaque attached to the elaborate gold-leaf frame indicated that the subject was Rufus Hatton. No artist was indicated.

"This looks Elizabethan," Lee said. The sitter's three-quarter pose, his clothing and the plain, rather murky brown background all suggested a sixteenth-century portrait.

"You have a good eye," Phelps replied.

"From the Rod of Asclepius, I assume he's a physician."

"That's correct. And you didn't call it a caduceus. I'm impressed." Despite the compliment, Phelps seemed eager to be rid of her.

"Are these all doctors?" She turned around, taking in the eight portraits, the most recent of which appeared to have been painted in the mid-twentieth century. All the subjects held a Rod of Asclepius.

"Yes, all physicians." He walked to the massive front door and opened it. Eager to be outside the gloomy house and yet intrigued by the gallery of physicians, she turned to the door and almost tripped over one of the great dogs. She hadn't realized that they were studying her as she studied the medical portraits.

"Toto! Maneras! Come here," commanded Phelps. At once the dogs turned from her and trotted to the door. She followed.

"I hope you find what you're looking for," Phelps said. His voice had turned completely neutral, as if he were dismissing a tradesman. He must have noticed that there was no car outside and yet he expressed no interest in how she had gotten there or how she planned to leave.

"I'll just call a taxi," she said, and when he merely nodded she added, "from my cell phone."

He closed the door.

CHAPTER 38

Lee took the taxi driver's card from her pants pocket and used her phone to call. After four rings, she got his voicemail and hung up. She turned back to the house, thinking she'd have to ask Dr. Phelps to call her a cab, but the great edifice looked unwelcoming, even impregnable. She still felt confused by Phelps's attitude toward her. He had seemed completely unsurprised by the premise of her visit, or even by the visit itself, as if people regularly showed up at his mansion asking questions about self-replicating viruses. He was largely uninterested in her line of inquiry, but suspiciously interested in whether or not she knew where the Semper vessel was located. And another thing: Why was Phelps living in a gothic revival palace more suited to a hedge fund plutocrat than an academic researcher?

She was about to try the cab driver a second time when a rustling of leaves or shrubbery distracted her. She turned abruptly to her left and saw nothing. Perhaps only a squirrel or bird. Still, evidence of life apart from Phelps was both reassuring and mildly unsettling. The house had been so still. Even the dogs seemed to glide about on a cushion of air. She stepped out into the driveway, hoping that Phelps hadn't let them out. What had he called them? Toto and Maneras. Odd names. Toto brought to mind Dorothy's little dog in The Wizard of Oz, hardly a fitting name for the giant beasts who'd stared at her as if she were dinner.

She pressed redial to try the cab driver once more.

And Maneras. Was it Spanish?

The phone rang. Once, twice.

She summoned forth her high school Spanish. Maneras meant "ways," she thought. Odd name for a dog. Perhaps it was a family name. Toto and Ways?

The driver's voicemail picked up. She clicked off and immediately felt the blood drain from her head, sudden lightheadedness almost knocking her over.

Both names were Spanish.

Not Toto, as in Dorothy's dog, but *Todo*, with a hard *d* sound, as in the Spanish word for "all."

The dogs were named All and Ways. Always.

Semper.

She turned abruptly back to the house, half expecting it to be transformed in some way now that at least one of its secrets was partially revealed. Phelps knew about Semper. Like Derek Martinson in Tunsbury, with that portrait in his living room, and like the old Filer House with the word spelled in bricks in the foundation, Phelps kept a secret reminder of Semper close by at all times. His loyal, vigilant dogs.

She felt suddenly exposed, each window in the big house an unblinking eye gazing down at her. She could start walking to the station, but the driveway alone was half a mile. Something the driver had said came back to her. A meaningless bit of chitchat a few hours ago, but now perhaps significant.

"Of course, I take many people here. People from all over. And I bring them back to the train," he'd said.

Was the house some sort of conference center? That might explain its extraordinary size. But who were these people? *Where* were they?

She pocketed her phone and headed for the back of the house. She'd try the driver again in a few minutes.

The long trek around the house took her past meticulously clipped shrubs and specimen trees and well-tended gardens of blooming perennials. The entire landscape, lit by pale moonlight, felt crisply perfect and vaguely unreal. All the while she had the distinct sense that she was being watched. It was the house itself, she decided, looming over her, following her progress.

At the side of the house the driveway divided in two; one direction led to the front of the house, the other to a four-car garage set about fifty yards from the house itself. She headed for the garage, a miniature version of the house, made of stone and with the same steeply pitched slate roof. Each of the four garage doors had three small windows. She peered inside and, once her eyes adjusted to the darkness, determined that the garage was full. She couldn't quite determine the makes of the cars, though one appeared to be an SUV, one a European station wagon.

Heading back to the house, she noticed that this spur of the driveway didn't in fact stop at the garage but wound around it. She followed it and discovered a small parking lot with capacity for eight cars, which was easy enough to determine as there were eight cars currently occupying it, filling every space. There were two upscale foreign models, but the others looked like American-made rental cars.

Twelve cars in all, counting the four in the garage. Either Phelps had a serious automobile habit or the house wasn't quite as deserted at it had seemed.

She walked back toward the house. There were no doors on the side facing the garage, and the shrubbery was quite thick, which would make it difficult to get close enough to look inside a window. She continued around to the back. Many of the windows were similarly protected by shrubbery, but the rear facade contained a series of six French doors that opened onto a large flagstone terrace. She moved quickly to the nearest door, flattening herself against the stone facade. Very slowly, she pivoted until she was just able to look in.

The interior flickered with the light of myriad candles, some held by chandeliers, others by oversized candelabra. A very long table ran down the middle of a large, rectangular room. She became aware of movement, a lot of movement. People were entering the room, moving around the table, standing behind chairs, not sitting.

She blinked several times, trying to focus. Something wasn't right. It was a kind of conference, but they weren't people.

She turned away, eyes closed, then looked back.

They were monsters, with the bodies of men, cloaked in long black robes, but heads like birds. No, goblins. Black heads with long, cone-like beaks. Tiny slits for eyes. She looked away a second time, trying to process it. A ritual. She took a deep breath, then another. When she turned back, they had taken their places around the table, these bird-men.

They appeared to be waiting for something, or someone.

Suddenly all heads turned toward one end of the long room as a new figure entered and stood at the head of the table. Though also dressed in a long black robe and headdress, he appeared to hold sway over the group, whose members stopped moving and stood facing him.

It appeared that the leader might be addressing the others, though Lee couldn't detect any movement under the black mask.

Were they fellow doctors, like the portraits in the foyer? But why the hoods and robes, which made them look like giant, predatory crows? Or vultures.

Doctors dressed as vultures? Why?

A moment later she answered her own question.

They were doctors, yes. *Renaissance* doctors. During the fifteenth and sixteenth centuries, physicians wore black hoods to protect against plague. The Renaissance equivalent of Hazmat suits, the long beaks with tiny slits for breathing designed to keep out the airborne pestilence that was believed to cause the unceasing series of plagues and other diseases that attacked Europe during the Renaissance.

She'd always imagined the terror of a sick person, fortunate enough to afford the attention of a physician, visited by one of these creatures, a vision of death more than healing.

Why had these people donned black robes and masks at least four centuries after their use went out of fashion? If only she could hear what they were saying beyond the French doors. Some sort of prayer or incantation, she guessed, from the way they all stood behind their chairs, facing the leader, whose arms moved about as if he were delivering a sermon. The candlelight added to the sense that she was observing the past, or an old movie, images flickering in and out of focus.

Then a kind of cheer erupted, all of the doctors chanting in unison. She couldn't make out the words at first, but they sounded foreign. As the chanting continued, she used the noise as cover, slowly turning the door handle and gently pushing open one of the French doors an inch or so. Now she could hear them clearly. The chant was repeated twice. "Dum spiramus tuebimur." Latin. Two years of Latin in graduate school yielded an uncertain translation: While we breathe we shall defend. When it was over, the men grabbed their hoods, all using their right hands, and in one coordinated motion pulled them off.

She saw at once that the leader was Reginald Phelps. Even without the mask, he looked bird-like, his gaunt face exuding a predatory hunger, his close-set eyes an anxious vigilance. The men—for they were all indeed male—placed their hoods on the table in front of them and took their seats. She looked slowly around the room. They were an older group, even for doctors, most with gray hair. All wore expressions of nervous unease, as if they were expecting bad news or even punishment. She studied their faces, one by one. There was something similar about them, all well-groomed and fit-looking, with an aura of self-satisfaction and comfort tainted with anxiety. But for the black robes and hoods on the table, it could have been a board meeting of a global bank or charitable foundation.

Her gaze reached the end of the table across from Phelps. Suddenly the urge to shout overtook her and she had to shove a fist into her mouth to keep from crying out.

He was younger than the others by a good decade but listening to Phelps with the same close attention. She stared at him as her mind replayed the events of the past few days in fast motion, trying to make sense of them. Trying and failing.

There was no making sense of what she was seeing.

Sitting at the end of the table, a black hood in front of him, and wearing a black robe, was Mark Warren.

CHAPTER 39

Phelps began talking the moment the hoods came off. "Lee Nicholson has been here." He waited for the reaction, which was immediate: a chorus of incredulity.

"We heard the driveway sensor," one of the others said.

"And you did what you are meant to do," Phelps said. "You returned to your rooms upstairs. She arrived here an hour ago. She found me quite by accident, through my research on self-replicating microorganisms. Well, not an accident exactly, but she certainly didn't realize that I know about Semper, nor that I want to find it as desperately as she does. More desperately, in fact, because I know what it is, and what it is capable of."

"And where is she now?" asked an elderly man with what sounded like a French accent.

"She left."

More incredulity.

"You let her go?" several people exclaimed.

"What was I to do, tie her up? In any case, she's no closer to finding Semper than we are. Isn't that so, Samuel?"

All eyes turned to the youngest man in the room, the man she knew as Mark.

He nodded slowly. Mark must have gone directly from Georgetown to Mount Kisco, taking a plane to beat the Acela.

"She learned more than any other civilian," Mark said. "She discovered where Semper came from and what it's capable of."

"But not where it is currently located."

"No one knows that," Mark said, a touch defensively.

"Why aren't you with her," the Frenchman asked. "Wasn't that your responsibility, to stay with her at all times?"

"She insisted on going her own way," he said quietly.

"Then you should have insisted on staying with her," said the man to Mark's left.

Mark pounded the table once, and most of the men started. "Do you have any idea what I've had to do these past days? Up in Tunsbury I drugged an innocent man named Mark Warren, shot him with enough Phenobarbital to render an elephant unconscious. He could have died, and that would have been on my conscience for life."

Lee felt her heart, already racing, begin to pound.

"We all took an oath when we joined our fraternity," Phelps said. "We all agreed that the power of Semper is so vast, sacrificing one life or even a hundred lives might be necessary to avert its deployment."

Dum spiramus tuebimur, Lee thought.

"Which is fine as an oath," Mark said. "But I'm the one who had to put it into practice."

"Not by choice," Phelps said. "By duty."

"Fuck duty," Mark snarled. "You sat here, mumbling Latin bullshit and dressing up like trick-or-treaters while I drugged a man, fled the police in New York, deceived a woman whose only crime was discovering an old poem… and what did it get us?"

"I say we should have killed her when we had the opportunity, back in New York." This was spoken by a trim Asian man wearing a red tie visible over the top of his robe. "There is still the chance that she may come across Semper."

"Calm yourself, Hideki; she has no evil motives," Mark said. "She needs to find Semper to exonerate herself. She's still wanted by the police for the murder—*our* murder—of that cameraman."

They killed Alex. Lee stared hard at Mark. Or had he done it himself?

"Exactly my point," the Asian man said. "She doesn't know what the power of Semper is, so she might place it into wrong hands to save herself. That is why we are here, why we have convened for centuries."

"And let's not forget that she's being followed," Phelps said. "Do we know who this person is, Samuel?"

Mark frowned and shook his head. "He's a freak, we know that. The last person we'd want to control Semper."

"But this Nicholson woman does not have Semper, nor does she know where it is," said a man across from Mark. His accent might have been German or Eastern European. "We have been here now for more than a week, virtual captives, and it appears that it's all for nothing. Most of us have medical and research positions to attend to. And families."

As the entire room voiced displeasure, Phelps stood up and walked to a cupboard opposite the row of French doors. One by one, as the others noticed what he was doing, they stood up. He removed a very large, old key from a pocket in his robe and inserted it into the cupboard. When the doors opened, he appeared to feel around the inside for something, perhaps a switch. A moment later the cupboard slowly moved to the right, revealing a safe. He turned around to face the others, a look of expectation on his face.

They immediately responded.

"Nos es tutela!"

The oldest man in the room, his face gaunt, the robe hanging off him like black curtains, shambled to the front of the room and jabbed a finger at the safe's key pad. Two others followed, then Phelps punched in. Lee heard a high-pitched whine, faint yet insistent, at which point Phelps pulled open the safe and took out a pair of thin gloves, probably cotton, which he slowly put on. He held up his protected hands for the room's inspection, turned back to the safe, and took out a book. Holding it in front of him like an offering, he slowly returned to the head of the table.

"Physicians, I have before me the diary of Rufus Hatton, Physician to Elizabeth, Queen of England, Scotland and Ireland. Nusquam mos sto in nostrum via!"

"Nusquam mos sto in nostrum via!"

They sat.

He opened the book and carefully turned the pages. When he arrived at the page he was apparently looking for, he removed something from inside his robe. A pointer in the shape of the Rod of Asclepius. He began to read.

> "6 September, 1602. What evil have I unleashed? And to what end? Have I, to ingratiate myself to Her Majesty, put the world at peril? To assuage a mother's tortured heart, have I set upon the world a power that might destroy thousands more? For when I told the Queen what I had discovered on the Lansdale, she hesitated not a moment. 'Secure it for me, Doctor,' she ordered. I endeavored to explain the fearsome power of this vessel called Semper, but my warnings only aroused her the more. 'If it should ever become known who Edward Filer is, he will be in great peril. The succession is at stake. My enemies will stop at nothing to discredit me.' Gently, I told Her Majesty that I understood the peril in which Filer lived. 'He will not live a day if his. . . .' Here she faltered, and I saw the woman beneath the Queen, behind the powders and creams and paints with

which she formed a royal mask. As her physician I know full well that the carefully applied facade conceals smallpox scars acquired in her twenty-ninth year. I know too that it conceals a great deal more.

I waited as she composed herself. 'He will not live if his… if his lineage were to be discovered. Even he must not know who he is, though I think he suspects.' Here she could not resist a faint smile, but levity soon faded from her face. 'I have given him so little, in comparison to what he deserves. He is a Tudor, after all.' I told Her Majesty that she had been most generous to Filer, and reminded her of the emeralds her own mother had been given by the late King Henry, and which she had given to her… to Master Filer. At this she shook her head, almost violently. 'Are we so stupid as to presume that jewels will save him, were his identity to be known? What you bring me today, this is true power. This will protect him and his son and generations of sons afterward.'"

Phelps looked up and glanced around the room. No one said a thing, or even moved. He returned to the diary.

"I had arrived at the Queen's quarters at Windsor prideful that I was able to bring her such a treasure as Semper. I never sought royal favor, but life at court has soiled my soul, I fear. Now I felt the full weight of my action. Should I not have grabbed the vessel from the captain and thrown it over the side into the Thames, where it would lie unknown for eternity? Now there was no retreat, for Her Majesty was set on acquiring this power for her… for Filer. I would of course do her bidding, but I felt I had to offer one final warning. 'Evil begets evil, your majesty, I have seen this a hundred times in my life, just as pestilence will consume a household, and then a street and soon enough an entire city. What may appear to be protection for Edward Filer and his heirs may come to be their downfall.' I saw her face harden at this. Her cheeks turned crimson. When she finally spoke, it was with a low, unsteady voice. 'Would I not destroy the world to save him, Doctor? The scale of my heart does balance his worth, and that of his heirs, with the lives of every creature on God's earth, and the balance tips in his favor. Get me this Semper, pay whatever is asked. Bring it to me.'"

Phelps carefully closed the diary and looked around.

"'The scale of my heart does balance his worth… with the lives of every creature on God's earth.' Such a line could be the motto of this monster who now seeks Semper, mutilating and then killing anyone who stands in its path. It is why we are here, why we live, to prevent this scourge from destroying mankind. It is our life's work. 'Evil begets evil.' Please keep this in mind before you complain of being *imprisoned* here at Henford."

Henford. The place was called Henford.

CHAPTER 40

The moment she saw Phelps remove the book from the hidden safe, even before she heard the two excerpts, Lee knew she had to read all of it. Texts had been her life, her passion. Texts had been her solace when her mother left, and a text had started her on the bloody road that led to this place. She felt certain that the answers she sought, the meaning of Semper and perhaps even its whereabouts, could be found in whatever Phelps had taken from the safe.

But how? Even from outside, she could see that the safe was opened not by a combination dial but by a keypad. Four of the men had entered numbers, the last being Phelps himself. She had to get it before Phelps replaced it.

Would Mark help her? Did he even know the codes to the safe? She couldn't risk letting him know she'd seen what just happened—the ancient hoods, the chanting, the ritualized removal of what looked like some sort of sacred book from a hidden safe.

Her only advantage was surprise. She could heave a rock through one of the French doors. Then what? Start a fire somehow? Even if she could, surely Phelps would safeguard the book above all else. Something bigger was needed, something more sudden.

She couldn't let him replace the book.

A plan took shape. Well, not a plan exactly, for that implied something fully worked out, a strategy. Call it an idea.

She ran back around the house to the parking area behind the garage. She tried to open the driver's side door of the closest car. Locked.

She tried the next car. This one opened, but there was no key in the ignition and none over the visor or on the floor.

She tried the next car, then two more. She was beginning to lose heart when she opened the unlocked door of a gleaming black SUV. An Avis rental agreement lay on the front passenger's seat. Next to it was a set of keys. She got in, buckled the seat belt, and started the engine.

The short drive from the parking area to the patio behind the house, headlights off despite the dark, allowed ample time for multiple rounds of second-guessing—decisions and revisions which a minute will reverse. But she pressed the accelerator, for what choice did she have? She had traveled so far from her comfort zone over the past few days, what she was about to do felt almost sane. *Almost.* And a small chance of success, of survival, even, seemed like reasonable odds at this point in her life.

She swung the SUV out into the center of the back lawn, turned it to face the house, and floored the accelerator. The car skidded on the soft lawn, the back wheels throwing up clumps of grass before gaining traction. Then the big V8 engine worked its magic. Within moments she was hurtling across the lawn toward the house, gripping the wheel, aiming for the double doors at the center of the dining room. If she was off even by an inch, the car would hit the house itself and come to a sudden, deadly halt.

The car sailed through the double doors with a scant inch of clearance on either side. She was only vaguely aware of what was happening because of the speed with which the car penetrated the room and because she'd thrown herself downward and to the side, onto the passenger seat, at impact, in order to shield herself.

The sound of shattering glass. People dove out of the way as the car slammed into the room. The table was thrown up against the far wall of the room, lit candles flying across the room before dying. Someone was trapped behind it.

Shouting. Moaning.

The car stopped suddenly, throwing her forward. The transmission shift dug into her abdomen. She heard screaming as she unbuckled her seatbelt, which had kept her from hitting the dashboard. The front passenger door wouldn't open because the chassis had been crushed on impact. She crawled over the passenger seat to the back and opened the door behind it.

She emerged into chaos. At least half the doctors had fled the room. There appeared to be a few injured men, but she had no time to study the extent of the harm she'd inflicted. She quickly made her way over a carpet of shattered glass and splintered wood toward the front of the upended table.

Phelps was nowhere in sight. Perhaps he'd fled, too. She rounded the end of the table. If the book had been on the table, it would have been thrown to the floor when the car hit.

The upended table had come to rest against the far wall, forming a kind of lean-to with a covered triangular space below it. That's where the book would be, she decided, only half aware that someone was shouting. "It's *her*! *Stop* her!"

Ignoring this, she got down on her knees and crawled under the table. She wasn't the first person there. Reginald Phelps, still in his long black robe, was feeling around the dark space for the book. When he saw her, he sat up and banged his head against the overhead table.

"Get away from here." Phelps lunged at her, knocking her to the side. His hands roved across the carpet, searching. She righted herself onto all fours and shoved him. He slammed against the wall. She heard his breath wheeze out of him.

Then she felt something. Soft leather with a slightly pebbly texture. The book. She grabbed it and shimmied out from under the table, unable to resist glancing at it. The cover was badly faded; it must once have been a deep burgundy, but was now the color of lightly sunburned flesh. No writing on it. Quite thick. The fall to the floor seemed to have loosened big chunks of pages, which overhung the cover at various angles. Under different circumstances she might have agonized over damaging what was clearly a very old manuscript. Not now.

Her instinct was to head for the front of the house, make a run for the street, and then flag down a car. Not much of a plan, given the length of the driveway and the lack of car traffic in the neighborhood, but what was the alternative?

At the far end of the room, several of the black-robed physicians were getting to their feet. She headed toward the door nearest her end of the table. Several men shouted at her, and she was aware that at least two of them were coming after her.

The dining room opened onto a short hallway, which in turn led to the front hallway she'd been in earlier. Clutching the book, she ran for the great wooden door. Before she got there, a man emerged from a side door and blocked her progress. He looked dauntingly sturdy, his arms folded across his black robe. Still, she figured she could barrel into him, knock him off balance, and buy enough time to get through the front door. She was long past subtlety.

But then two more men appeared, blocking her path. There was no way she could charge through them. She stopped abruptly, just a foot or so in front of them.

Their expressions were as dark as their robes. In fact, their eyes gleamed with rage. The man on the left, who was Asian, took a pistol from a pocket in his robe and pointed it at her.

"Hand me the diary, Miss Nicholson."

It felt odd and, even under the circumstances, reassuring, to hear her own name, her real name.

"There is much more at stake than you," the man in the middle said in a rather sinister European accent—French, she thought. "Give it to us and spare yourself a lot of anguish."

"I don't have Semper," she said. It was all she could think to say.

The man with the accent stepped forward to take the book. She cradled it to her chest. Unable to take it, he grabbed her arm instead.

"Get your hands off me!" She slammed her right foot into his left shin. He yelped and stepped back.

"That was foolish, Miss Nicholson," he said. "Your life is worth nothing now. But you have made it easier to do what we are about to do." He nodded to the Asian man, the one holding the pistol. "Shoot her, Hideki."

Hideki stepped closer, his arm thrust in front of him, and adjusted his aim. Lee, without thinking, moved back a step. The left side of her face was throbbing, and she felt as if her heart was going to pound its way out of her chest.

So this is how it's going to end.

From the moment the sonnet slipped from the book in the Taylor-Shipford house to now—it all seemed inevitable, somehow, as if the road to Mount Kisco, through New York, Henford, Tunsbury, and Washington, had been pre-ordained. She was meant to be there, to hold the diary, to die holding it.

Hideki's finger tightened around the trigger. She felt a huge sadness come over her, a sense of regret that erased fear. Odd. Now that death was imminent, she wasn't afraid, just terribly sad. She closed her eyes and held the diary tight to her chest and began to silently recite the lines from Sidney that had always, strangely, comforted her with their tragic faith in self-delusion.

And now employ the remnant of my wit
To make myself believe that all is well,
While, with a feeling skill, I paint my hell.

The gunshot rang through her head before she could finish the passage, as if traveling in slow motion from ear to ear. *To make myself believe that all is well.* She staggered back, then opened her eyes.

Hideki had fallen to the floor. His left hand was clutching his right shoulder, which was oozing blood. The gun had fallen to his side.

She turned around.

Behind her, Mark held a pistol aimed at the other two men.

CHAPTER 41

Everything went still. The two men who remained standing didn't move, their faces locked in expressions of deep shock and dismay. Hideki, the gunman, bleeding on the floor, seemed frozen in some combination of physical agony and disbelief. Lee was immobilized by too many emotions to register: fear, of course, and panic, the instinct to run, the desperate need for answers. Even Mark, having fired the pistol, seemed unable to move, his arm still thrust forward, holding the weapon.

Finally the physician with the European accent broke the silence.

"Don't do this, Samuel. She has the diary."

Samuel. Despite everything she found herself furious over this one deception.

"You lied to me."

He hesitated a half second. "You need to get out of here." With his free hand, he hiked up his robe and dug into his pants pocket, extracting a set of car keys, which he threw to her. "Here, it's a rented Ford, silver. Give me the diary, get in the car, and keep driving."

"I'm not leaving the diary," she said.

"Don't be stupid, Lee, put the diary down and get the hell out of here."

The patronizing tone was infuriating.

"Why should I trust you?" She let this sink in for a moment. "The only way to save myself—from all of you, from the monster who killed David, from the police—is to find Semper. Until I do I'm either a dead woman or a fugitive."

"You don't know what you're talking about. This is bigger than you."

More patronizing.

"I know a lot, and this will tell me more." She patted the diary. "I'm not leaving without it."

"Then you're not leaving."

She looked carefully at him. How much of what had taken place over the past days had been an act? All of it? Some of it? The way he'd assaulted Miles Truman in Washington had revealed a violent side of him that had surprised and frightened her, with good reason, as it turned out. Was that the real Mark… no, not Mark, *Samuel*? And the affectionate, empathetic companion, the gentle lover, was *that* the actor? These questions were of more than academic interest, given what she was about to do. So she looked deeply into his eyes, seeking a sign.

And saw nothing to help guide her actions.

She had no real choice, then. She'd have to trust that at least part of him, a significant part, in fact, actually cared about her. That the Mark Warren she knew was at least partially real. She took a deep breath, turned back to the door, and began to walk toward it, circling around the two standing doctors.

"Leave the diary, Lee," Samuel called after her.

She kept walking, half expecting a bullet in her back. *To make myself believe that all is well.*

"I don't want to shoot you!"

She turned the doorknob and started to pull open the massive door.

"No, Lee!"

When the door was a third of the way open, she slipped through and pulled it shut behind her. Then she ran.

Within moments, she was aware of someone coming after her. Turning around without slowing down, she saw, with a mix of feelings, that it was Mark. *No, Samuel.* The pistol was at his side.

He was gaining on her. The parking area was about fifty yards ahead, across a long expanse of open lawn. If he wanted to shoot her, he'd have a clean shot and ample time. The moon cast enough light to illuminate his target—her. Clutching the diary close to her in one hand, the rental car keys in the other, she willed her legs to move faster, but she sensed he was still closing the distance between them.

She reached the parking area. He hadn't fired the gun. Why? She looked right and left, still moving quickly. There, toward the far end, a silver sedan. Closer to it—yes, a Ford. She circled to the driver's side; used the key fob to unlock the doors. He was about ten yards behind her.

Inside she tossed the diary onto the dashboard and shoved the key at the ignition, missing the first few times. *Fuck.* Finally it went in.

He was next to the car, passenger's side. She fumbled for the automatic door-lock button. Gave up and reached across to manually lock the passenger door. Too late. He opened the door.

She turned the key, starting the engine, and yanked the shift into reverse. The car lurched back just as Mark/Samuel lunged inside, basically hurling his body at her. His legs were still outside as the car spun back and around. She threw it into drive, hoping the sudden reversal would throw him back out of the car. It didn't.

Her left hand on the wheel, she tried to grab the pistol from him with her right. He jerked it away from her and scrambled completely inside the car, facing her. Bracing both hands against the wheel, she slammed on the brakes, hoping to throw him against the windshield. The car jerked to a halt; his body hit the dashboard with a dull thwack. The gun dropped to the floor on his side of the car.

Before he had a chance to regroup she lunged for it, taking her foot off the brake. He began kicking at her hands, his shin and knee banging into her face. She was dimly aware of the car moving forward, gaining momentum.

Where's the goddamn gun?

Her body, hunched over the passenger side, prevented him from full access to the floor on his side. So he flailed at her with his legs, thrusting her head against the underside of the dashboard. She considered biting him but then felt the gun. Grabbed it.

A sudden noise and she was thrown forward, her entire body hurled against the underside of the dashboard. The car, after picking up steam, had hit something.

She was practically on her back, facing up at him. Without the gun.

She tried to move. He pressed his knees against her chest, immobilizing her.

She squirmed and tried to free her arms to hit him. But she was essentially stuffed into the floor of the passenger's side, on her back.

"Get off me!" she yelled.

"Lee, listen to me. I could have shot you. I didn't." He was panting, practically whispering. "They'll be here any second. All of them. With guns. Now that you've seen the diary, they'll kill you."

She continued to struggle.

"I can save you. Otherwise you won't leave this place alive. They won't let you."

"Why should I trust you? Let *go* of me!"

"Stop fighting me. They'll be here any… oh, hell."

She felt his hands encircle her neck and begin to squeeze it, the pressure going from gentle to firm to constricting. She flailed hard at first, her fists doing nothing more than banging at the car door and the front of the seat. Not touching him. The sides of her head began to throb. She felt her diaphragm twitching.

She stopped struggling, just let her body go limp. *While with a feeling skill, I paint my hell.*

"I'm going to let go, but if you struggle again…"

Threatening *and* patronizing. Her arms came back to life as if on their own, swinging madly, trying to make contact with him, failing.

"Lee, stop it now and I'll let go."

She felt her vision start to cloud over. No choice now. *Fuck.* Her arms fell to her side.

He waited a few seconds, then released her. She gasped so deeply it felt like a seizure wracking her body. Tried to say something. Couldn't.

He pulled her up, practically shoving her back onto her side of the car. By the time she could focus, she saw that he had the gun in his hand.

"Let's get out of here," he said. The gun rested on his right leg, pointed at the dashboard.

She glanced at him, trying to read him. He looked fierce and determined.

"Drive!"

"Don't tell me what to do, okay?" she said. The words more or less leapt from her mouth; under the circumstances it really didn't matter who was in charge. The car had slammed into another vehicle during the struggle. She reversed away from it, then headed out of the parking area.

Near the end of the long drive, she saw a gate stretching between the two great stone pillars on either side. It had been open when the taxi brought her there.

"I can smash through it," she said, hoping it was true.

"It's reinforced steel. You'll kill us both. Pull over."

As she slowed the car, she noticed one of the men standing to the right of the gate in his black robe.

"Pull up to the gate and stop there," he said.

Mark/Samuel got out of the car and walked over to the man. He was short and stocky, with a thick head of steel-gray hair.

"I've got this situation under control, Andrew." He showed him his gun. "She's not going anywhere."

Andrew cast a skeptical glance at the car.

"Tell her to get out of the car."

"I'm taking her out of here. There's no reason she has to die."

"That's against policy, Samuel, as you well know."

"Open the gate, Andrew."

Lee saw the man shove his right fist into a pocket in the folds of his robe.

"Open the gate."

"The others are on their way," he said. Mark/Samuel looked back along the driveway. Lee followed his glance. Two cars were speeding toward them.

"Open it!"

Andrew stepped back. Mark/Samuel raised the pistol and brought it down on his head. He staggered to the side for several steps. Mark/Samuel hit him again and he crumpled to the ground. He reached into Andrew's robe and took something out of a side pocket. About the size of a TV remote. He aimed it at the gate, which began to open.

He got into the car. Lee put it in drive and checked the rearview mirror. The two cars were about twenty yards back.

"Open!" Mark/Samuel yelled at the gates, banging his fists on the passenger door. The gates, which swung inward, seemed to move in slow-motion. Lee allowed the car to creep up as close as possible without impeding the arc of their movement.

The two cars were almost on top of them. One swerved out to the right, the other to the left. Then, having moved fifteen yards or so away from the drive, they both turned back, heading right for the car.

"They're going to pin us here!" she said.

Both cars were heading directly for them, one on either side. In a second or two they'd be trapped. Or dead on impact. With no choice but to charge ahead she floored the accelerator.

"Not yet, Lee!" Mark/Samuel shouted, but she ignored him.

The rear wheels skidded on the gravel before finding purchase. The car lurched forward.

Lee held her breath and focused on steering the car between the gates—an opening that might be too narrow to get through. She braced for a crash into the gates, which were now pointed almost directly at them and looked suddenly quite thick and heavy, clearly capable of bringing a speeding car to an immediate and deadly halt.

She let out a furious scream. Mark/Samuel did the same. There was a loud crash as the left gate caught the car's left front bumper. The back of the car fishtailed right. She managed to straighten it out in time to allow the car to clear the gates with an inch to spare on the right side.

Once outside the gates, she turned right, instinctively heading back the way she'd arrived in the taxi.

"They're following us," Mark/Samuel said.

She pressed the accelerator.

"They'll try to run us off the road, so don't let them catch us."

"Thanks for the brilliant advice," she managed to sneer, despite everything. Then, on a more practical note: "I think the village is up ahead. We'll be safe there."

"Not true. They won't hesitate to shoot you even in a crowd. They've taken an oath. They have no choice."

"You took the oath, too," she said.

He said nothing for a few seconds as she navigated a series of curves and turns on streets bordered by long driveways that cut through perfectly green lawns in front of impressive houses.

"Turn left here!" he shouted, and this time she obeyed without hesitation, the car screeching as it crossed a deserted intersection. "I think there's an entrance to a highway ahead. We can lose them there."

The two cars were still close behind, gaining on them. To her left was a highway, which she was now paralleling. A low metal rail ran alongside it.

"There's the entrance!" she said and started to slow down. The small green sign said "Saw Mill River Parkway North."

"No, don't get on. Drive past it."

"But you said—"

"They'll catch us on the highway, their cars have more power. Keep driving."

She sped past the entrance. A glance in the mirror confirmed that the cars were getting closer.

"Okay, now do exactly what I say. When I say 'go,' turn sharply left."

To their left a long patch of grass, perhaps twenty yards wide, paralleled the highway.

"*Go!*"

She jerked the wheel to the left. The car swerved onto the grass. It was all she could do to maintain control.

"Get on the highway!"

"But—"

"Floor it!

Her foot responded before her brain could object. The Ford lurched forward, crashed through the metal barrier, and careened onto the highway. She heard a screech of brakes to her left—oncoming traffic, probably—but she couldn't afford even a second to confirm this, because their car was headed directly across the two lanes of the highway toward the center divider. She jerked the wheel to the right. Mark/Samuel had already grabbed hold of it and was turning it with her. The car canted up onto its two right wheels and missed the divider by inches. She spun the steering wheel to the left, and the car righted itself with a heart-sickening thud. The back of the Ford was still fishtailing, so she eased up on the gas until she felt in control.

"We lost them," he said, facing the back. "Nice work."

She let the car slow further until she was doing a comfortable fifty miles an hour. Her hands, she realized, were shaking, and her face was damp with sweat. She tried to speak but couldn't find her voice. She kept driving, waiting for her heart rate to slow, waiting for her brain to catch up with the events of the past hour.

"We need to talk," he said after a long silence.

She could only nod.

CHAPTER 42

They drove north on the Saw Mill River Parkway. Lee, still at the wheel, moved the diary to her lap and occasionally touched it, as if just the feel of it—soft as silk—would protect her, perhaps by showing her what to do next. She had no plan or destination, but driving along the curving two-lane highway felt purposeful.

"Talk to me," she said without turning to him.

"My name is Samuel Dobson, I'm a physician. I specialize in infectious diseases. I live in Baltimore." He glanced quickly at her, but she refused to acknowledge anything that he'd said, lest even a noncommittal response convey a sense of absolution. "The Society exists to prevent Semper from ever seeing the light of day. We're all physicians. We live in six different countries, but Phelps summoned us all to Mount Kisco because of everything that's been going on. We knew from the diary that there was a sonnet, and that it might have something in it about Semper. He read the press release Columbia put out. That's when he called us all to Mount Kisco. And when you read your sonnet on the air, we became convinced that you were going to discover it."

"So you tried to kill me and murdered Alex Folsom instead."

"That wasn't me."

"Oh, well, everything's great then."

"As a member of the Society, I endorsed the initiative."

"The initiative?" A surge of rage quickened her breathing. "You *endorsed* the *initiative*?"

"I took an oath, Lee. *Dum spiramus tuebimur.* Nothing will stop us from defending mankind from Semper. Your life—the life of the cameraman, as it turned out—is a small sacrifice compared to the potential devastation that Semper could cause."

"So you believe in Semper?"

He hesitated. "I believe that it might exist, and that even the possibility of its existence is sufficient to justify extraordinary steps. The Society was formed over three hundred years ago, after the discovery of this diary. A chain of physicians stretching down the centuries who are told of the power of Semper and dedicate themselves to preventing its use. Since I've been a member, we've never done anything other than meet annually and act out our silly dress-up scenario. It was really little more than a fraternal organization, a secret society and a good justification for an annual boondoggle to New York. Then you read the sonnet, or a portion of it. We had to stop you from reading more. Reginald Phelps sent someone to steal the sonnet."

"Who?"

"That I can't tell you."

"Bullshit."

"I can't tell you because I don't know. It was someone Phelps knew locally, I suspect a handyman or gardener. He always implied that he had someone on the payroll who could 'do things' if it became necessary."

Lee glanced at him. Was he lying? "Did you think I was stupid enough not to have copied the sonnet?"

"But without the original, no one would take you seriously, or so we hoped. You'd never have an opportunity to read it in public again. Whoever Phelps sent that night saw you leave the next morning. That's when he went up to your apartment and was surprised by the kid."

"He had a name. Alex Folsom."

"We never authorized murder. We never told him to bring a gun. The guy claimed Folsom went after him. He panicked."

"How did the name 'Henford' end up on a piece of paper on the floor?"

He gave her a half-smile. "I'm surprised a master at word games didn't figure it out." She let this pass. "Henford is the name of the Mt. Kisco home, which is named after—"

"I know, the Filer estate in England."

"But it's more than that. It's also Phelps's phone number. 436-3673. Phelps gave it to him as a reminder. He was told to call when he got the sonnet. Instead he called to say he'd discovered Folsom in your apartment. He wanted to know what to do."

"Phelps said to kill him."

"In fact he argued to keep him alive, but Phelps's man had been recognized. He made it clear there was no way he was going to let him live."

She wasn't sure if she believed this. "And the whole ruse, making me look like the killer?"

"We didn't know that you had only gone out for coffee. For all we knew you had left for the day, or for the week. So Phelps arranged for it to look like you were the killer, which included forcing Alex Folsom to record the message that said you were threatening him."

"Why? What was the point of getting me arrested?"

"We didn't know if you had seen the hidden reference to Semper in the poem, but we had to assume that someone else out there had. Worst-case scenarios are our stock in trade. We needed to get our hands on the rest of the sonnet before anyone else did. We decided our best recourse was to frame you for the murder so that you'd be in police custody. Once there, we'd find a way to get to you, and the poem. We're very well connected."

"And when this didn't work…"

"You were followed to England. Phelps's man again. We tried to stop you there, at Henford."

"That time you intended to kill me." When he didn't respond, she added: "And when *that* didn't work?"

"They sent me."

She focused on the road. In those first terrifying days, she'd clung to the idea that she was in control. Rather than let herself be taken into custody and framed for something she hadn't done, she'd seized her destiny and made her own rules. Or so she'd thought. In reality she'd been duped, played.

"What about Mark Warren?" she asked.

"I needed a local identity in Tunsbury in order to get close to you. He was in the right place at the right time. Or wrong time, I suppose, looked at from his perspective. I found his street more or less by accident. His lawn needed mowing; the house looked in bad repair. I had a strong sense that a man lived there alone, and I was right. I rang the doorbell and gave him a story about my car breaking down. Pretty soon he was telling me about the sad state of the fishing industry and his lack of a job."

"Which you dutifully repeated to me."

"The closer I stayed to the actual facts the safer I was. He was drinking when I got there, and it was simple to spike his vodka with Phenobarbital, enough to knock him out. I dragged him down to the basement, tied him up, and injected him every six hours after that for the two days I was up there. Not my finest hour, morally speaking, but it did the trick."

"You left him tied up in the basement?"

"On the way back to New York, when I told you I needed a

bathroom? I called the Tunsbury police from a rest stop. I told them where to find him. As far as I know, he's okay."

"As far as you know."

"If it means keeping Semper out of the hands of a maniac, then a few days in the basement is a small price to pay for—"

"Blah, blah, blah. Don't ever use the words 'small price to pay' with me again. I'm not a small price. And neither was Alex Folsom, and neither was Mark Warren."

"I had to do what I did, Lee."

"Did that include sex with me?"

A beat, then: "No, that wasn't part of the job."

"A side benefit, then?"

"Lee, what happened between us—"

"Stop talking." A tense silence, then: "What about the attack on me at the Filer House?"

"Not us. I don't know who or what that was. Our plan was to let you pursue whatever angle you got from the sonnet, and stay close by. We didn't want to harm you."

"Not after you'd failed to kill me in New York."

Another tense silence. Finally, Samuel spoke, sounding tentative.

"Do you have a destination in mind?"

"Tunsbury," she said. The plan had only just taken shape. "Make yourself useful and enter the town into the GPS."

He took the portable unit from its dashboard holder and began punching in letters.

"Everything points to the Filer family. They're the only direct link to the sonnet, the Hever Emeralds, and Semper. Someone followed me when I was up there, someone local. If it wasn't your medical cabal that attacked me, it had to be someone local. And I want to read the diary."

It still lay on her lap, and if Samuel made a move to take it from her she was prepared to scratch his eyes out. The answer was in the book. The answer was *always* in the book.

"Tell me about the diary," she said.

"It's what started everything. In the eighteenth century there was an auction of books and manuscripts in London. The diary was among the items up for sale. It was purchased in 1728 by a London physician named Oliver Firth who had an interest in old medical manuscripts. He had become alarmed about the possibility of a new form of plague. There hadn't been a plague outbreak in England since 1666, but there were outbreaks all over Europe even during the eighteenth century. In his own diary, Oliver Firth records his alarm at a plague outbreak eight years earlier in Marseille. It was bubonic plague, most likely, and it killed at least 100,000 people. Now here was a diary from a century earlier purporting the existence of a new kind of plague, an even more virulent strain."

"I heard Phelps say it was written by—"

"Rufus Hatton, a physician during Elizabeth's reign. He confirms what you discovered on your own, that the queen had a child out of wedlock, while still a princess. Hatton attended the queen during her confinement, as it was called then, and watched over the child until he reached adulthood."

"Edward Filer."

He nodded, and she sensed he was staring at her.

"We were amazed at what you were able to learn without the diary."

"*We.*"

"The Semper Society. The existence of a bastard son of the Virgin Queen has been a secret for nearly five hundred years. You uncovered it in a few days."

She refused to acknowledge the praise, waiting for him to continue.

"Hatton was introduced to Semper by a sea captain and brought it to the queen. She was desperate for a means of securing the safety of her illegitimate son and his heirs. If their connection to her was ever discovered, they would be in great danger. The succession to the throne, already a murky issue, was at stake. When male monarchs spawned bastards, they made them dukes and granted them great estates. Henry VIII had a son by Bessie Blount—"

"Whom he named Henry Fitzroy. Meaning 'son of a king.' Words always had multiple meanings for the Elizabethans. Fitzroy was made Duke of Richmond by his father. Please try to remember who I was before I became a fugitive."

"Sorry if I seem to be talking down; it's rare that I get to discuss this stuff." He took a deep breath. "So Elizabeth wanted to give her son something that would make him safe, even powerful, without tipping her hand as to who he really was. Even the Hever Emeralds weren't enough to secure his safety."

"So she gave him Semper?"

"She gave him Semper. The ultimate power, the power to end the world."

"But if Semper was a secret, how could it protect him?"

"It wouldn't be a secret once he was threatened. This was a time of plagues, remember. The Elizabethans believed in potions and spirits and malevolent vapors. Think about the vessel we saw in the museum, what Truman described. All of that would have found a very credulous audience in Elizabeth's time. And in fact we still believe Semper may be real."

"But how has this remained hidden all these years?"

"Because the diary is the only known reference to both Edward Filer's lineage and Semper. Or was, until you discovered the sonnet. Oliver Firth showed the diary to a small circle of fellow physicians, no one else. They all saw the threat that Semper posed. They didn't know where it was, of course. The diary indicates that Hatton somehow managed to safeguard it, even from the Filers. But they immediately dedicated themselves to preventing its ever coming to light. That meant never sharing the secrets of the diary with anyone outside their circle, which eventually became the Semper Society—physicians pledged to protect the world from a potentially deadly pandemic."

"How were you recruited?"

"My specialty is infectious diseases. I'm associated with Johns Hopkins in Baltimore. As a kind of hobby I've done some research on plagues, particularly bubonic plague."

"Nice hobby."

"Keeps me out of trouble." He looked at her. If he was expecting a smile he was disappointed. "Or so I thought. When Phelps contacted me at a medical conference I thought he was insane. Other than the diary there isn't a lot of evidence for Semper. What you and I discovered in the past few days just about doubles what's known about it. But it seemed harmless enough, and we go to some nice places—we've met in Vienna, Bangkok, Cairo, and of course Mount Kisco. The Society has a small endowment, accumulated over the years from member donations, that pays for the trips."

"Where you dress up and what, spin conspiracy theories?"

"There haven't been any theories. We mostly discuss medical issues, share our interest in the history of infectious diseases, enjoy the strippers."

She looked quickly at him and confirmed, from his grin, that he was joking. She did not smile.

"We're a pretty tame bunch, as you might guess. But then Phelps saw that press release about the sonnet, and you read a few lines of it on the news. We've been trained to be alert to anything to do with Semper, and Hatton's diary describes a sonnet by Shakespeare. Phelps told us that the clue jumped off the page, once he'd written down the portion of the poem you read from a recording he made."

"Does the diary mention the Ateeka?" she asked. He nodded. "Then why did you go with me to Washington? Why rough up Truman? You knew so much already."

"Because as much as we knew, we still didn't know where Semper was. We thought the answer might lie in the sonnet, which you had, and which you seemed uniquely able to decipher. So I had to stay close."

"And humor me by playing ignorant, accompanying me to Washington, even assaulting an old man." When he started to protest she shook her head and said, "Don't talk."

The GPS had directed them to Route 84 East, then navigated them through Hartford, heading south to the New England Throughway. They were driving across Rhode Island, about a half hour from Tunsbury, when Samuel broke a long silence.

"I'm not married," he said quietly.

"Well, that's a considerable relief," she drawled. "In fact, your marital status makes up for everything that's happened. You've lied to me, one of your members tried to kill me, earlier today you threatened me with a gun—but at least you're single, thank god for that. And a doctor, yet. Looks like I struck gold."

"Lee, I'm sorry, I don't know—"

"Do not apologize. There's nothing you can do or say, so don't try. Am I clear?"

The next voice was a woman's, with a British accent: "Take the next exit, on the right."

The GPS had brought them back to Tunsbury.

They checked into a Marriott Courtyard on the outskirts of town, not the place she'd stayed (or at least booked) during her last visit. She wanted no reminders of Mark the fisherman and Lee the dupe. She insisted on separate rooms, and he didn't argue, paying with his own credit card. Both rooms were on the second floor.

"I'd like the diary back," he said as she tried to unlock her room with one of those plastic cards that never seem to work on the first try. She held the book in her left hand, close to her body.

"No."

"Lee, try to understand what the book means to us. It's our bible, our constitution. We can't let it get away from us or, god forbid, become public."

A tiny green light flashed after the third swipe.

"I won't read it on the news tonight, if that's what you're worried about. I've learned that lesson."

"Please, Lee, I need the diary."

"I won't let it out of my sight," she said as she slipped into the room. "Enjoy your evening."

Immediately after shutting the door, she crossed to one of the two double beds and sat down. Fuck him and his Semper Society and his rationalizations. She kicked off her shoes and let out a long, slow sigh. She felt that she hadn't breathed all day and now, finally alone, the pressures of the last twelve hours descended upon her like a sudden fever, draining what was left of her energy and focus. Then she glanced at the diary, ran the palm of her hand over its ancient leather binding, and felt reenergized. Another old manuscript in which to lose herself. Only this one would lead to her future, not the past.

She made a cup of coffee from the in-room machine, then opened the book.

CHAPTER 43

29 September 1602
Hampton Court

I awoke this morning at Whitehall with my heart full of trepidation, for on this day I was to present to Her Majesty a power like no other, if the captain of the Lansdale is to be credited, and I believe he is. But fate had far worse in store for me than I could have imagined. My servant Lucy brought my morning meal to my room and asked about my uneasiness, which was all too apparent to her. "You not been right since that man come here," she said, and pointed to the small crate in which the captain had packed his evil vapor, itself inside a jewel-covered vessel. I assured Lucy that the crate had nothing to do with my ill humor, though I was impressed by the power of her observation. An ignorant African she may be, but she is as knowledgeable of the human soul as any poet or scholar. She placed a hand on my shoulder and gently rubbed. Her touch often led to carnal exertions involving regions of my anatomy far removed from the shoulder, but on this day I pushed off her hand. "Today I am to see the Queen," I told her. The hand returned to my shoulder. "Then today you need comfort," she said in that lilting patois that transformed her every sentence into a charming ditty. Again I removed her hand. "Leave me be," I said, perhaps too gruffly, for her face, always expressive, showed great disappointment, her heavy lips turning down, so too her great onyx eyes. Oh to spend the day in my chamber with Lucy, who lives to enchant me, than with that other woman, whom I live to serve. But since called to attend to a pregnant woman some thirty years past, my days have not been my own, any more than Lucy's belong to her, plucked as she was from her tribe by Portuguese bandits.

I had stayed behind at Whitehall to finish negotiations with the captain of the Lansdale and arrange for the packing and delivery of his vile bottle. But the Queen and her court had moved on to Hampton

Court, and there I went after breakfast in my rooms.

I boarded the Queen's barge at Blackfriars. The sky was dark, though it was only morning, with black-edged clouds moving swiftly downriver. The boatmen were accustomed to ferrying me. Most often I went to attend to the health of the Queen or one of her court. Today I carried a crate, neither heavy nor large but with a cargo quite fragile. I paid two men to bring it from my house to the embankment and place it on the boat, admonishing them frequently to take care. What they imagined to be inside that would cause such anxiety I cannot myself imagine, for even the richest jewels are not fragile things.

The trip was interminable, though it took but several hours. The Thames was choppy and sprayed water often upon me. A dozen times I thought to toss the cursed crate overboard, so that the evil within it would rest for eternity at the bottom of the Thames. Was it loyalty to the Queen that prevented such an action? Or mere vanity, the desire to please and be esteemed? I take pride in my indifference to power, yet am I not a slave to it? Perhaps I have been poisoned by proximity to power and those who seek it. I leave it to my maker to decide.

The noon bell from a nearby church was ringing as we arrived. Two members of the Queen's guard escorted me up the long walk to the palace, one of them carrying the crate. Their faces looked unusually long, and I thought to inquire of them if anything was amiss. But they were never a cheerful band, these servants to the Queen, so I kept to myself as we entered the palace.

I do not think Hampton Court is among Her Majesty's favorite houses. It was her father's darling, the object of his lavish attentions and purse, and so perhaps it holds unpleasant associations for her. Her mother, Anne, spent time there as well, not all of it happy, which is perhaps another reason the Queen avoids it. Then again, Her Majesty would be hard-pressed to avoid her family's history anywhere she stayed. Her past is like the wind, sometimes benign, other times destructive, touching everything in England.

In truth I have always found it a delightful house, with its beautiful gardens, spacious courtyard, and the old King's tennis court which, though rarely used these days, always speaks to me of a more carefree time. Any pleasure I might have taken from the palace was quickly quashed by the arrival of Kat, still her mistress's most loyal and devoted servant. She ran to meet me even before we had entered the royal apartments.

"Good Doctor, praise God you are here," she said. I have always liked Kat, ever since we first met that awful night so many years ago. Her good heart and loyalty tend to bubble over into hysteria, as a woman's temperament will, and yet today I felt her humour not entirely unjustified. I saw terror in her eyes, which looked red and watery, as if tears had only recently been stanched.

"What is it, Kat?" I enquired.

"My Lady is in a very bad way," she said, having never lost the habit of referring to Her Majesty in this way. "I am glad you have come."

I did not explain to her that I had not been summoned to minister to the Queen but to make a delivery. In her anguish she had overlooked the crate carried by the two guards standing behind me.

"What has caused this distress?" I asked.

She only shook her head and beckoned for me to follow. The guards stopped outside the door to her privy chamber. Before entering, I took the crate from them and brought it with me inside.

"Your Majesty, see who is here."

I saw at once that the Queen was anguished, though her back was to the door. She sat at her writing table, or rather I should say she was collapsed upon it, for her head rested on it, as if she were asleep. Yet she slept not, for I could see her shoulders heaving and hear a faint whimpering.

"It is Doctor Hatton." Kat could speak to the Queen as no one else in the realm could, with the familiarity of a friend, or perhaps sister. But this day even she sounded timid.

Her Majesty's shoulders froze. When no one spoke, I felt I had to.

"It is indeed I, Your Majesty. Are you unwell?"

"Unwell?" She spoke without turning to me. "My soul is dead. How can I be unwell when I am dead?"

"Perhaps if Your Majesty would allow me to examine—"

"Can you examine my soul, Doctor?" She spat the name of my profession like an unwanted apple pip.

"Of course not, Your Majesty, yet I—"

"Then you are useless. Leave me."

I looked quickly at Kat, whose face was now covered with tears. She shook her head to indicate that I should remain.

"What has happened to cause such anguish?" My voice trembled.

She said nothing for some time, and I fought a powerful urge to flee. The crate holding Semper was on the floor beside me. I could leave it and retreat, never to return.

Then she spoke.

"I have failed, Doctor. All is lost."

"What has been lost, Your Grace?"

"Everything!"

She turned suddenly around, and I forced myself not to gasp. My Queen had become an old woman. Where always a veneer of white powder made of her face a porcelain mask, now, without it, there was only sallow flesh, furrowed with age. Where red paint had made rose petals of lips, now her naked lips were gray, puckered worms. I had never before appreciated the effort required to make herself a Queen, and now I felt for her a deep sympathy.

"Have you not heard?" she said. Even her voice was faded.

"I have heard nothing, Your Majesty."

"Tell him, Kat, for I have neither the heart nor voice for it."

Kat stepped closer to me, as if about to share a dangerous secret.

"Edward Filer has been murdered."

With this a cry escaped from the Queen, as if she were hearing the news for the first time. I gave Kat an inquiring look, seeking more information.

"Stabbed he was while riding on his estate at Henford. Taken from his horse, and a dagger thrust into his heart."

Another cry from the Queen. I placed a finger to my lips to silence Kat.

"Who?" was all I could ask.

"We do not know." Her Majesty slowly shook her head. "His purse was missing, so it is thought that robbery was the cause. There have been reports of roving gangs of brigands in the countryside near Henford."

"They must be brought to justice," I said.

Before the Queen could answer, Kat stepped forward.

"It was Stuarts who did this, barbarians they are, and ruthless."

Mary Stuart of Scotland was many years gone, sent to the chopping block by her cousin the Queen, but her son was next in line to the throne, by some reckoning. But how would murdering Edward Filer further the Stuart cause? He could never inherit the throne. Filer's identity was still a tightly held secret, or so I assumed.

"Has someone talked?" Here I couldn't help but glance at Kat.

"How dare you!"

"Now, Kat, there can be no doubting your discretion," the Queen said. Kat glared at me, her tiny hands balled into fists. "But there are rumors. The emeralds, I should never have given my mother's emeralds to him, but he's my… how could I help myself? They are his by rights."

There was indeed still much talk at court of the Hever Emeralds, no matter that it had been many years since the Queen had given them to Filer. Only a fortnight ago his wife, Lady Sarah, had worn them to a ball, where they eclipsed the jewelry worn by all the gentry. A most injudicious display, under the circumstances, although neither Filer nor his wife knew the true story of Edward's birth, though undoubtedly they had suspicions, given the Queen's attentions and his red hair and pale complexion.

"I have failed him," the Queen moaned. "I have failed."

"Your Majesty could hardly protect him at all times," I offered.

"I have served England yet failed my son. I count myself a dismal failure on balance."

Kat and I started to protest, but she waved us off.

"Do not console me," she shouted. "Your empty words make deeper my suffering." The sudden explosion seemed to shake the room itself.

After a few moments, I dared to speak.

"What about the son?" I asked softly.

"He lives, but for how long?" The Queen's eyes betrayed something I had never seen in them before, a great insecurity. She felt impotent, this most potent of women. Suddenly she turned to Kat. "The Holbein, Kat, the Holbein!"

Kat gave a quick curtsey and hurried across the room to a great chest. I hardly thought she had the strength to raise its top, but raise it she did, and from it she took a small picture, framed simply in dark-stained walnut, which she brought to her mistress, handing it to her like a precious document, a treaty newly arrived from the Continent, perhaps, or a fragment of parchment in a saint's hand.

Her Majesty's expression softened as she considered this picture, which I could not see. I had not yet accommodated myself to her appearance and felt ashamed that I put so much stock in it. I dared not speak, and she seemed lost in contemplation.

"Come here, Doctor," she said suddenly.

I approached her, and she turned the picture toward me. It was a fine drawing of a young boy, perhaps ten or twelve, shown in profile.

"Does he not look like me?"

"He has Your Majesty's strong profile and intelligent eyes," I said.

I could see this answer did not please her. I studied the portrait more closely, glancing between it and Her Majesty. For a moment the two images merged in my mind. The old Queen and the young boy became as one.

"'Tis uncanny," I said. "The lips, the nose, the high brow."

She smiled for the first time and slowly nodded.

"Is it Edward Filer as a boy?" I dared to ask.

"His son," she answered quickly. "Charles, now ten years of age."

The Queen's own grandson. Her heir, if only she could acknowledge him.

"And a more handsome boy you will not find in all of England," Kat said with a touch of defiance.

"I fear he is frail," the Queen said, turning the portrait back toward her and moving a long finger over its surface. "He has his father's tendency toward shivering."

So the boy had the father's affliction. I wondered that the Queen herself never showed the symptoms. She must have read my thoughts.

"His… the father, he seemed most comfortable by a fire, even in summer's heat. The smallest breeze would set him trembling. And I understand Miles Stafford had a similar affliction."

A family curse, then, from the father's side. Poor Miles Stafford, who'd never lived to see his son. His only legacy a tendency toward ague.

"This changes nothing, Doctor," she said as she handed the picture to Kat, who crossed the room and placed it back in the chest, laying it down like a sleeping infant. "This vapor you described a fortnight ago, do you have it?"

I indicated the crate, which sat on the floor by the entrance to the chamber.

"I have brought it, Your Majesty."

"And does it work? Will it protect Charles?"

"I cannot say for certain, Your—"

"Have you not tried it?"

My Queen's knowledge of the laws of science was not on a level commensurate with her governing prowess.

"Were I to open it, your grace, the vapor would escape, killing all in the vicinity and perhaps letting loose a plague that might destroy the entire city. This is what I have been told, in any case. Semper, as it is called, can be unleashed but once."

I thought of the Ateeka savages, felled along with the Spanish adventurers in one great massacre, and of the bodies piled in the hull of the Lansdale. Perhaps if the vessel's ruby stopper was replaced in an instant, some of the vapor would remain inside, prepared to wreak further destruction. Or perhaps the vapor is no longer inside the vessel. Who can know for sure? But I dared not convey this observation to the Queen.

"It is the threat of it, of Semper, that gives it power," I said.

"Show me," she said, and sat down again on her chair.

I bowed and backed away from her to the crate, which I carefully opened.

"It is filled with old rags, Your Grace, to protect the vessel. I am sorry for the mess."

She waved away my apology as I reached through the fabric and firmly grasped the thing with both hands. I blew gently to clean its surface, not daring to shake it, and placed it on the Queen's writing desk.

She brought a hand to her lips, for it was indeed a fearsome thing, a frightful effigy of a seated man, naked as Adam, a deity, perhaps, encrusted by jewels of countless colors and shapes. The crown was a ruby stopper that seemed to bathe the room in rose-colored light.

The sides of the figure were decorated with paintings of a grim nature, which the Queen began to inspect, more fascinated by these crude drawings than by the stones themselves. She peered so closely I feared her nose would touch the vessel and topple it over. If it should break, I felt certain we would all die at once, and perhaps loose a plague on all of London, for I had come to believe in the power of Semper.

"What is the meaning of these designs?" asked Her Majesty.

"If I may." I stepped forward so that I was standing next to her. Kat, I observed, was keeping a wary distance, her back against the far wall, a look of torment upon her face.

"It appears that the savage who created this effigy painted an image of the vessel itself onto the side. Here." I pointed to a small picture, rendered with primitive skill, of the vessel, sitting on a pedestal of some sort, as if it were the image of a god.

"But as you can see, the round top has been removed. It is lying next to the vessel. Something appears to be rising out of the vessel."

"A vapor," the Queen whispered.

"Now, if you will allow me to turn the vessel around...."

"Yes, yes," the Queen said.

Carefully, I turned it so that the opposite facade now faced the Queen.

"Good God," she said, for this facade, the figure's back, revealed a scene of great horror, made worse, in my mind, by the primitive nature of the rendering. The artist, if he could be called that, had changed his perspective to show more than the vessel. Now we could see that it was surrounded by bodies, many bodies, lying on the ground, their mouths distended as if they had died in great agony.

"I believe this was painted as a warning, Your Grace. It was intended to show us what would happen should the vessel be opened."

"'Tis quite horrible," she said, but something in her voice told me that she was already calculating to what use she could put the thing.

"It must never be opened," I felt the need to say.

"No, never," she replied, but I could see that her mind was elsewhere, perhaps with her grandson at Henford. If Semper were real, and clearly, like me, she credited its power, then whoever possessed it would hold great power.

I felt a hand on my arm, clutching it with surprising vigor.

"Your Majesty?" I said, suddenly fearful, for she was staring at me with unblinking eyes that looked right through me to some distant place, and her pale lips were quivering.

"With this, this Semper," she whispered, "I could make him King."

CHAPTER 44

Lee woke up on top of the bedspread, fully dressed, not sure at first where she was. Harsh sunlight beat down on her, causing her to turn away. Slowly the room came into focus as her mind caught up with the events of the previous day that had brought her to the Marriott outside of Tunsbury.

She'd fallen asleep reading the diary. It had been very slow going. Rufus Hatton's handwriting was admirably neat but badly faded, with Renaissance idiosyncrasies and flourishes that challenged even an experienced reader of old manuscripts. The doctor's sporadic use of capital letters, what scholars called majuscules, was particularly irksome. Sometimes, at the beginning of a paragraph or entry, he'd use a double miniscule in place of a capital letter, particularly *ll* and *ff*. Other times he wouldn't, and sentences and paragraphs ran into each other. Punctuation was completely lawless, as it was in much Renaissance writing, even important legal documents. He tended to abbreviate words, as was customary at the time, but with no apparent logic or consistency to the practice, also typical of the period. "Her Majesty" might be spelled out in one line, then written as a confusing but ultimately comprehensible "HR Mesty" in the next, and then as a nearly impossible-to-fathom HRM in the line after that. Lee could easily picture Hatton's hand flying across the page, stopping only to dip his quill (a swan's feather, most likely, given his station, rather than the cheaper goose quill) into an inkwell. With the story he had to tell, who could blame him for eliding over the occasional—well, frequent—letter or syllable? Lee had read countless manuscripts from the period, most of them transcribed into modern type and with modern spelling and punctuation added. But reading original manuscripts was, for her, the surest route back to the Renaissance; the writer's hand, with all its quirks and oddities, was a wormhole into the past. No wonder she'd woken up unsure where she was.

She'd gotten about two-thirds of the way through before nodding off. Now, she picked up the diary, prepared to continue reading, when there was a knock at her door. She walked to the door, relieved that she'd remembered to engage the chain lock, and asked who it was.

"It's me," came the answer, then: "Samuel."

She unlocked the door but not the chain, and opened it a few inches.

"How did you sleep?" he asked.

She said nothing. Hadn't they moved way beyond small talk?

"Right. Can I come in?"

She shook her head.

"How about the restaurant downstairs, fifteen minutes?"

After a pause, she nodded and closed the door.

He was already seated at a booth by a window when she got to the hotel's coffee shop. The diary was in her purse, which she held close to her. She sat down and ordered coffee, scrambled eggs, and rye toast.

"Did you read the diary?" he asked after her coffee arrived. Then, with gratifying nervousness, he added, "Is that an okay question?"

She sipped coffee; put down the cup.

"I got through most of it."

"Amazing, isn't it?"

"All night I dreamed about Rufus Hatton, holding first one secret, then another. It was the strangest thing. I felt I was with him, listening to him tell his stories."

Her food arrived, and she dug in right away. "Does the diary end without indicating where Semper is?"

He nodded. "If it told us where to find Semper, the Society wouldn't need to exist. For all we know Hatton *did* toss it into the Thames, in which case our work has been pointless. But we don't know."

"If it isn't at the bottom of the Thames, then it's got to be here, with the Filers. I read through the part of the diary where the doctor gives the vessel to the queen. Her intention was to give it to her grandson. Don't we have to assume she did?"

"The Society has existed for three centuries. You can also assume that we've investigated every square inch of Filer property. And turned up nothing. No one here seems to know anything."

"But I was attacked when I started asking questions. They must have something to hide."

"You were looking for the emeralds at the time, don't forget. They may be here with the Filers. We know that at least two stones have turned up on the market, one years ago, one more recently, through Maurits Immersheim, so someone knows where the necklace is and is selling off stones. My bet is on the Filers."

"And they attacked me to keep me from finding them?"

"They're worth a fortune. Elizabeth Taylor's jewels were auctioned for ten times their estimated value because of who owned them. The Hever Emeralds were worn by *Elizabeth I*. They haven't been insured, as far as we know, and I'd bet no taxes have been paid on the sale of the individual stones. No inheritance tax, either."

"Or maybe the family knows where Semper is and attacked me to keep the location secret. I need to talk to them."

"They're not a communicative bunch. In fact, most of them are freaks. Very insular, and some of them are always bundled up like it's the middle of winter."

Like Edward and Charles Filer, she thought. *A tendency toward ague.*

"If they do have Semper," she said, "do you think they know what it is?"

"Doubt it. They don't have the diary, and as far as we know that's the only reference to Semper other than the Ateeka relics we saw."

"And the sonnet."

"And the sonnet," he said.

She hadn't looked at the sonnet in days, which seemed odd, since it had started the awful mess that had brought them to this place.

"Your society has had the diary for centuries and hasn't been able to locate Semper," she said. "The Filers don't have the diary but they seem very secretive, perhaps because of the Hever Emeralds, though perhaps they do know where Semper is. We saw the word on the foundation of that house, so there's definitely a connection with this town."

"Nothing's turned up for three centuries."

"The doctor gave Semper to Elizabeth to give to her grandson, Charles Filer."

"There's nothing in the diary that proves she did that," Samuel said. "The doctor only wrote about what he witnessed. He never saw the queen give the vessel to Filer. And later in the diary he hints that he found a way to safeguard Semper from ever being used as a weapon." She hadn't read up to that part yet. "We just don't know what he did."

"The answer is here in Tunsbury," she said, as much to convince herself as Samuel. "Remember I told you about land sales, huge tracts of land that no one seems to know about? I want to find that land."

"If there is still land owned by the Filers, and if it's as large a tract as you described, then how will you find a small vessel on the land, assuming it's even there?"

"At least I'll be closer." She stood up, still clutching her bag with the diary. "I'm going upstairs to read more of the diary. If you want to come with me later to look for the property, fine." She headed for the exit.

"Lee, wait." He caught up with her in the small lobby. "Maybe it's time to give this up. You're not going to find Semper here. We've been looking for three hundred years and we're no closer than we ever were."

"Looking? You mean sitting on your asses in big houses playing dress up. I'm still wanted for murder, *Samuel*. Have you forgotten that? Will you step forward and tell the police that one of your devoted members was the killer? Will you?"

"We take an oath," he said.

"Not the oath again." She could only shake her head. "I'll be back down in an hour. Have the car ready."

CHAPTER 45

20 March, 1603
Richmond

It seems I am always at the Queen's side, though she does not invite me to it. Her Majesty is gravely ill. She refuses all food and drink and will not rise from the bed her ladies have made for her on the floor of her bedchamber at Richmond, Her Majesty being unable to find peace atop her own bed. Her breathing is labored as if from hard exercise. But she will have no treatment from me or anyone. I fear she is anxious to die.

The palace fairly vibrates with whispers. Everyone is here, the entire court, all with a stake in who will succeed her. Some wish her dead, I know, for they have already allied themselves with James of Scotland, whose own mother, the traitor Mary, lost her head to the Queen's executioner. He is now waiting at the border for word that he may safely ride south to claim the crown that eluded his mother. Others would see the Queen live on, fearing the diminution of their own status when the Stuarts take power. Inside the gates of Richmond, a horse stands ready to fly north to the Queen's cousin with the news that all expect.

I whisper to no one, though I am oft asked my opinion as to Her Majesty's condition. It is very grave, but the Queen is a lion, I say, and say nothing more. In truth my heart is breaking, for when the Queen is buried a great bloodline will go into the coffin with her. I think of her father and his father, whose gifts for statecraft she wore with lightness and authority in equal measure. Is it not an injustice that these gifts be buried with her? Charles Filer might possess them, I suppose, but he will never be free to exercise his blood right. And he seems a frail sort, bundled at all seasons in furs and cloaks as if the merest breeze could bring on sickness.

She will see no one, my Queen, and shoos me away before I can even read her pulse. Yet there was one visitor this week. I confess I was astonished to see Master Shakespeare approach her quarters and gain entry. The playwright was summoned by Her Majesty, said Lord Burleigh, not a little jealous, I could see, that a mere author should be granted an audience while he was kept waiting for his summons outside her door. There were whispers that she was to commission a new play, and many saw this as a sign that her health was improved. They all look for signs like sorcerers reading the shapes of clouds or examining the entrails of fowl. Perhaps she wanted only some pleasant memories among so much gloom, for her ladies are inclined to tears when in her frail presence, and her advisors, when allowed to see her, wear serious faces made long by the issue of succession.

Perhaps she was recalling the Lord Chamberlain's men, who performed for her at Greenwich to such success decades previous. Will Shakespeare was among these players, some felt the most accomplished of them, although I never had the privilege of seeing him. Later he performed his own dramas for Her Majesty. Her love of Falstaff, the source of much merriment in two plays about King Henry IV, caused her to command a new play of Shakespeare so that fat, vainglorious knight could fall in love. It is said she has a stone for a heart, but I do not credit this, for I know her to be her heart's servant as much as any woman, and I know why she has never taken a husband. It's childbirth she fears, not the love of a man nor the prospect of sharing power. *The Merry Wives of Windsor* so delighted the Queen she bade the poet create still another entertainment for *Twelfth Night*, not two years ago. This one was a sumptuous performance of much singing and dancing and rich costumes that greatly pleased the Queen, I am told, for I was not among the hallowed courtiers invited to the royal performances, and I do not attend the Globe or other theatres, which attract a decidedly wicked and lowborn element of London.

So perhaps he had been summoned to her bedside to answer a call for a new drama. This would indeed be encouraging news, for even the prolific Shakespeare requires many weeks for a new play, as the Queen must know. He passed a goodly time with Her Majesty and when he left he made his way through the whispering courtiers without a word. He appeared lost in thought, which I took to be a good omen.

No sooner had the playwright departed than I too was summoned to the Queen by Margaret Russell, the Queen's Maid of Honor. Kat Ashley has long since gone to our maker, but I miss her each time I am shown into the Queen's chambers, for she and I shared a grave secret, and now that secret is mine alone, and doubly grave, having gone to the grave with her, and weighs the more for it. The Queen's chamber was so dark I feared I would stumble on a chair or table as I crossed it to the royal bedside. I was pleased to see her in her bed and not on the makeshift floor pallet she more often prefers. The only illumination came from around the edges of the curtains drawn shut against the daylight.

"How is Your Majesty today?" I said when I reached her bedside, though I need hardly have asked. She seemed a tiny thing, so pale she was nearly lost among her white sheets. The blanket pulled over her lay flat, as if there was nothing beneath it. Pink circles ringed her eyes, which were themselves dimmed like dying embers. Wisps of white hair escaped from beneath her cap. Truly, my heart ached for this sad specter, once as splendid as the sun itself, now obscured by the clouds of age and illness.

"You of all people know best how I am," she said. Her voice, though soft, still commanded respect. "How am I, then, Doctor?"

"Your Majesty is not well, I fear." There is a time for flattery, and a time for truth.

"You are a brilliant physician, then."

I felt my face warm at her mocking tone.

"You are not much younger than I, and yet you appear in robust health."

"Appearances can deceive, Your Majesty. My joints do cause me agony, and I find my body desires sleep more and more often, and for longer spells, even as my mind grows restless and no longer allows it. But my health matters not besides your own. I beseech your Majesty to allow me to do what I can to heal you."

"There is nothing you can do, Doctor, beyond adding to the torture I already endure." The effort to speak stole the wind from her.

"Yet I have medicines that can soothe your anguish."

"I want no medicine." Here she turned to Margaret Russell. "Be away." When the good lady hesitated, the Queen summoned all her strength. "Be away!" A moment later we were alone.

"I have had Will Shakespeare to see me this morning," she said in a quieter voice.

"I saw him quit your chamber not an hour ago."

"Yes, I imagine the full court is outside my door, watching. Waiting."

"They gather to wish Your Grace a speedy recovery."

"If that is what you think, then you are a poor judge of men after all, Doctor." She breathed heavily for some time while I waited. "I bade him write a poem for me. A sonnet." She paused to regain her breath.

"A lovely idea, your Grace."

She glanced around the room to be sure we were alone.

"It is a gift for my grandson." Another pause.

"Charles Filer," I whispered to fill the silence.

"He plays with words like a musician with notes, this Shakespeare. I have told him to conceal messages in the poem, hidden messages for Charles, from me."

"I am sure Charles Filer will be pleased."

"I want you to present the poem to him. I would do so myself, but how could I bring him here, with every eye trained on my door. How would I explain the presence of this young squire of indifferent birth?" Her chest heaved beneath the blanket.

"Your Majesty, if you would let me examine you, I may be able to relieve your shortness of breath."

"There is no relief but knowledge that I have done right by my charges. I have instructed Master Shakespeare to deliver the poem to you, Doctor, and I command you give it to Charles Filer, with whatever explanation is required."

"I will of course do as you wish."

"To be a Queen is to comprehend the full nature of power," she said after a long silence. "To be a mother is to know its limits."

"You have done so much for the Filers," I said, thinking of the Hever Emeralds, the greatest treasure in England, and of course Semper, the greatest evil.

"And yet Edward is dead, we know not whether from a thief's sword or that of a traitor. His son is yet a young man, soon to be without my protection. Can I deem myself successful if I have failed at such a personal mission?"

Her face, already wizened with age and illness, appeared to contract with anguish. I could not allow her to go to her grave, for thence she was soon to be, I was certain, in such an agony of regret.

"There is perhaps one additional measure of security you could provide young Charles Filer, Your Majesty."

Her eyes, nearly closed, opened quickly.

"You could arrange for him to leave England."

"He is the grandson of a Queen—a Tudor, no less. He cannot leave England."

"Not English rule," I said quickly. "But English soil."

"Speak clearly, Doctor. I have precious little time."

"I refer to the New World, Your Grace. The Crown owns vast lands there, as I understand it. Your Majesty could grant Charles Filer an estate in the Massachusetts Bay Colony of such expanse that would make him the envy of the Dukes of Norfolk or Somerset."

In truth I doubted that either duke would covet forested land thick with savages, but the Queen could hardly grant young Filer vast lands in England. His connection to the Crown was already suspect, as his father's had been.

"Do you think he would be safe there, in Massachusetts?"

"I believe that the jealousies that plague our old world are unknown across the sea," I said, omitting mention of the savages. In truth I would sooner trust my fate to naked cannibals than the men standing at that moment outside the Queen's bedchamber.

"It would be a new beginning in a new world. And he would start as one of the greatest landowners in the colony."

"I shall think on this," she said. "And quickly, for time is not my ally. It pains me some to think of him so far away, but then I will be far away as well." Here she gave me a sly grin, which I could not return or even acknowledge. Her face turned serious, and I felt her hand on my arm, as delicate as a child's. "You have been our good friend, Doctor."

"I have always endeavored to serve Your Majesty."

"You have kept our secret, when to divulge it might have more favorably booted you."

"Nothing could be more valuable to me than Your Grace's trust. Might I not see to your breathing, which I fear is growing more labored each minute. A poultice, perhaps, to loosen the phlegm."

She slowly shook her head.

"I need rest, and time to think on your proposal. Away with you for now, old friend." She closed her eyes, and at once her breathing grew hoarse. Her Majesty had fallen directly to sleep.

I didn't leave her for some time.

Here sleeps the most powerful woman in Christendom, I thought, as great a ruler as ever lived. It has been my privilege to serve her, to keep her great secret which will die with her, and then, when the good Lord determines that my stay on earth has reached its end, with me, for this diary shall be destroyed when I die. I have told Lucy that she is to burn it before I am in the ground. Keeping company with it has been my great comfort, for to imprison all that I have seen and known within my skull would have been as torture to my soul. Yet I must be as vigilant a protector of Her Majesty's reputation after her death as before. I must not imperil Charles Filer and his heirs, for surely they will never be safe so long as they can lay a claim, however weak, to the throne of England. Lucy, who cannot read English nor any language, I think, will destroy this diary when I am gone; she has given me her word. The thought saddens me with its futility, for I have written my soul into these pages. Vanity, all is vanity. Were truer words ever written?

CHAPTER 46

Lee put down the diary, at once exhilarated and exhausted. For a PhD candidate, one of the challenges of focusing on Elizabethan England was the fact that every possible angle of the period had been dusted off, examined and, more and more frequently of late, turned into a major motion picture. But Rufus Hatton's diary was a glimpse into the life of the Queen that only a handful of people, all of them sworn to secrecy, had ever been privileged to see. The Queen as a vulnerable, troubled mother and grandmother. The entire history of the reign would have to be rewritten through the prism of the diary.

Lee would have liked nothing better than to spend the day finishing it. But reading the diary was very slow going and particularly hard on her eyes, which burned and teared from the effort. She called Samuel at ten.

"I'm heading down to the lobby." She hung up and locked the diary in the room safe.

He was there when she arrived, wearing an unfamiliar shirt and looking far more refreshed than she felt.

"I did some shopping," he said. "New shirt, new jeans. New man." He smiled gamely.

"Who are you this time?"

The smile vanished.

"I want to go back to the Tunsbury town hall," she said. "Something clicked while I was reading the diary just now. I talked to a young woman who worked there; her name was Grace. She had a space heater under her desk turned up full blast in the middle of June. And she had on a wool sweater. Something the Queen told the doctor—"

"That Charles was like his father, Edward—neither could ever be warm."

"Grace claimed at first that she'd never heard of the Filer family, but her boss scoffed at that and mentioned that everyone knew about the Filer House, which is obviously the case. So why was Grace so secretive?

She could be a Filer herself, for all we know, given the physical link to Charles."

In the car, Samuel driving, it occurred to Lee that he was a doctor, a fact she still wasn't entirely reconciled to.

"Could a genetic trait be passed down from the sixteenth century to today?"

"You mean the inability to feel warmth? Potentially. Many diseases are caused by mutations in a single gene, which is passed down from generation to generation."

"What would cause someone to feel constantly cold?"

"Don't know. The hypothalamus gland controls internal body temperature. Though it's located at the base of the brain, it responds to signals from temperature receptors in the skin and deep inside the body. There could be a problem with the gland itself, or with the receptors. The sweat glands, technically sudoriferous glands, help the body regulate temperature. I suppose there could be some inherited disorder involving these glands. None of these is my area of specialty."

"I'm still not completely comfortable with the idea that you're a doctor."

"Lee, we need to talk about this."

"No, we need to find Semper so I can reclaim my life."

"It's been missing for four centuries."

"So was the sonnet I found, which the diary confirms is by Shakespeare. I have proof." A surge of sadness came over her. This fact alone, proof of what she'd been claiming all along about the sonnet, should have elated her. Instead, it felt irrelevant next to all that was happening.

The GPS led them to the Tunsbury town hall. Lee parked in front, along the sidewalk. At the front desk she leaned close to the thick, cloudy Plexiglas barrier and asked the receptionist, the same one who'd been on duty the first time, for Grace. She couldn't recall her last name, but it seemed unlikely there was more than one.

"What's the nature of your business?" the receptionist asked. She seemed more tired than suspicious and gave no indication that she recognized Lee.

"Personal," Lee said.

The receptionist glanced from Lee to Samuel and back again, then rose from her chair with a deep sigh and exited the vestibule through a door at the back, which she left open. Lee recognized the open office area from her last visit but couldn't see any of the desks or workers. A minute later the receptionist returned.

"She's not here." Her eyebrows arched slightly, as if she were challenging them to doubt her.

"Is she out sick?"

"What does it matter?" She lowered herself onto her chair and began typing energetically on a keyboard.

"When will she be back?"

"I don't know," she said, still typing. "If you tell me your business, I can find someone else to assist you."

"It's urgent that we speak to her," Samuel said. "Do you have a cell phone number?"

"Not that I can give out."

Lee scanned the small lobby. The only entrance to the office area, other than through the receptionist's cage, appeared to be a single door about ten feet away. Lee forced herself to thank the receptionist and headed with Samuel for the exit. At the last second she turned and sprinted to the door. It was locked.

"I have to buzz you in," the receptionist said with evident pleasure.

"And I'm guessing you're not going to do that."

She shook her head slowly, without looking away from her monitor.

Out front, Lee asked Samuel for the keys, wanting the distraction of driving. She started the engine but couldn't bring herself to put it in drive.

"Grace is in there. Why won't she see us?"

"Remember your last visit here? The natives weren't exactly welcoming."

They sat there for several minutes. Lee felt a looming sense of hopelessness. Why did she think she could find Semper when an entire organization dedicated to nothing else had been unable to do just that for hundreds of years? And if she failed, what would become of her? The search for Semper wasn't a sideline for her, as it was for the doctors, a chance to travel the world and play dress up. It *was* her life.

"Derek Martinson!" she said suddenly, recalling the man who lived in the Victorian house with the map that contained a coded "Semper." "His servant was wearing a wool sweater in June, but Derek denied knowing anything about the Filers." She put the car in drive.

"Lee, there's no point to asking people the same questions over and over."

"But we know more now that we did then."

Just as she pulled away from the curb, a maroon Honda sedan came tearing out of the town hall parking lot and made a right turn without stopping. Lee caught a glimpse of the driver.

"That was Grace!"

She accelerated to catch up with the Honda, careful to keep a discreet distance.

"She's in a hurry," Samuel said.

"And eleven in the morning is a strange hour to be leaving the office."

Grace led them through the mostly empty Tunsbury shopping area and then continued north on a road that quickly grew rural as two-family homes gave way to dilapidated farmhouses and eventually woodland.

"She must have figured out it was me asking for her," Lee said as she drove.

"But why would she run? That dragon of a receptionist wasn't going to let us back."

"She panicked, obviously. She needed to get out of there."

Lee had to concentrate to keep from drawing too close to the Honda. The farther they drove from town, the more deserted the road became, and the more obvious their presence behind the Honda. After seven miles or so she let the car come to a near halt in order to allow Grace get a substantial lead. When she accelerated again, the Honda was a quarter-mile ahead, occasionally drifting out of sight around turns or over small hills. There were few turn-offs, so Lee felt confident of not losing her.

About ten miles north of town, the Honda disappeared. Lee accelerated until she was sure she would have caught the Honda if it were still on the road.

"She must have turned off," Samuel said.

Lee slowed the car and turned it around just beyond the point where the road crossed a stream, identified by a small sign as the Crownmead River. As she began slowly to retrace their route, a line from *A Midsummer Night's Dream* came to mind, one of her favorites from that play.

"'Met we on hill, in dale, forest or mead, by paved fountain or by rushy brook.'"

"What?"

"The start of Titania's diatribe about jealous rage. I once memorized it."

"I'll bet you did."

She drove slowly, looking for a turnoff where the Honda might have gone. They were in a densely forested area with no houses or buildings of any kind on either side.

"It's the word 'mead' in the name of the river, Crownmead, that triggered the memory. Mead to Shakespeare was a field."

"There's the turn-off!" Samuel shouted. At that very instant, jerking the car to the right, Lee also shouted.

"Field!" She turned into a dirt road, not much more than a broad path between a grove of pine trees. The road was deeply rutted and barely wide enough for the car. "Mead means field and a crown is a hat."

"So?"

"Crown… hat. Mead… field. The Crownmead River is the Hatfield. Where Edward Filer was born in England. The river was named after the birthplace of the Filers."

"You're amazing," he said. She was aware of him watching her.

"No, the Filers are amazing. They can't help themselves from hinting at their origin. In the ledger books in the town hall, there were erasures where the location of the Filer land purchases had been noted. They began with a capital *c*. Crownmead."

About fifty yards in she saw a sign, hand-painted on a board attached to a metal stake in the ground: Private Property. Another hundred yards in, another sign: "Tresspassers will be prosecuted." With an extra *s* before the *p*.

"Lee, are you sure you want to do this?" She pressed on the accelerator, feeling more confident about navigating the narrow road. "What are we going to do when we find her, anyway?"

"I won't sit around and wait for something to happen, the way you and your fellow jokers have done for all these years."

The pine forest gave way to a dense area of maples and oaks as they drove deeper into the property. The trees formed a canopy over the road, cloaking it in deep shadow. Lee noticed a stone wall running along the right side of the road, about ten yards in the woods. She pointed it out to Samuel.

"This was once farmland," she said. "That wall would have been built with rocks cleared from the land."

They drove for several minutes. After a gentle turn in the road, the forest ended suddenly, replaced by an astonishingly broad, well-tended lawn. Lee slowed the car to a crawl and shielded her eyes with a hand against the sudden sunlight. When her eyes adjusted to the brightness, she was able to make out a white farmhouse about two hundred yards ahead, atop a slight rise.

She pulled the car to the side, driving across a stretch of lawn that sloped downward, back toward the woods. This spot appeared to offer some cover from the house. She stopped the car and got out.

"This must be a thousand acres," Samuel said as he walked around the car to join her.

"It's the tract of land that Elizabeth granted to the Filers, the land there's no record of in any of the Tunsbury recorded deeds. I want a closer look." She headed for the big house, close to the edge of the tree line.

The land gradually rose as they approached the house, still hugging the perimeter of the cultivated area. At one point the entire landscape was visible. In addition to the large house they had first spotted there were four smaller buildings, all white clapboard.

A hidden compound not found on any local tax rolls. Semper had to be close by.

She saw the maroon Honda parked behind the first house they'd seen, which was the largest one by far. When they were as close to it as possible, while still partially shielded by the trees that ringed the lawn, she signaled for Samuel to follow her and sprinted toward to the house. It took less than a minute to reach it. She flattened herself against the side; a moment later Samuel joined her. Then, moving slowly, she sidled over to a window and looked in.

It appeared to be a living room, quite large. The ceiling was low, the floors dark wood. Colonial-era furniture was neatly arranged into two seating areas. She had the sense of viewing a museum rather than an occupied home. It looked authentic but unlived in.

She edged along the perimeter of the house, heading toward the back. The next room was a dining room. At the center was a two-pedestal table, early nineteenth century, she guessed, surrounded by eight shield-back chairs. Another empty room.

She turned the corner to the back of the house and passed two more dining room windows. The next set of windows, she predicted, would look into the kitchen.

She was right. And this room was not empty.

It was a large kitchen with white-painted, nickel-hinged cabinets that appeared to have been built in the 1920s. On an inside wall a large, open-hearth fireplace was in full flame; next to it was a tall pile of logs. There were two figures in the room. Grace and a man who looked to be about fifty stood in front of the fire.

Lee sidled away from the window and turned to Samuel.

"Did you bring the gun?" She meant the one he'd taken from Mt. Kisco.

"Lee, we can't just break in there and—"

"Did you bring it?"

He nodded.

"Give it to me." When he hesitated, she grabbed the waist of his pants, yanked him toward her, and patted down his front pockets. The pistol was in the right pocket. He pushed her hand away before she could get it.

"I'll handle the gun, Lee."

The condescension was infuriating. She edged back to the window and, reassured that Grace and the man were still in the kitchen, crouched down and crawled below the window, Samuel close behind. There was a door to the kitchen ahead. She stood up and began to move faster, Samuel directly behind her.

"I'll go in first. Then you follow with the gun. I doubt the door's locked."

Instead of Samuel's voice she heard an explosion, then felt tiny flecks of wood from the side of the house bite into her cheeks.

A second explosion. She looked down the hill, away from the house. A man was running uphill toward the house, a rifle trained directly at them.

"I'll fire again, and this time I'll aim *for* you, not above your heads," he shouted as he continued to approach.

"The gun," she whispered at Samuel, whose empty hands hung at his side.

"He's got a rifle, Lee. Aimed at our heads."

That wouldn't have stopped her.

The kitchen door opened, and Grace and the man she'd been talking to emerged. The man with the rifle was a few yards away. He looked familiar.

"Derek Martinson," she said a moment later. The town historian with the wool-clad servant who knew nothing about a large tract of land belonging to the Filers.

"You should have stayed away," he said when the rifle was just a few feet from her chest. "Now it's too late."

CHAPTER 47

"Edward, check them for weapons."

Derek Martinson had seemed almost avuncular in his home in Tunsbury. Now he came off as anything but kindly. He was still dressed like a fussy old antiquities collector in starched blue oxford shirt and crisply pressed gray slacks. But his expression was rigid to the point of fury, just barely holding back an instinct to attack.

The other man, the one who'd been talking to Grace in the kitchen, walked over to Samuel and patted him down. He found the pistol, which he placed in his own pocket before turning to Lee. She suddenly realized that she'd seen him before: the contractor who'd threatened her at the Filer House in town, Edward Aspinall. Despite everything, she had to marvel that Aspinall might well be a direct descendant of the greatest monarch in English history, named for the first Edward Filer, perhaps, who had himself been named for the queen's beloved younger brother and predecessor on the throne. Was there a dynastic resemblance? Edward was tall and thin, with pale skin, and his hair, while thinned with middle age, had a reddish tinge. There was an Elizabethan delicacy to his features—long, narrow nose, pale, thin lips, faint blue eyes. Grace, who looked to be in her mid-twenties, shared these qualities, and it occurred to Lee that she was probably Edward's daughter. But her fearful expression, hunched posture, and buttoned-up cardigan sweater were anything but regal.

"This way." Derek Martinson nodded away from the house, back toward the edge of the woods. When Lee and Samuel hesitated, he raised the end of the gun so that it pointed directly at her face. "*Walk*."

As they walked, he followed close behind.

"Go back inside, I'll take care of this," Martinson told Edward and Grace. Edward immediately protested, and in his brief flash of defiance Lee recalled the earlier encounter in Tunsbury. He'd been dressed in a suit, then, the formal attire lending him an air of authority that he lacked now. No wonder he'd been given a sweetheart of a deal to develop the Filer property in town. He *was* a Filer.

"I'll handle this," Martinson said, cutting off debate. Aspinall took Grace's elbow and led her back into the house.

Martinson was taking them to the woods to execute them and didn't want Grace to see it. When Lee started to turn around, Martinson jabbed the rifle into her.

"Keep walking and don't turn around," he barked.

"Are you a Filer, too?" Samuel asked as they walked.

"We're all Filers here, by birth or marriage. My mother was a Filer. Some of us live in town, others here. But this is our home."

"Do you know who you are?" Lee asked. "Who you're descended from?"

"Charles Filer settled here in 1614. We are all descended from him."

"And before that?"

"Before that we came from England."

"But do you know who you're descended from?"

A momentary pause, then: "Farmers in the Midlands."

Lee almost laughed. "You're Tudors, you're direct descendants of—"

"We are Filers. Americans. Whatever we were in the old country is of no interest to us here."

Why was he so emphatic about denying the connection to Elizabeth?

"Is it Semper? Are you afraid that you're in danger because of Semper?"

"I don't know what you're talking about." The voice was flat.

"You might as well tell us," Samuel said. "You're going to shoot us anyway. We saw Semper on that mapmaker painting in your home, and written in brick on the foundation of the Filer House."

"Semper is the family's motto," he said with a defensive edge. "It means 'forever.'"

"We know what it means," Lee said. They were only ten yards or so from the edge of the woods. "But why the secrecy? Someone attacked me when I was last here. And now this. It has to be Semper."

"I don't know what you're talking about." He was clearly lying, and yet there was something in his voice that rang true, a sense of puzzlement as well as defensiveness.

"Then it's the emeralds," she said, "the Hever Emeralds."

He said nothing for a few moments. When he next spoke, they were at the edge of the woods.

"Keep going," he said. Meaning into the woods themselves. Where their execution wouldn't be seen from the house. From one corner of her eye, Lee saw something odd. A white house, two stories high with a peaked roof. It looked out of place in what was otherwise a settled-in landscape, ancient trees and old buildings comfortably occupying the terrain like interlocking puzzle pieces. This house didn't fit, and in a moment she understood why: it was the Filer House, from town, the one Edward Aspinall had been arranging to move to make way for a new subdivision. The house with "semper" in the brick foundation. It must have been moved only the day before.

"You don't have to do this," Samuel said. "We mean you no harm. We'll leave and never come back. You have our word."

"That's what they…." He stopped himself.

Lee leapt right in. "That's what they all say? Who? Who else has been here asking about Semper?"

"No one."

He sounded firm and, for a change, not defensive. She believed him.

"But you were about to say—"

"No one in my lifetime. But they have come before, many years before."

"Looking for Semper?" she asked.

"That's right. They come, they make inquiries, just like the two of you, they promise to leave us alone, and when they don't find what they're looking for they attack us."

"Who did this?" Samuel asked as they continued walking into the woods. The air was suddenly cooler, musty with moldering leaves, and the tall canopy of trees dimmed the light.

"We don't know who it was. This happened more than a century ago. Half of the family, everyone on this property at the time, were killed. We have been warned that others would come, generation after generation, but nothing happened. And then you showed up, asking questions. Okay, this is far enough."

He was going to shoot them in the back.

Lee turned around to face him.

"You don't want to do this."

Martinson's face looked resolute, however, and the rifle was raised directly at her chest. He stood about two yards from them, too far for her to make a successful lunge at him. If she and Samuel ran in opposite directions, there was a chance that one of them might survive, depending on how good a shot Martinson was. But then what? It was at least a mile to the road.

"You're a Tudor," she said. "You and the rest of them here, you're the only descendants of one of the greatest dynasties the world has ever known. Why do you hide away like this? You have stories to tell—great stories. If you kill us you condemn yourself and your family to hiding out for another century. Why are you hiding? You should be proud of who you are."

"We are proud. But also private. And we intended to remain private."

She needed to say something, anything, to keep him engaged.

"The warm clothes, even in summer. Edward Filer, Elizabeth's son, had the same affliction, did you know that?"

His eyes narrowed, and the gun lowered just a hair. He didn't know.

"We have a diary," Samuel said. "Written by the physician who witnessed the birth of Edward Filer. He describes Edward and Charles Filer as frail and always cold."

"We knew it went back generations. Some of us escape it, but many do not. Where is this diary?"

"I can take you to it," she said.

His eyes lost focus for a moment, then: "You're not leaving the property."

"You don't have to do this," Lee said. "I study the past; I want nothing to do with whatever you have going on today. None of this interests me." She waved an arm to encompass the forest and the cultivated compound behind them. "Please."

"We have our own history," he said. "It talks of men coming to search our property. It talks of thieves and government agents."

"Looking for Semper?" Samuel asked. "But no one has known about Semper for centuries."

"Not for Semper," Martinson almost whispered.

She suddenly got it. "For the emeralds. They came looking to steal the emeralds. And the government came to investigate them—where you got them, whether tax was owed."

"We learned to keep to ourselves."

"Because you live off the emeralds. You've sold them, one at a time, over the years. Each one could support this place—" again she waved an arm—"for years."

"We know about the murder of the emerald dealer in New York," Martinson said. "A horrible death. It followed your visit here. It confirmed that no one must be allowed to penetrate our world."

"But you're not invisible in Tunsbury," Samuel said. "You work in the town, or some of you do."

"This place isn't on any local property maps," Lee added.

"We are very generous to the local community. What we avoid in property taxes we more than make up for in other ways. The Filer name itself disappeared long ago, which has made it easier to maintain our anonymity. One generation produced only girls."

"The Tudor curse," Lee said.

"Keeping our heads down has worked for us for four centuries. And it will continue to work." With this he raised the barrel of the rifle, which he'd allowed to drift lower. "I'm sorry," he said. "I wish I didn't have to do this."

Samuel stepped toward him. "Please, wait—"

A muffled bang, like the crack of a whip, reverberated through the silent woods. Lee turned to Samuel, expecting him to collapse from the gunshot. But he was apparently unharmed. She looked back at Martinson just as the rifle fell from his hands. A second later, he crumpled to the ground. The back of his head was gone. In its place was a mass of blood and brain.

CHAPTER 48

Lee looked beyond the fallen body of Derek Martinson to the Filer compound, but saw no movement. Whoever had shot him was either hiding behind a tree or had retreated so quickly he was already beyond their range of vision.

Samuel picked up the rifle. "Let's get out of here. The car is that way." He pointed in the opposite direction of the compound. "We can get to it through the woods."

"Who shot him?" Lee asked as they quickly threaded their way through the woods. Running was out of the question, given the density of the trees and the uneven ground.

"Don't know, and we're not waiting to find out."

Had one of Martinson's relatives killed him? Why? Preventing their murder by murdering one of their own hardly made sense. She tried to think it through as they speed-walked, but only a minute ago she had mentally prepared herself for a gunshot to the chest. Nothing felt logical, or real, any longer.

"Are you sure this is the right direction?" she asked after they'd been moving for at least five minutes. She felt completely disoriented.

"You got a map?"

They kept going. After another few minutes she saw a clearing ahead, lit as if from giant klieg lights suspended above, and felt encouraged. But it wasn't the road, only a small patch of land, about the size of a baseball infield. When her eyes adjusted to the sudden brightness, she saw that it was full of tombstones.

There were about fifty of them, perhaps more, neatly lined up in rows spaced a casket-length apart. All were identical granite rectangles engraved in the same style. As she hurried across the clearing she caught many of the names. About half were Filers, with birth dates going back to the eighteenth century. Below the names were the dates of birth and death. Below the dates, on every tombstone, was a single word.

Semper.

The more recent names were not Filers. One generation produced only girls, Martinson had said.

Samuel had used the clearing as an opportunity to pick up the pace. He was almost beyond it, back into the woods on the far side, when something caught her attention.

A group of older-looking headstones, not quite erect, listing with age, was clustered off to one side. They were more haphazardly situated; no doubt the people who'd dug those graves had not anticipated how crowded the cemetery would one day become. The shape and lettering were the same, however, with "Semper" at the bottom of each one. As she ran by Lee noted the birthdates. December 3, 1649. August 10, 1703. May 25, 1699. Most of these bore the name Filer. She slowed almost to a halt, the scholar in her drawn to these ancient markers.

A rustling, coming from the woods behind them where they'd just been. Then a faint, rhythmic thudding. Footsteps.

"They're chasing us," she shouted at Samuel, who was at least twenty yards ahead of her, already beyond the clearing.

She started to run.

And then stopped.

At the very edge of the clearing, at one end of the section of old headstones, was a much larger and more elaborate marker. In fact it stood sentinel over the entire cemetery, like the head of a marching army. As tombstones went it wasn't particularly ornate, just significantly taller than the others, with a rounded top that supported a simple cross.

"Lee, come on!" Samuel had stopped about ten yards into the woods on the far side of the clearing. Behind her, the crunching of dry leaves grew louder, and she heard voices.

The inscription was longer than the others.

EDWARD FILER
Born June 22, 1555
Died March 1, 1582

Here, as before, for all time.
With God I be
A cross I am
Ever my hopes repair.

Edward Filer, Elizabeth's son. But he had died before the Massachusetts colony was settled. What was his grave doing in Tunsbury?

Only that morning she'd read in the diary of the queen's intention, suggested by Rufus Hatton, to bestow an estate in Massachusetts Colony. Here was proof that the queen had indeed made the gift. But how had Edward's grave ended up in this place?

"Lee, let's go!"

She ran her fingers along the front of the headstone, over the name "Filer." She reread the inscription and took out her phone to snap a photo of it. Then a sharp crack, not a gunshot but a branch breaking underfoot, jerked her back to reality. She sprinted across the clearing and into the woods, quickly catching up to Samuel.

"What the hell are you thinking?" he shouted as he resumed running.

She kept close to him, praying that they were heading in the right direction. Every few yards, she glanced back. The third time she saw something, a flash of color. Clothing.

"They're catching up," she panted.

As if to confirm this, the sound of a gunshot pierced the forest, then another.

"Look!" Samuel pointed ahead as he ran. There was a brightening about twenty yards farther on.

Fortunately, the trees were spaced close together, forcing them to zigzag as they ran and providing good cover from the rifle shots, which now occurred every few seconds. With each explosion, Lee expected to feel a bullet in her back and fall.

The clearing was the dirt drive, but their car was nowhere in sight.

"This way!" Samuel shouted, pointing to his right.

"Are you sure?"

He turned sharply right and continued running. By keeping within the forest, about ten yards in, they retained the cover of the irregularly spaced trees.

A gunshot was followed almost instantly by a small explosion about chest high in a tree just to her left.

What if the car was in the opposite direction? It seemed to Lee that they were heading back toward the compound, not toward the road. Another gunshot. She didn't dare turn around, but the explosion sounded closer than before.

"There!"

Ahead, barely visible through the trees, was a splash of blue. The car. Samuel took out his keys while running.

"Lee, here." He slowed a bit to let her catch up and then, while still moving, he handed them to her like a runner passing a baton. "You drive,

I'll give you cover. Wait until we're right next to the car before leaving the woods."

They ran for another thirty seconds, then he shouted "Now!" and turned abruptly to the left, toward the car.

The pursuers were getting closer. She followed Samuel to the car, circling it to get to the driver's side. She opened the door and slid in, then started the engine.

"Get in!" she shouted through the closed passenger door.

Now she saw them, two men with rifles. One of them was Edward Aspinall. Both stopped at the edge of the woods, about fifteen yards from the car. Samuel, using the car for cover, fired at them with Martinson's rifle, missing. The two men dove for cover behind the trees.

"Drive!" Samuel shouted at her.

Did he expect her to leave him there? She put the car in drive and floored the accelerator. The car lurched forward. Immediately she swung it to the right, toward the two Filers, who were still taking cover behind trees. Then she yanked the wheel to the right again, so that the car was now facing the opposite direction it had been parked, between the Filers and Samuel.

"Get in!" she screamed just as a rifle shot shattered the window behind her on the driver's side. She saw both men step out from behind the trees, rifles trained directly on her.

She lurched her body to the right for cover, so that her head was almost resting on the front passenger's seat. Looking up, she could just make out Samuel, crouching behind the car, firing back at them. There was a momentary lull in the shooting—the two men must have retreated behind the trees. The rear door opened and Samuel dove in.

Without sitting up, she jammed her right foot down on the gas pedal. The car lunged forward. Gunshots erupted; the driver's side window shattered. Shards of glass rained down on her, biting into her face and hands.

She didn't dare sit up even as the car shot forward. She prayed the car didn't hit a tree. If it did, the two men would be on top of them.

"Go right! Turn the wheel *right*!" Samuel was sitting up, navigating for her. With her left hand, she jerked the wheel to the right. The car swerved.

"Now left! *Left*!"

She palmed the wheel left, and the car swerved.

Gunfire continued, but it sounded a bit farther off.

"Okay, hold the wheel steady."

The back window exploded.

"*Shit*!"

Was he hit? The car was still hurtling forward. The risk of slamming into a tree was at least as great as getting hit by a bullet. Either way, she'd be dead.

So she sat up. The car was skirting the right side of the road, less than a yard from the tree line. She jerked the wheel to the left. A bullet hit somewhere on the trunk. She straightened the car, her foot still hard on the gas pedal.

In seconds they were out of range.

"Samuel? Are you all right?" No answer. "*Samuel*?"

Finally he answered.

"Yeah, I'm all right."

She glanced in the rearview mirror at Samuel, crouched in the back. His left hand, covered in blood, was pressed against the left side of his head.

CHAPTER 49

"What happened to you?" Lee glanced at Samuel in the rearview mirror once they were safely back on the public road, heading toward Tunsbury. "Are you okay?"

"Surface wound," he answered. "Bullet grazed my skull."

"We'll find a hospital."

"No hospital. Stop at a drug store. I'll tell you what to get."

His voice sounded shaky but resolute. She had many questions, beginning with who had saved their lives by shooting Derek Martinson, but he was in no condition to talk. So she drove at a fast pace, stopping at a Walgreens in a strip mall just outside of town. It took her less than five minutes to get the antiseptic gel, gauze pads, scissors, disposable razor, adhesive tape, and aspirin. At the hotel, she dropped him off at a side entrance that offered access to guests with a room key; he'd attract far too much attention if he crossed the lobby holding a bloody hand to his head.

Up in the room, she finally got a good look at him. Once she managed to get beyond all the blood, which covered most of the left side of his head, matting his hair into wet clumps, she could see that the bullet had skimmed his skull, cutting a path through the thin layer of flesh that protected it.

"I don't think it broke your skull," she said, feeling vaguely ridiculous giving a diagnosis to a physician.

"My skull more than likely deflected the bullet, just enough to prevent it from breaking the surface. I did my ER rotation at Maryland General in Baltimore. We saw a lot of surface wounds to the head. The pain was from the bruised skull."

"Are you in a lot of pain?"

He closed his eyes and nodded slowly.

She filled a glass with tap water and handed it to him with two aspirins. He asked for the bottle and emptied a handful of pills into his palm. He swallowed them with one long gulp of water.

"Ready to play nurse?" His voice was hoarse.

Truthfully, she felt queasy just looking at the wound. But she'd been out of her comfort zone for days and figured she could get through dressing a wound. He walked her through the process, from cutting away the hair around the wound and dabbing it with antiseptic to applying gauze and strips of bandages. When she was done, he got up and checked out her handiwork in the mirror over the bureau.

"I don't look too frightening, do I?"

"You look like someone who was shot in the head." She sensed that she was more rattled by the procedure than he was. But a moment later, he lay down on the bed and said he needed to close his eyes.

"Don't let me sleep more than an hour, in case I have concussion." He was out moments after his head touched the pillow.

She took a hot shower, scrubbing his blood from her hands and under her fingernails. She felt both encouraged and frustrated. Semper was on the Filer property, she felt certain—otherwise, why was the family willing to kill them to prevent them from leaving? It wasn't about the emeralds. She strongly suspected that Semper might be buried in the cemetery, but she wasn't about to dig up a grave on a hunch. As the hot water washed over her, she felt frustration begin to smother more positive feelings. Semper was both within reach and out of range and she'd never be vindicated—or safe—until she found it.

She dried off and considered getting back to the diary. Then she recalled the headstone of Edward Filer. What was it doing in Massachusetts? True, it was not uncommon for earlier settlers to bring the remains of their parents with them to the New World, rather than abandon them to an eternity of neglect. Had Charles Filer brought his father's coffin to the New World?

And that strangely worded inscription. She retrieved her phone from her pants pocket. The photo was tiny but quite clear. Holding the phone close to her face, she read the strange inscription.

Here, as before, for all time.
With God I be
A cross I am
Ever my hopes repair.

Strange enough as poetry, but as an epitaph it was bizarre. "A cross I am?" What could that mean? Ditto "Ever my hopes repair." She'd come across nothing like it in all her readings of Elizabethan literature. She got a paper and pen from the desk and copied it out. The entire nightmare had begun with a poem. Perhaps this bit of verse also contained a clue.

Approach it like a scholar. Let the text inform the reader, not the other way around.

She began with the first line. Right away one thing jumped out at her: the alliteration of "for" in two words: before and for. Nothing in Renaissance poetry was accidental, and certainly not when it was etched in a granite headstone. So, why the repetition of the "for" sound? Just a poetic conceit, or was there hidden meaning? A reference to something that came before? Something that was lying "before" the headstone? But if the repetition of the "for" sound was deliberate, then it wasn't either of the two words that the writer wanted to call attention to. The two words were calling attention to something else.

What?

She put down the paper and closed her eyes, so frustrated she felt herself trembling.

And the moment she shut out the visible world, she heard it.

Here.

She sat up and grabbed the paper. The key word in the line, the *instruction*, was the first one: here. With her eyes closed the word could sound like "hear"—to listen. And in Elizabethan times, *here* and *hear* were often spelled interchangeably.

The writer wanted her to *hear* the inscription. So she read it out loud.

"Here, as before, for all time.
With God I be
A cross I am
Ever my hopes repair."

It made no more sense aloud than when read silently. She read it a second time aloud, then a third. Nothing. Perhaps the instruction to "hear" referred only to the first line. She read that aloud: "As before, for all time." She closed her eyes again and read it from memory. "As before, for all time."

The alliteration struck her more powerfully with her eyes closed. *Before. For.*

She opened her eyes. She had it.

Before.

For.

Four.

She was meant to *hear* the words, not read them. *Four* was the buried clue. A number.

What to do with it? She tried every fourth word, beginning on the next line and came up with: "Be am repair."

Even odder than the original. How about every fourth letter instead? She used the pen and paper to record the letters, and when she was done she almost sobbed with relief, her suspicion confirmed.

h i c s e m p e r

She rewrote the letters, adding a space.

hic semper

She tossed aside the pen and paper and crossed to the bed, where she shook Samuel awake.

"I know where Semper is," she said the moment his eyes opened. "I've found it."

CHAPTER 50

At a Home Depot several miles from downtown Tunsbury they bought two spades, two pairs of gardening gloves, two flashlights, and two packages of AA batteries. They had an early dinner at a chain steakhouse and sipped coffee until darkness fell. Then they headed back to the Filer property.

It had taken Lee less than a minute to explain to Samuel the message hidden in Edward Filer's headstone. And although he'd tried to temper her conviction that 'hic semper'—here semper—meant that the vessel was buried with Edward Filer, she sensed that he agreed with her; they'd found it at last.

"If we find it we have an obligation to destroy it," Samuel said as they drove. "I've taken an oath."

"Right, the whole Elks Club thing."

"It's not a joke. There's a possibility that Semper could be a viral strain we've never seen before and therefore have no immunity to. No government can have it, not even ours. No one can be trusted with it. You heard Martinson talk about men coming for Semper a hundred years ago."

"Was that your society?"

"No. But over the centuries there have been rumors of others who knew about Semper. We don't know how they learned of it. There might have been an oral tradition, passed down from the captain of the Lansdale."

"But I need it to prove that I didn't kill Alex Folsom or anyone else. If one of your lodge brothers would come forward and tell what really happened in my apartment that night, I wouldn't need to be grave robbing right now. But none of you will say anything, including you. I need to connect the murder in my apartment to Semper—that's how I can prove I had nothing to do with it."

"We've been through this. If I tell what I know I'll bring down the entire organization. I can't do that."

"Instead, I go to jail for life."

"This thing may have the power to destroy mankind. Next to that—"

"Just drive, okay?"

"And there's someone else out there looking for Semper, the maniac who killed David Eddings and Maurits Immersheim. It's not just the Semper Society. I'll get you out of this, I promise."

She said nothing, and certainly not what she was thinking, which was that she had never counted on anyone to protect her and wasn't about to start now. If the events of the past week had taught her anything, it was that she was on her own and always had been.

Samuel pulled the car off the road about twenty yards past the entrance to the Filer property. There was a grassy shoulder, perhaps ten yards wide. He drove the car as close to the edge of the woods as he could, and angled it between two trees as far in as possible so that most of it was obscured from the road. They got out, retrieved the shovels and gear from the back seat, and headed back to the dirt driveway, hugging the edge of the woods for cover.

"I hope I can get us back to that cemetery," Samuel said. "I'm guessing it's about a quarter mile ahead. I know it's off to the right, but I have no idea where to turn in."

"We have all night," Lee said, walking briskly ahead of him. "We'll find it."

The night was windy, overcast, and starless, but a blurry half-moon occasionally made an appearance as clouds blew across the sky, casting the long, straight road in quivering luminescence.

After ten minutes they turned into the woods, their progress slowed by the almost complete darkness caused by the dense tree cover. Only when they were at least a hundred yards into the woods did they dare turn on the flashlights. The two beams of light somehow made them seem smaller, more vulnerable. They trained them on the ground, enabling them to walk faster without fear of tripping over a root or fallen branch. Lee used the shovel as a walking stick.

After ten minutes or so, they hadn't come across the cemetery.

"I think we've gone too far," Samuel said. "We should turn around and walk more in this direction." He pointed to his left. Lee had no idea if left was the way to go or even if they'd gone too far into the woods already. She followed him for another five minutes in silence, trailing the beams of their flashlights.

"Okay, let's try this way." Samuel sounded frustrated and uncertain as he headed off to his right without waiting for Lee to respond. The woods felt enormous. As they walked quickly, almost running, she had the oddest sense that she was stationary while the trees were moving toward them, faster and faster. She began to feel light-headed and stumbled a few times. She grazed her shoulder on a tree, caroming off it as if drunk. She needed a break.

"Samuel, I think I need to—"

"There it is!"

He aimed his flashlight straight ahead and fanned it back and forth. The beam illuminated one tree after another, from a few feet in front of them to twenty yards ahead. But at the center, roughly straight ahead, the light found no purchase. A clearing.

He practically ran the last thirty yards, Lee doing her best to keep up. When she got to where he was stopped, she waved her flashlight over the tiny cemetery. In the darkness it felt particularly defined and isolated, like it had been carved from the dense forest by a fallen meteor. She walked among the dozens of closely laid tombstones, reading the inscriptions. The dates ranged from mid-seventeenth century to the most recent, ten years earlier. The last tombstone bearing the Filer name was from the mid-1950s; the inability to bear male heirs, the Tudor curse, lived on along with the shivering condition.

A line from the diary came back to her, a quote from the dynasty's founder: "How can I protect him? How can I make certain that the line continues?" Elizabeth had succeeded in this as with most other things: her line lived on, if not the name itself. Filer—son of ER. The land she'd granted to her grandson was still Filer land. The necklace she'd given to her son Edward continued to support generations of Filers. And Semper, the ultimate power, was still with him.

"Let's get started." Samuel's annoyed tone snapped her back to the present. She joined him at the largest headstone and reread the inscription. Now the important letters, every fourth one, jumped out at her. *Hic semper.* She ran an index finger over them, feeling a distant but almost visceral connection to their author.

She started at the sound of Samuel's shovel digging into the ground in front of the headstone. The entire forest seemed to shudder in response.

"Try to keep the grass intact," he said as he carefully lifted a foot-square piece of sod from the ground and laid it to the side. "We can put it back when we're done, and in a few days no one will know we were here."

She began digging close to the headstone, not entirely comfortable committing what was certainly a sort of desecration. The soil was loose and gave easily to the rounded edge of the shovel. She laid each piece of sod to the side, as Samuel had done, essentially reconstructing the top layer several feet away from the grave itself. When they had uncovered a rectangular area roughly four feet by six feet, they began to dig straight down, piling the soil between the grave and the sod.

Each time their shovels dug into the ground, the sound echoed off the surrounding trees. Lee felt certain that someone was listening. Occasionally she'd stop digging to listen.

"Samuel, listen!" she whispered when they had dug about a foot below the sod.

He stopped, cocked his head, and shrugged.

"I thought I heard something," she said. The woods were reassuringly dark; if someone was out there, wouldn't they need a flashlight?

A moment later, her shovel hit something hard. Samuel heard it and thrust his shovel straight down. It hit a hard surface with a sharp, metallic sound.

"Careful!" Lee said. "It's almost four hundred years old."

"If it's still intact then it's not wood," he said.

"I won't deface something this old and sacred." He shot her a look that bordered on disdain and she added, "Just don't jam your shovel into it, okay?

He didn't answer but used a less violent, more horizontal movement as he cleared the remaining layer of soil from on top of the casket. It took them about ten minutes to remove the entire surface. The coffin, which was buried about a foot down, was an unornamented rectangle. It appeared to be made out of some sort of metal, which wasn't surprising; wealthy Elizabethans were often laid to rest in lead coffins, as the metal was believed to preserve the body more effectively. This was especially true for those buried inside churches. Survivors didn't want to face the unpleasant odors of a rotting casket or decomposing corpse.

"It's too heavy to pull out of there," Samuel said. "I'm going to try opening it without moving it." He teased the shovel between the coffin and the soil; shimmied it until he found the groove under the coffin lid. "I'll be careful," he said, shooting her a quick glance before pressing down on the handle, forcing the blade of the shovel up.

His first attempt resulted in an eerie creaking sound, like old floorboards in winter. His shovel slipped out of the groove and shot up, causing him to lose his grip. He picked up the shovel and reinserted it along the side of the coffin. This time he ran it back and forth along the groove under the lid.

"Here," he said. "There's a deeper space under the lid."

He pushed the shovel into the groove, rotating it back and forth to get the deepest possible purchase, then pressed down on the handle. The creaking was louder this time; it sounded like nails being wrenched up slowly, unwillingly. The center of the lid began to arch.

"Take your shovel and jab it in next to mine," he said. She walked around him and inserted her shovel a few inches to the right of his, first shoving it straight down between the dirt and the coffin, then angling the blade until she found the groove. As she pressed down on the handle, she felt the lid begin to give a bit. Though made of metal, it was less than an inch thick.

"Okay, hold it there." Samuel removed his shovel, walked around her, and placed it a few inches to her right. The lid was looser now, so his shovel easily found its way under it. Without waiting for instructions, she pulled out her shovel and walked around him and repeated the process. Then he moved in the opposite direction, so that within minutes they had loosened the entire length of the coffin lid.

"Okay, now you take that end," he said, pointing to the end closest to the headstone. "I'll take this one. Try to get the shovel in as far as you can." The lid loosened, and she was able to insert almost half the shovel blade. "Now let's pry it off together."

They pushed down on the handle together, and the lid lifted an inch or so.

"Angle it around to the end, like this." He shimmied his shovel around the corner of the coffin until it was at the short side of the rectangle. She did the same at the opposite end. "Now push!"

The entire lid began to rise.

"It's not hinged," he said as he continued to jimmy his shovel deeper under the lid. "But it's heavy as hell." He slid his shovel around the next corner, and she did the same, so that they were now prying up the long side opposite the one they'd started on. As they pumped the shovel handles up and down, she felt the lid begin to rise.

Her arm muscles were straining to the point of pain. Little by little the lid began to rise from one end, as if it were in fact on a hinge. As it rose they pushed their shovels forward to get better leverage. When it was about a foot open on one side, Samuel asked her, "Can you hold it by yourself?"

She couldn't talk through the strain of holding it open with his help, but she managed to nod.

"Okay, I'm going to let go on three. One… two… three."

He let go, and the full weight of the lid came down on her shovel. She felt as if the pressure of holding down the shovel handle was about to break her wrists. But she managed to hold steady as Samuel got to his knees and placed both hands on the open edge of the lid. With a loud groan, he pressed his entire body against it. Almost immediately Lee felt the weight lighten. The lid angled up slowly with a groan almost as loud as Samuel's. Then, suddenly, it was almost vertical, resting on the far side of the coffin. The shovel fell from her hands. Samuel gave it one more push, and the lid slipped an inch or two between the edge of the coffin and the dirt. Samuel almost fell into the open casket, but he was able to push off the lid and tumble back onto the ground.

A dry, musty odor wafted up from the grave. They both coughed. The air felt powdery, like fine sawdust. For a moment she feared that Semper itself had been released. Then Samuel stepped forward and peered down into the casket, training his flashlight on it.

"There's no vessel," he said.

She leaned over the open grave and looked down.

"Oh, God," she said, covering her mouth as the coarse air continued to drift up.

"Semper isn't here," Samuel said. "Shit."

It wasn't the absence of Semper that made her unable to breathe. Nor was it the gritty air.

It was what she saw inside the casket.

CHAPTER 51

"Two people," Samuel whispered as he and Lee stared into the opened coffin.

But it wasn't only the presence of a second body that had astonished her to the point of muteness. The skeletons were lying side by side, facing each other, one significantly taller. The taller one's arm appeared to be draped over the other.

"The one on the left..." he jiggled his flashlight over the smaller skeleton, "is a woman. See the broader pelvic bone?" He moved his flashlight over the midsection of the smaller one. "Look at the skeleton on the left. The shoulders are broader, the ribcage longer." He directed the light from one end of the coffin to the other. "But no vessel. A total waste of time. So much for 'Hic Semper.'"

The beam of Lee's flashlight hadn't moved from the left hand of the smaller skeleton, the female. Nor had her eyes moved from it. Was she even breathing? On the fourth finger was a ring, dangling loosely at the first knuckle. She'd immediately recognized it but... how could it be?

"I need to see the ring," she said when she was finally able to speak. She got down on the ground, the grass damp and unexpectedly cool. She shimmied forward until her head and shoulders dangled over the open grave. But her arms were a few inches too short to reach the skeleton. She shimmied forward a bit more and felt herself sliding into the casket.

Samuel caught her by the ankles. "Lee, you don't want to fall in there."

She was less worried about herself than damaging the skeletons.

"Lower me a few inches more." She stretched her right arm toward the ring.

When he relaxed his hold just a bit, she used her left hand to push off the edge of the opened grave.

"A few inches more. Keep going." Her stomach was at the edge of the open grave, pressing into the earth and making it difficult to breathe.

"More," she managed to gasp.

Samuel allowed her to sink another inch. Her fingertips grazed the skeleton's hand. "Almost there…." Another inch and she was able to touch the hand. She didn't want to risk moving the hand, or any part of the frame, lest she damage it. Stretching her arm, hand and fingers, she managed to connect her middle finger with the top of the ring. The hand was folded across the skeleton's chest, so the ring had clearance both above and below. She carefully pushed the ring toward the fingertip, not wanting to disturb the bones themselves. When it was at the very end, she shimmied another half inch forward, praying she wouldn't fall in and do irrevocable harm to the ancient remains, and brought her thumb to the end of the skeleton's finger. Gently, she used her middle finger to ease the ring off the bone, closing her thumb against her middle finger to secure it. Afraid of dropping it by trying to manipulate it back into her palm, she managed to slip it over the tip of her index finger, which she immediately closed into a fist to keep it from falling off.

"Okay, I have it."

Samuel began to pull her back. As soon as her shoulders were safely on grass, she picked up the flashlight and scrambled to her feet, pulling her shirt over her stomach, which was badly abraded by the dirt and grass. No matter. She trained the light directly on the ring, which she slid easily on to the fourth finger of her left hand. Though it was badly tarnished, the sudden light brought it alive.

She wanted to say something but couldn't.

"Lee, what's the matter?"

She shook her head, unable to look away from the ring.

"But you're crying."

She'd been unaware of the tears but now felt them on her cheeks, clouding her vision, causing the ring, despite centuries of tarnish, to sparkle for her.

She held the ring close to her face. It was round, about half an inch in circumference. Around the perimeter were what looked like tiny pearls, though they were blackened with time. Embossed on the center of the ring was a regally attired woman atop a horse, riding side-saddle across a field of flowering plants.

"It's Elizabeth," she was finally able to say, in a breathy whisper, still unable to take her eyes off the ring. "A replica of the great seal. Look, surrounding her…." She held the ring closer to Samuel. "The rose is the symbol of the Tudors. The harp is for Ireland. The fleur de lys for France, which the Tudor's claimed was theirs. The inscription around the edge is taken right from the great seal: 'Elizabetha Dei gracia Anglie Francie et Hibernie Regina Fidei Defensor…' Oh, my God."

"What is it? Lee, what's the matter?"

"It's true," she whispered, struggling to find her voice.

"What's true?"

"Elizabeth had a son, Edward Filer. It's here. Look."

She held the ring to his face. After a few moments he looked up at her.

"I see one person. The queen herself, I assume."

"But the inscription. It's taken directly from her great seal, but it includes extra words. 'Elizabetha Dei gracia Anglie Francie et Hibernie Regina Fidei Defensor.'" She had to fight a jangle of emotions to talk coherently. "'Elizabeth, by grace of God, Queen of England, France and Ireland, Defender of the Faith.' Then these words: 'et Mater EF– mother of Edward Filer.' She had those words added."

"Why would she risk disclosing her relationship with Filer this way? Wouldn't the goldsmith or whoever have wondered what she meant?"

"How would a goldsmith know the meaning of EF, or even understand Latin? And even if he knew Latin, sometimes Elizabeth was referred to as the mother of England. The *e* could be England, the *f*, France."

They both turned back to the open grave. After a long silence, Samuel asked the question that she didn't dare voice.

"Is that…." Even he couldn't finish, so she did it for him.

"Elizabeth?"

The notion that the skeleton lying below them, age-yellowed, unexpectedly small, almost pathetic, could be Gloriana, Edmund Spencer's Faerie Queene, Lee's touchstone since childhood, when her mother read her stories from the great monarch's life, seemed cruel in its irony. Not to mention highly, highly unlikely.

And yet.

"Who else could it be? Edward Filer's wife is buried over here." She trained her flashlight on the marker a few feet away: "Abigail Filer, 1584–1645."

"Elizabeth is buried *here*?" He glanced around, taking in the isolated and humble cemetery. "*Here*?"

"It explains why Charles Filer brought over the remains of his parents, Edward and Abigail. He must have known who else was buried in the casket with his father."

"But the reference to Semper being here…" Samuel pointed

into the gravesite.

"I don't think Semper meant to them what it means to us," she said. "For them it was a motto; it stood for the eternal bond between them. Semper is 'here' because Elizabeth is here." Lee looked down at the two skeletons, which now struck her as being locked in a somewhat desperate embrace. "She's here," she whispered.

"So we're no closer to finding *our* Semper."

She ran her right index finger over the surface of the ring. Elizabeth had long, slender fingers, often remarked upon as a sign of aristocratic birth.

How lonely she must have been! For surely she had asked to be buried with her son—no one would have dared done so except under orders. She had contemplated burial in Westminster Abbey, where her father and sister were interred, and had chosen instead to spend eternity in an obscure country church a day's journey north of London, with her unacknowledged son. Had she known that he would be moved from his original burial place, and she with him, across the vast ocean to the New World? Had she anticipated that fate, and endorsed it, rather than be left behind in England, where she was merely a queen, but not a mother?

So many books, so many letters, so many visits to so many palaces and churches. Yet only now did the great Elizabeth feel viscerally alive to her—ironically, in a grave. Here was the key to the soul of the woman, lying in an open coffin. Not merely ruler of England, Ireland, and France, but *Mater EF.*

A sudden rustling behind them. A small animal, perhaps, a branch falling from a tree.

The rustling grew louder, closer. Not just behind them now but in front, and to the left. Footsteps. Without speaking they both turned off their flashlights. Darkness fell on them like a shroud. Unable to see anything, her hearing grew sharper—or were the footsteps getting closer?

"What do we do?" she whispered.

Before he could answer, the small clearing lit up. She squinted but could see nothing behind the beams of harsh, white light, which were trained directly at them.

"Put down whatever you're holding, take off your jackets, and empty your pockets so we can see them."

The male voice, from behind them, was deep and steady. When they didn't immediately move, more from fear than any intention to disobey, there was an explosion directly in front of them. A bullet hit the pile of dirt they'd just dug up.

They dropped the flashlights and took off their jackets. Then, one by one, they inverted their pants pockets to show that they were empty. Samuel held up his wallet and let it fall to the ground.

A moment later a hand grabbed Lee from behind and pulled her away from the grave.

CHAPTER 52

"You trespassed onto our property. You murdered one of our elders, Derek Martinson. And now you desecrate the grave of our patriarch. Can you offer a single valid reason why we should not kill you immediately?"

The question was posed by Edward Aspinall who, like the three other men who'd discovered them in the cemetery, carried a hunting rifle.

They were in the dining room of the main house, having been force-marched there from the cemetery with four rifles trained on their backs. They'd entered the house through the kitchen, in which three women were occupied doing dishes, although it was long past dinner time. There was something oddly *colonial* about the scene, modern dress notwithstanding—the men patrolling the grounds with their rifles, the womenfolk back in the kitchen scrubbing pots and pans into the night.

No words had been spoken since leaving the cemetery, not even after each of the four men had taken a close look into the open grave. The ring was still on Lee's fourth finger, which she curled into a concealing fist.

The house smelled of old wood and lemon furniture polish. In the dining room these odors were joined by the damp musty scent of an old fire. She saw the source right away, a beautiful old fireplace topped by an intricately carved wood mantel, a Victorian addition, Lee guessed, historian even at gunpoint. In the center of the room was an oval double-pedestal table, mahogany, and in perfect condition. Over the table hung an incongruously elaborate crystal chandelier, another Victorian addition, more than likely. Around it were a dozen shield-back chairs with butter-yellow muslin seat cushions. There was an open-shelf china cupboard displaying a set of white porcelain plates decorated with blue flowers, and a waist-high sideboard that held an elegantly simple and gleaming silver tea set.

The four men were about the same age, in their mid-thirties to mid-forties. Two of the men seemed to have inherited the Filer shivering ailment, as they wore heavy wool cardigans buttoned to the neck.

Aspinall and one other man were dressed more appropriately for the warm evening in short-sleeved shirts. All four were on the pale side, and slight, and two of them had reddish hair. Elizabeth's coloring, she couldn't help thinking, and then, still holding the ring, she glanced at their hands, which seemed disappointingly normal—nothing like the long, slender fingers so often remarked upon by the queen's contemporaries.

Samuel seemed less fascinated by the pedigree of their captors.

"If you kill us you'll never be left alone," he said. "People will come after us. There'll be inquiries, investigations."

"And if we let you go?" So far only Aspinall had spoken. He had apparently assumed the mantle of leader following Derek Martinson's gunshot death, which didn't bode well, for his face was set in a scowl of disdain that seemed personal, intent on settling an old score. Lee recalled the territorial rage he'd displayed at the Filer House, as if she'd trespassed not only his property but his very soul. That rage was evident now, in the rigid calm of his voice.

"We'll say nothing," Samuel said.

The four men exchanged skeptical glances, not surprisingly. Lee's only hope lay in the fact that they'd been brought back to the house and not shot in the woods.

"You want to know what we know," she said, forcing herself to make eye contact with Aspinall, the apparent leader. "That's why you brought us here, isn't it?"

He observed her without answering. It seemed almost a matter of pride to him not to respond at once, as if in doing so he'd cede a small but crucial advantage.

"Are you all Filers?" she asked, glancing at the others. When they didn't respond she added, "I know who you are, and you." She pointed at the two men in sweaters. "A lot of you seem to have trouble maintaining body temperature. Did you know that there's a reference to this same condition in the diary of a sixteenth-century physician? One of the first people with this malady was named Filer, Edward Filer. He's buried here, on your property. His grandfather, Miles Stafford, is the first recorded person with the affliction."

"Edward Filer had CAPS?" one of the men said.

"Caps?" she asked.

Aspinall answered in a gruff, impatient voice. "An acronym. Chronic acryopyrin-associated periodic syndrome. An autoinflammatory disorder. When exposed to low temperatures, even mildly cool ones, we get feverish and our joints become inflamed."

"And rashes," offered the other sweater-wearer.

"About half of us have CAPS, but every Filer is a carrier. There is no cure or treatment. As best we can tell, the disease is restricted to a handful of families in the US and England. And to answer your original question, yes, we are all Filers. Second and third cousins, in fact."

"Do you know how your family began?"

"You mean Elizabeth?" He whispered the name, invoking a deity. "We know. We have no diary, no written account. But it has been a part of our family history for four centuries."

"I have proof," she said. "Written proof."

"Where is this diary?"

"Not here," Samuel said quickly. "If you kill us you'll never find it."

Aspinall pondered this for a moment, then: "We've never wanted any special attention because of our ancestry. In fact, we shunned it."

"Why?" Lee asked.

"No proof, for one thing. We would have been ridiculed. Our claim to this land was always tenuous, based on a grant made in the sixteenth century for which no documents survive. For a long time we were treated as freaks because of our condition. Devils. Filers were shunned by the good citizens of Massachusetts. Only in this century have we integrated into the world in any meaningful way. It helps that none of us bears the actual Filer name. And there were financial reasons."

"Missing pages in the town ledger books," Lee said. "Records having to do with this property, I assume."

"If the town knew the actual size of our land, we'd go slowly broke paying taxes."

"And no one has bothered to assess it all these years?"

"We have family members in the town offices. You met one of them, Grace. My daughter. And there are other ways to ensure that a blind eye is turned."

"Payoffs," Samuel said. "Paid for with emeralds. The Hever Emeralds."

Aspinall said nothing, but his shoulders stiffened.

"You've supported the family by selling off emeralds," Samuel said. "You sold one recently to a dealer in New York. I'm guessing you didn't pay taxes on the sale, or any of the sales."

"You murdered Maurits Immersheim."

It was as good as an admission that the family had the emeralds, and were harvesting them, one by one, to enable the extended family to remain on the Filer land.

"We didn't kill Immersheim," Lee said. "Or Derek Martinson. And Immersheim's killer wasn't interested in emeralds. He was looking for Semper. As are we." She waited for this to sink in, then continued. "We thought Semper was buried with Edward Filer. There's a coded message on the headstone."

"A message?"

"'Hic Semper'—here is Semper. It's buried in the inscription."

"Semper is our family motto. It means 'always.'"

"It's also the name of a potentially lethal element. A virus or similar microorganism that was brought back from South America in the sixteenth century and purchased by Queen Elizabeth, who gave it to Charles Filer as a form of eternal protection against his enemies—enemies of the queen."

"Absurd." But his rifle, along with the other three, had gradually lowered as all four men became engaged in the story.

"We don't know what kind of organism Semper is," Samuel said. "And it may in fact be a legend. But the Spanish and English explorers who discovered it saw firsthand proof of its destructive power, and the Elizabethan physician who bought it for the queen believed in it. If it *is* real, then it's likely that we have no immunity from it. It must not be allowed to infect our world."

Aspinall let his gun hang at his side, his expression a mix of relief and sadness.

"This explains so much," he said quietly. "There were attacks on our family in the century after we arrived here. We always assumed they were motivated by dynastic concern with the succession, given our ancestry, though this must have seemed bizarre to the settlers living in what was then a very remote and sparsely populated area. What sort of threat could we have posed from this godforsaken wilderness? It's another reason we learned to stay apart. But each time, the attackers not only killed family members, they also ransacked our homes. We assumed they were looking for the emeralds, but accounts passed down over the centuries talk of 'semper.' They were looking for Semper. We never knew what this was, only that it was extremely valuable."

"Was any of this written down?" Lee asked.

He shook his head.

"Another defensive habit long ingrained in our family—we write nothing down. But even so, we've managed to attract the two of you. What will you do if you find Semper, sell it to terrorists?"

"I'm a historian," Lee said quickly. "I discovered a clue to the whereabouts of Semper and was attacked because of it. I was also accused of murder. I need to find Semper to clear myself."

She could see still more skepticism fighting with credulity in his eyes. Her story was implausible, but then so was so much else about the Filer's history. What was one more lunatic showing up with a story about an ancient vessel whose contents could destroy the world? His silence reassured her that credulity was winning out.

"We don't want to expose you," she said, taking a step toward him. He did not raise his rifle. "But we need to find Semper. And so do you. There's someone else looking for it. He's killed at least two people already, and if he finds Semper before we do, I fear what he'll do with it."

"Did he kill Derek?"

She looked at Samuel. Was it possible that the monster had followed them to Tunsbury? How? And if he had, why had he saved them?

"I don't know," she said. "But the killing will not end until Semper is found. That won't happen if you kill us."

"We can search for Semper on our own," he said.

"It's not here. I thought it might be in the grave with Edward Filer. Obviously it isn't. Let us go. We will find Semper and destroy it. And you can live in peace."

"Too great a risk," he said softly, slowly shaking his head. His evident sadness at what he felt he had to do was more chilling than his earlier anger.

"It's not a risk. Here, look at this."

She walked to within a few feet of him. His rifle stayed by his side, but his three cousins immediately raised theirs. She held out her left fist and unfurled it, revealing the ring on her fourth finger.

"Take it."

He slowly extended his hand and took the ring off her finger, peered closely at it.

"It was on the ring finger of the left hand of the woman's skeleton in the cemetery. It's Elizabeth's great seal. No one else would have had such a ring. To duplicate the seal, even for a ring, would have been considered treason."

He turned the ring in his fingers, then held it out for his cousins to admire. They shuffled closer to him, rifles now at their side.

"The inscription is Latin. 'Elizabetha Dei gracia Anglie Francie et Hibernie Regina Fidei Defensor et Mater EF.' "

Aspinall murmured the translation: "Elizabeth, by God's grace, Queen of England, France and Scotland, Defender of the Faith…" He stopped and looked up at Lee, who nodded slowly. He cleared his throat and continued, "And mother of EF."

The four cousins looked like they'd just received a one-in-a-thousand diagnosis that was too good to be true.

"It's true," one of them said. "Let me see."

Aspinall handed him the ring. Immediately the other two moved over to examine it.

"We've never had proof," Aspinall said. "We've known, but we never had proof."

He looked over at his cousins, whose faces seemed to glow from the reflected magic of the ring.

"I believe that Elizabeth is buried here, with her son," Lee said. "Of course, there are tests that can be done to prove this beyond doubt."

"No tests. We don't want attention and we don't need the approval of others."

"But this could rewrite history."

"It confirms our history; it does not rewrite it." His expression, which had softened as he contemplated the ring, turned rigid with disdain. "There will be no tests."

"And so you'll murder us to keep your history private?"

He said nothing.

"Look at them," Samuel said to Aspinall, nodding at the three cousins, still gaping at the ring. "She's given them a gift. All these years you never knew what that gravestone inscription meant. You never dug up the grave. You never found the second skeleton and you never found the ring, the proof of who you are. For all that, you're going to murder this woman?"

"We cannot allow—"

"You cannot *allow*?" Samuel exploded, taking a step toward Aspinall, who immediately raised his rifle so that it almost touched Samuel's chest. "You may be a queen's descendant, but this isn't your kingdom. You don't decide who lives or dies."

Aspinall's eyes continued to reflect a dawning sadness, but he said nothing.

"I won't tell anyone, you have my word," Lee said.

"But you said you're a historian. This could make you famous."

The sonnet was going to make her famous, not this. "Not at the expense of your privacy," she said. "Besides, you have the ring, and the grave is on private property. All I have are words. No proof."

"And there's something else," Samuel said. "Semper. Until Semper is found you will never be left alone. Someone will show up, maybe not tomorrow or next year, but eventually someone will come. And they'll keep on coming. We know for a fact there's a maniac out there now willing to slaughter people to find it. For him and people like him your ancestry is irrelevant. It's about the power to kill on a mass scale."

The cousins had finally looked up from the ring and were now staring at their leader, awaiting a verdict. It was impossible to tell what they were thinking. Finally, Aspinall spoke.

"Charles, wait here with them. If they try to leave, shoot them. You two, come with me."

Aspinall led two of his cousins into the kitchen. Lee heard voices from that room and leaned forward to have a look. The kitchen was crowded with men and women, all looking expectantly at Aspinall. She couldn't make out what anyone was saying but assumed they were discussing the fate of their two captives.

She saw Samuel glance around the room, looking for a way out. The one remaining Filer cousin, the man called Charles (another Charles!) had his gun trained directly at her. His body was frozen, but his eyes darted nervously from her to Samuel. He had a long, thin neck and prominent Adam's apple; his maroon cardigan, buttoned to the neck, seemed to prop up his head, which looked almost too heavy for his reedy neck.

The room's only door led to the kitchen. There were two windows that opened onto the back of the house. Perhaps she or Samuel could smash through one of them and make it out alive, but the other would surely be stopped by a rifle bullet.

The voices from the kitchen occasionally flared into shouts, then subsided. At least there appeared to be some argument over their fate. She wanted to hear what they were saying and started to move slowly toward the door.

"Stop," Charles said in a flat, quiet voice.

Movement at the kitchen door caught her eye. But it was only a little girl, perhaps three or four, wandering from the kitchen where her elders were too engrossed in arguing their fate to notice her absence. She wore a pale yellow sundress and lavender plastic sandals. Her strawberry blond hair was cut into a short bob. She had light blue eyes and was quite pale. Lee noted that she was not wearing a sweater; apparently she had escaped the Filer genetic legacy.

The little girl stopped about two feet into the room. Lee saw that Samuel was staring at her and realized that their guard, standing across the room, couldn't see her, his sightline blocked by the long table.

The arguing in the kitchen continued.

Samuel slowly extended his right foot toward the girl, sliding it along the floor. Then he brought his left foot forward. He was inching toward her. Lee knew what was about to happen.

Samuel had found their way out.

CHAPTER 53

"Don't do it," she whispered to Samuel, barely moving her lips.

But he continued to slide one foot and then the other along the floor, closer to the girl who had stopped at the end of the long table and was staring up at them.

Lee stared back at the little girl, mesmerized by her fragile, almost ethereal beauty: the pale complexion, the rose-colored hair, and the light blue eyes. Tudor coloring. Were Elizabeth's genes asserting themselves through this little girl five centuries after her death?

"Don't touch her," Lee whispered to Samuel, who continued to edge closer to the girl.

The guard, Charles, sensed something was happening and started to move toward them. In one quick movement Samuel sprung at the girl, snatched her up, and pressed her to his chest so that she was facing away from him. Immediately he placed his right arm under her chin. Lee heard her try to scream, but Samuel's arm stifled anything louder than a faint gurgling.

"I'll snap her neck," Samuel whispered as Charles raised his rifle so that it pointed directly at his head. "She'll be dead before the bullet hits me."

The guard lowered the rifle a few inches. From the kitchen, the heated debate raged on.

"Give her the rifle," Samuel said, nodding toward Lee. When the guard hesitated, he jerked on the little girl's head, causing a muffled cough. Tears were pouring from her eyes as her legs kicked ineffectually against Samuel hips and thighs.

The guard lowered the gun and handed it to Lee. Wanting no part of what was happening but with no choice but to go along, she grabbed the rifle by the barrel.

"Now open that window," Samuel said, still whispering.

Lee circled the table and opened one of the room's two windows.

"You go first," Samuel said, then turned to face their guard, who was frozen on the other side of the room, looking humiliated and terrified. "One move, one sound, and I'll snap her like a twig."

Lee swung one leg over the window sill, which was about two feet from the floor, straddled it for a moment, still clutching the rifle, then angled her body outside. She swung her other leg through and stood up.

Samuel bent at the knees so that she could see him through the window, though he kept his eyes on the guard, and his arm clamped around the girl's neck.

"Aim the rifle at him and shoot him if he makes a move," he said. He waited for her to acknowledge this with a nod, then crouched down, sat on the sill, still facing the guard, and swung his right leg over the sill.

"I've still got her neck," he whispered to Charles. "Do you understand?"

Charles slowly nodded.

In one smooth move, Samuel ducked under the top sash of the window and swung his left leg across the sill. The moment he was standing on the outside, he said "Run!" and took off to the left, hugging the side of the house. Lee followed, carrying the rifle.

Behind them she heard Charles shout. Within seconds she was aware of voices, first muffled shouts from within the house, and then much louder sounds.

Suddenly a wailing pierced the night air. A woman's voice, anguished.

"Elizabeth!"

The girl's name was Elizabeth.

They rounded the corner of the house and took off in the direction of the dirt road. It was obvious to Lee and no doubt to Samuel as well that they couldn't outrun the entire Filer family, particularly with Samuel carrying the girl. *Elizabeth.* There would be a standoff. It would not end well.

The front door of the house flew open, and a woman emerged. Lee just caught sight of her as she ran: about thirty, slim, with shoulder-length blonde hair. She wore a heavy cardigan sweater over loose jeans.

"Don't take my daughter," she shouted from about fifty yards away. Her voice was harsh with panic.

In an instant, Lee made a decision. She grabbed Samuel's arm. He almost tripped, regained his footing, and started to run again.

"No, Samuel, stop. I have a plan."

Without waiting for him to follow she ran toward the woman, who was herself sprinting after them.

"Those cars," she said, pointing to two cars parked in front of the big house. "Do you have keys?"

Samuel, still holding Elizabeth, had stopped and was facing them.

The woman studied her for a long moment, then pointed to a maroon minivan.

"Keys are in that one," she said.

"I won't harm your little girl," Lee said. She got into the minivan, dropped the rifle between the front seats, found the keys on the passenger seat, and started the engine.

A group of men, several with rifles, had circled to the front of the house.

"One shot and I'll snap her neck!" Samuel shouted.

"Don't shoot at them!" the girl's mother screamed as she ran toward the men, waving her arms.

Lee drove the minivan across the lawn to Samuel. She stopped it, reached across, and opened the passenger-side door. He got in, still holding the girl close to his chest, his right arm wrapped around her throat.

"Let her go," Lee said.

"Not until we're out of here," he panted.

Lee put the car into park. In the rearview mirror she saw the men slowly walking toward them, rifles raised. There appeared to be about six of them. The girl's mother was in front of them, arms akimbo to shield her daughter from potential gunfire.

"Let her go, or we're not moving."

"For Christ's sake, Lee, you'll get us killed."

"I won't get *her* killed." *Elizabeth*. Pale, red-haired, blue-eyed Elizabeth.

The men had stopped a few yards from the minivan.

"Lee, I beg you, get us out of here."

Her heart was beating so intensely she thought it might rupture her chest. Gripping the steering wheel didn't stop her hands from trembling. But she kept her focus on the girl, tiny Elizabeth, whose unblinking eyes betrayed a fear far deeper than anything she was experiencing.

"Fuck!" Samuel shouted, and then, in a quieter voice, "Okay, I'm opening the door. You put the car in drive. The moment I release her, floor it."

She shifted into drive, foot on the brake.

Samuel let go of the girl's neck but immediately grabbed her around the waist with his left hand. Then, with his right hand, he opened the door a crack.

"Wait until I say 'go,'" he said.

"Don't hurt me." Her neck finally free, the little girl—*Elizabeth*—spoke for the first time, in a tiny, plaintive whisper.

"No one's going to hurt you," Lee said, with as much conviction as she could summon given that the little girl was about to be tossed from the car.

Samuel placed both hands around the girl's waist. He lifted her off his lap and used her body to push open the door. She let out a short scream as her body met the door, and another yelp when she tumbled to the dirt driveway.

"*Go*!" he shouted.

Lee floored the gas pedal. Samuel slammed shut the passenger door just as the car lurched forward. "Two of them are getting in the other car. Don't slow down."

A terrifying, dizzying minute later, the public road came into view. She didn't slow down until ten yards or so from the intersection. Then she hit the brake and skidded into a right turn. The back of the minivan fishtailed to the left, and for a sickening moment she thought they were going to do a complete one-eighty and end up face-to-face with their pursuers. But the car straightened out, and she floored it again, heading back into town.

"They stopped!" Samuel yelled. "They're not coming after us."

They had stopped where their world ended, at the edge of the property deeded to them by Elizabeth centuries earlier.

She eased up on the gas pedal and allowed the minivan to slow to a comfortable, and legal, speed.

CHAPTER 54

29 April 1603
Henford

It is over. Yesterday our Queen was laid to rest in the Abbey, one month following her death. I took no part in the procession but observed it with the multitudes, who thronged the streets and leaned out the windows of their homes as her statue, lying upon the coffin, passed by. There was a great weeping and sighing as she passed, such as I have never before seen. Grief at her absence was matched by fear for what the future holds without her steady hand.

Today I arrived in Hertfordshire and called on Charles Filer. My purpose was to deliver a certain poem. Master Shakespeare had completed his sonnet for Charles, with some small contribution from me, and it was my duty to present it to him following Her Majesty's death. It is a most clever thing, this sonnet, thick with meanings inside meanings that I suspect will elude Charles Filer. But the Queen wanted it so, it seems, her devotion immortalized but not recognized. She was a lover of words and enjoyed watching them play on the page and stage, as do I, and William Shakespeare is a jeweler of words, fitting them into intricate settings so that they sparkle for all to see but hide their true import from all but the cleverest of readers. Charles Filer is not one of those readers.

Yet he seemed pleased with the lines, for he knew that though their author was the young Shakespeare, their inspiration was the old Queen, whose patronage of his family was as lavish as it was mysterious. I wonder if one day these lines will be fully comprehended. I find myself of two minds on this. They tell a story of great devotion, with a glimpse into the tender heart of a woman who appeared to the world to have none. But they also hold danger, for they speak of riches and power and therefore of jealousies and threats. Perhaps one day this will not matter, and the sonnet may be read as a simple love poem. I pray that day comes, though I know I will not live to see it.

I bade farewell to Charles Filer and his family in the great hall at Henford. I wonder if I shall see them again? He has been granted a large tract of land in the New World. He calls it an estate, but I fear it is nothing of the sort, merely dense forest thick with savages. Someday, he tells me, he will take his place there, across the great ocean. There is a small hostelry nearby, the Coach and Horses, to which I repaired for a night's rest and from which I pen these sorry lines. Tonight I cannot sleep, but I trust I will rest easier when there is an ocean between the Queen's grandson and England.

CHAPTER 55

Lee carefully laid the diary on the bed. Reading even a few pages of the doctor's dense, faded handwriting made her eyes watery and tired. But her mind was never less than fully engaged.

They'd gone directly from the Filer property to the hotel. She didn't want to be alone and had invited Samuel to her room, where they talked about the insane night, trying to make sense of what they'd discovered. The great Elizabeth, buried in a simple country graveyard in Massachusetts along with her unacknowledged son. Whose idea had that been? If the queen's, then had her entire public life, one of the most illustrious, not to mention well-documented, in history, been but a distraction, her true soul that of a mother more than a monarch? The story of history's most written-about ruler would have to be rewritten.

But Samuel was less concerned with the soul of the queen than with the whereabouts of Semper. He kept bringing her back to the most important truth: they had not found Semper in the grave, despite the promising headstone inscription.

"What do we do now?" he asked as he sipped water from a bathroom glass. "After everything we've been through, we're at another dead end." His tone had an accusatory edge.

He fell asleep on one of the double beds. Still restless, she'd retrieved the diary from the room safe and picked up where she'd left off the night before. She read about Charles Filer's departure for the New World, along with the lead caskets, one of which she and Samuel had just dug up.

When her eyes began to give out, and drowsiness made her head suddenly heavy, she stopped reading and, still dressed, got under the bedspread.

Now what? The question clawed through her exhaustion. *Now what?* Samuel had fallen into a restless sleep. She briefly considered moving to the other bed. Was all this going to end with her in custody, charged with murder after all? She'd spin wild tales of ancient curses and a modern psychopath, and who would believe her? She wondered if Samuel would come to her defense, or instead side with his fellow doctors, pledged to secrecy until Semper was found. Would the doctors even allow her to testify, or would they get to her first, and silence her? Samuel wanted Semper destroyed to save the world; she wanted only to save herself. She sat up and opened the diary to the page on which she'd left off. If only he'd written what he'd done with Semper. Had he destroyed it? Unlikely, for if he had he would probably have written so. He'd mentioned his reservations about dropping it into the Thames. Certainly the Semper Society was predicated on the belief that Semper had been hidden, not eradicated. And how would you go about destroying it? You'd bury it, more than likely. Not in the casket with Edward Filer, as she'd originally suspected from the inscription on the headstone.

Then where?

She returned to the diary and read the final portion.

CHAPTER 56

March 1630
Plymouth

Today I took up with two old acquaintances long neglected. One is this diary, which has sat unopened in a drawer in my bedroom for many, many years. Many is the night I have been tempted to destroy it, but never could. Perhaps I knew, in the way of a prophesier, that I had one last entry to make. That entry is this one, written with a hand grown thin and spotted with age. I have lived beyond my allotted three score and ten. I wonder, in moments of vanity, if I have been granted this surplus in order to bear witness to what transpired this day.

The second acquaintance renewed was with Charles Filer. He is now a stout man of middle years, still prone to fits of shivering, as are two of his four children. He had sent word through a messenger that he was departing for the Massachusetts Bay Colony, taking possession at long last of his great properties there. He wondered if I would see him off at the dockside. He offered no explanation for this sentimental request, but I suspect he knows that I am the one link between him and our late Queen, gone for so long but hardly forgotten. Before severing all ties to his benefactor, he wanted one last taste of royal favor. So I suspect, in any case.

I made the journey to Plymouth with some difficulty, being in frail health. I have outlived my wife and daughter, my Queen, my Lucy and, hardest of all, my usefulness, for I have abandoned my practice and now pass the days looking back over my long life so as not to look ahead, where lies only greater frailty and then blackness. Three nights I spent at roadside taverns, arriving on the very day of departure. I found the port in great commotion, most centered around the Mary and John, the ship on which the Filers were set to sail. I was told that 150 souls were leaving on the ship for Massachusetts, most of them from the West

Country. Few of them appeared to know one another, though all were civil enough. The Filers held themselves apart, I noticed. Charles did not recognize me at first, nor I him. But when I made myself known, he embraced me warmly and introduced me to his children, three grown women and a son—the typical Tudor mix, I thought with a treasonous smile. He led me on board and thence to a private cabin belowdecks. He seemed much proud of this small space in which he and his brood would pass the crossing, having secured it at great expense. "I will be the largest landowner in Massachusetts," he told me. He still does not think to ask why the Queen bestowed so large a grant on his family, but he knows that his father Edward was a great favorite of Her Majesty and I think he knows the truth. I of course do not think to confirm his suspicions, even after all these years. He feels it is his right to own a vast tract of royal land, and he is correct in that, though perhaps not for the reason he suspects.

All about the room there were chests of fine clothes and books and china ready for transport. Somewhere hidden among those belongings is a necklace of emeralds and diamonds worth more than the ship itself and all its cargo. More than the Massachusetts Bay Colony itself, I think. Charles seems to believe he will be a gentleman squire in the New World, his life no more strenuous than the one he is leaving behind. I wish him well among the forests and savages. Sometimes delusion is a stronger tonic than courage.

He led me farther below to the great hold of the ship. Amid the boxes and chests and barrels there were two items that stood out. They were caskets made of lead. Charles had them removed from their place inside the church in Henford to bring them across the Atlantic to the New World. "The land was given to my father," Charles informed me, "and so he and my mother will rest there with me for eternity. I cannot bear to leave him here, for we are a small family, new to the country. Who will remember them if not their own son and his sons and their sons?"

I of course offered my fervent endorsement of this plan, for it was I in fact who first planted its seed in his pliant mind many years earlier. I even provided him with a fitting inscription for the monument to his father, telling him the Queen herself had written it, and he assured me he would make of these words his father's eternal epitaph when he arrives in Massachusetts.

All was proceeding as I had hoped and planned. Charles Filer was leaving the country, along with his father's coffin. He would bring with him something else, or perhaps I should say someone else. I didn't dare write of this back then, when the Queen was fresh in her grave. But I find I must write of it now. For I had been busy that dark month in 1603, and I still marvel that I found the energy to accomplish all that I did, even as a much younger man. I had to pay bribes to countless guards and sentries and diverse others. None knew what I was about. None but my poor servant Lucy, whose aid I had no choice but to enlist. Her horror at my undertaking afflicted her until her death a few years back. She was with me at Richmond, and later in Henford, when I made my secret visit, having avoided Charles Filer at that time. It did little good to tell Lucy that I was merely following the Queen's command. She was a superstitious woman, my Lucy, and though I introduced her to the glory of Christ our Lord, and had her baptized into our faith, she never fully cast off the false ideas of her savage upbringing, and oftentimes I caught her making imprecations to the heavens that I fear had nothing whatsoever to do with our Christian God and his only Son. She was a nervous partner in my doings, at times near to hysterics, but I had no one else I could trust.

I certainly could not trust Charles Filer. He was ignorant of the intrigues and machinations that swirled about him as flies circle a corpse. Like his father Edward, he is a good man, but weak. Weak men are far more dangerous than strong, for they will do anything to protect themselves. My late Queen surrounded herself with strong men, for she knew them to be more loyal and trustworthy, though harder to control. I had made up my mind that the Filers could not be trusted with the power known as Semper, which Her Majesty had bade me give to Charles shortly before her death. I knew he would be a poor custodian for Semper, even in the forests of the New World, far from the intrigues of court. Who would not be tempted to open the vessel and observe its power?

'Tis a scourge most awesome and grave, I am convinced, one that must never be released into the world. I wish I could kill it, but I can only ensure that it sleeps for eternity, never to be resurrected. I have been sorely tempted to drop it into the Thames, but the river has powerful currents that might yet drive it to shore, and some years it shrinks to a mere stream from want of rain, exposing its reeking bottom to the city. Perhaps I should follow Charles Filer to the New World and drop it overboard in the great Atlantic. But I am far too old and cowardly for such a journey, so I disobeyed the Queen and merely hid it.

Did I betray my Queen in doing so? No, for I am her partner in throne and grave, and I serve her subjects, God's children all, which is perhaps a better thing.

CHAPTER 57

"Partner in throne and grave." The words echoed a line from the sonnet:

> A plague when I uncap the bottled thing
> From throne to grave no soul shall comfort know.

The line made sense in the sonnet. But they were an interesting choice of words for a physician. Would even a court physician refer to himself as the partner of a queen? Well, he had been a kind of co-conspirator since the day she gave birth. But a partner?

Lee closed the diary and put her head down, but she couldn't sleep for a moment, let alone the eternity the doctor had written about. "Partner in throne and grave." The line was a direct connection between the sonnet and the diary. It had to be significant.

After ten minutes, she got out of bed and quietly left the room. She took the stairs one flight down to the lobby, which was deserted except for a single person behind the check-in counter. Squinting in the harsh overhead light, she walked to the hotel business center, which was located off a long corridor that led to several meeting rooms. About halfway to the business center, she heard someone behind her, but when she turned the hallway was empty.

She used her plastic room key to open the locked door to the center, which was a single small room with three desktop computers and a shared printer. The door closed behind her. She sat down in front of one of the computers and navigated to Google, where she typed in five words: "partner in throne and grave."

She clicked on the first link, which took her to the official site of Westminster Abbey. She scanned some text that summarized the life of Elizabeth I before she found what she was looking for. Elizabeth was buried in the Abbey (or so it was universally believed) in a shared tomb with her older half sister, Mary. On the base of the tomb was an inscription:

Partners in throne and grave, here we sleep,
Elizabeth and Mary, sisters, in hope of the Resurrection.

She'd visited the tomb several times, and it had always struck her as ironic that Elizabeth should be buried with Mary, her archrival for the English throne who had kept her a virtual prisoner during her bloody reign. Yet perhaps it was fitting, for not only were they sisters, they were queens who had ruled in their own right, not as wives. Partners indeed in a very exclusive club.

The doctor's reference to the inscription could not have been accidental. Nor were the words "throne and grave" in the sonnet. Hadn't the doctor written that he'd made a small "contribution" to the sonnet? He must have meant these words, since they alone also appeared in his diary. The sonnet was pointing to the diary, to a specific line in the diary.

She reread the epitaph and thought he might have made additional allusions to it in the same passage. She pressed "print," retrieved her document, left the business center, and headed down the long hall to the lobby. A self-described lover of word games, as was his queen, both of whom liked "watching them play on the stage and page," Rufus Hatton had been unable to resist leaving a clue to the whereabouts of Semper, even though, having outlived his servant, Lucy, as he had most of his contemporaries, he must have known that his diary might endure. And the sonnet as well, like a commentary on the diary, pointing to and illuminating the key passage. Halfway across the lobby, walking toward the elevators, she decoded the clue. She stopped suddenly and worked it through.

In the diary, Hatton described hiding Semper using words that directly referred to the tomb inscription. He wrote "throne and grave," an explicit reference to the inscription. He called Semper a *grave* scourge. He wrote that he could not destroy it but could only ensure that it rested for eternity, never to be resurrected. It was almost as if he needed to share the cleverness of what he'd done with the world, but his diary was his only outlet. And it wasn't really an outlet at all, because he wrote early in the diary that Lucy had been instructed to destroy the diary upon his death. Of course, this never happened.

Lee turned and sprinted back to the business center, where she searched online for flight schedules from Logan Airport to London. After printing them, she hurried back to the elevators, impatient to tell Samuel what she had found: the location of Semper.

The Abbey

Men die, but sorrow never dies;
The crowding years divide in vain,
And the wide world is knit with ties
Of common brotherhood in pain

—Sarah Coolidge
Inscription on the Cradle Tomb in Westminster Abbey

CHAPTER 58

Lee stood at the entrance to Westminster Abbey, reluctant to step in. Though she had no idea what she was going to do, she sensed that entering the great cathedral would be an irrevocable step, the last of many she'd taken over the past several days.

It was ten in the morning. She had slept very little on the overnight flight from Logan, paid for with Sarah Cooper's credit card, and entered the country, for a second time, as Sarah Cooper. She hadn't told Samuel what she was planning and left while he was in the shower. She wanted to do this alone. Count on no one—perhaps the most enduring lesson she'd learned from her mother, or rather her mother's desertion.

She'd taken a taxi directly from Heathrow to an inexpensive hotel in Bayswater that she'd stayed in several times while doing research at the British Library. Following a quick shower, she'd taken the Circle Line tube to the Westminster stop.

A small line had already formed in front of the ticket booth just inside the gate. When she got to the front, she paid the twelve-pound fee using Sarah Cooper's credit card. This would, she hoped, be the last fraudulent charge she'd have to make. She entered the north transept and stood still for a few minutes, taking it in. She'd been to the Abbey several times, and was always struck with a kind of scholar's guilt that she wasn't more thrilled to be there. Yes, it was beautiful, spectacular, unique, historical—choose your gushing adjective. But tourists flocked to it not for the architecture but for the people buried there, poets, soldiers, statesmen, and monarchs. She'd stand before their tombs and plaques and feel… nothing. Bones in marble—so what? On either side of the transept, closely spaced marble tombs and statues of dead luminaries jostled for attention. She preferred palaces and ordinary homes, old streets and pubs where history lived, or at least asserted its right to the present. The Abbey was a shrine to death.

Of course, this time was different. The Abbey contained more than old bones, she felt certain. This time she sensed the presence of Semper. There was a sinister pall to the great church that she'd never picked up before, an aura of foreboding in the streaming dust motes shooting down from the great windows above, in the hushed roar of voices swirling around the gothic vaulting. The great marble statues along the north transept seemed to speak to her. Pitt. Palmerston. Cavendish. Gladstone. Each called out a warning she had no choice but to ignore.

When she finally headed deeper into the Abbey, toward the Lady Chapel to the left, behind the altar, her sense of foreboding intensified.

Or was it perhaps a sense of helplessness, the knowledge that Semper was here, in this very building, and yet inaccessible to her? Without Semper, would she ever be beyond suspicion, or safe? It was here, but so what?

She walked slowly through the north transept, circled the great altar, a nineteenth-century addition to the Abbey, and saw ahead of her the entrance to the Lady Chapel. To the left, she knew, in a side room, was the tomb of Elizabeth and Mary, *partners in throne and grave.*

"Chapel" hardly conveyed the size and grandeur of this part of the Abbey. She walked slowly up a short flight of stairs to the entrance, passing through a pair of bronze gates displaying Tudor emblems. It was at once more intimate than the Abbey and more magnificent, a very large space topped by a fan-vaulted roof with carved pendants. She stood at the top of the stairs, once again almost paralyzed by the sense that her next step would take her somewhere from which she could not easily return.

Straight ahead was the centerpiece of the chapel, the great tomb of Henry VII, who'd built the Lady Chapel in honor of the Virgin Mary and his wife, Elizabeth of York. His ladies. Both sides of the chapel were lined with two tiers of oak pews festooned with banners representing the Knights of the Bath. The colorful banners were festive and welcoming, but Lee avoided the Lady Chapel and instead made her way into the small enclosure to the left. It was a weekday, and early, so there were relatively few people milling about the small, narrow room. Ahead was the tomb. And to its left—Lee took an automatic step back, stifling a gasp.

The monster from David Eddings's apartment. How had he found her? Why was he there?

He stood about three feet from the rail that circled the tomb of the sister queens, staring intently. His body was completely still, his gaze focused directly on the tomb, planning something. Did he know about Semper? How?

An image of David, sprawled on the floor of his living room, his head destroyed. She turned and left the small enclosure, retracing her steps down the stairs to the nave. Once she was beyond the monster's range of vision, she began to walk quickly, back through north transept. She pushed her way through a small crowd of tourists waiting to pay and, once outside, broke into a run. Heading to her right, toward the Parliament building, she threaded her way across Parliament Square, narrowly avoiding an enormous double-decker bus. Adjacent to the Westminster tube stop were a number of tourist shops she'd seen earlier. She turned into a mid-sized store that offered everything from kitschy bric-a-brac to small electronics and guidebooks. Out of breath, she charged down the first aisle to the rear of the store, then back down another aisle toward the front. Midway, she stopped and grabbed a hooded sweatshirt with the Union Jack emblazoned on the front. At the end of the aisle was a vertical rack of cheap sunglasses. She chose the most inconspicuous pair on display and walked to the register. Sarah Cooper's card would foot at least on more charge.

Back outside, she ripped the tags off her purchases, pulled the sweatshirt over her blouse, and put on the sunglasses. Then she ran back to the Abbey and presented her ticket stub at the entrance.

Inside, it took a few minutes to get used to the near-blackout caused by the sunglasses. When she felt able to navigate, she proceeded along the north transept. At the altar, she pulled the hood over her head and continued to the chapel behind it.

The monster was close to where she'd left him, leaning on the wall to the right of the royal sisters' tomb. She moved to the side to let what was now a steady stream of visitors pass her and studied him. He was a menacing presence. Even leaning casually, he projected a coiled aspect that suggested limitless power held, just barely, in check, power that could obliterate anything or anyone who came too close. And his eyes. They darted continually from side to side, missing nothing.

What was he thinking? Why was he there?

She watched him for several minutes, waiting for something to happen. Finally she got up and walked back into the main section of the Lady Chapel, feeling safer with more distance between herself and the monster. When he decided to leave the side chamber, he'd have to walk across the entrance to the Lady Chapel, so she would be able to monitor his movement without having to be with him in the small chamber itself.

She slowly walked around the chapel, trying to focus on the tombs and inscriptions but always with one eye on the front of the chapel, where the narrow doorway led to the side room with the sisters' tomb. She'd grabbed a handful of brochures on her way in the first time and read every word as she passed the time. The last admission to the Abbey was at 6:00. It was going to be a long day. She checked her watch at least every ten minutes. Every half hour or so she walked to the entrance to the side chamber, insinuated herself into a cluster of tourists, and entered the tiny chapel, reassuring herself that the monster was still there.

At about one o'clock, he left the side chamber and began to walk slowly through the Lady Chapel itself, glancing around, making a mental survey. He paid particularly close attention to what looked like surveillance cameras mounted halfway up the walls. There were eight of them, small white plastic-looking objects situated all around the chapel.

After he'd slowly circled the chapel, he left it, walking briskly back to the main portion of the Abbey and, turning left at the front of the altar, heading past Poets' Corner and the Abbey museum to the exit. She watched him leave, keeping a safe distance back. She considered following but thought better of it. He was coming back, she was sure. Instead, she positioned herself outside the only public entrance, the Great North Door through which she'd entered that morning, and waited for him to return.

The wait felt interminable, but at least she was outside. The day was warm and sunny and the throngs of tourists offered a needed distraction—and needed cover.

He returned just over two hours later with a duffle bag. He wore a loose-fitting windbreaker that effectively disguised his imposing size, but he still looked threatening and egregiously out of place, as if a special light were trained directly on him, illuminating his menace. Still, no one paid him any notice as he entered. She waited a few seconds and then went back in, flashing her ticket stub to the guard.

She saw him halfway down the north transept, his height making him an easy mark. He circled the altar and, as expected, climbed the short flight of stairs that led up to the Lady Chapel. As he slowly circled the chapel, he once again focused on the plastic cameras mounted on the walls. Then he walked to the side chamber that held Elizabeth and Mary's tomb. When he was gone, Lee approached one of several red-robed vergers posted throughout the Abbey, who she'd watched all day answering questions from tourists. Hers was a bit unusual.

"Those small cone-shaped, plastic-looking things," she said, pointing up to one of the objects that had so fascinated the monster. "What are they?"

He didn't miss a beat. "Seventeenth-century security devices. Installed by James I."

She managed a smile and hoped he knew the true answer.

"I thought they were nineteenth century," she said, playing along. "Late Romantic."

"Actually, they're multi-directional motion sensors. Passive infrared. Quite modern, obviously."

"They trigger an alarm?"

"Absolutely. Any motion at all sets off an alarm and brings the beadles in."

"Beadles?" The irony almost brought a genuine smile: infrared alarms summoning Dickensian beadles.

"They're posted just outside."

Not inside. The Lady Chapel would be deserted after closing time. But what about the sensors? How was he going to get around them?

She thanked the verger, who seemed completely unfazed by the nature of her question, and decided to stroll around the Abbey itself for an hour until closing time. That was when the monster would make his move.

By six o'clock, when a recorded voice over the public address system announced that the Abbey was closing, most of the visitors had already left. She walked quickly back to the Lady Chapel, which was nearly deserted. Even the verger had left. But the monster was there, at the far end, to the left of the tomb of Henry VII and his wife. Fearing exposure, Lee pressed herself along the right wall at the entrance to the chapel.

A second announcement declared the Abbey officially closed. The stern voice echoed down from the high, vaulted ceiling. The moment the announcement ended, the monster pulled himself up and over a richly carved masonry wall that separated the main portion of the chapel from a small side chapel that held an elaborate tomb. George Villiers was the occupant—she'd memorized every inhabitant of the chapel over the course of the long day. The wall gave him cover, making Villiers's tomb an effective hiding place.

What should she do? A part of her wanted to notify a guard. That would mean blowing her own cover, of course, and she'd find herself telling the London police about a deadly virus buried where the great Elizabeth's bones were supposed to be.

Scratch that. She, too, would have to hide and see what happened. Next to Villiers's tomb was a large organ in its own niche. A plaque, which she must have read ten times that day in an effort to pass the time and appear occupied, indicated that it had been donated by the British-American Society in 1965. Hugging the right side of the Chapel, along the front of the oak stalls, she walked quickly but quietly to the organ. If the monster looked above the masonry wall he'd be able to see her, but he seemed intent on keeping down and out of sight. She reached the organ apparently undetected and crouched behind it.

After a few minutes, she heard the clop of footsteps on the stone floor. Someone had entered the Lady Chapel. The footsteps stopped for a moment, then resumed as whoever had entered left. Then a voice: "All clear in back. I'm heading out."

One of the "beadles" had made his final inspection.

A moment later, there was a thud by the Villiers chapel where the monster had hidden. He must have leaped back over the masonry wall. Then footsteps. Cautiously, Lee peeked around the corner of the organ, then walked quickly across the length of the chapel to the entrance to the side chamber, where she flattened herself against the wall next to the opening and waited until she felt calm enough to slowly turn and look inside.

The monster was already at work.

CHAPTER 59

He was alone. And yet he acted like someone being observed, moving furtively, glancing from side to side, a wary bird. Again she was struck by how tall and powerfully built he was, shoulders unnaturally wide over a narrow waist. Handsome in a cold, squinty way, with that deep, angry scar running from his jaw nearly to his left ear. This was the monster who had followed her from the beginning, the creature who had killed David Eddings and Maurits Immersheim.

The Abbey felt haunted. Silent and very faintly lit by weak light from the stained-glass windows above, it felt alive with spirits, all them watching the monster.

He walked slowly to a far corner of the chapel and looked up at an infrared sensor. From his duffel bag he removed a small fire extinguisher, raised it above his head, and sprayed a thick layer of foam over the device. He moved methodically around the chapel, muttering the entire time, spraying foam over one device after another. When he reached her side of the chapel, he seemed to freeze for a moment, an alert dog sensing a presence, then resumed his work.

"Thermal sensors," she heard him mutter. "Did it occur to *anyone* that heat cannot be detected through water?" He sprayed another sensor. "Fools. You'll live to regret your ignorance. Except you won't." He sniggered and continued to move around the chapel, still muttering, though she could no longer make out what he was saying.

When he had covered every sensor with foam, he put down the extinguisher and walked over to Elizabeth's tomb, which was surrounded by a square railing made of age-blackened steel, about four feet high. Along the top of the railing was a horizontal steel strip inlaid with gilded icons and topped by gilded Tudor roses and fleurs-de-lys. Four black marble columns supported an elaborately decorated canopy that covered the entire tomb. A reclining effigy of Elizabeth lay on a platform that was held up by four small carved lions that sat atop the tomb itself, inside of which were the bones of the sister queens. Well, at least one of them—and Semper.

He tossed the duffel bag over the railing. It fell to the hard stone floor with a loud clatter. He looked up at the nearest motion detector. Lee followed his gaze and saw a milky red glow—it had been activated. He froze for a few moments, probably waiting to see if an alarm sounded or if anyone came to investigate. When no one came he took off his windbreaker, tossed it to the floor, grasped the top of the railing with both hands, and pulled himself up onto it. It must have taken considerable arm strength to lever his body against the railing so that he could bring his legs up to the top horizontal bar. Once he'd done this he swung around and pressed off from the top. He executed the maneuver flawlessly. If he had faltered he would have been impaled by one of the steel roses or fleurs-de-lys.

He turned toward the tomb. The two queens, half sisters, enemies, had been buried together for eternity by Elizabeth's successor, James I. The first Stuart king had a sense of humor. Elizabeth's coffin was on top of Mary's, appropriately enough. The beloved Elizabeth was thought to be pressing down on the despised Mary, prompting some debate as to whether or not the tomb should be opened and Elizabeth's casket trussed up in some way.

Two queens might be crammed into the tomb, but only one rated an effigy. Elizabeth, of course. She looked quite old and beak-nosed, with a half-smile that suggested she was in on some sort of eternal joke—perhaps the knowledge that she'd spend eternity outshining her older half sister. Her head rested on two pillows sculpted from marble. In her long fingers she held a gold scepter, and on her head was a gold crown. Her neck was engirded by a ruff, carved quite effectively from marble.

Above the effigy, the high canopy was supported by eight black marble columns topped by gold capitals decorated with acanthus leaves and scrolls. The canopy itself was a massive structure, also made of marble, with a lengthy inscription that was essentially a list of Elizabeth's accomplishments (nothing on Mary), ending in an acknowledgment that her successor, James (son of the rival she'd executed, Mary of Scotland, who was interred in a similar chamber on the other side of the Lady Chapel), had erected the entire folly.

Lee sensed her legs beginning to lose feeling and shifted very slightly to get the blood circulating. The monster continued to consider the tomb with clinical detachment. The recumbent marble effigy of Elizabeth, supported by four short pillars, was on a platform. Under that platform were the coffins. He moved a finger along a two-inch-long section of a seam separating the top panel from the base. Even from across the chapel Lee could see that the marble on the bottom of the seam had been chipped or abraded, as if some sort of implement had been placed there to pry off the top. Or perhaps this was where a hoist had been connected to the top when it had been lowered onto the bottom centuries ago.

The monster reached into the duffle bag and retrieved what appeared to be a short tire iron and a large rubber-headed mallet. He placed the flat end of the tire iron against the bottom of one of the four carved lions that held up the effigy and gave it several sharp jabs with the mallet. Nothing moved, but each jab discharged a small cloud of dust, probably plaster of some sort, indicating that he'd possibly loosened the pillar a bit. He applied the same process to the other three lion pillars, then put down the mallet and tire iron.

He anchored his feet against the railing and leaned into the statue, pressing against it with both hands. At first, nothing. Then a cracking sound, very faint, then a bit louder, like paper slowly torn.

The queen stirred, almost imperceptibly. The monster repositioned his legs to reestablish purchase and once more leaned into the statue, this time with a roar that reverberated throughout the small chapel. The statue shifted a millimeter, then perhaps an inch. Even from across the chapel Lee could see his arm muscles straining, looking like they would burst through his skin. Slowly, the statue began to shift along the tops of the pillars, which themselves began to wobble.

He let out another roar, and the effigy slid off the two pillars closest to him. No doubt to prevent it from collapsing onto the base, he carefully slid his hands under the lip and pressed up so that it rested on the two pillars farthest from them. Then he pushed forward, and it began slowly moving forward. When it was balanced evenly on the far pillars, he heaved it.

The queen began to slide… then, in a sudden downward acceleration, she crashed to the floor, wedged in the narrow space between the rail and the tomb itself.

He didn't check to see if the fall had damaged the statue. Instead he focused on the marble panel that covered the top of the tomb. He ran a finger around the seam and appeared to find a compromised spot which he leaned closer to to inspect. A few seconds later, Lee watched him jam the tire iron into what must have been a break in the seam and begin to tap it with the mallet.

His efforts produced a fine spray of marble dust, or perhaps pulverized grouting of some sort. It wafted to her end of the chapel carrying a strangely sour odor. Within a minute he had two inches of the tire iron under the panel. He went back into his duffle bag and took out a small object. A doorstop, she guessed. He jammed it right up next to the tire iron, using the mallet to pound it in until it was halfway under the panel. It seemed to loosen the pressure on the tire iron, which he pulled out.

Next he placed the tire iron on the seam about two inches to the right of his original incision and began to pound it with the mallet. After quite a few hits, he inserted a second doorstop to secure the opening and removed the tire iron.

The process seemed to grow easier with each doorstop, as the lid resisted less and less. When he had six doorstops wedged along the length of the tomb, he attacked the two sides, beginning with the ends nearest the opened length. He inserted three doorstops into each end, then stepped back to survey his work.

The panel or lid was now at a visible angle, with a two-inch gap along one side. He went to work on the fourth side, inserting four wedges under the lid. When he was done the entire lid was elevated. A strange odor leeched out of the tomb, spoiled fruit and moldering leaves. The sickly smell of time, she thought. Or was it death?

He positioned himself on one long side of the lid and began to lift it. His arm muscles began to twitch with the effort, but his face was preternaturally serene as he made steady progress. History itself was surrendering to him. Even the thick cloud of sickly sweet dust that was billowing up from the opening didn't appear to deter him.

When one side was open about two feet, he let go with his right hand, reached down, and picked up the tire iron, which he wedged into the opening. Then he let the lid slowly come down until it stopped, propped open by the iron.

The tomb was open for the first time in centuries.

After a few moments reflecting on his victory, he leaned over the tomb and looked inside.

CHAPTER 60

Lee wished she could look inside with him. The coffins of Elizabethan nobles were usually made of marble and quite plain. She imagined Elizabeth's coffin lying on top of that of her hated half sister, reduced for eternity to a prop.

The monster once more reached into his duffel bag and took out a claw hammer. He leaned into the open tomb and seemed to struggle for a few moments. Then there was a scratchy, whining sound—marble against marble, she imagined. She heard him grunt as he applied his entire body to the task, no doubt prying the top off the coffin. After several minutes of effort he placed the hammer on the raised platform, leaned back into the tomb and, with a hoarse, feral moan, he slowly raised the coffin lid to where she could see it over the lip of the tomb.

He stared inside, mute for a moment. Then, in an angry voice: "What the fuck?"

Lee could have told him: there was no body inside, no bones.

He raised the lid until it suddenly slid away from sight, probably down the gap between the coffin and the wall of the tomb. He took a flashlight from his bag and shone the light into the coffin.

"Yes," he hissed, leaning in. "There you are."

Not a body, but he'd seen something.

He shimmied to one end of the casket and began pulling something from it. He was so focused on what he was doing that Lee felt safe stepping forward a bit. He was removing what looked like cloth, but it appeared to disintegrate into fragments, dust even, in his hands. He tossed several pieces onto the floor. Then he retrieved a few of the doorstops that had fallen to the floor when he'd moved the tomb lid and used them to hold open the top of the coffin. She watched him put both arms into the coffin, then he moved his shoulders, adjusting his hands and grip. Very slowly, he pulled his arms back, clearly struggling, as if lifting something heavy at an awkward angle.

His forearms began to quiver from the strain. Then Lee saw what he was struggling to remove from the coffin. The top of a box, just clearing the space beneath the raised coffin lid. When he had the box entirely free of the coffin, he pulled it toward himself and enlisted his arm and chest muscles to hold it close.

He appeared to savor the moment, holding the box tight against his chest before placing it, very carefully, on the floor between the tomb and railing. There, he regarded it with an expression that mixed awe with smug triumph. Lee couldn't make out any lettering or decoration on the box, which struck her as a somewhat pathetic container for what she assumed it contained.

The monster inspected the lid, running a finger along the perimeter before pressing the tips of his fingernails into the space between the base and the lid. With what looked like only a slight effort, he was able to pry it off.

A thin haze of dust shot up from the box, as if fired from a small cannon hidden inside. Even from across the chapel she smelled wet earth laced with sweet spices, cinnamon or cloves, perhaps. Odd. It seemed to sting his eyes, which he rubbed with both fists. When he was able to see clearly, he reached inside the box and began to remove more of the fabric that Lee now realized must have been used to secure the box within the coffin, and was also used to secure whatever was inside the box itself. Again, it broke into fragments. He pulled several chunks of it away before lifting out the box's contents. It was all she could do not to step closer.

A ceramic vessel, about two feet high and half as wide. Even in the gloom of the chapel it glistened with encrusted jewels, which seemed to generate their own light. The largest jewel was the stopper itself, a ping-pong-ball-sized orb that appeared to be made of a single carved stone, the ruby described in the diary. Wrapped tightly around the stone and continuing down to the neck of the vessel was some sort of string or wire, clearly intended to secure the stopper.

He studied it for a few minutes. She wanted to do the same. Then he placed the vessel on the stone floor. Its base must have been a bit uneven, as it wobbled for a moment. He steadied it and then went back to his duffle bag and retrieved a gas mask and hood. He pulled the hood, bright yellow like a rain slicker, over his head, then fitted the mask on his face, pulling the strap over his head.

He was going to release Semper.

There had to be guards patrolling the grounds of the Abbey. She could make a run for the exit and summon them. But if the monster heard them approaching he might open the vessel before they got to him, or simply smash it on the hard stone floor. Her eyes scanned the dimly lit chapel for something she could use to stop him and came to rest on the mallet he'd brought.

As she weighed her next step, the monster began the process of getting the vessel back over the railing without breaking it. He carefully placed it in his duffle bag and then jammed in some of the old cloth he'd taken from the box. After zipping the bag shut, he very slowly lifted it over the top of the railing and then hung the straps over one of the rose finials. Choosing a part of the railing several feet from the bag, he hoisted himself back over, then freed the bag from finial and slowly placed it on the floor.

He crouched next to the bag, unzipped it, and gingerly took out the urn, placing it beside him on the floor. As before, he kept his hands on it until it stabilized. Though she couldn't see his face behind the mask, he seemed totally absorbed in studying his prize.

This was her moment. Her heart pounded in her chest—surely he'd hear it and turn around. She debated between making a run for the mallet, which would be noisy but quick, and moving slowly but quietly. The latter seemed the better course, since even a moment's warning would give him an advantage over her; she'd seen what his strength could do.

Overcoming a paralyzing reluctance to move, she stepped into the small chapel and froze, waiting to see if he'd detected movement. When he didn't react, she took another step. Then another.

He was crouched next to the railing, the mallet three feet behind him, about ten yards from her. Each step felt like a huge commitment, a decisive move from which there was no turning back. Her sneakers were almost silent on the hard stone floor, and the dull hum of wind coursing through the upper reaches of the chapel muffled what little sound she did make. Maybe the gas mask dampened his hearing. Still, as she moved closer he was bound to detect something.

When she was within two feet of the mallet, she decided to lunge for it. He was an animal; even through the mask he'd sniff out her presence if she waited another second. In one swift movement, she jumped forward, picked up the mallet with her right hand, and leapt toward the monster. She brought it down directly on top of his head.

For a moment he didn't appear to respond, just sat there, frozen, staring up at her from behind the mask. She raised the mallet to strike him a second time when he fell to the side.

It felt too easy. The monster unconscious on the stone floor, Semper next to him, waiting to be picked up.

No time to count her blessings. She squatted next to the vessel and carefully raised it. It felt lighter than expected—but then, it likely contained nothing more than infected air. As she slowly lifted it, she saw that it was in the shape of a seated man, as described by Rufus Hatton. She recognized it from the urn at the Smithsonian. Its eyes were incised into the pottery, broad almond shapes with black-painted pupils. The nose was disproportionately large and slightly convex, giving it a hawkish appearance. Its mouth, also incised in the clay, extended from one side of the face to the other and was slightly open; it could be smiling or grimacing, expressing joy or anguish. If joy it was of a diabolical sort, joy in the pain of others. The figure was fearsome, emanating a sense of menace disproportionate to its stature.

Every inch of its surface, which appeared to be made of pottery glazed to a luminous shade of reddish orange, was incised with detailed drawings that were enhanced with finely applied coloring of some sort. The drawings showed near-naked men in the throes of what appeared to be horrible pain. Large almond-shaped eyes, like those of the vessel itself, wide open, pupils too big to fit within. Exaggerated noses with enormous nostrils. Ears with big hoops dangling from them. Mouths distended, baring teeth in what could only be interpreted as agony. The drawings were clearly meant as warnings.

The illustrations formed a sort of story, beginning with men admiring the very object she was holding, then in obvious agony, then lying dead. The surface was rough and surprisingly cool to the touch. She took note of the jewels, particularly the large ruby that served as a stopper.

Wanting to study it more, but aware that she needed to leave quickly, she slowly lowered the vessel into the monster's duffle bag, which he had stuffed with old rags to protect it, and stood up.

She felt something on her leg.

The monster's hand, gripping her just above her ankle. He was lying on his side, looking up at her.

"Put down the bag." His voice was deep and flat. With his free hand, he tore off the gas mask. When she didn't answer, he tightened his grip, his hand easily circling her leg. She felt certain he could shatter her shin with one hand. He started to get up, moving slowly. He could have yanked her down to the floor, but he was obviously worried that her fall would destroy the vessel.

"Stop," she said with all the authority as she could muster. "I'll drop this." She felt his grip weaken just a bit. "You know what will happen."

"Ecophagy," he said. The word she'd heard first from Phelps. "End of days. No one will survive." A deep breath. "What I live for."

She needed to buy time until she figured out how to get away.

"You've been following me. David Eddings, Maurits Immersheim. Miles Truman."

His grip tensed for a moment.

"Dad." He spit the word like a piece of gristle.

"Miles Truman was…." She should have figured this out, and yet. "You're Daniel Truman. But he said you were—"

"Beautiful? I was. I was perfect. But he changed that." With his free hand, he ran a finger along the scar. Back and forth, enjoying the sensation. "With a piece of Ateeka pottery after I broke his precious urn. It was an accident, what I did, but he didn't care. He told the doctors a cabinet of pottery had fallen on me. Who were they to doubt the eminent Miles Truman? He ruined me. No one could look at me, after. I was a pariah."

Miles Truman had told her and Samuel that he didn't know why his beautiful son had been teased in school. But he knew.

"I know what he told you. I forced him to talk, after you left, the way the Tudors forced their prisoners to talk." His eyes met hers, and behind the blue coldness she detected for the first time a spark of something almost human, a connection.

"You know all about Tudor information gathering techniques, don't you Lee?" The sound of her name from his lips was almost sickening. "He also told me where you were staying in Georgetown." The finger still tracing the scar from jaw to ear. "He hated the sight of me, once I'd destroyed his precious urn. He wanted to destroy me in return, but this is all he could do." A note of contempt had crept in. "I'd seen the urn, all of it. I knew the power of Semper. I devoted my life to finding it. Using it." He waited for a reaction. When she remained silent, he said, "Reginald Phelps, did you know I was there, too?" The voice still flat, a dull hum. "He told me what you wanted. He's with the others now. And so is Derek Martinson. Yes, I followed you to Tunsbury. I couldn't let him kill you, not when you seemed to be getting close to finding Semper."

No time to digest this. "How did you find me?"

"You left a trail of Google searches. Semper. Ateeka. I'd been waiting my whole life for this."

It had started with a lost sonnet by Shakespeare. The sonnet had brought the monster.

"How did you know what—"

"I cultivated people who could help me. In intelligence, police work. And once I found you they kept me informed about where you were. Rental car GPS, police bulletins. It wasn't hard. No one is invisible." A short silence, then: "Now give me the bag."

He began to pull her down.

"I'll drop it," she said. "I'll throw it."

"Go right ahead." But she'd heard a moment's hesitation.

"You don't want to die."

"I deeply want to die."

"But the gas mask…." She glanced down and saw something approaching a smile, his index finger still sliding along the scar.

"I want to see it." He let out a long breath, a sigh. "The suffering. The death. You saw the carvings on the urn, and on the vessel? I want to see that, here, in the Abbey. And then I'll take off the mask. My work will be done."

"But it's just you and me."

"And when it opens, this place, this house of God…." A slight surge in volume. "It will fill up with people, and I will watch them writhe and cough blood and I will know that the virus will find its way outside and I will imagine the thousands, perhaps millions of wretches meeting a similar fate." The finger was moving quickly now, back and forth. His eyes had lost focus. If she was ever going to get away….

"Okay, I'll give it to you," she said. "Here." She held the bag in front of her, at waist level.

"Put it on the floor."

She bent her knees and leaned forward, the bag still at her waist. Slow, deliberate, but clutching it tightly, both hands gripping the loose canvas. His hand relaxed very slightly on her leg. She pivoted left as she slowly lowered herself and the bag until her knees were bent at ninety degrees. She was aware of his breathing, an expectant dog awaiting a treat.

"On the floor," he said.

"I don't want to drop it." Buying a few seconds.

His free hand moved from the scar toward the bag. His eyes followed. "Drop it if you want, I don't—"

With her free leg, she kneed his face. He groaned. A second knee to his face, directly on his nose, pushing upward. A crunching, a trickle of blood. She felt his grip loosen and yanked her leg hard, freeing it but almost stumbling. She staggered a few feet, clutching the bag, and managed to right herself. Without looking back, she ran, her footsteps echoing sharply on the stone floor as she left the side chapel, crossed the entrance to the Lady Chapel, and began to circle the great nave. Keenly aware of leaving a trail of sound, she cradled the bag to her chest, both hands wrapped around it. Ahead was the entrance she'd come in through hours earlier, four modern doors set into the ancient entrance. Each had a panic bar—she wasn't locked in.

Less than ten yards from the exit, she heard something behind her. Turning, she saw him, barely five long steps from her.

Just before hitting one of the doors, she turned around and slammed her back into the panic bar. The door flew open, and she practically fell through it. When she'd regained her equilibrium, she saw that she was in a small vestibule with another set of doors to get through. Again, she turned at the last moment so that her back hit the panic bar, the vessel safe in the bag. The monster was coming through the first set of doors. In his right hand was the mallet.

Finally outside the Abbey, she ran straight ahead, unsure where to go or what to do, other than get away from him. She heard a shout behind her, then a muffled groan. Turning briefly, she saw a security guard standing to the side of the entrance crumple to the ground. He must have been alerted by a motion sensor in the nave. Already leaving him behind was the monster, mallet raised.

The area in front of the Abbey was deserted. In the small, open park, she felt exposed and vulnerable. The night was dark, the air cool. She had no clue where to run, only that she couldn't stop. Then, an idea. She turned abruptly to her right, toward the Thames. If forced to, she could throw the urn into the river.

She sprinted across the lawn toward the darkened Parliament building. The Thames was straight ahead, perhaps a only few hundred yards away. Hopefully nearer, because the footsteps were getting closer. She didn't dare break stride to turn around.

She turned right onto Bridge Street, toward the river. A car pulled onto the street, heading toward her, headlights forcing her to squint. She tried to shout but was too winded to make much noise. The car cruised right past her, throwing the street back into darkness.

He was gaining on her. She could hear his breathing, each pant accompanied by a low grunt, a feral animal ready to pounce. She forced her legs to move faster. The river came into view, or rather the wide road that ran parallel to it. She turned left onto it, the Victoria Embankment, and then ran across it toward the river.

A car approached along the embankment. She couldn't let this one pass. She turned and headed directly into its path. If she hadn't been carrying Semper in the duffle bag, she would have waved her arms.

The car, which she couldn't make out behind the blaring headlights, didn't slow down. She was running right toward it, and it was coming directly at her. When they were perhaps ten yards apart, she darted to the right. But not in time. She heard the screech of brakes, then felt an impact on her left hip. It was a glancing hit, but enough to send her sprawling onto the cobblestones. She fell on her back, still cradling the duffle bag to her chest. The car stopped several yards beyond where she lay.

The monster was on top of her now. Reaching over, trying to pry the bag from her arms.

"Noooo!" It was all she could shout as she tried to fend him off. He made low, rutting grunts. In the darkness she couldn't make out his face, that ugly scar.

Then another voice, a man's.

"What the hell?"

The driver. He must have left his car. Footsteps approaching. The monster left her for a moment to deal with the interloper. She scrambled to her feet, prepared to run.

Then another idea.

The car door was open, the headlights still beaming, clouds of exhaust drifting up into the night air. Aware that the monster was attacking the driver, who was still standing, fighting off blows from the monster's fists, she raced to the open driver's door and got in. After placing the bag on the floor behind her seat, she put the car in drive.

The driver collapsed to the ground, and the monster turned to face the car in front of him, walking toward her, arms thrust to the side, prepared to stop the oncoming vehicle with strength alone.

She floored the gas pedal. The car lurched forward, slammed into him, and for a second she thought she might have succeeded, for the car jerked to the right on impact. At that moment she saw his face clearly, the headlights illuminating it from below, casting it in super-relief. The scar looked almost translucent. She thought of the distorted faces on the side of the vessel.

Time froze at the moment of collision, just her and the monster, eyes locked. The impact threw him off to the left, his body catapulted at least five feet into the air.

She regained control of the car and kept driving along the embankment. In the rearview mirror, she saw him stand up.

Just leave, she told herself. *Get as far from him as possible, as quickly as possible.*

But she couldn't leave the monster alive.

She slammed on the brakes, causing the car to spin around so that it faced him. Now the gas. He didn't move from his spot in the middle of the road. He assumed the same defensive stance, prepared to stop the car in its tracks.

This time the impact sent him straight up in the air and then, a long moment later, back down onto the hood with a thud that sent a tremor through the steering wheel and up along her arms to her shoulders, which jerked back. His face was against the windshield, one eye seemingly pressed against the glass. It looked straight at her, glassy as a dying fish, as she continued to steer the car along the embankment. Then it blinked, and the monster's arms began clutching at the windshield, finally finding purchase in the recess where the wipers retracted.

Slam on the brakes or accelerate? Which would dislodge him? Suddenly, his right hand began pounding on the glass directly in front of her, his fist like the mallet head. On the second blow, tiny cracks appeared and immediately spread across her line of vision. On the third blow, pieces of glass flew into her face. He was pummeling his way into the moving car.

She took her foot off the gas and jammed it down onto the brake pedal. She hoped he would fly off the hood and onto the street in front of the car, but his left hand managed to hold on.

The car was almost stopped. His right hand continued to decimate the windshield in front of her. Blood dripped from his fist. Soon there'd be nothing left between them.

She floored the gas pedal and the car lurched forward. After half a block, she slammed on the brakes. Again he managed to hold on with one massive hand, and immediately resumed demolition, opening a gap in the windshield about a foot in diameter.

She stomped on the gas pedal as his right hand thrust through the glass. She pressed herself back into the car seat, but he managed to pull his body forward with his left hand, which still gripped the edge of the hood. As the car accelerated, his hand inched forward until it touched and then gripped her neck. The smell of blood, the warm breath of something not quite human. He squeezed, his hand so massive it gripped her neck like a child's wrist.

She tried to swat his hand away with her left hand, but it was a vise, unmovable, and she needed both hands on the steering wheel to control the moving car. She hit the brake pedal and brought the car to an almost immediate halt, but this time he had two braces—the hood edge and her neck. The sudden stop jerked him back, bringing her head with him. Somehow he managed to tighten his grip, huge fingers now squeezing it as easily as a sponge. She tried to inhale but couldn't.

The monster was choking the life from her. Bursts of black, like ink blots, shot across her vision, eyes beginning to close.

In a single panicked moment, as she pressed the gas pedal, she calculated that she had one more chance left to jerk the car to a stop and hope it dislodged him.

Simply stopping short wouldn't work. His hand was fused to her neck, his other hand a clamp on the edge of the hood. But there was another option.

Still accelerating the car, she jerked the wheel to the right, toward the river. The brakes squealed, and the monster's body flailed off to the left, pulling her head to the side. She straightened the car and floored the gas pedal. Her vision began to flicker. A second or two of consciousness remained. Ahead, the waist-high limestone wall that ran along the embankment appeared to be flying toward the car.

It took every bit of resolve she had left to keep her foot down on the gas. The flickering morphed into a steady dimness, the world contracting to a few feet in front of her. The pressure on her lungs was awful.

The monster's face was an inch or two from her own face, bits of glass sparkling on his skin.

Then, in a flash, the wall was there. Close to unconscious, she braced for impact.

The explosion felt like it came from within her, so all-encompassing was the sound, the impact. Her entire body lurched forward, and in what must have been a nano-second she prepared for the impact, and for what would follow.

But the impact never came. Instead, when she managed to open her eyes, she saw nothing. Darkness engulfed her, and she realized right away what this had to mean.

Or perhaps not. She was able to move a hand. Tentatively she brought it to her neck—or tried to. It wouldn't move. She wasn't dead. Worse, she was paralyzed.

Then she got it and almost sobbed with relief. The impact had deployed the airbag.

Once this sunk in, she began beating it with both hands. The sound of her own panting meant that the monster's hand was no longer choking her. Finally she was able to push the airbag off to the passenger side. She turned quickly to the duffel bag on the floor of the back seat. It looked unharmed; the vessel remained swaddled in cloth.

Facing front, she saw him, to her left, his blood-streaked face in the driver's side window. Before she could process this, he reached his left arm around to the hole in the windshield.

She put the car in reverse and it lurched back, throwing the monster off to the side. He almost fell to the ground but righted himself. She jerked the car into drive and floored it, turning the wheel to the left. The instant she slammed into him she hit the brakes. The car stopped a few feet from the embankment wall, but he flew into it. She heard the thud of impact through the gash in the windshield.

But the monster remained standing. Even took a step toward the car.

She waited until he was a yard away, and hit the gas, slamming him back against the wall. This time he collapsed onto the sidewalk. She backed up the car and watched as he slowly got to his feet. Blood ran from the back of his head down his shoulders. His shirt was in tatters, blood leeching from his chest.

He lurched forward, toward the car. His face was expressionless, eyes boring into her through the punched-out windshield. She waited until he was halfway between the wall and the car, then stepped on the gas. The car jumped forward and hit him just as he reached the edge of the sidewalk. He was thrown against the wall and collapsed to the sidewalk.

She backed up the car and waited.

"Get up!" She was surprised by the strength in her voice. "Get the fuck up!" She wanted one more shot at him.

He complied.

This time, standing was a long and slow process. His arms appeared to be useless to him as he pressed his back against the wall, using only his legs to force himself up. His head looked wobbly, and when he began to move toward the car he staggered more than walked, lurching from side to side. And still he stared at her, directly at her eyes, even as blood obscured most of his face. No evidence of pain or fear. Only rage.

When he was a few yards from the car, she floored the gas and drove into him. He flew into the air, perhaps eight feet off the ground, hit the wall with his back, and fell forward, landing on his face.

She backed up and waited.

"Get up, fucker!" she yelled, thinking of David Eddings and Maurits Immersheim. "Get up!"

This time it took him at least a minute to stand, his legs now almost as useless as his limp arms. But by pressing himself against the wall he was able to stand, and once he'd righted himself he came at her, staggering, unblinking eyes lasering into her.

She put the car in reverse, wanting a head start for the next hit. When she was ten or so yards from him, across the embankment, she put the car back into drive and began the final assault.

It seemed to unfold in slow motion. As the car flew toward him, his expression never changed, not even when the car hit him square in the gut. At the moment of impact, their eyes locked. In that instant she saw a depth of wrath that she knew, even then, she'd never be able to forget.

"Rot in hell!" she screamed as his body flew off the car. It sailed up into the night sky, easily surmounting the wall, then plunged down toward the river on the other side.

She put the car in park and ran to the wall. The monster had landed on his back on the hard, dry ground that ran along the Thames, arms splayed, legs bent at the knee. A pool of blood spread out from under his head. And still he stared up at her, oozing hatred and blood even in death.

CHAPTER 61

For two days, numbness alternated with chest-pounding panic. During the long, blank stretches it was as if Westminster Abbey had never happened, as if she'd never encountered the monster or even found the sonnet. And then, sudden as a camera flash, it all became vividly clear, and the pressure on her chest made it difficult to breathe. In the hotel room's small closet, still swaddled inside the monster's gym bag, was the source of the horror, the jeweled effigy. She hadn't looked at it since returning to the hotel in Bayswater. Wasn't tempted. In fact, she wanted it away from her. Gone.

At some point during the second day she turned on the television. Every channel was given over to round-the-clock coverage of the Elizabethan Desecration, as it was being called. The tomb of the most beloved monarch in British history despoiled, the casket itself emptied of the great queen's bones. The effigy atop the tomb would be repaired, experts reassured a shaken nation. Security would be beefed up. But the queen's bones, would they ever be recovered?

At least they had discovered the man who'd perpetrated the horror. Among other clues, his fingerprints were all over the tomb. His broken body was found on the edge of the Thames. He carried no identification. The car with his blood on it was mentioned. It was thought that he'd taken the bones from the coffin and then perhaps thrown them into the river. Or had someone else taken them, an accomplice? The monster's body was badly damaged, multiple bones shattered, deep gashes across his face and arms. Had the person who'd done this to him also taken the royal remains? A second body, found lying dead on the embankment, his head crushed, belonged to a government auditor heading home after working late. He was assumed to be an innocent victim.

The perpetrator was identified within twenty-four hours: Daniel Truman, son of Miles Truman, the eminent archaeologist. An analyst for the CIA, honors graduate from Yale with top-level security clearance.

No wonder he'd so easily managed to follow her. There were crews from British and American news services outside his father's home in Washington, where Miles Truman's torture and murder were breathlessly covered. News crews were camped outside the Abbey, of course, which was closed to visitors.

Lee waited for the knock on her hotel room door. But no one came for her. Perhaps surveillance cameras from the Abbey would be consulted, and they would reveal a blond woman wearing dark glasses in her late twenties, early thirties entering the Abbey and never leaving. She carefully worked through the events of the past several days. Was there any connection between her and the monster, something the British police could turn up? Perhaps he'd written her name somewhere. His Google searches could be investigated. It was out of her hands.

Lee clicked off the TV and waited for the numbness to return. During these blank periods she slept for short, blessedly dreamless spells. And gradually, while awake, she began to process the recent past with decreasing panic. She began to formulate a plan.

Day three, as Lee thought of it. Three days *after*.

She felt small and inconsequential as the fishing boat she'd hired motored out of Tilbury harbor. Tilbury was near where Elizabeth had made her famous address to the troops in 1588 while awaiting the expected invasion by the Spanish Armada. It had seemed a fitting place for what she had in mind, but now she wasn't so sure. Tilbury turned out to be one of Europe's busiest container ports. Huge, unwieldy ships, their decks stacked high with steel containers, loomed over the port. Several cruise ships, too, were moored there. The small fishing boat she'd hired felt like an ant maneuvering among massive furniture.

Tilbury was on the Thames, about an hour by train east of London. She'd told the boat's captain, a white-haired man in his late sixties named Dave, that she wanted to head out to open water. That would take an hour or so, he'd said, and cost her two hundred pounds. He hadn't asked her what her intentions were, other than to ascertain that she was not interested in fishing.

"Not exactly your charming English port," Samuel said as they left Tilbury harbor. The growl of small boat's engine forced them to shout. Lee didn't have much to say and used the noise as an excuse to keep to herself. She'd invited Samuel to accompany her not because she wanted him there but because she needed a witness.

"Somewhere over there is where Elizabeth addressed her troops." She pointed to a high spot of land, east of the town, now covered with houses and warehouses. *We have been persuaded by some that are careful of our safety, to take heed how we commit ourselves to armed multitudes, for fear of treachery.* It was the longest passage Lee had memorized as a teenager, the famous speech by the queen whose reign, with its poets and playwrights and soldiers and statesmen and explorers, would be her life's work.

While holed up in Bayswater, she'd made exactly one phone call—to Samuel. Tomorrow, back from Tilbury, she'd turn herself in to the authorities in London, tell them everything she knew, beginning at the end, in Westminster Abbey, and working back to the beginning, with a trip to the Taylor-Shipford house with a dimly recalled bond trader named Matthew and the serendipitous discovery of a sonnet in a book of love poetry.

As they motored east toward the sea the landscape became less populated, and in places quite lovely. She found it easier to imagine Elizabeth, dressed in warrior's garb astride her white horse, itself draped in armor, inspiring the troops as they awaited the expected arrival of the Spanish. She doubted that any member of the Filer clan had been among the troops that day, but Elizabeth's thoughts had no doubt turned to her progeny as she surveyed the sea of young men. Was she pleased that the Filers were safe in Hertfordshire, or did she, like so many monarchs, ache to see a young prince of her blood bearing arms for the crown at the head of an army? Frail Edward, the first of a shivering dynasty, would never fill that role. Nor would his heirs.

It was an hour before open sea came into view. She and Samuel said little, and in truth she would have preferred to be alone. She'd begun the journey on her own and wished she could finish it that way. He must have sensed her diffidence, for he had made few attempts to speak even when she'd picked him up at Heathrow and on the ride from the airport to Tilbury. She looked forward to dropping him off at a hotel and having nothing more to do with him. She might need him to verify her story, once she'd gone to the police, but there would be no more personal relationship. It had begun with him using her. It would end with her using him.

"How far out were you thinking?" the captain asked.

"Until the sea bottom drops off," she said. "To where it's deeper than a fishing line can reach."

Dave shrugged at the strangeness of her request but said nothing.

• • •

A half hour later, the sudden silence when Dave turned off the engine intensified everything: the sounds of seagulls in the distance, the slapping of the current against the side of the boat, the sparkles of sunlight glancing off the water, the rhythmic back-and-forth of the boat atop the choppy sea. There were no other boats within a half mile of them.

"It's too deep for an anchor," the captain said, "but the tide's heading out to sea. We'll be fine."

Yes, we will, she almost said back to him. She ducked into the low-ceilinged cabin where she'd earlier placed the duffle bag and brought it back onto the deck. She'd left the vessel in the monster's duffle bag, which had successfully protected it even during the frantic chase outside the Abbey.

"Can I see it now?" Samuel had asked several times already, and each time she'd said no.

She wanted to say no one last time, but in truth she desired a final look. *The* final look. Carefully, she placed the bag on the deck and unzipped it. The vessel was swaddled in the old cloth she'd seen the monster pull out of the crate. She gently pushed it to the side and, with both hands firmly gripping the center of the figure, she raised it from the bag.

Samuel expelled a long sigh. Five hundred years of mystery and anxiety, bottled up in a South American jungle and now held in her hands.

"It's hideous," he said, almost whispering. The effigy was indeed fearsome, with its leering smile and maniacally large eyes, and the faces incised and painted on the side of the vessel were ugly, primitive depictions of agony. Somehow they canceled out the glory of the encrusted jewels, even the magnificent and no doubt priceless ruby stopper.

A bigger-than-usual wave heaved the boat to one side and she stumbled forward into Samuel. Alarmed, she sat down on one of the benches that ran the length of the boat, still cradling the vessel.

"We'll never know if it was true," Samuel said, unable to take his eyes off the urn. "It could be nothing in there, or it could be Armageddon. The scientist in me wants to know."

"And never will," she said, looking intently at him.

"There are laboratories that could handle this. Analyze it."

"Where someone like that monster could get hold of it. Or an accident could occur. I won't let that happen."

After a long beat, he nodded.

"Here are the weights you brought along," the captain said, coming from the stern. "Christ, that's an ugly thing. All those gaudy fake jewels and nasty drawings. S'no wonder you want to bury it."

One of those "fake" jewels could support her for years, as the Hever Emeralds continued to support the Filers. The ruby stopper alone could set her up for life. But she hadn't been tempted to pry even a single stone from the vessel. What if doing so opened up a tiny hole in the clay? And in any case, she wanted nothing to do with anything connected to it, literally or figuratively. It was evil. It needed to disappear.

Dave dropped a canvas bag onto the deck with a loud thud. Lee had bought a hundred pounds of barbell plates, ten plates weighing ten pounds each, at a sporting goods store in London.

"Rufus Hatton held this," she said. "It was carried from South America to London, and he held it in his hands, Elizabeth's personal physician. The queen herself saw it, perhaps even touched it." Lee ran her fingers along the vessel's jeweled surface, as if reading Braille for a long-hidden message. "Hatton knew what these pictures meant, and he tried to ensure that Semper would never do harm."

The vessel might be evil, but it had touched glory. Reluctantly, she placed it back in the duffle bag and arranged the old cloth around it.

"I called Edward Aspinall yesterday," she said, also in a quiet voice, as if she, like Samuel, was concerned about rousing old spirits. "I told him I would try to protect the family's privacy. All they want is to be left alone. I think we owe them that."

Again she looked intently at him, and again, after a pause, he nodded.

"Burying a truth like this is agony for a scholar," she said.

"Sometimes life has to trump the past," he said.

Her thought exactly. As if to prove this point, she grabbed the handbag she'd brought along and took out the diary, which she'd placed inside a small, heavy-duty plastic bag with a ziplock closure.

"You're going to bury that, too?" Samuel asked.

"Life trumps the past," she said. "Rufus Hatton wanted it destroyed when he died. But he outlived his servant Lucy, and anyone else who might have carried out his wishes. At least I can do that for him. And if I published this, it would lead the entire world to the Filers' doorstep."

"But it could help you prove your innocence."

"I'm not worried about that."

She waited for him to acknowledge what she'd said. His testimony, and that of his Semper Society colleagues, could corroborate her story. He waited a full minute before nodding. She started to place the diary next to the urn in the duffle bag but hesitated a long moment. Why not just keep it to herself, a treasure, her secret? The sonnet had led her to the diary, and it had trained a spotlight on the one line in the diary that indicated where Semper was: "partner in throne and grave." The Semper Society had always had the power to find Semper, but only she'd uncovered its secret, led to it by the sonnet.

"You had the information all along," she said to Samuel, holding up the diary. "But you didn't have knowledge."

She placed the diary in the plastic bag and then, reluctantly, put it next to the vessel. The plastic bag would only protect it for so long, and then it would succumb to salt water and time. Life trumps the past. But she couldn't send it to the bottom of the sea unprotected. She swaddled the vessel in towels she brought from the hotel and then, one by one, she placed the iron plates very carefully around it, with the towels acting as a buffer. She managed to get eight plates in the bag.

"Eighty pounds should do it," she said. Then she reached into the side pocket of her windbreaker, another London purchase, and took out a second heavy-duty plastic bag. Inside was a piece of plain white paper.

"I wrote something for the occasion," she said as she took out the paper.

"Read it," he said.

She hadn't planned to read it again, but now it seemed the right thing to do, a eulogy. She unzipped the bag and took out the paper, which was folded in quarters. She spread out the paper and stood up.

"Hear, Queen, for word I bring from distant time and place.
The augur clasps the common man in firm embrace.
Honi soit qui mal y pense.
You, friend, of gold are made in France."

When she was done, she couldn't help smiling, though, oddly, she felt tears on her cheeks. Samuel was looking at her as if she were insane.

"That makes no sense."

"Well, I'm not Shakespeare, obviously. But I've learned a few things about word games. I think Rufus Hatton would know what it means. And the queen." And the hidden message would please Her Majesty, she might have added.

"What does it mean?"

She folded the paper and put it back into the plastic bag. After she'd closed it, she tucked it into the duffle bag.

"What does it mean?"

"Figure it out." He frowned and started to insist, but she interrupted him. "Help me with this."

They lifted the duffel bag from the bottom, both using two hands. They first hoisted it onto the stern-side bench. The side of the boat was about a foot and a half higher than the bench.

"We want to lower it gently," Samuel said. "If it hits the water with too much impact, the weights could smash the vessel."

They both got onto the bench, on either side of the bag, and knelt facing it. Then, slowly, they raised the bag to the edge of the boat and extended their arms over the side.

"Wait for the boat to come down from a roll," Samuel said, his voice pinched from the strain of holding the bag. "Okay, not yet… okay… now!"

They let go of the bag at the same moment, just as the water rose to meet it, as if the sea itself were eager for this latest offering. The bag floated for less than a moment, but it seemed an eternity. And then, finally, it began to sink.

They both watched as it fell away, and continued to stare at the spot where it had vanished.

"Rest in peace," Samuel whispered.

She could only nod in agreement.

The Heir

"I know the truth of that Madam, you need not tell it me. Your Majesty thinks if you were married you would be but Queen of England; and now you are both King and Queen."

—Sir James Melville, Scottish Ambassador

"I must not omit to say also that the common opinion, confirmed by certain physicians, is that this woman is unhealthy, and it is believed certain that she will not have children."

—Bishop Alvaro de la Quadra,
Spanish Ambassador to England,
January 1561

CHAPTER 62

After all that had happened, Lee assumed she was immune to shock. But the sight of Matthew the bond trader standing at her door on a Saturday morning, two weeks after she returned from London and following countless hours of lawyer-assisted meetings with cops and district attorneys in New York, made her head swim.

"Surprised, huh?" he said.

Well, he hadn't been the most articulate lover she'd ever had. But he was still undeniably good-looking, albeit in a casual, scruffy way that was very un-Wall Street.

"It's Matthew," he said shyly but with a touch of pique; he was unused to being forgotten, clearly. "We spent a weekend together a few—"

"I remember."

"Can I come in?"

The police had recommended a cleaning service that specialized in crime scenes. After spending several nights in a hotel, she'd moved back to her sanitized apartment. She'd had a new bed delivered and splurged on cheerful, high-thread-count linens. But she'd slept on the sofa in the living room and didn't know when if ever she'd feel unsqueamish in the bedroom. She wished she could afford to move, but her fellowship at Columbia was in doubt, now that David Eddings was no longer there to sponsor her, and her reputation, though clear in a legal sense, was hardly one with which an Ivy League English department wished to be associated. The sonnet was in police evidence, but it would be returned to her eventually. Perhaps it would be her ticket back.

"I'm not really looking to…" In fact, no one had been inside her apartment other than the cleaning crew, and certainly not a lover.

"No, no, nothing like that. I have something to tell you." When she didn't respond, he handed her an envelope. "And I wanted to give you this."

She took it. It was addressed to her, still sealed. The handwriting, neat, precise, with the distinct northwestern thrust of a leftie, was immediately familiar.

"Where did you…."

But she couldn't finish. Instead, she walked back into her apartment and sat on the sofa on which her new quilt and pillow were still piled. He sat on a chair across from her.

"I should have come to you sooner," he said. "When I read what happened here…." He glanced nervously at the bedroom, then back at her. "I didn't think it had anything to do with our night together, or finding the poem. It seemed like a coincidence, your going home with that guy and him ending up getting killed. I'm glad it all worked out, by the way."

By the way. Samuel had come through for her, at least, corroborating the key points of her story. The police and the FBI were able to trace the monster's movements from Washington to New York to Tunsbury to London. There was still no evidence of the monster traveling to New York the night Alex Folsom had been murdered in her apartment, but the assumption was that he'd driven up, killed the cameraman, set up the frame, and left the same day. She knew that it had been the Semper Society, but part of the deal she'd worked out with Samuel was that he'd support her story only if she didn't implicate his brethren in the Folsom murder. We did what we did for the greater good, he kept telling her. The Filer family had likewise escaped with their privacy intact; the shooting death of Derek Martinson was attributed to robbery and never connected to the case. Their illustrious ancestry remained a secret.

"Where did you get this?" She clutched the paper so tightly between her fingers that her hand was shaking.

"Like I was saying, I didn't—"

"Where did you *get this*?"

He looked up at her with an expression close to panic. His eyes darted to the bedroom door—what if the newspapers had it wrong and she was, after all, the killer? She almost smiled at his sudden fear. Taking a deep breath, she sat down.

"Talk to me."

He nodded sheepishly. "I'm not a bond trader," he began. "Not even close. I'm an orderly at a nursing home in the Bronx, the Riverdale Senior Center."

Another handsome, smooth-talking imposter. For someone with trust issues, she was easily deceived.

"It's not the most glamorous job, mostly transporting patients to and from therapy, helping out with personal care, shaving and stuff, sometimes restraining them when they become unruly. That's what I do during the day, but I'm really an actor."

"No kidding."

He rolled his eyes. "I haven't had much luck getting parts. My look isn't really what casting directors want, at least that's what I'm told."

Too generically handsome, she thought, almost an anachronism, like a dad from the fifties. She waved the envelope at him to get him back on track.

"Okay, so one of the patients, a Mrs. Dillard, she and I got to know each other. Nice old lady, well, they're all old, but she was more or less lucid, which was kind of rare. She was at the home for a few years and we talked about the theater and movies. About six months ago, she started to go downhill. Cancer, I don't know what kind, I don't really get involved in the medical stuff. Anyway, she was transferred to the hospice ward a few months ago and I figured I'd never see her again. That happens a lot; you get used to it. One day they're there, the next, gone. But then I got a message from a nurse who worked hospice that Mrs. Dillard wanted to see me. During a break, I went to her. She didn't look too bad, but she told me she didn't have long, and her voice was kind of faint. 'I have a role for you,' she said when I sat down next to her. She asked me to open her locker. All the hospice patients have a locker for their things. The key is on an elastic band around their wrists. Which doesn't always prevent some staff from looting them, but I guess it makes them feel like they still have some control. She pulled the key off her wrist and asked me to open her locker and take out a book. The book was the complete works of Shakespeare, very old and worn. I handed it to her and helped her to sit up. She opened it and took out a piece of paper, also old-looking, like parchment. She had it sandwiched between two pieces of plastic wrap. She told me it was a sonnet written by Shakespeare. Naturally I had my doubts, but what was the point of arguing with a woman with a few weeks at most left to live? Then she told me I needed to give it to you, but without your knowing that it had been arranged."

"You arranged for me to find it?"

"I had to work fast. She didn't have long to live and I was only going to get paid—five hundred bucks—once the sonnet was in your hands. She told me where you lived and I—"

"She knew where I lived?"

He nodded. "And I followed you for a few days, until I saw a chance to make contact."

"At the Starbucks here—"

"On your corner. You weren't exactly ..." He shook his head and looked down.

Hard to get, he was going to say. "Go on."

"She told me that I should take you to the Taylor-Shipford house, where you'd discover—" he made air quotes with both hands "—the sonnet. She told me there was a gift shop there with a lot of used and new books and that you were into Shakespeare and poetry and stuff."

"All you had to do was convince me to go away with you."

His half-smile was equal parts sheepish and proud. "She made it clear that we didn't have to spend the night. She kept referring to a day trip." Another half-smile.

"Excuse me." She got up and walked quickly to the bathroom. A surge of nausea had overcome her; she retched a few times over the sink but didn't throw up. She splashed cold water on her face and glanced in the mirror. She'd dyed her hair back to its original color, more or less, but still didn't fully recognize herself. Every glance in the mirror involved an effort at reacquaintance.

When she was back on the sofa, she nodded for Matthew to continue.

"While you were looking around upstairs at Taylor-Shipford, I went to the gift shop and found a book of Elizabethan love poems. She told me the kind of book to look for. I put it on a table near the front of the store and put the poem in it, and prayed you'd open it, which you did."

"And if I hadn't?"

"I was going to discover it myself, and show it to you. Not as effective, but I wasn't going to leave that house without you having found the poem. But you did open it, and you found the poem."

"Did you get paid?"

"She gave me a check for five hundred dollars, yes. Easiest money I ever made. A few weeks later the news hit that you were wanted for murder." A quick glance at the bedroom. "The press hadn't connected the murder with the sonnet itself, and I didn't think there was a connection, but I was pretty freaked out that I'd known you, even for a weekend. I didn't tell anyone about us. It seemed smart just to keep my head down. About the same time I heard that Mrs. Dillard had stopped eating. A lot of hospice patients do that when they know it's almost over. I figured the next thing I'd hear about her was that she was dead, but I was wrong. I got another message to go see her. She looked even worse than before, much weaker. I sat real close to her and asked what she wanted. This time she told me to open the drawer next to her bed. Inside was an envelope, the one you're holding. She asked me to give it to you. No fooling around this time, no acting. I was to hand it to you and then let her know that you had it. She offered me money, but I told her I would do it for free. See, by this time you were a fugitive and I didn't know how I'd get it to you. I figured I'd just humor the old lady and make her last hours a little less painful. I wasn't sure if she'd seen the news about you or not. I kept the letter, and I didn't open it, as you can see. When I read that you were back in New York and no longer accused of anything, I figured it was time to make good on my promise."

"And Mrs. Dillard?"

"She died two days after giving me the letter. Did you know her?"

"I think so," she whispered, glancing at the handwriting.

"I'm sorry about what happened, and if I had any part in—"

"Forget it, okay? You need to leave now." She stood up, and he immediately did the same.

"If I had known that—"

"I said forget it." She walked to the front door and opened it. He seemed reluctant to leave without absolution. Best to give it to him and get him out of there. "You're an actor, you played a part. Goodbye." When he still seemed unwilling to leave, she added, "Look, you did the right thing, bringing the letter." She forced herself to add, "Thank you."

Visibly relieved, he stepped out into the hallway, and she shut the door. For a moment, it seemed possible that he'd never been there. She stood still and closed her eyes, trying to clear her mind and, by extension, erase the last half hour. But when she opened them, the envelope with the familiar handwriting was still in her right hand, the unused bed was still visible through the bedroom door, and the events of the recent past were still staking a claim on her mind, and probably always would. Now everything would have to be retrofitted to the unexpected but patently credible tale told by yet another liar.

She made a pot of coffee, each step in the process a buffer against the moment when she would have no choice but to open the envelope. She made buttered toast even though she wasn't hungry and put the coffee cup and plate on a tray along with silverware and a napkin. All very nice; all very pointless. After setting the tray on the living room coffee table, she sat down, picked up the envelope and, following a long wait, peeled it open.

CHAPTER 63

The familiar left-canting handwriting filled two sides of an unlined page. The words and lines were densely spaced, covering almost the entire surface, as if there had not been a second piece of paper available. The writing was precise but faint, the work of a determined but frail hand.

My dearest Leslie,

May I call you that? I ceded any claim to your heart the day I left you twenty-five years ago, but you are still dear to me. My dearest.

If I ramble and seem incoherent, it is only because I am writing from a place where I have been brought to die. Moving my hand across the page is a struggle, but the words themselves pain my heart far more than the effort to write them strains my body. Still, they must be written, and I have little time left. I have spent my life running away. Now, at the end, I will not run.

I left your father because I had to. He wasn't a bad man, but he was bad for me. I was suffocating. That sounds selfish, I know, even to me, but that is how it was. I considered taking you with me but I had no money, no place to live. It seemed better for you to stay with him in Pennsylvania. He was a kind man, and he loved you. At least that is what I told myself. There is no forgiveness possible for what I have done, so I will not ask for it.

I came to New York and got work at a small book store. Eventually I married its owner, Bob Dillard. He wasn't as kind as your father, but he was interesting to me in a way your father never was. We had an interesting life together. I was too old to have more children then, which seemed to suit him. He died almost ten years ago, and I've lived alone and comfortably since.

That's the end of the story, but not the most important part. You see, Leslie, leaving you wasn't the first time I ran. More than forty years ago I ran away from home. Fled would be a more accurate word.

Oh, my energy for writing is draining like the ink in this pen. I will write quickly, and to the point.

I was born in Tunsbury, Massachusetts. I told your father, when I eventually met him, that my maiden name was Stafford. It wasn't. I was born Elizabeth Filer. By now that name may mean quite a lot to you. The newspaper stories haven't mentioned the Filer connection, but I suspect you've figured it out. I was the only child of Edward and Margaret Filer, the last of the family to carry the Filer name, as it turns out. Edward was named for his father, also Edward, who was named for his father, another Edward, and so on back to the sixteenth century.

And so now you know.

I wish I had the time and stamina to tell you what this legacy meant, but I have neither. So I will only write that I hated it. The Filers were an insular, clannish group, mistrustful of the outside world, plagued with a physical affliction for which they sought no medical help lest it expose them to unwanted attention. I lived on a compound outside of town—perhaps you've been there?—and though I attended the local public school I was never allowed to talk about who I was, and I was never allowed to bring friends back to the property. We were a cult, a cult not of god but of family. Everyone knew we existed, this odd family who lived apart, but they left us alone, which is what we wanted.

Outsiders like my mother were brought into the fold after careful vetting, the way spouses are chosen for members of a royal family. As the sole heir of Edward Filer, and direct descendant of… I can feel my hand start to cramp just having to write this… of the great Elizabeth, the selection of my husband was of monumental importance to the entire Filer family. I was headstrong, Leslie, like you I imagine, and I resisted every candidate brought to me. When I passed the age of thirty, my family laid down the law. They had found a man for me, a distant cousin, Derek Martinson. I didn't mind him so much, but I wanted to choose my own husband, and I feared that marrying a blood relative, no matter how distant, would increase the likelihood that our offspring would carry the shivering curse, as the affliction was known to us. So I ran.

I wandered around the northeast for a few years, taking odd jobs to support myself. No matter where I settled I was aware that my family was looking for me. I saw marriage to your father as a way to acquire a new name in an anonymous town in the middle of nowhere. I wish I could write that it was more romantic than that, but it wasn't. He was a man who asked few questions; that was his chief attraction.

I brought only one thing with me when I left Tunsbury, a sonnet that my parents told me was by Shakespeare and had been commissioned by Elizabeth for our family. I never showed it to you. I wanted nothing to do with the Filers, and I wanted you to have nothing to do with them, either. But perhaps I was more a part of them than I thought, because I found myself reading Elizabethan poetry to you, and histories from that time. And you loved it, far more than the usual fairy tales and children's stories that other kids wanted to hear. As your father grew more brutish, mostly due to drink, I think I retreated into that world, the world of the past, and brought you along with me.

I took the poem with me when I left your father. And you, my dearest, I left you, too. When I was diagnosed with pancreatic cancer a few months ago, I was overtaken with the urgent need to get it into your hands. Otherwise, where would it end up? It belonged to you, the heir. In fact, the last two lines, the rhyming couplet, inspired your name. But I didn't want to give it to you in person. I had hurt you once, when I left you. I didn't want to hurt you again by presenting myself as a sick woman at the end of her life, asking for pity. I thought about sending it to you—I found your address on the Internet. One of the orderlies helped me. But that would have made you suspicious, perhaps led you to investigate. You see, I wanted you to have it, but I didn't want you to know that it connected you to the Filers and to Elizabeth herself. That knowledge had been a curse for me. I didn't want to bequeath that curse to you. You had to find the sonnet on your own, by accident.

So I hired Matthew, a young orderly at the hospice in which I am now confined. If you are reading this letter then you know what I asked him to do. I asked him to take you to the Talylor-Shipford house because I knew it well and figured it wouldn't be inconceivable to you that an old manuscript might fall out of an old book there.

If you are reading this you also know that I have most likely died. I am in a better place, as they say.

I never for a moment thought the sonnet would cause you trouble. I never knew that it held hidden meaning. But I did know that you were a clever girl, and headstrong as hell, so if there was meaning to be found, you would find it. I would never have given it to you if I'd known what it contained, or what it would do. You have escaped the shivering curse, but I have inadvertently given you the curse of knowledge.

Stay away from the Filers, Leslie. They are an insular and ignorant clan, and they will suck you in and keep you within their cloistered world. I do not believe they know who you are. Keep it that way. If you do, then perhaps I have given you not a curse but a magical gift. For you are the direct heir of the greatest monarch who ever lived. Like her you are a warrior and a scholar and a wizard with words. You are beautiful and determined and fiercely independent. I hope you find love, as she never did, and the strength to surrender to it. If you do, then there is no curse. This is the thought I will take with me as I lay down this pen and wait for death.

There was no signature, only three words to end the letter, crammed into the very bottom of the second side:

All my love.

Too late, she thought, then read the four lines that had been squeezed in next to them, which she immediately recognized from Sonnet Seventy-one. They were final instructions from a woman who had never stuck around to offer advice or comfort or even safety.

Nay, if you read this line, remember not
The hand that writ it; for I love you so
That I in your sweet thoughts would be forgot
If thinking on me then should make you woe.

Okay, then, she would not give in to tears. But she did succumb to an even stronger impulse. She put down the letter and walked quickly to the mirror that hung over a small table next to the front door. The face that greeted her there had changed, somehow, since she'd splashed cold water on it less than an hour ago. It had changed, but it finally looked familiar. Her hair, russet once again. The long, narrow nose. The pale complexion and pale blue eyes. Yes, she knew this person, perhaps for the first time. With her right hand she pushed her hair behind her ears, and then peered closely at it, with its long, slender fingers. Why had she never noticed them before, *really* noticed them? How had she overlooked them all this time?

Watching herself, she recited the last two lines in the sonnet, *her* sonnet, from memory:

"When all the world in bootless ruin lies
I'll lie not more, but less my love belie."

When Semper was released—"uncapped"—then, and only then, the world in bootless ruin, would Elizabeth no longer have to deny her love for the object of the sonnet, her son. It was a futile desire, an idle threat, as surely she must have known and conveyed to Shakespeare. But it perfectly expressed the vastness of her stifled love and the depth of her frustration.

And it contained the final clue in the poem, embedded not by

Shakespeare but devised by her mother centuries after the sonnet's creation: her very identity, the source of her name.

Still gazing at her image in the mirror, seeing herself for the first time, she said it aloud.

"Leslie."

ACKNOWLEDGMENTS

I would like to thank the amazing team at the Jean V. Naggar Literary Agency, starting with Jean herself, who has been my steadfast agent and friend for (gasp!) more than twenty-five years. A big thank-you to Jennifer Weltz who, amazingly, shares so many of Jean's best qualities. And to Tara Hart, whose enthusiasm and perseverance helped immeasurably.

I've had the perhaps dubious distinction of working with many publishing companies and editors over my career. The Diversion team has been right up there with the best. Special thanks to Randall Klein, whose thoughtful, meticulous, and opinionated editorial advice was invaluable. Susan Schwartz also provided keen editorial guidance that improved the novel significantly.

Speaking of editors, Jane Margolis once again proved to be an insightful reader and (given that she's my sister) a surprisingly objective critic. A more intelligent and supportive reader no writer ever had.

A number of sources were very useful in helping me to spin my mostly fictional tale. In particular, I drew upon *Elizabeth's London: Everyday Life in Elizabethan London* by Liza Picard; *Elizabeth I* by Anne Somerset; *The Life of Elizabeth I* by Alison Weir; *Sir Philip Sidney: The Major Works* edited by Katherine Duncan-Jones; *Burghley: Tudor Statesman* by B.W. Beckinsale; *Henry VIII: The King and His Court* by Alison Weir; *Jewels: A Secret History* by Victoria Finlay; "Pathways of Discovery: Infectious History" by Joshua Lederberg; and *The Spanish Lake: The Pacific Since Magellan, Vol. I* by O.H.K. Spate. Clearly, I took enormous liberties with these meticulously researched books. Also very helpful, in very different ways, were *Modern Identity Changer: How To Create And Use A New Identity For Privacy And Personal Freedom* by Sheldon Charrett and *The Dictionary of Wordplay* by Dave Morice.

Finally, thanks and love, as always, to (in order of appearance) Carole, Maggie, and Jack.

MORE FROM SETH MARGOLIS

FALSE FACES

Alison Rosen, a young, single Manhattan department-store buyer, first met Linda Levinson seven years ago when both answered the same Village Voice classified ad for a Fire Island "share." Since then, they've been returning to Seaside Harbor every summer weekend.

One night, after leaving Crane's, the singles bar that often serves as a pickup place, Linda Levinson is found murdered. Is her killer a spurned suitor whose advances Linda rejected? What about the mysterious lover back in the city about whom Linda had spoken but whom Alison has never met?

Long Island police officer Joe DiGregorio is assigned to work undercover on the case, posing as a yuppie accountant. Together, Joe and Alison, who is unaware of Joe's masquerade, set out to find the murderer before he strikes again. In the process, they find out that Linda was a woman of many secrets—and find themselves falling in love in an atmosphere in which nobody can be trusted.

DISILLUSIONS

In his atmospheric, complex, and suspenseful psychological thriller, Seth Margolis delivers the story of a woman fleeing an abusive relationship, only to find herself with a man whose dangerous past is obscured by his seductive charm—and who may be framing her for murder.

Gwen Amiel had only wanted a job, a haven, a fresh start. But inside a wealthy family's elegant home, a crime is committed that is so shocking—so seemingly random—that a tiny upstate New York town will never be the same. Gradually, evidence will lead the authorities to Gwen, the family's new nanny, a woman whose past is shrouded in mystery…and violence. Now, with a police investigation swirling around her and no way to prove her innocence, she turns to the one person who seems to believe her, and the one place she feels safe. But as Gwen struggles to find answers, she'll discover that nothing is what it seems, that no one can escape from the past, and that trusting the wrong person can destroy your sanity… and your life.

PERFECT ANGEL

Back at college in the '70s, they called themselves "The Madison Seven"—a close circle of friends inseparably linked by trust, loyalty, and love. Then one night, years later, they gathered at Julia Mallet's Manhattan apartment for a "Come-As-You-Were Party" and decided to play a game…

Tough, beautiful and independent, Julia Mallet feels her life is nearly perfect. She holds a high-profile executive position in an important advertising firm. She is raising a beautiful little daughter, Emily, without the inconvenience of a husband. And now "The Madison Seven" have come together once again to celebrate her thirty-fifth birthday…and to bring back a past that should have been left dead and forgotten.

Less than twenty-four hours later, a woman Julia barely knows is brutally and senselessly slain by a faceless psychopath. NYPD Detective Ray Burgess is a man pursued by shadows, a good cop who has stared too deeply into the face of evil, and his obsessive dedication is drawing him closer to Julia, even as a crazed killer strikes again and again.

The maniac has left a calling card behind that only Julia Mallet can read: the result of a post-hypnotic suggestion inadvertently lodged in six subconscious minds—the dark residue of a harmless party game gone terribly wrong. Now Julia knows without question that one of her six dearest friends is a murderer…and is coming after her next.

VANISHING ACT

When retail tycoon George Samson appears in detective Joe DiGregorio's office asking for help in faking his own death, the wary private eye knows enough to refuse. Joe D. has been having second thoughts about his move from the Long Island police force, where he'd been a lieutenant, to trying to make it as a private detective in Manhattan. Joe had made the move to be with Alison Rosen, whom he met while working a homicide case on Fire Island (*False Faces*). Though wonderful in many ways, their relationship is strained by Joe D.'s lack of work and income. The Big City doesn't seem to need one more private investigator.

But George Samson's proposition isn't easy to forget. So when Samson is found murdered, the struggling P.I. is convinced that his would-be client found another "killer." Thing is, there's no doubt the man is dead. What happened?

Intent on the truth, Joe D. offers his investigative talents to the new CEO of Samson Stores, who accepts, and Joe D. embarks on a case that could be the making of his new career—or the end of him.

Printed in the USA
CPSIA information can be obtained
at www.ICGtesting.com
JSHW031706140824
68134JS00038B/3550

9 781682 300565